C000291901

AFTER
THE
FIRE II

A STILL SMALL VOICE

AFTER THE FIRE II

A STILL SMALL VOICE

JOHN LOCKLEY

WORD PUBLISHING
WORD ENTERTAINMENT LTD
Milton Keynes, England

AFTER THE FIRE II: A Still Small Voice.

Copyright © 1996 by Dr John Lockley

Published in the UK by Word Publishing, Milton Keynes, England, 1996. Reprinted 1999

ISBN 1-86024-075-5

All characters in this publication are fictional.

Front cover illustration by Michael Setchell.

Frontispiece map drawn by Brian Maunders.

Reproduced, printed and bound in Great Britain for Word Publishing, by Cox & Wyman Ltd, Reading.

99 00 01 02 / 10 9 8 7 6 5 4 3

Acknowledgements

Grateful thanks (in alphabetical order) to Kathleen Carter, Charles Dort MD, Chris Garraway, John Goddard, Revd John Greenway (for background information on organic farming), Keith Howlett, Dr Edwina Kruszewska, Philip Lockley, Stephen Long, Tricia Massey, John Metcalf, Andy Metianu, Mr Bernard Palmer, Ron Roper (for a wonderful day spent learning how to work Bromham Mill), Andrew Underwood (for a great deal of background information on Ampthill) and to all the others too numerous to mention who have provided specialist information and advice on a wide variety of subjects.

Particular thanks are due to all those residents of Ampthill and Buckingham who have so willingly allowed me to use their homes and buildings for the purposes of this book: without exception they have demonstrated unfailing kindness and interest. May I emphasise that none of the fictional characters in this book is based on the real-life inhabitants of any of the houses!

Corporate thanks to David Willcox of 2V Microsystems Ltd of Toddington for information on his wind turbines—though some of their capabilities have been altered (both up and down) for the purposes of this book.

Thanks, as always, to Nancy Watkin my loyal secretary, who always manages to read my mind and get information before I ask for it, and Win Kennedy, my editor, who has a mind like a filing cabinet and seems to know my books better than I do!

Part I

*T*he woman sitting at the desk by the window was on edge to the point of agitation, restlessly shifting in her chair, crossing and uncrossing her legs and from time to time gnawing at her upper lip. Several times she reached hesitantly into the drawer to take out some writing paper, but each time she withdrew her hand, as if bitten. Nevertheless it had to be done, she reasoned, it had to be done: otherwise the memories would fade and the story would be lost forever. And with time on her hands, if only temporarily, she was the one best-placed to do it.

But the remembering: that would be......... difficult.

Suddenly determined, she reached into the drawer again, lifted out a sheaf of paper, picked up her pen, and with an involuntary shudder, began to write.

It was in October last year that the plague struck. At first we thought it was an organism that had escaped from a germ warfare laboratory, but eventually it turned out to be a natural strain of Legionnaires' disease which had suddenly become much more deadly and, unlike the original, could pass from person to person

*The outbreak started after an accident at Southill Hospital in London. First to be infected was the head of the laboratory, then **his** contacts, and then **their** contacts... It took two weeks for the plague to become fully established in the community, but after this cases multiplied by the minute. On that first dreadful Thursday night tens of thousands died in London: the rest of the population fled in terror, hoping to escape but instead taking the disease with them. Many fell ill on the journey, collapsing and dying—often inside their cars. Because of the risk of infection, no one dared get into the vehicles to move them out of the way, and soon all the major roads out of London were blocked.*

The remainder of the population had no option but to escape on foot. Soon, those living in the towns and villages around London faced a horde of potentially infected refugees streaming out of London towards them and in turn took flight, adding to the panic and the confusion.

There was little that anyone could do except run away and hide. The Department of Health did nothing. By the time they realised they had an epidemic on their hands—and they seemed to be the last to find out—it was far too late: the plague was out of control. One or two special antibiotics did give some protection, but supplies of these soon ran out.

Within a day the plague had spread throughout the whole country. Those infected would incubate the illness for forty-eight hours, then without warning went into paroxysms of coughing until within half an hour they collapsed and died. The dead lay everywhere—in the streets, in their houses, in their cars—wherever they had been taken ill.

There were a few survivors: we are testimony to that! Some were already immune, others were living in isolated areas and never came into contact with the plague; and a few were already taking the special antibiotics, but for other illnesses.

Even now, one year later, we can't be sure of all the details. The devastation was such that many individuals thought they were the only people left alive in the country. Each of us heard the radio stations stop broadcasting one by one—not just in England, but abroad, so we knew the plague had spread world-wide...

It was some time before Susan realised that she had stopped writing, and was staring straight ahead, sightlessly, remembering just what those first few awful days had been like. She came to with a shudder, and looked round for her husband. Where was Alan? Late as usual, she thought. He'd vanished, as always, just when she could do with some help. Making an irritated noise with her tongue, she turned back to her diary and began writing again.

A week after the plague struck two small groups of survivors met quite by chance here in Ampthill: Derek Jones and his family—who had survived because they were marooned on a narrow-boat on a canal—and Paul Greatorex and his partner Jane Tomlins who had been confined to their flat with flu, together with Martin Freeman, whom they'd met on their journey out of London. A few days later Paul reconnoitred the area using a light aircraft and attracted some more survivors. Others stumbled on us by accident—such as Kevin Jensen, an East End lad; Mary Harper, who before the plague was a librarian; and Peter Abrahams, an ex-policeman who had lost all his family. All told, by the end of November about a hundred people had gathered here.

Even so, precious few of the population remain...... Some are here at Ampthill, in Bedfordshire, but we know of other communities of survivors: there's one at March in Cambridgeshire, another in Harpenden, and probably many others elsewhere. There may well be survivors of whom we know nothing, who made it to isolated places like the glens of Scotland. Like a grass fire, the plague appears to have burned itself out, leaving small pockets of people unscathed.

The first few months here were awful. With few exceptions, none of us had any experience of living in the country and off the land. Quite frankly, we never thought we'd make it through that first year. All we needed was for the harvest to fail—just the once—and we'd have nothing to fall back on.

Luckily, we met up with Neil Rawsthorne, who turned out to be a farmer, and his expertise has proved invaluable. However, we still didn't have a doctor, which was important because Jane, Paul's partner, was in the early stages of her first pregnancy. Worse, in November Derek's daughter Alison became severely ill. Cleverly, Derek used the Public Library and the books in the Health Centre to work out what was happening to her, diagnosed her diabetes, and managed to treat her successfully, using medicines from the local pharmacy. After that, it was obvious to all of us who ought to be the one to learn medicine! Derek took a lot of convincing, and agreed to be our doctor only on condition that no one blamed him if anything went wrong.

Paul has been extremely important, too. A stockbroker before the plague, he had no skills that were directly useful in our new situa-

tion—except that he's got an extraordinarily organised mind, and is
our chief planner. Another survivor was Martin Freeman, who was
originally a vicar in London. He lost his faith at the time of the
plague and became very depressed afterwards, though both Derek
and his wife Anne played a major part in helping him through it.

Mostly we've had a peaceful time here with no outside interfer-
ence. The only exception was last Christmas, when a group of four
bikers led by a man called Lew Pritchard tried to steal from us, but
Kevin—the East End lad—managed to see them off, rather ruth-
lessly as it happened. It's about the only useful thing that Kevin's
done: I'm afraid he's a bit of a layabout.

In April we decided to see if we could get back into London
again, as we were starting to run short of several important items
that we couldn't make or grow. We weren't able get in by road
because of all the crashed and abandoned cars, so Derek led a
group in by narrow-boat, along the Grand Union Canal.

That summer, Jane went into labour, but complications set in and
tragically both she and the baby died. Derek, our 'doctor', wasn't
to blame, but he took it very hard. To add to his misery, his daughter's diabetes became worse—the insulin that kept her alive was
deteriorating in the hot summer. We couldn't find any more supplies,
though Paul and Kevin spent a long time travelling around looking,
and she too died shortly afterwards. Derek was devastated. He also
kept saying that we were trying to blame him for Jane's death. We
weren't—everyone was quite sure that he'd done as much as anybody could, but he kept on repeating that when we first asked him
to be our doctor we'd agreed not to criticise him and yet we had an
inquest after Jane's death. Lucky for him he did all the right things,
he said.

'We', by the way, are the council; by the spring the community
here had enlarged to several hundred. It was becoming impossible
to get decisions made if everyone wanted to have a say, so reluctantly we elected a governing body. Many of us—especially Mary—
liked the freedom and lack of constraint that had come with our new
way of life here, and we didn't want to go back to rules, regulations
and organisation. But really, we had no option.

The council soon decided to dispense formally with the previous law of England, which nobody knew in detail any longer. Peter and Mary were instrumental in guiding us into adopting a simple system of laws which everyone could remember, and which was easy to apply. One of our great principles is that nobody should do anything which is against the interests of the community as a whole. This seems to have been very effective. It even allowed us to punish Paul, who at the time was our Chairman! He'd been pilfering pethidine and morphine from the chemist's shop—we discovered later that he'd had a cocaine habit before the plague—so when his partner Jane needed pethidine during her labour there was none left. As if that weren't bad enough, he tried to blame the theft on Kevin, but Kevin turned the tables on him (he seems to have a habit of doing this sort of thing, does our Kevin) and showed everyone that it was Paul who was the addict. We don't have a prison—we can't afford the time for anybody to be away from work, nor for someone to be a prison warder—so we whipped Paul there and then as punishment.

In the meantime Derek has become very low. It's the death of Alison, of course, but also the loss of Jane, his patient, and our reaction to it. I have to admit that he's had a lot of work to do—I've been ill with gallstones and he's been called out to me at all hours, so he's been under considerable stress physically and mentally, poor chap.

That summer the weather turned nasty. It rained through most of July, and for a time we thought we were going to lose the harvest. Fortunately—almost miraculously—the weather cleared up in early August, and although the harvest was late, we got it in eventually. There was a lot of it! So it looks as though we're safe for some time, even if next year's harvest isn't so good: that's a real comfort.

Something odd appears to have happened to Martin, though. Three months after Derek had diagnosed my gallstones—but didn't have the expertise to operate on them—we came across a surgeon, Nicholas Poulton, who was travelling around performing operations in a mobile operating theatre. He's solved the problem of getting through the traffic jams—he travels in a convoy of three large vehicles, and has fitted the first one with a snowplough, with which he simply pushes crashed cars out of the way! However, he demanded an exorbitant amount for taking out my gall bladder. Martin, the one-time vicar—whom I should have said was an ardent pacifist and CND member—suddenly started threatening Nicholas with a shot-gun if he didn't do the operation. Needless to say, Nicholas agreed to do it! At the time we thought Martin had gone mad: yet, surprisingly, he made sure afterwards that Nicholas was paid an appropriate amount for his work. Martin seems to have undergone a total change of heart in some sort of way which I don't quite understand. He certainly looks a lot happier for it.

Despite the altercation about the fee, Derek and Nicholas have become good friends. Derek is glad to know that there is a proper doctor around, to whom he can turn for advice and Nicholas seems to have quite a respect for Derek in a disdainful sort of way! But Martin is the one who seems to have been most affected by the encounter: suddenly his depression and alcoholism appear to have lifted. He certainly did a lovely harvest service the following week.

But I'm going on too fast... How did we live in those first few months? It's only the older houses which are any good now—the ones with open hearths, ranges or Aga cookers: without gas or electricity the newer houses are hopeless, and few of them have open fires. Of the older houses, one of the biggest, next to the church, is Dynevor House, which has really become the centre of our community, and it's where Derek and his family live. But after we'd been nearly a year in Ampthill the original owner of the house, Henry Courtauld, suddenly turned up...

She put down her pen and leaned back in the chair, wincing slightly as the movement pulled on the scar at the top of her abdomen. The late afternoon gloom was already encroaching on the room. She rubbed her aching eyes. How difficult it was to write under these circumstances! she thought as she crossed the room to light one of their precious mutton-fat candles. Through the window the sky was fading from the crisp blue of early afternoon to the sluggish red and orange of a November sunset. Outside it was almost silent except for the high pitched twittering of a couple of sparrows, and the creak and snort of a horse pulling its load up the hill beside the terraced house. Trevor Smith, one of the farm-hands, was holding the reins as with a little whinny the horse left a pile of droppings steaming on the road in front of her window.

The pain increased for a moment and almost involuntarily Susan's hand went to the scar in the upper right side of her abdomen where her gall bladder had been. It was six weeks since the operation, and it was still aching. Mind you, Derek had always said it would be sore for a bit—and for some considerable time in the future, too. Slowly she eased her considerable bulk out of the chair and stretched cautiously, wincing yet again. That was enough writing for the moment. There would be time for more tomorrow.

With the cart gone, the road outside became silent again. The sky slowly dimmed, the branches of trees, now losing their leaves, showing stark against the orange sunset. It was going to be another cold night. She shivered, and by the dim light of the candle in her hand went to put another couple of sticks on the tiny fire in the wood-stove on the hearth.

*   *   *

At the other end of the town Derek and Anne were also staring gloomily at a fire, this time in the morning room at Dynevor House. They loved the house—a fine Georgian exterior surrounding an earlier building—which was both gracious and welcoming. But their minds were in disarray. With the arrival of Henry, claiming his house back, they were put in a quandary—where would they go? All the old-style houses were already occupied. If they had to leave Dynevor House they would have to live in one of the modern houses which, as everyone in the community knew, were useless. About the only way to cook in them was to build an open fire outside, but then its heat wouldn't warm the house itself: nor was there any other way to heat a house which had only gas and electric central heating.

All in all, it looked as though Derek, Anne and the two children were to be consigned to a cold, inhospitable modern house. And they were one of the pillars of the community!—the first family to take up residence in Ampthill. Anne picked up the poker and angrily jabbed it at the smouldering logs, while Derek, exhausted from his day's work, which also had included being called out in the middle of the night, dozed fitfully in a chair as the dusk settled outside.

It was the beginning of winter—and didn't they know it. Before the plague winter had been a time of closeness, of well-lit, cosy houses, settled and gentle, protected against the outside weather. Even though the day outside might have been spare and cold, a womb-like warmth always awaited their return, with light available at the flick of a switch, the central heating pre-programmed to come on before they got home, or else just before they woke up.

Now it was different. In the winter it was impossible to heat a huge house like Dynevor. Individual rooms could be made warm—mostly, and as long as their occupants were near the hearth—but the hall was like an icebox and the general rule was that anything that got cold stayed cold for the next six months. But to add to the cold, the gloom had descended, unrelieved by the single candle that was all that they could afford for light. It wasn't that they weren't well-off—like everyone else in the community they ate well enough, and shared everything—but there just wasn't the lamb-fat to make enough tallow candles. Now everyone in the community had to use daylight as much as possible, taking care to do in the day those jobs that needed good vision, and in the evening using as few candles as they could. As a result, with the onset of winter a thick gloom had started to permeate the vast spaciousness of Dynevor House, a gloom that they could almost feel. It felt as if a cold, yellow-green miasma had descended, thick darkness that was only partially penetrated by the flickering yellow light from the smelly candle perched on the table beside them.

In the gloom the house creaked from time to time. No wonder that medieval man had become so obsessed with spirits, ghosts, demons and things that go bump in the night, thought Derek. There's less room for superstition when visions of ghosts disappear with the flick of a switch as the room is bathed in 200 watts of light:

but in a dark echoing, cold, damp, cavernous house things just didn't seem quite the same...

Involuntarily he shuddered. He didn't believe in ghosts, but the onset of winter terrified him. The previous year it had been different: then it was a fight against the world in order to survive. The novelty of the situation had at least given them determination, and a capacity to ignore immediate hardships that had helped them withstand the shock of winter. But now they all knew what was coming. Instead of warmth, light and long evenings, they had six months of cold, damp and gloom to withstand—a cold that would penetrate deep into their bones, a dampness that wouldn't be shaken off until late into the next spring. No wonder that in the past, people dreaded the onset of winter, with its cold, damp, pneumonia and sickness.

And now they were going to lose their house...

Derek pulled himself forward in the chair. 'God, I can't stand it,' he said.

'I do wish you wouldn't say that,' retorted Anne from the other side of the fireplace, looking furiously at Derek and then at Sarah, who was playing on the hearth rug and who hadn't heard.

'Why not? Martin's not here, is he?'

She looked daggers at him. 'You know exactly what I mean.'

Derek grimaced. 'Oh, I'm sorry... Anyway it's how *you* feel, Anne. You're just as full of despair as I am.'

'Yes, but I don't put it that way.'

'Does it matter how you express it? We both *feel* the same—what's wrong with me *saying* it as angrily as you've just poked the fire?'

'Derek, you're really getting irascible in your old age.'

He shrugged and gave a half-wry smile. 'I'm just tired, I suppose.'

'What you need is a holiday.'

'Sure. How about Acapulco? We could fly there this weekend... No... Greece perhaps? Don't be silly. Holidays are a thing of the past. Anyway, why should it be just me who needs a holiday? You need one just as much as I do.'

There was a silence. The fire suddenly flared up, spitting and hissing.

'I wonder how long it'll be before we can get a holiday,' said Anne wistfully.

'More to the point, will we ever get a holiday again in the rest of our lives?' The thought depressed Derek even more as visions of year upon year of unremitting slog suddenly rolled out in front of him. 'Do you know, I don't think I've ever worked as hard as this. I mean—back in the days when I worked at the Patent Office I'd commute in and commute out. Sometimes I'd have to work late and I'd feel hard done by, but it was nothing compared to this, nothing. And I don't mean just for me, I mean for everybody... Up at the crack of dawn or earlier; using every bit of light there is, come back shattered at the end of the day; collapse into bed; get up the next day, do the same thing... On and on and on. It's not even particularly enjoyable when we do get home because it's so cold and miserable and gloomy.'

He stared out into the middle distance with unseeing eyes. 'What I could do with now is to curl up in front of the fire with a nice light so I could read properly instead of straining to make out the words.'

There was another silence, punctuated by a loud bang from the hall as their son David came in. Now thirteen, he had that same cheeky face as always, but had started his pubescent growth spurt and was shooting up in all directions, gangly arms and legs everywhere. He'd also reached the hollow-leg stage.

'Hi Mum, hi Dad. What's for tea?'

Derek groaned.

'What's the matter with you?' asked David. 'Tired out again, I suppose, and irritable too.'

Anne turned round to remonstrate.

'I know when I'm not wanted,' said David, before she could open her mouth. 'It doesn't matter what anyone else says, being a doctor's son is no fun at all.'

'I keep on telling you David, I'm not a doctor,' replied Derek wearily.

'All right, all right, I know, I know. When's food? Oh... all right,

I'll go off and get some myself.'

'Shut the door,' shouted Derek and Anne in concert, but by now the meagre heat in the morning room had dissipated into the black hole of the hall. Anne shut the door, then returned disconsolately to poke at the smoky fire again.

'He's right, Derek; you *are* getting irritable.'

'Oh, I'm sorry. It's the winter... and the job... and Alison... And losing our house... and being up all night... and not knowing what I'm doing half of the time.' He leaned forward and threw another log on to the fire, none too gently. 'I don't want to leave this place, and I certainly don't want to leave it for something much worse. Life's difficult enough as it is—and when all's said and done we *were* here first.'

'Not before Henry, though,' said Anne. 'After all it *is* his house.'

Derek sighed and leaned back in his chair.

'You have a nap, I'll get the food.'

He heard her footsteps go out into the black hall and then to the kitchen, followed shortly afterwards by a wail. '*David! Come and clear up this mess...*'

*   *   *

What a change a month makes! Thirty days earlier it had been sunny and warm. Ampthill had been basking in an Indian summer amidst the mists and mellowness of the coming autumn. Their first harvest had just been brought in—a good harvest, against all the odds. It was a warm and optimistic time. Derek and Martin had been walking in the gardens of Dynevor House after the Harvest Festival, revelling in the success of both bringing the harvest in and having survived a whole year without external support.

And then...

They'd been chatting in the garden when Henry had arrived. Derek answered the door expecting to see yet another patient, and there stood Henry, dapper and immaculate despite his long overland journey from Scotland.

'How do you do?' he said. 'May I introduce myself? My name's Henry Courtauld, and you appear to be living in my house.'

Derek stood there speechless, totally lost for words.

'Er... you'd better come in.'

'Yes, do,' said Martin, similarly taken aback. 'Come in.'

Looking every inch the local squire, Henry came into the hall-way and gazed round in vague astonishment. Anne, brushing the crumbs from her apron, bustled out from the kitchen to see what the fuss was about.

'Hello, I'm Anne Jones. Welcome to Dynevor House.' Not the best thing to say under the circumstances. She turned to Derek who was standing behind Henry, slowly shaking his head at her. 'Why, did I say something wrong?'

'This is Mr *Courtauld*,' said Martin, carefully emphasising the last word.

'Courtauld?' said Anne. 'Should I...?' and then her hand flew to her mouth. 'Oh. Mr Courtauld. Yes... Oh dear.'

There was an awkward silence. In spite of the constant trickle of visitors into the town, this was the first time that a survivor had returned to Ampthill to reclaim his own property. A few moments earlier Derek and Anne had been leaders in the community: now they felt like thieves and criminals. They'd broken into this man's house, helped themselves to his store of food, coal and wine, used his bed, and read his books. To be fair they'd looked after the place pretty well—apart from the smashed lock in the morning-room door where they'd broken in on that first night—but even so they suddenly felt an overwhelming sense of shame and unease, coupled a few seconds later with insecurity as they realised that they would no longer be welcome in the house that for the past year they'd called their home.

It was Anne who broke the silence. 'Well,' she said brightly, recovering her composure, 'It's good to know that you're alive. Do come in. We were just about to have lunch and I'm sure it'll stretch to another person.'

Henry followed her into the dining room, looking round care-fully to see what was missing or damaged. Fortunately he didn't spot anything of great importance. David and Sarah were there, lay-ing out the plates.

'Hello,' said Sarah, running up to him in the affectionate way eight-year-olds do, 'my name's Sarah Jane. What's yours?' and she looked up at Henry and smiled. Then she caught Derek and Anne's faces and suddenly looked crestfallen, as though she'd somehow been infected with the guilt that had settled on both of them. There was an awkward pause and then Henry held out his hand.

'Hello, young lady. I'm Mr Courtauld. Do you live here too?'

'Yes,' said Sarah. 'I've got a room upstairs all to my own. It's very pretty. Have you seen the garden? We've got ever such big fish in the pond. I've got a special one. I call him Hamble.'

Anne smiled and said apologetically to Henry, 'It was supposed to be called Hannibal, but she couldn't get her tongue round it.'

To Anne and Derek's surprise Henry happily followed Sarah out onto the patio. 'There you are,' said Sarah, pointing. 'There's Hamble. He always seems to know it's me,' and as if on cue the great Koi carp obligingly rose to the surface nearby, expecting a few morsels of food.

'He looks very well,' said Henry thoughtfully. 'You've looked after him very carefully for me, Sarah, haven't you?'

'He's not yours, he's mine,' replied Sarah indignantly, then stopped as she saw Derek and Anne's faces. 'Isn't he?' Her face displayed all the confusion that Anne and Derek felt inside. 'He is mine, Auntie Anne, isn't he...?'

Henry looked round the garden and then turned to face them again. 'Well, you'd better tell me what you've been doing with the place.'

'Yes,' said Anne anxiously, brushing some more non-existent crumbs from her apron. 'Yes... do come back inside. David, will you pull up an extra chair for Mr Courtauld?'

Derek, still totally taken aback, stuttered, 'Mr Courtauld... I... I'm sorry if we've done anything to your house that we shouldn't have. You see we didn't know that you'd survived...' He gave a despairing shrug of his shoulders and sat down, lost for words.

'Well I have, as you can see. So what's been happening in Ampthill?'

'Let me tell you that,' interjected Martin quickly, thinking that as the only one there not personally involved with Dynevor House, he was in a position to be more dispassionate, if not actually fluent, bearing in mind that Derek and Anne were still in a state of shock. He proceeded to tell Henry in a few succinct words how the community had grown, yet in all this time none of the original inhabitants of Ampthill had come back.

'It's really quite a shock, you understand... I mean, seeing you here, one of the original inhabitants, in the flesh... We'd made a rule, you see, that we wouldn't take anything from someone who was still alive.'

Henry stared at him over his half-moon spectacles. 'But you'd never *met* any of the original people... so how would you know if they were likely to survive or not?'

'I know we hadn't met them,' replied Martin, 'but we always said specifically that we weren't going to take anything from anybody whom we *thought* might still be alive... There wasn't much chance of them surviving, was there? And nobody came back...until now, of course. If we'd known that you had survived then we wouldn't have dreamed of using your house. And I'm sure that Derek and Anne will be the first to say that you must have your house back immediately. Obviously, nothing else will do, and we can only apologise for any damage that we've caused, and for everything that we've consumed. And we'll try to make good...'

'There's no need for you to worry,' interrupted Henry. 'To be honest I think I'm just as glad to be alive as you are, and it's nice to be back in the old house after all these months.'

'Let's eat, shall we?' said Anne, slightly relieved. 'Martin, would you like to say grace, seeing as it's Harvest Festival?'

Martin obliged.

'Harvest Festival, eh?' mused Henry. 'So you got the harvest in then?'

'Oh yes,' continued Martin a little too enthusiastically, betraying the inner unease he still felt. 'We were very fortunate. Two months ago we thought we were going to lose the lot because the weather was so bad. But then it brightened up and now we've got a really good store of wheat. At a pinch it would do for another two or three years if we need it... But what happened to you? Have you a family?'

Henry's face suddenly went still.

'I'm a widower,' he said. 'Have been for about five years. We have a daughter... *had* a daughter... but I haven't seen her since the plague started. She worked in London, you understand...'

There was a silence round the table. Which of the bodies in London was hers? thought Martin, wondering if it was one they'd inadvertently driven over when getting out of the city.

Henry continued. 'We'd seen the programmes on the television and heard the news stories, and I knew immediately that that fellow... the doctor... what was his name? Mike something...?'

'Williams,' chipped in Derek.

'That's right, the doctor fellow. I knew instinctively he was right and that the thing to do was either to stay isolated, or move out quickly. Staying here wouldn't work because everybody else was coming up from London and we'd just have been infected by them. So a group of us went round Ampthill, telling everyone that if they wanted to save their skins they'd better move, and move quickly. We did a good job too. We got them all out before the refugees came up from London.'

'Does that mean there are other people waiting to come back and claim their houses, then?' asked Derek warily.

'I shouldn't think so. I made a point of staying out of the way as long as I could. I doubt if anyone else is likely to have waited that long. I went to a shooting lodge on the Scottish estate of a friend of mine, and kept out of the way for a whole month.' He chuckled. 'Even he didn't know I was there, I don't think, poor chap... I'd got the car radio, and like you I heard all the radio stations fail one by one, so I knew it was unlikely to be safe to come out for quite some time.

'Then when I *did* venture out... well, there weren't as many people around as before. Mind you, there were a lot more people alive up in Scotland than down in England. Some refugees grouped themselves into enclaves in the glens and refused entry to anybody from outside. They just shot at them until they went away. Quite a few groups avoided the plague like that.'

'So what did you do in the meantime?' said Anne. 'I mean, that only takes you up to November.'

'I have some good friends up in Scotland. Fortunately one or two of them had survived and I stayed with them. The roads are dreadful—all blocked with cars, the major ones especially—so I lived up there for some time. We didn't think anyone was alive in the south of England, so there wasn't any point in coming back. I'd got no family left, and nothing really to come back to... apart from the house.'

'So what made you decide to return?' asked Martin, tucking into a second helping of greens.

'We'd heard persistent rumours that there were survivors in the south. There was even somebody who'd been to Ampthill, quite recently I think, and he told me that there were people living there, so I decided I'd make the trip. So, here I am. And this is my house,' he added significantly, in a tone which brooked no contradiction.

'Oh... Yes...' said Derek. 'Well, we'll get out just as soon as we can... I'm sorry if we appear to have stolen your property.'

'That's all right,' said Henry. 'Don't worry. I'm not upset that you've been living here, so long as you return it to its rightful owner.'

'Yes,' said Anne, 'but unfortunately we don't have anywhere obvious to go to. I wonder whether perhaps we can organise it over a few days? We have to find somewhere to live that's got an open hearth where we can cook, and there aren't many houses like that left. And it's a bit difficult because you see my husband is the town's doctor, and he's very busy.... So it may be a few days...'

Henry turned to her. 'Anne,' he interrupted gently. 'I do understand. So long as I can have my house back. And Gates House, as well.'

'Gates House?' said Martin, choking on his last mouthful of potato. 'Why Gates House?'

'Because I own that as well,' said Henry. 'I'd just bought it. It was going to be a wedding present for my daughter...' His voice tailed off.

'I'm sorry to ask this,' asked Martin. 'I don't want to appear to doubt your word, but do you have any proof you own *both* houses?'

'That might be a bit difficult, considering everything that's happened over the past year.'

'Deeds?' asked Martin.

'With my solicitor, unfortunately,' replied Henry immediately. 'In London—Lloyd, Bloom and Rumark, of Hallam Street. They'd just completed the sale... of Gates House, that is. I've been here in Dynevor House for a long time, but unless you've got anyone who knew me from that time it's going to be a difficult thing to prove, isn't it? Mind you, there are all the old photographs and family albums and things like that. You'll be able to recognise me from them.'

'We can do better than that,' replied Martin.

'Really?' said Henry, raising his eyebrows.

'Yes. We've got a survivor from Ampthill. Neil. Neil Rawsthorne.'

'Neil?' said Henry, with a start, as if taken aback. 'Why... but that's wonderful.'

'It's been wonderful for us, too,' said Martin. 'He's been our salvation. He's the only real source of farming information we've had and we'd never have got through the past year without him.'

'Well, well, well,' said Henry lost in thought. 'Well, well, well. Neil Rawsthorne... Is he still farming up at Haynes West End?'

'That's where he started,' said Anne, 'but he's now moved his base to King's Farm at Maulden so that he's nearer to the rest of us. More cabbage anyone?'

*   *   *

After the meal they went out to have acorn coffee on the patio behind the house, which allowed Sarah to show off her trick with Hamble again. Henry sat on the bench there, basking in the warm, early autumn sunlight. 'It really is a lovely day today,' he said. 'It *is* good to be back here.'

Derek and Anne exchanged sideways glances.

'I grant you this—you've really looked after the place well.

Though I can see it'll take some time for you to clear up and move
out. Well, there it is,' and he suddenly stood up. 'I want to go off and
try to find two of my friends out near Norwich. It'll take me some
time—about a month, I reckon. So I'll expect you to be out of the
house by... shall we say... the tenth of November? Good. Then that's
settled. By the way, you will be repaying me for the consumables
you've taken, won't you? The food, the fuel and the wine? And rent
for the place, of course? Good. Thank you for the meal Anne, and I
look forward to taking over my house in the middle of November.
Oh, and by the way, I also need rent for Gates House as well. So can
I get you to broach the subject with the present occupant, whoever
he is? Splendid. I knew I could rely on you. Good day.'

And with that Henry turned abruptly on his heel, walked back
through the house and let himself out of the front door. On the patio
they could hear the Range Rover starting up, purring gently as it
swung out into the Maulden road and headed off east. The three
adults just collapsed into their chairs.

Anne heaved a sigh. 'I feel as if I've been hit by a human whirlwind. How *do* people like that manage to do it? Here we are—
we've only known him an hour and a half and he's got us eating out
of his hand already.'

Derek didn't answer. He was staring ahead into the middle distance. No matter how brightly the sun might be shining, the gloom
of winter had already descended into his heart.

- 2 -

The Council met in the middle of the next week, with two unexpected additions to the agenda.

Item: what to do about Henry.

Item: what to do about Derek.

As usual they met in the courtroom in Woburn Street. The chair-
woman, Chris Wilson, a blonde twenty-eight-year-old, began in her
usual brisk style. 'I'd like officially to welcome Paul back after his

absence, and I'm sure I speak for every one in saying that we want bygones to be bygones. The past is behind us—let's leave it there.'

Paul nodded gratefully and said nothing. He'd learned his lesson. He was over the pethidine addiction, and he'd paid the penalty for trying to blame its theft on Kevin.

'The first item on the agenda is Henry Courtauld. Over to you, Derek.'

Derek recounted the events of the previous Sunday. It was the first time that most of the council had heard the tale in detail and they all listened attentively. Neil Rawsthorne, the farmer, almost fell off his chair on hearing that Henry had returned.

'Good heavens,' he said. 'Old Henry alive? I can quite believe it. The man's bomb-proof.'

'And, it would seem, bacteria-proof as well,' muttered Alan Rogers from the other side of the table.

The other person who was surprised, but for an entirely different reason, was the Major. A crusty, white-haired man of seventy, he was the current resident of Gates House, which he perceived to be the best house in the town and the one where 'The Squire' would naturally choose to live, which was why he'd chosen it. He was considerably put out to find that someone else might have that privilege, and his face reddened at the thought.

At the far end of the table, Martin took a more sanguine view of events. Putting his long thin fingers together and brushing away the lock of fair hair that constantly seemed to fall across his forehead, he delivered a pithy assessment of the situation.

'I have to say I'm a little cautious about this,' he said quietly. 'It does seem strange that one of the old inhabitants should suddenly come back out of the blue to claim what he says is his rightful property. Why has it taken him so long to travel back from Scotland? *Does* he own Dynevor House? For that matter, does he own Gates House as well? Is he who he says he is? Or is he a con merchant? Neil, you say you'd recognise him?'

'Oh yes. Without any doubt whatsoever. From Derek's description it sounds like Henry, anyway, though I have to say I didn't know anything about Gates House.'

'Well, it *was* supposed to be a surprise,' said Derek. 'For his daughter. A wedding present...'

'And we can't check that out,' said Martin, 'because he hasn't got the deeds. They're with his solicitors in London, apparently.'

'It does sound as though he's the man he claims to be,' said Chris. 'And we always said we'd never take or use anything that belonged to anyone who was still alive, so we'll have to give him his house back, I'm afraid.'

Derek and Martin had been firm friends for a long time, and Martin knew just how keenly Derek would feel the loss of Dynevor House. Martin flashed him a look as if to say 'I'm sorry', only to find Derek staring down dully at the tabletop.

'So where are we going to live?' mumbled Derek.

'That's just what I was thinking,' said Alan. 'You're our doctor. We can't have you miles away, where we're settling the new people. You've got to be in the centre somewhere. The trouble is, there aren't any decent houses going spare at the moment, are there?'

'You could all come up and stay at the Old Rectory with me,' said Martin. 'You'd be very welcome.'

Derek looked up at him. 'No, Martin, thank you. That's very kind... but you still need space and quiet. You won't be wanting the noise and bustle of our family, never mind the disturbance from patients coming to consult me at all hours of the day and night. No, we'll just have to make do with one of the more modern houses and see if we can adapt it. Maybe we can find one that once used to have proper fireplaces and put them back in again.' His voice sounded dull, empty, exhausted. He obviously didn't relish the prospect.

'What about Gates House?' said Mary.

'But I'm living there,' expostulated the Major.

'No, I didn't mean that,' said Mary. 'I meant, what about payment for it.'

'Payment?' spluttered the Major, his white moustache bristling. 'You don't mean I'm going to have to *pay* to live there?'

'It's that or getting out, isn't it?' said Derek tartly, wondering why it was that the Major thought he could live free in Gates House while Derek had to vacate his own residence. 'And who's going to pay for it? Come to think of it, who's going to pay Henry for all the stuff we've used that was his? I haven't got anything that I can give him.'

'I wonder if he'd take a cheque?' said Paul dryly.

'Don't be silly,' said Mary, 'he wouldn't be able to cash... Oh, I see.' She went red.

Chris tried to stifle a smile, murmured 'Paul, you're irrepressible,' and attempted to recover her composure, all at the same time, anxious to support Derek and relieve him of his misery. 'Look, the whole community's in this together. It wasn't Derek and his family that took over Dynevor House—it was all of us: Derek just happened to be the one who was living there. And Derek's right. He doesn't have anything of his own to give Henry in repayment: in any case we've all benefited from the food and wine that Henry had stored away in the cellars. No, we'll *all* have to pay—or, rather, the community will have to pay. We'll just have to ask him what he thinks would be adequate compensation.'

'*How* are we going to pay him?' asked Paul, somewhat angrily. 'We're still not using money, despite what I said six months ago: we just share everything. So how is he going to be more rich? If we give him fifty bags of wheat now, how does that repay him? We all have enough to eat and there's no point in having extra when you've already got enough.'

'I suppose he could sell the grain outside the community. He seems to be a man who travels around a lot,' said Alan.

'There is that,' said Paul. 'But it does highlight what I've been saying for ages—we ought to get back to using some form of money. It would make things a lot easier. Then we could pay people like Henry, and it would automatically deal with those who won't work.'

'I really don't see why we have to start talking about money all over again, 'interjected Mary, crossly. 'You all know what I feel— it will be such a shame if we have to stoop that low. We're getting on fine without it—why reintroduce the idea, Paul? Or don't you care what I think?'

'That's a separate subject,' said Chris, hastily. 'Maybe we can return to it on another occasion.' Mary subsided slightly.

'I still can't quite get over the effrontery of it all,' mused Alan. 'I mean—he comes into our community and without a "by your leave" suddenly takes over one of the houses and demands rent for the use of another one. It really doesn't seem very fair.'

'It depends how you look at it,' said Peter in his usual self-effacing manner. 'See it through his eyes. He's got his house—or rather, houses. He's paid for them: why shouldn't he expect to return and find them intact, even if he has spent a year away? They were originally his, after all.'

'But we're sharing everything,' said Mary.

'Yes,' said Peter gently. 'But don't forget that's the way *we've* chosen to live since we came here. Henry isn't a party to that, is he? He wouldn't necessarily be expected to agree with what we'd chosen to do.'

Mary pursed her lips in reluctant acceptance.

'So are we agreed?' asked Chris, looking round the table. 'Derek has to vacate Dynevor House: and we'll try to find him a place as soon as possible. And we'll have to pay Henry for the fact that the Major's living in Gates House. Unless the Major chooses to live elsewhere,' she added mischievously. The Major looked apoplectic.

'I don't want to move,' he expostulated. 'I'm happy where I am, thank you.'

'Well, just as long as you realise the community is going to have to pay rent for your house, and for you alone.'

Grim-faced, the Major nodded.

'On to the next item. Now that we've had our first year here we need to meet to discuss where we're going—an Annual General Meeting, if you like, to assess how well we're doing, to make sure that we're still going in the right direction and to see what ideas we have for the future... forestall problems that may come up, that sort of thing.'

'Yes,' said Neil, taking up the theme. 'For example, we need to make sure that we're planting the right crops in the right amounts. Now I've got my own ideas, but I think we need to hear from every-body else.'

'And not just crops,' added Alan. 'What about medicines? Have we got enough of them?'

'We're running out,' said Derek. 'There are quite a number of items we can't get hold of any longer and some medicines have gone completely out of date...' Pictures of Alison flickered spontaneously into his mind, the daughter he couldn't save because the insulin had all degraded with the heat and the passage of time. With an effort he brought himself back to the present. 'We're not going to be able to make most of the complex drugs that we used to rely on, so we'll have to go back to herbal medicines and things like that.'

'Oh good,' said Mary. 'I like that, treating things naturally. What a splendid idea. I'll see if I can find some books on the subject.'

'Then there's always the matter of petrol,' chipped in Paul. 'Our stocks are running out fast. We really do need to spend a lot of time thinking about this one. Yes, I think we ought to have an AGM—a planning meeting—call it what you will.'

'I thought we'd done all this last year,' said the Major.

'To some extent we did,' said Paul. 'But to be honest I never thought we'd manage to get this far. If you must know, I thought we'd all be dead of starvation by now. But since it looks as if we aren't going to starve for the time being, then perhaps we ought to be making slightly more detailed plans for a long-term future. In any case, now we've had a year here we know more of what we're up against, so a new meeting will be able to make better-quality decisions.'

'I think that's an excellent idea,' said Chris. 'Shall we call a general meeting of the whole community for a week on Saturday?' Everyone nodded. 'Then I look forward to meeting everybody there.'

*   *   *

Beside the dying embers of the stove the cat woke up, yawned and stretched. Above it on one side was the towering figure of its mistress, Susan, snoring. On the other side of the hearth from his wife, Alan was trying to read in the half-light of the candle, enjoying the chance of some time to himself for once. Originally a science teacher, he'd always retained his inquisitive nature, and was currently immersed in a book about Peru—which was, he recognised sadly, about the nearest any of them was likely to get to that country ever again. He shifted his long thin frame in the chair.

The silent movement of the cat caught his eye and he put down his hand to stroke its back. The cat looked up at him, walked over to the door which was slightly ajar, pawed at it until it opened, then padded off into the hall, white feet and throat visible long after the rest of its black body had melted into the surrounding gloom.

The snoring stopped. Susan came to with a start. 'I don't know why you let that cat wander round the house letting all the cold air in.'

Alan shrugged, knowing his half hour of peace was up.

'*And* you've let the fire go out, too.'

'Have I...?' Alan put down his book. 'I'm sorry, I was reading. I got carried away...'

'I don't think you care about me at all, do you? All I have to do is go to sleep and everything goes to pot—fires go out, doors left undone. Really Alan, you don't care a bit, do you?'

Alan came to the conclusion that sadly this was possibly now true, though he tried to make the expression on his face deny the thought.

'And *why* you put up with that cat, heaven only knows...'

They'd had the cat since early summer—or, more specifically, the cat had had them. It had wandered in one day, taken a liking to them, and stayed. Alan had fed it a few scraps of left-overs and let it lie in front of the fire: in turn the cat had paid its way by keeping mice and rats away from their stored food.

Two weeks later it disappeared—so suddenly that they feared it had had an accident: Alan was quite put out as he'd got quite accustomed to its presence. Three weeks afterwards, it reappeared again just as suddenly. For the next eight weeks it made sudden appearances and disappearances, totally unpredictably. At any one moment they never knew whether it was alive or dead.

Alan, who'd been reading a book on quantum mechanics at the

time, christened it Schrödinger. It was just another of those things about Alan that irritated Susan intensely. What a stupid name, she thought. *Schrödinger*. What a name—for a cat, of all things!

She turned over and went off to sleep again, wincing intermittently as the scar pulled at her.

She'd just drifted off when, out in the hall, Schrödinger decided he'd come back into the dining room again and did so, pushing the door open and letting the cold air from the hall rush in. With an insouciant gaze he looked round the room, then wandered off again in search of food. There was silence in the house, apart from the snoring and the tick of the clock in the gloom of the hall.

- 3 -

*L*ike the others, Derek had been expecting the Annual General Meeting to be a corporate pat on the back. Flushed with the success of the harvest and with the knowledge that they'd managed to survive the first year on their own, most community members went to the meeting feeling very positive, looking forward to an even rosier future. Whilst the last year hadn't exactly been the epitome of easy living, nevertheless they'd not done badly: they hadn't starved—in fact they'd eaten well, they'd produced food for the future, and more than anything, they'd grown accustomed to the new ways of living. So as they filed into the magistrates' court—those who had bothered to turn up, for it's usually only protest meetings that are well attended—they were all chattering amiably about the successes of the past twelve months.

What came next was a shock to all but two of them. Chris rose to begin the meeting and after giving a brief summary of the previous year, invited Neil to start the ball rolling by talking about agricultural plans, following which Paul would lead a discussion about all other matters.

Neil rose to address the assembled company. 'Firstly I'd like to congratulate everyone on the way you helped to get in the harvest

so effectively. I can see by the look on your faces that you feel
we've achieved a great deal. Well, we have. But I also have to tell
you that from now on it's going to be a lot harder, in ways you may
not have expected.' A light burble of consternation rose from the
audience.

'Last year we had it easy. The wheat was planted for us, and all
we had to do was watch it grow. We had weedkiller, pesticides, fertiliser, fuel for the vehicles, and more fields planted with wheat than
ever we could have harvested, so that even if the crop in one or two
fields hadn't been up to standard we'd still have had other fields to
pick from.

'But the bad news is that now we've got to do it all again—but
this time we've got to sow our own fields. We've got to use our own
seed-corn, too, which won't be specially prepared and may well
have quite a lot of weeds in it; and because we're following on from
chemically intensive farming there's going to be a lag time while
the soil recovers its natural fertility.' Mary nodded—the only other
person in the audience already to have realised what was about to
happen.

Alan interrupted. 'I'm sorry Neil, I don't quite understand what
you've just said, and I'm sure there are others here who don't follow your train of thought either. I certainly concede that when we
don't have weedkillers and pesticides our yields may go down, but
I don't follow what you said about the land recovering its natural
fertility. Surely it will just go *back* to its natural fertility, rather than
have the super-productivity that all the dressings and weedkillers
gave it in the past?'

'Thank you for that, Alan,' replied Neil graciously. 'I'm sorry if
I haven't made it clear. Let me explain. What we think of as "soil"
is actually a mixture of many different things. What gives it its
structure are inert grains of sand or other finely divided rocks: the
smaller the grains, the more clay-like the soil. In between these
grains is water.

'But there are lots of other things in the soil as well—broken
down vegetable matter, the remains of animal manure, bacteria,
seeds, weeds. The dead organic matter is called humus, by the way.

Then there are the bigger animals—earthworms, insects, and the like.

'On its own, the sand with the water around it is quite unsuitable for growing things in. The grains of sand are inert and don't dissolve. There's nothing to feed the plants. And, like us, plants need food. So they use the humus in the soil; but often this humus has first to be broken down by bacteria or earthworms before the nutrients it contains can be used by plants.

'Land can be very rich in plant nutrients without the use of artificial fertilisers. A piece of land that has never been cultivated is actually quite stable—it grows grass or weeds or bushes or scrub or whatever: then the leaves fall and the plants die, and are broken down within the soil to provide nutrients for next year's plants, and so the whole cycle continues in a steady, secure way. The jungle is like this—jungle usually grows on very poor soil, but because it's well adapted for recycling its own waste, it keeps on growing well.

'So far, I've been talking about uncultivated land. If we want to cultivate this land we've got to do three things. We've got to clear it of the old weeds, which otherwise would use up the nutrients that the new plants need; we have to protect the new crops against diseases like fungi which would otherwise attack them; and we've got to protect the plants against insects that will eat them as they're growing.

'Let's say we're trying to grow crops on land that doesn't have much humus in, or else we've harvested the previous crop and not allowed much to die back. In other words, we've taken away the nutrients that originally came from the earth, without giving anything back. Now in the recent past this was where all our modern agricultural chemicals came in. By feeding the land with extra fertilisers—nitrates, for example—we could artificially put back a lot of the goodness that we'd taken out through intensive farming. With nitrates we can get crops to grow much more luxuriantly. In the past we also used weedkillers to stop competing weeds from using up the goodness that the crop wants, and pesticides to stop pests eating the crop. But when we do that we're altering the balance of the land and making it into quite an artificial environment. For example, while killing off other bacteria, if we also kill off those useful bacteria that convert nitrogen in the air into a form that plants can absorb, then there won't be enough naturally produced nitrogen in the soil and we'll have to put more nitrates on directly to make up the balance.

'Before the plague, if you looked at a field of wheat or vegetables you were looking at something that was growing very artificially, in a very strange environment, however natural it might have looked at first.

'Unfortunately the land around us is used to being farmed in this artificial way. But things are very different now, and it will take some time for the land to get back to its original state. During the next few years it will be neither one thing or the other—neither intensively farmed, nor back to a natural level of nutrition either. It will have the problems of each type of farming and the benefits of neither. During this time we'll find that our yields drop dramatically.'

The level of consternation amongst the audience rose considerably. Derek interjected. 'I seem to remember from my history lessons at school that in the Middle Ages they used crop rotation so that one crop would put back what another crop took out. Can't we go back to doing that?'

'Yes,' replied Neil. 'That's what we'll have to do. But it'll take some time to set up. The character of the soil has been changed quite dramatically by all the intensive agricultural methods that have been used.'

'I always said these methods were wrong,' said Mary, pointedly. 'Now we're just finding out the hard way.'

'No,' said Neil patiently, 'I disagree. The old methods were perfectly sensible, provided they were carried through properly. They gave high yields, and they stopped the crops getting attacked by all sorts of unpleasant pests. Our problem is that we've got to change *suddenly* from one type of farming to another—a bit like getting on the plane in Spain where it's boiling hot, and two hours later getting back to England where it's cool. We notice the difference especially over such a short time. It's because we've got to make the change over a short timescale that we have the problem.'

'So, as Derek said, can't we establish a rotation system like they did in the Middle Ages?' asked Chris.

'Yes, we can,' said Neil. 'In fact we've *got* to do it—for two reasons. Firstly we've got to make sure that the land doesn't get depleted of any of the essential substances that the crops need—and we can put some of these back by growing different crops in different years, and by spreading manure on the fields. The other matter, which nobody here seems to have realised, is that each crop has its own natural enemies. To make certain that diseases don't spread, we need to rotate the crops so that, if a crop in a particular field gets infected, we don't plant the same crop the next year and pick up the infection again.'

'So it's a bit like human illnesses,' said Derek thoughtfully. 'The way most of us have stopped ourselves getting the plague is by keeping out of the way. You can stop a crop getting an infection by isolating it—by not planting the same type of seeds in the same field two years running.'

'That's exactly right, but there are other things that will help as well. At the moment all the fields around us are large, because in the past this suited the big agricultural machines we used to have, like combine harvesters. In the past we could stop diseases spreading by using pesticides and weedkillers, but now we haven't got them we'll have to make sure that if a disease gets in at one end of a field it can't do too much damage if it spreads. So what we need to do is to make fields a lot smaller, and not plant the same crop on either side of the hedges, so infections can't simply jump across, or be blown on the wind, or get carried across by animals. If we leave wild spaces on either side of the hedges it'll also provide somewhere for the natural predators of crop pests to live. It may even be a help to leave a wild space down the middle of each field...'

'Hang on a minute,' interjected Paul. 'Aren't you going over the top? Does it really matter if we get a few predators and reduce our yields by a few per cent? I mean, come on, be realistic. What sort of percentages are we talking about?'

'Do you remember what I said last year?' asked Neil. 'About

how much of the crop we'd lose if we didn't use pesticides and weedkillers?'

'Vaguely.'

'It was thirty per cent. In fact, I think that's probably an under-estimate at the moment, at least in our second year of production. Bearing in mind we've got soil that wants artificial feeding and won't get it, to be honest I don't know what the figure is—thirty per cent, fifty per cent, sixty per cent.'

'Sixty per cent of our previous year isn't bad,' said Paul.

'I wasn't talking of our previous yield, I was saying sixty per cent *loss*.' There was a gasp from the audience as the enormity of it all sank in. 'That's assuming that we get a good summer again. And the point I want to make is that every little counts. Let's say we lose thirty per cent of our yield because we can't use fertilisers any longer. If we then lose ten per cent of the remainder to predators we're starting to get very high losses, aren't we? Every little helps. Trust me, Paul, I know what I'm doing.'

Mary murmured something under her breath about agro-chemical farmers and soil damage, which Neil pretended not to hear.

'There are other protective measures that we need to employ in order to be able to work the fields properly. We're not going to be able to use tractors very much which means we've got to be able to hoe the crop—the vegetables in particular—so we'll need to plant as they did in the Middle Ages, in long strips of about five feet wide...'

'Why?' interjected Peter. 'Why can't we just walk among the crops, treading carefully?'

Neil was just starting to lose his patience with all the interruptions from those who'd never tried farming themselves. 'Because if you stand on soil you compress it, which means that air and water can't get through—so you can't grow plants on soil you've stood on repeatedly. The best way is to leave lanes in between the plants so the workers can use these and not damage the looseness of the soil in which the crops are growing. There are all sorts of other mea-sures that I suggest we take, such as putting animals in the fields to let their manure fertilise the ground naturally...'

'Talking of natural, I still think you farmers have a lot to answer for,' said Mary, 'the way the agribusiness interfered with the natural balance of nature in the past.'

'*All* agriculture interferes with the natural balance of things,' replied Neil evenly. 'Anyway what do *you* mean by natural?'

Mary waved her arm around in no particular direction. 'The countryside around us.'

'The English countryside isn't natural,' expostulated Neil. 'Everything you see is man-made, or did you think that hedges just grew like that? And did the fields in the Pennines just happen to grow with dry stone walling round them? And the woods were all natural, were they?'

'Well, yes,' said Mary. 'Woods certainly.'

'Rubbish,' said Neil. 'How many woods do you know where there are lots of different types of trees? Most of them are actually plantations, if you look carefully. No, Mary, I know what you mean, but I'm afraid you're mistaken. Most of what you see *isn't* natural. The English countryside looks the way it does because of what we've done to it over hundreds of years. Agriculture itself is about interfering with the natural balance of things. When you clear out scrub and grass in order to plant a field of wheat or rye you're interfering with the natural balance. When you make compost in your garden and feed that round the plants, you're doing something which is unnatural. When you put on extra chemical fertiliser you're interfering with the natural balance too. So what's the difference? Mary, you've got a bee in your bonnet about things "being natural", but you don't know what the phrase means. You're using it emotively.'

Mary subsided like a pricked balloon, her face going even redder.

'I'm sorry, Mary,' said Neil. 'I didn't mean to be rude, but I do know what I'm doing. Also, I *did* know what I was doing in the past, and with all due respect you've been trained as a librarian, not a farmer. But let's get back to my original point. Whatever the rights and wrongs of fertilisers, chemicals, pesticides and weedkillers, the fact is that we don't have any of these things now, and our yields are going to be severely depleted as a result.'

He sat down. The buzz from the audience increased.

'Derek, I think you wanted to ask something at this point,' said Chris.

'Yes,' said Derek, standing up. 'I'm anxious to make sure that we start to replace our medicines. I'm sure we'll have to go back to using herbs.'

'Which ones do you want?' asked Neil, picking up his pen, 'and how do we know which are useful?'

'I've made a list from a book of medicinal herbs. That might do for starters. I thought maybe if you took a trip in one of the narrow-boats down to the Chelsea Physic Garden you might be able to get cuttings from the plants there. Then we could grow them here and see if they were any use.'

'Much more natural,' said Mary pointedly and almost inaudibly—but not quite. Derek hadn't the patience nor the resilience of Neil, and nearly exploded.

'I don't think you've got the vaguest idea about that word, Mary,' he said angrily. 'Neil's quite right. It's all very well talking about "natural" this and "natural" that but you don't have a clue what you're talking about. You say something is "natural" because it comes from a plant—but it doesn't necessarily mean it's good for you. Try eating deadly nightshade berries and see what it feels like. I'll tell you, if you didn't know already: it'll kill you. And just because some things are "chemical" doesn't mean that they're bad for you either. Ascorbic acid is a chemical, isn't it?'

Mary nodded.

'Well, it's vitamin C and it's vital for your health.'

'But isn't it better to use the existing natural flowers and herbs that nature has provided instead of chemicals?'

'Rubbish,' said Derek. 'What's the point in using a "natural" product that's full of other substances you don't want, when you could isolate the one substance that's important, purify it or synthesise it artificially, and then give the pure form alone, as a medicine? When you use a plant extract you're giving many other impure substances. Sometimes these substances are things that you don't want, things that will damage you. Anyway when you use the word "chemical" you don't realise what you mean.'

'I do,' retorted Mary angrily.

'No, you don't,' said Derek. '*Everything* is made of chemicals. It's just that you've decided to call certain things chemicals and other things not. Every time you open your mouth and eat a "naturally produced" wholewheat loaf you're eating chemicals. The proteins are chemical, the carbohydrates are chemical, chemicals make up the water, the milk and the yeast—and the carbon dioxide made by the yeast that causes the bread to rise is a chemical too. It's just that you've got this silly idea that just because something is a "chemical" it's nasty and that because something is naturally produced it's somehow good. It *isn't*.'

He subsided irascibly into his seat and then looked up again. 'Mary, you've got us off the point again. I was trying to say that we don't have many of our original drugs left in the chemist's and I need some new supplies. For a start the old sort are going off'— visions of Alison flashed again, unbidden, into his mind—'and we need to have something to replace them. Mary, I'll grant you that plants are better than nothing, but I'd rather have nice purified "chemical" medicines any day than rely on plant extracts. Plant extracts are variable, they don't necessarily do what you want, they're contaminated with all sorts of other substances and they don't work anything like as well as the "chemical" medicines that we used in the past.

'And to get back to the point, we need to provide ourselves with a sheltered area—another Physic Garden if you like—where we can grow the more important plants to provide us with those medicines that we're going to need for the future.'

'As I said before, what sort of things are you talking about?' asked Neil.

'I've got a long list. I'll see you later about it.'

'No, no,' said Neil. 'Just give me an idea.'

'There's all sorts of things,' said Derek. 'Many of them grow locally already. There's willow bark, from which we can get aspirin;

foxglove leaves are a source of digoxin, which is a heart drug; feverfew can be used in migraine; dandelions for making you pass more urine—all sorts of things. Big plants, small plants, trees, shrubs, annuals, seeds, roots...'

'Some of them are what we used to think of as weeds, and I've heard it said that a weed is a plant in the wrong place,' replied Neil dryly. 'It all comes down to a matter of definitions, like the word "natural".' Mary went pinker and bit her tongue. 'In answer to your question, Derek, yes, I'll happily go down to London and take cuttings of the rarer plants. You'll have to give me your list.' Then courtesy took over, and he held out an olive branch to Mary. 'Mary you're obviously into this sort of thing, aren't you?'

She nodded silently, tight-lipped.

'Perhaps you could help Derek by providing a list of the plants you know about that might be of use to him. It won't be the sort of information he'll find easy to acquire from his modern text books.'

Mary nodded again, avoiding both Derek's and Neil's eyes.

'One final thing on farming,' said Paul. 'What about a supply of fuel? The coal will run out eventually. It would be a good idea to plan now to use wood in the future.'

'I've already thought of that,' said Neil. 'I think we ought to do what they did in the old days, and use a technique called coppicing.'

'What's that?' asked the Major.

'They'd grow a young tree, then cut it back, so instead of a single, big main trunk it would produce a lot of smaller trunks which would grow, bush-like, quite quickly, and which could soon be cut down for use as firewood and staves and anything where they needed small straight pieces of wood.'

'I think some of the woods on the way to Ridgmont have been coppiced,' said Alan. 'I saw them a few weeks ago. Massive great trees they were too.'

'Ah, well, it's too late to use them for things like staves, then,' said Neil. 'Coppicing like that was done many years ago and has just been left. The sort of coppicing I'm talking about is where the tree is finally cut down after a few years—it shouldn't be left to go on to become a mature set of trunks. We *will* be able to use the wood from the trees you spotted, Alan, but not for the thin laths you can get from a properly maintained coppice.

'But we'll set to work on this. Time's on our side here, for once. For the moment we can still chop down ordinary trees in the woods to provide us with fuel. We've just got to make sure that we replace what we cut down—something with which I'm sure you'll agree, Mary.'

Mary nodded again, not quite sure whether she was being deferred to or patronised. She decided it was probably the former.

'All right,' said Chris. 'Let's move on.' She beckoned to Paul who was sitting next to her. 'Your turn.' Paul rose and looked round at the members of the community packed into the crowded court-room.

'Right,' he said. 'We got through the first year, didn't we? And it's not gone too badly, but we haven't made any really long-term plans yet and I think it's about time we did. To be honest, like many of you, I didn't really think we'd survive the first year. But we did, and we can be proud of it. Now we've got to look really long term. What are we going to do after the diesel runs out? Because it will do one day. What are we going to use for tyres? We've no supply of rubber, and rubber tyres perish in the light after eight or ten years.

'There are any number of items like this, and we need to look ahead carefully to make sure we don't get caught out—like we did last year, remember? Wasn't it surprising how some things ran out before we realised how important they were and took steps to conserve them? Newspapers for instance. How many of us realised that we'd miss newspaper? Not for the news, but for things like cleaning, or to protect a floor, or for lighting the fire? We used to have a continuous "free" supply of it posted through our door every day: then suddenly it wasn't there, and only later did we realise how much we depended upon it. So we need to make sure that we conserve carefully those things that we can't easily replace.

'The good news is—we've got a genuinely all-round supply of knowledge, skills and trades. We've even got ourselves a doctor...' he motioned towards Derek who smiled and nodded, '...in Nicholas,' said Paul pointedly, wiping the smile off Derek's face,

'...and of course we've got Derek.' A ripple of laughter ran round the courtroom. At least Paul had got the old spark back in him, thought Chris happily. Derek coloured a little at being set up, but then reflected that it was Paul's way of dealing with people, and he knew he didn't mean it.

Paul's face suddenly became serious again. 'Other than food and medicines our main problem is going to be fuel—or energy, call it what you will. Our stocks of both petrol and diesel are running very low, and what we've got now we really must keep for the future. There are no two ways about it—we'll have to use animal power wherever possible, and we've got to make a rule not to use any of the vehicles unless there's a pressing reason why nothing else will do.' He looked pointedly round for Kevin but Kevin wasn't there. He was probably burning up and down a road somewhere on his Harley-Davidson, thought Paul bitterly.

'On the other hand, we can make various alternative fuels available. I understand from Derek, whom you know in a previous incarnation was an engineer...' there was a little titter of appreciation from the audience '...that we can convert petrol engines to use methane gas and we've got a good continual supply of methane from the waste dump to the north by Elstow. Have you seen the flares at night? They're still burning. That's because the rotting of the waste material underground is producing a more or less constant supply of methane. I also understand there's an electricity-producing plant there but whether we'll ever be able to get that connected up so that we could supply electricity to ourselves I'm not sure: I think we ought to look into it. But we ought to look at collecting the methane from those dumps instead of flaring it off, because, believe it or not, you can put a gas-bag of methane in the back of the car and use it to drive around instead of petrol.

'Most of the agricultural machinery works on diesel but some of it doesn't. A few very older types of tractor can work on petrol so we could convert those to methane. And I gather you can also run certain types of engines on castor oil and rapeseed oil, so in the future we can think about growing that. Maybe that's something for Neil.

'But to be honest I think our main need is to try to provide a source of electricity. We could do so much if we had this. We'd have light, heat, and we could use electrical equipment like drills and lathes. We'd also be able to provide ourselves with a bit of recreation in the form of CD players and even videos. So all in all I think we ought to try and get that electrical plant up at Elstow working. I'm sure it would make a lot of difference.'

He sat down to a burble of discussion. For the next quarter of an hour they discussed the pros and cons of what Paul had said, and all the while Derek became aware of a feeling he'd not experienced before—a profound lethargy, a sense of disinterest that somehow this was all happening to other people and that his involvement in it was only marginal and minor. He looked outside at the wind blowing the leaves off the trees and shivered. Winter was approaching.

- 4 -

Mary had an uneasy night and was troubled when she woke up, the more so because too little sleep puts the emotions on edge; and in reality so many people make decisions not by logic but by emotion. It was Sunday, a day on which the community tried to do only that work which really had to be done. It wasn't set aside for any great religious reason, but from the purely pragmatic viewpoint that human beings need a rest at least one day in seven. So after feeding her chickens Mary walked purposefully down the road into Ampthill. It was a bright and sunny October day with a sharp breeze—the sort of day that makes people glad to be out in it, but also glad to get indoors afterwards. Opposite Dynevor House on Church Street was Foulislea Cottage where Chris had taken up residence. Mary knocked purposefully on the door. A few moments later Chris opened it.

'Hello, Mary. Do come in. Would you like a hot drink? I was just about to make one.'

'Yes, please,' said Mary conscious of how cold it had been outside. 'What have you got?'

'No coffee or tea left, I'm afraid.'

'I don't know anyone who has,' smiled Mary.

'I've got some acorn coffee. Would you like that?'

'That would be fine.' Chris went off to put a kettle of water on the stove, leaving Mary gazing round the inside of the cottage, watching the sun slanting in through the French windows.

'I've never been here before,' she said after a moment.

'Nice, isn't it?' said Chris.

'It's bigger than it looks from the outside.'

'It is *much* bigger than it looks from the outside: a bit like the Tardis, really.' They went into the tiny morning room with its diagonally placed hearth and homely clutter of prints and paintings on the walls. 'Now what can I do for you?'

'I suppose I came to have a moan, really,' replied Mary. 'I'm just getting a little fed up of the way everybody seems to be ignoring everything I say.'

'I wasn't aware of that.'

'Maybe you weren't, but it's happening anyway. First it was Neil, now it's Derek. And Paul.'

'I'm not really aware that anyone's ignoring you. What are you saying that you feel we're not listening to?'

'Oh, everything,' she said, her lips thin-set and the grey bun of hair bobbing up and down as usual. 'I'm not a fool, you know. Before the plague I took a great interest in "green" issues. I *do* know what I'm talking about. About how to grow things naturally for a start. I used to be a librarian. I had time for these things, time to read them, time to look them up, to put on exhibitions and talks.'

'And what precisely do you think we ought to do that we aren't doing?'

'I don't think Neil understands the problem. He's so bogged down with the mind-set that says "agro-chemicals are good for you" that he hasn't the vaguest idea of how to work without them. I *know*. I've read the books. I knew everything that he was saying about the soil, and all about the problems that we're going to have next year because of the poisoning of the place with fertilisers and weed-killers, but nobody seems to be listening to me.'

'I think Neil is,' said Chris. 'Biscuit?'

'Thanks,' said Mary, munching away absentmindedly. 'And then there's Paul, little upstart, talking about money and people earning it. Why, before the plague he was one of the most dishonest of the lot, wasn't he? A stockbroker. Never produced a thing, simply sponged off everybody else. And then he has the gall to talk about those who don't work. Really—'

'I think you'll find it was quite hard work,' said Paul, materialising as if by magic from the stairwell behind where Chris was sitting. Mary nearly dropped her plate. Crumbs spluttered everywhere.

'Where did *you* come from?' she said, her cheeks reddening again.

'I was upstairs in the study. I assure you, being a stockbroker is very hard work. Many of my colleagues couldn't do it for more than ten years. In at twenty-two, out at thirty-two, burned-out. Maybe you don't think we produced anything very much but we did provide a service that a lot of people wanted and a lot of people used: and if *we* weren't working then neither were council officers or NHS managers or secretaries or any other administrator you care to name. We were all doing something that somebody wanted. Come to think of it, you weren't doing anything productive, were you?'

Chris turned a disapproving look towards Paul, who ignored her. 'You were only a librarian. I'm sure we'd have found the books ourselves if we hadn't had you lot around—'

'Oh, do be quiet Paul,' said Chris.

'Just making a point,' said Paul acidly, pouring himself a cup of coffee. 'But you're wrong Mary. I don't have it in for you and I certainly *was* listening to what you said in the meetings. It's just that, like Derek, I disagree with you about "natural" medicines—basically because I think you're wrong.'

'I'm not wrong,' said Mary brushing the crumbs off her sweater, 'and I'm not wrong about the crops either.'

'Why should you think that you know more about agriculture than Neil, who's been doing it all his life?' asked Chris.

'Because he's had his head turned by all those wretched people from the chemical companies. He's never been taught green economics.'

'Aren't you assuming rather a lot?' asked Chris. 'After all, he did it for a living, and has been doing for a very long time.'

'He just thinks I'm a fool,' said Mary, 'and he won't listen.'

'Well, maybe you are,' said Paul. 'Maybe you're just an interfering old busybody.'

'*Paul*!' interrupted Chris.

'No, I mean it,' said Paul. 'How you have the gall to think that you know more about farming than Neil does, when you've spent all your life inside a library and he's been out in the fields doing it for real, I don't know.'

'Don't experts get it wrong?'

'Sometimes.'

'And don't experts get it wrong when they get their heads turned by marketing men from conglomerates?'

'Yes, sometimes, but that doesn't mean that they *always* get it wrong, does it? Anyway Mary, I'll tell you what Neil really does think about you, if you want: if you want to listen, that is.'

'Go on,' said Mary her lips pressed together even more tightly than usual, preparing for the worse.

'Actually he thinks you're quite nice. Well-meaning. Caring. Concerned. He was very grateful to you for bringing up some of your points, and if you must know, he agrees with a lot of the things you've said. He'd have said them himself if you hadn't got in first. But there are some areas where he thinks you're totally wrong and he's not going to let everybody else get hijacked. The bottom line is that if you lead everybody on what seems to you to be the right course and it turns out to be wrong then we'll all starve. To *death*. Right? So you've got to be absolutely certain that you're right before you dare to criticise what Neil is doing. And I'll go along with Neil because so far his track record is good. You may be a good theorist, but it doesn't matter to me whether your ideas work in theory: his ideas work in practice, so I'll stick with that. I always was a pragmatist.'

'Paul's right,' said Chris gently. 'Neil *has* listened to much of what you've said. But why don't you go and chat with him directly? Go with a list of the things that are bothering you and a set of suggestions and see what he says. He's listened to you about herbal medicines, hasn't he?'

'Derek didn't,' retorted Mary.

'That's not true either,' said Chris. 'Derek asked Neil to go to the Physic Garden and take cuttings.'

'He didn't think much of herbal medicines.'

'Simply because they're not as potent as the pharmaceutical ones, but he knows, and you know, that it's all we've got now, so we'll have to make do. It's not what he'd like but it's as good as he'll get. So *we* need your advice. *He* needs your advice. We *all* need your advice.'

'It still doesn't sort out the problem of the money,' said Mary bitterly.

'Yes, it does,' said Paul evenly, totally unaware of how deeply he'd wounded her. 'And exactly the same thing applies. Your ideas about not needing money may work in theory, but if they don't work in practice there's not much point in having them. What's the statement that Derek's always quoting whenever he studies his medical books? "Many a fine theory has been slain by a cruel fact." When the ivory tower and the practical man meet, give me the practical man every time.'

'You used to be a librarian, didn't you?' said Chris, desperately looking for a way to change the subject.

'I think so. In an earlier existence, though I might well be wrong,' replied Mary testily, taking a sip from her cup. 'Apparently I usually am.'

Chris ignored the barb. 'I've got something to show you. Come with me,' and she led Mary up the winding staircase leading off the back of the morning room. It ascended directly into a barn-like room that had obviously been a study, packed from floor to ceiling with shelves of books, loose-leaf folders and card indexes, and lit only by a tiny strip of window in front of which was an old-style desk.

Rooms are like people—they seem to give off hidden vibes. Some rooms manage to be ugly and forbidding even though on paper they ought to look nice. Others are higgledy-piggledy with no order, no right angles and no straight lines but still manage to be homely, welcoming and above all, human. And this room was welcoming. Mary fell in love with it at first sight. It was like a return to the womb, a womb packed with information. As her practised librarian's eye surveyed the shelves, taking in the meticulous detail with which everything had been marked, codified, indexed and annotated, she suddenly felt totally and completely at home. 'Good heavens,' was the only thing she could manage to say after thirty seconds of silence. 'Well... I say...' Deftly she pulled out a drawer of the card index to the right of the desk, a card index that looked as though it was made out of apothecary's drawers—which indeed it had been. Searching through the groups of files labelled 'People', 'Places' and 'Events' she pulled out one at random. '*Railways*' it read. '*Railway comes to Ampthill*,' with the reference. '*Closure of the station*', with the reference. '*Last ticket bought*', with another reference. The references were obviously to the loose-bound folders on the shelves to her left. She looked them up. Inside were further references, but no original documents or articles. 'There's something else,' she said, puzzled. 'Must be. These are just references to where everything's kept. The actual documents must be in another room.'

'Yes, they are,' said Chris. 'Come through here,' and ducking down she led Mary through a five-foot-high door under one of the crossbeams holding up the old roof. They went through into a bedroom, then to a further landing and to two rooms beyond.

'It's incredible,' said Mary. 'This place is about three times bigger on the inside than it looks on the outside. It's even bigger than I thought.'

'That's right. Actually a lot of it is let into the big house next door.' She led Mary to a bedroom which overlooked Church Street. Inside were racks of box files stuffed with documents, objects and photographs.

'This is *wonderful*,' said Mary, her eyes glancing around as she opened files, studied the contents, then replaced them carefully. She hurried back to the main card index. 'But this is incredible. This is what we've always wanted.'

'What?' said Chris and Paul together, by now totally mystified.

'This is a record of the things that have happened in the past in Ampthill. Obviously an antiquarian's collection of local facts.'

'What's so clever about that?' said Paul. 'It's history. It's boring.'

'Not a bit of it,' said Mary, without looking up. She was still rummaging around in the card index. 'This'll tell us things that we never knew. Look! Look!' and she pulled out cards one after the other. '*Sites of local wells... Sewage system... Shops... Field names.*'

'*Field names*?' chorused Chris and Paul in unison.

'Yes, field names. Didn't you know? Names of fields mean things. They tell you about the fields themselves—which were wet; and which looked fertile but weren't. Look, *Snow Hill* in Maulden. That's the area between Ampthill and Maulden on the north side. It would be called "Snow Hill" because in winter snow would remain there for longest.'

'I'll drink to that,' said Paul. 'That's just where we kept all the sheep last year. The shepherds will testify to the hours they spent out in the snow last February.'

'Look!' said Mary, eyes aglow. 'You wanted fish? This is a list of all the fish-ponds round here—that is, if you insist on fishing.'

'Let me see that,' said Chris, almost grabbing the card off her and holding it up to the sunlight that slanted in through the low window with its insets of medieval glass. ' "Fish ponds..." There was the Stew—that's for Dynevor House. Hey—that's the pond on the left of Holly Walk as you look towards Martin's house.'

Paul nodded. 'Yes, I know it.'

'And the Westminster pond. That was supposed to be very deep—it's at the western edge of Ampthill, on the bypass. Then there's one at the bottom of the hill in the park—that was attached to Park House.'

'I still don't really see the significance of all this,' said Paul.

'Then you're losing your touch,' said Chris tartly. 'They were all ponds to feed the big houses.'

'What, perch for dinner?' said Paul. 'Pull the other one.'

'No,' said Chris scornfully. 'They farmed fish just like we farm the fields.'

'That's right,' said Mary. 'In the old days they'd be full of carp. They'd feed them regularly, fatten them up and that would give them a constant supply of fish. They didn't have to go to the sea for fish—not that they could. We're about as far away from the coast as you could possibly get in England. And I don't know why I'm telling you all this,' said Mary, 'after all you've said to me.'

'Yes, you do,' said Chris, 'it's because you care about us all.'

'There is that,' replied Mary, somewhat embarrassed to have to admit to a positive emotion for once.

'So the old houses used to stock fish in the fish-ponds and fatten them up for a ready supply,' mused Paul. 'I bet you couldn't use the pond—what was it called?—the one up Holly Walk...'

'The Stew,' said Chris looking up from the card.

'I bet you couldn't use it now. It looks far too shallow.'

'Maybe we ought to dredge it,' said Chris, 'then stock it with fish. Then it's something else we've got, another supply of food in case we have a bad harvest.'

'See?' said Mary 'Who said you don't learn anything from history? You'd forgotten all about fish-ponds as a source of food, hadn't you? You know the maxim, don't you? "Those who don't learn the lessons of history are condemned to relive them." We've just rediscovered fish-ponds.'

'Wells,' said Paul. 'You said something about wells.'

'Yes,' said Mary, hardly looking up now, her face content, still concentrating on the pieces of paper in front of her on the desk. She waved her hand vaguely in the air. 'There's a list of wells, many along here in Church Street.'

'Where's the list?' said Paul.

'On the card. Look for yourself.' Paul bent down and pulled out a drawer. He thought it was a long card-index drawer, but it wasn't: it was an apothecary's drawer, and about a quarter of the length he'd expected. He pulled it right out of its housing and all the cards spilled on the floor. Mary looked at him with that special hardened

look that librarians managed to achieve after years of practice, fix-
ating at twenty yards those who chew crisps in the silence of the
reading room. Paul went red and began stuffing the cards back into
the box.

'In order, Paul, in order. What's the point in having an index
that's been randomised?'

'Sorry,' said Paul, cowed, and began the laborious task of putting
them back in their correct sequence. 'Hey, look at this,' he said
showing the card to Chris, who nodded '...and this... and this...' He
sat back on his heels. 'You're right, Mary, this is wonderful.'

'What else is there here?' Chris wandered round the room. She'd
looked at the room in the past of course, but in a superficial uninterested way. History had never been one of her strong points at
school; and local history had always seemed much less important
than national and international history, so the first time she had
come to Foulislea Cottage she'd looked vaguely round the books
and then put the information to the back of her mind. Suddenly she
saw them afresh and wondered why she'd never recognised them
for what they were. Martin's phrase about 'seeing things with
different eyes' suddenly surfaced as she realised that she too was
looking afresh at how life really was lived—this time village life,
rather than Martin's 'theology seen through real life'. Village living,
rather than theology, but in its own way just as important, because
the one couldn't do without the other. There was no point in theological truths if all the theologians had died of starvation; nor was
there any point in simply existing without understanding why. And
in that second Chris suddenly stopped feeling that she was living
just in modern times, solely a product of the end of the twentieth
century, and began to understand that her way of life, her very existence even, was rooted in the past: that she was nothing but another brick on top of a wall built on the lives of those who had lived
before her, and that her very existence rested on the experience,
wisdom and knowledge of her communal ancestors. She ran her fingers over the books on the shelves and with an approving glance
pulled out book after book, surveyed them and put them back again.
'Here you are, Paul,' she said finally, handing him a pink-backed

book entitled *A history of everyday things in England*. 'Nirvana.'

'What do I want with this?' asked Paul.

'Read it, silly.' Paul opened it at random at a set of diagrams of different types of carts and how to build them. He turned back a page, to find a model of a horse-powered thresher and a cut-away drawing of the mechanical principles it used. He flicked through a few more pages.

' "How to make an ice house",' he said. 'I didn't know you could store ice without electricity or gas.'

'*Ice house*,' repeated Mary, going across to the index that Paul had just replaced in its holder. 'There was one at Avenue House.'

'Ice house?' said Paul. 'Without a refrigerator?'

'Yes,' said Mary. 'The ice was cut in the winter from the top of the ponds, and the ice house was specially constructed to keep it as cool as possible so that there was a supply throughout the summer.'

'Well, I never,' said Paul turning over another page. 'Look, here's a set of instructions on how to build an oven.' And suddenly the penny dropped. *These are things we can make ourselves*, these are things we can make *simply*. We can do it. We can do it ourselves. It was as if the whole world had blossomed out in three dimensions and Technicolor in front of him. No longer did they have to make do and mend what remained of the technology of the twentieth century, technology that was so inelegant and unfitted for use in a world without electricity or gas—such as plastic containers that were ideal for cooking in microwave ovens but totally useless on a range or if pushed into a fire; or grinders, shredders, splitters and sharpeners that only worked with electricity instead of by hand.

'I must show this to Derek,' he said finally.

'Derek?' said Mary. 'Why? There's not much to do with medicine here.'

'No, but Derek *used* to be an engineer, didn't he?' replied Paul. 'He'll be able to assimilate this much more quickly than I can. Look! *How to grind corn*. We'll need that. I must admit I was wondering how we'd do it.'

'That's simple,' said Chris. 'There's a working water-mill at Bromham. You knew that, didn't you?'

'Yes,' said Paul, 'I did, *but I didn't know how to use it*. I remember going round a demonstration mill once and they said that they set it one way to provide seed for the animals and another way to provide fine ground flour. And if you got the setting wrong you'd set the whole place on fire. A bit worrying, that.'

'Well, it looks as if you've got the answer,' said Chris, putting the book back on the shelf.

'This is wonderful,' said Mary her eyes still fixed on the papers in front of her. 'Just wonderful.'

'We'll leave you to it,' said Chris.

'Yes, do,' said Mary absent-mindedly, turning over yet another page.

'Gone,' said Paul. 'Totally gone.'

*   *   *

Derek, more than anyone else, was aware of the onrush of winter. Because he was called out so much he experienced night-time more than most: as he'd morosely remarked to Anne, there seemed a lot more night around than he'd remembered in the past. And it wasn't just the physical absence of light in a world without electricity. Frequently Derek was up and about at times when all sensible mortals were tucked up in bed, then spent the next day trying to keep awake, wishing he were in bed able to sleep his tiredness off, only to be called out again the next night. It was just another of the stresses mounting up against him.

His medical knowledge was another problem. For the past year he'd struggled to make sense of medicine. He'd found that while he understood the individual systems well enough—the cardiovascular system, orthopaedics, the urinary system, the nervous system—seeing their inter-relationships was another matter entirely. Although he understood the effects of, say, heart failure on the cardiovascular system, it was only with an effort that he remembered what, if anything, it could do to the kidneys. Similarly, when six months earlier, he had had an elderly patient with a bad leg injury, he had had to force himself to remember the effects of immobilisation on the rest of the system, such as the increased likelihood of blood clots in the legs or lungs. It wasn't easy. Many times Derek wished that he had that easy facility of Nicholas in realising how a problem in one area of the body would have knock-on effects elsewhere in an entirely different system.

Like so many things in medicine, it was in the night when the change occurred. On one particular night Derek got an uninterrupted night's sleep. Perhaps this helped, giving time for his subconscious to assimilate the information it had in its possession, time to reorganise it, make connections, lay down new thought patterns and eradicate old and incorrect ones—but for whatever reason, when Derek went to bed that night, his understanding of each system in the body was separate, curiously unconnected to the others. The next morning when he awoke they were together in one whole system! All the interconnections were there—and for the first time it required no special effort on Derek's part to realise that a hole in the heart might damage the workings of the lungs through back pressure, or that there was an intimate relationship between heart failure and kidney performance, or that diabetics get more infections, or sufferers with severe multiple sclerosis more chest infections...

As he woke up, and as he realised what had happened overnight, Derek smiled the biggest smile Anne had seen for many a long month. He *knew*! Now he *knew* how the body fitted together in all its detail.

He smiled again, then turned over and gave himself an extra five minutes in bed as a congratulatory present. Winter might be coming on, but his new-found understanding would make it a little more bearable.

*   *   *

There was one man for whom the onset of winter didn't hold any real fear—at least, not this year. Martin hadn't really expected to go back to being a priest but somehow naturally gravitated into it. If he were honest, he rather enjoyed the physical work of farming, milking and looking after the animals, and didn't want to give it up. But now the community had got through the first year and once its physical needs were beginning to be met, other needs—both emotional and social—were surfacing, problems to which someone like Martin could perhaps provide better answers than others.

For the first few months he was still enjoying the recent turn-around in his emotional fortunes. To the outsider Martin had 'got religion'—a most unfortunate phrase and one that didn't get even remotely near the truth. To the ones who knew Martin better it seemed that he'd suddenly become more enthusiastic about his beliefs—but even that wasn't the whole story. As he'd already explained to Derek, at last he understood how religious principles truly fitted in with worldly ideas, and so he no longer felt pulled in six different directions at once.

This meant that, from being a complex, ambivalent, indecisive person, Martin had suddenly changed. No longer did he lie awake at night worrying about whether he was doing the right thing. No longer did he feel anxious about what to do, nor did he have difficulty making up his mind on small issues. Things somehow slotted into place a great deal more easily—at least, up to a point. There were still problems and crises, but now they seemed to be on a different level. Whereas in the past Martin had become bogged down with silly obsessional problems, now he could turn his full attention to the more major difficulties.

But the thing he was currently enjoying more than anything was the sense of unity and peace which had descended upon him, an absence of inner strife which made the whole of his existence so much more restful.

Some would have said it was because Martin had found God. Others would have said it was because God had found him. Now that Martin had found himself, and realised how God fitted into that scheme of things, he could rejoice in it all and, in the words of St Augustine, had learned not only how to know God but how to enjoy him. To the outsider this looked like getting religion. To Martin it felt like refuelling.

True to his promise at the Harvest Festival, Martin had gone back to reread the Bible, trying to see it through the eyes of the people who had written it. And, like his personality which had previously been ambivalent, higgledy-piggledy, with everything inside him pulling in six different ways at once, and which now suddenly seemed fitted together and centred, the Bible similarly adopted the same sort of nature. Passages which he'd never really noticed in the past suddenly became much more significant, welding his theological concepts solidly together instead of their being connected with the loose stitching which in the past had roughly pulled them together, usually with lots of creases. Far from being a dry, dusty, stuffy book Martin found to his immense surprise that the Bible seemed to come alive in his hands. He could see in its narratives reflections of the life that they were living, reflections of the personalities that were around, reflections of the problems that they were facing.

In the past he'd not paid that much attention to the background of the social life in the Bible, but now he began to feel a great empathy for its people, extending over a gap of several thousand years, as their spokesmen talked of threshing floors, and oxen, and sheep, and wells, and all those important things of life that in the past he'd taken for granted. How necessary it was to have a well! How important that it shouldn't be salty! How vital to have a threshing floor where the grain could be knocked off the ends of the wheat, then be thrown into the air for the wind to blow away the chaff, leaving the pure grain to descend alone.

But there were still parts that caused him problems: why were the laws in Exodus and Leviticus so strict and so barbarous, stipulating, for example, that an adulterer should be stoned to death? Why? Why not forgiveness, understanding, reconciliation? It seemed odd. On the other hand, as so much else in the Bible seemed to fit together with a remarkable sweetness, he was prepared to leave some of the knottier problems for a later date. After all, these laws were part of the Old Testament and many had presumably been modified with the coming of Jesus.

As autumn continued Martin simply devoured the Bible, enjoying every minute of it. To an outsider he would have been thought fanatical: yet it wasn't fanaticism that drove him on—it was love, just as a husband is attracted to his wife not because he is fanatical about her but because in his eyes she is all and everything he wants.

And unlike fanatics, Martin had an open mind, a mind that wasn't afraid to see the difficulties, to appreciate those areas where things didn't yet seem quite to fall into place, where there were still questions, loose ends, uncertainties—but because he was now a much more mature and centred person he was able to accept those uncertainties. Fanatics reject those areas that cause problems because they don't fit in with their way of looking at things. More mature people recognise the existence of problems without letting them upset the overall scheme of things.

*   *   *

On the appointed date, as expected, Henry returned. Anne greeted him at the door with a forced smile, barely able to conceal her disappointment. She'd hoped that perhaps he was just a bad dream, or else he would stay on with his friends in Norfolk, or get lost or waylaid on the road back—but here he was, standing on her doorstep, immaculate as always.

They'd already done the packing—not that there was much to do. They only had a small number of personal items which they'd obtained by returning to their own house in Twickenham six months after the plague had struck. Apart from this, and other than the medical books, there wasn't much: everything else in the house was Henry's.

And they hadn't got anywhere to go to either. There were just no suitable houses available. Although there were empty houses by the hundred in the modern estates, these were entirely unsuitable for current living. What they needed was an old house, built at a time when gas and electricity hadn't been invented. The nearest house of that type that they could find was on the far side of Clophill, four miles away—and that was no use as a dwelling for the town's doctor! Derek needed to be in the centre of things, readily available.

Henry's knock was followed five minutes later by Martin, who always seemed to be around whenever he was needed. He'd noticed the Range Rover standing once again in Church Square. The gentle and sad Peter, sensing also that he might be able to help, followed close on his heels. 'Have you found anywhere to go yet?' he enquired.

'No,' said Anne, 'not apart from that house in Clophill.'

'Well, there's nothing left for it then,' said Martin. 'You'll just *have* to come and stay with me.'

Small actions can have profound results. Small kindnesses can also have profound results. It was unfortunate that, despite his undoubted wisdom, Martin didn't have any powers of prediction because this small kindness was soon to have effects beyond anybody's wildest dreams, and not all to the good.

Derek protested, thinking only of Martin's needs.

'No,' said Martin gently, noticing Anne and Derek's hesitation. 'You must come. I've got a large house that's quite big enough. We can all live separate lives; you won't interrupt me; there's lots of space for the children; there are outhouses at the back; I've got a study that you can use as a consulting room, and I'd be *delighted* to have you staying with me. It'll only be a temporary measure anyway—sooner or later one of the houses in the town will fall vacant when one of the older inhabitants dies.'

'Well...' began Anne doubtfully, thinking of all the psychological upheaval that Martin had gone through in the previous year, and not wanting to do anything which might upset that particular apple cart.

'No,' said Martin, 'do come. I insist. You've paid me enough kindnesses. It's time I did something in return.'

'But we don't think of it like that,' said Derek. 'We'd hate to think that you felt obligated to us.'

'I don't,' said Martin, his eyes flashing that nice relaxed smile that had come over him a lot in the past few weeks. 'I don't feel obligated at all. I'd just like to be able to repay some of the kindness you've shown me. If you don't want to come, I won't mind either. But I don't like to see you being thrown out of your house; I don't think it's right for you to go to the outer reaches of Clophill; it would be nice to have your company up at the Old Rectory; and I'm sure it's the answer to a difficult problem.'

'Well...' said Anne, still hesitating. 'As long as it's only for a short time.' She looked up at Derek, who nodded.

'It's very kind of you, Martin. I hate to say it, but I don't think there's much else we can do.'

And so it was settled. Within twenty minutes they'd cleared their belongings on to a wagon, to be towed up the short distance to the Old Rectory by horse.

Sarah was the last to leave. Of all of them, she was the one, who, silently, was feeling it most. It was yet another upheaval in her life, yet another reminder of the transience of things. A year earlier she'd lost both her parents in the plague and had had to move from her old house along to Dynevor to live with Derek and Anne. Now, having found a certain stability, she was having her roots pulled up again. She was just about to go out through the front door when her eyes filled with tears and her lips started quivering.

'I'm not going to see Hamble again,' she cried.

'Well, you'd better go and say goodbye to him, then,' said Anne, and Sarah rushed off in the direction of the garden. Henry had just come into the hall and overheard the conversation. He followed her out to the pond.

'You don't have to say goodbye to Hamble, you know,' he said kindly. 'You can come and visit him any time you want. Just come in through the side door into the garden. I shan't mind.'

Sarah looked up at him, her eyes blurred with tears. 'Can I? That would be nice.' Then she stamped her foot. 'But if you weren't being so horrid, wanting your house back, I'd be able to see Hamble all the time,' and she rushed back through the house, and out to the front door where Derek and Anne were waiting.

It was actually quite fun moving into the Old Rectory. A large house, much extended, it sat on the top of a hill with fine views over to the east, and woods behind. There was a courtyard at the back, with many outhouses, a pleasant terraced lawn at the front, and a long drive, shielded by holly trees and laurel bushes. It had been far too large for Martin of course, and he'd really only wanted it for the solitude but now that his depression had lifted and he'd sorted out some of his problems, his need for isolation, peace, and quiet had disappeared—and if the truth were told, he was glad to have some company.

He'd actually used only a few of the many rooms in the house, so it was quite easy to allocate the rest for the Jones family. Sarah seemed particularly pleased by her own bedroom, which was a relief to Anne who'd only just realised how upset she'd been by the enforced move. After amiable consultation they decided that Martin would continue to use his existing bedroom—the one with low windows that looked over the front lawn—together with the old dining room (with the wood stove and the piano). Derek, Anne and the children would occupy the other bedrooms, and have the lounge at the north end of the ground floor as their own living area. The kitchen was to be a communal room: vast and high-ceilinged, it was an obvious central focus: and it certainly made more sense if Anne cooked for both families, leaving Martin and Derek more time for their own specialised work in the community.

*   *   *

Half a mile away the watcher in the woods put down his binoculars, and wrote something on the pad in his hand.

*   *   *

With the information they'd gleaned from the archive at Foulislea Cottage they soon made preparations for all manner of things they'd never even dreamt of even a week before. At long last they'd found how to use a water mill to grind corn correctly: how farm carts were made; how to keep ice; and a thousand and one other things that had long ago passed out of the oral tradition of farming and village practices. Plans were well under way to take the first load of grain up to Bromham. They'd decided it was better to grind the corn as they needed it rather than grind too much and risk the flour going off.

However... The human mind is excellent at dredging up convenient excuses for not doing things its owner finds difficult. Creative artists find it so much easier to tidy up their desks rather than sit down to write the next article: and it's much less stressful to dream up new plans for the colour scheme for the front room than actually to get down to making the final decision.

It was exactly the same about grinding the corn. Growing and harvesting it—these were easy. For a start, Neil knew what he was doing: and everyone had seen wheat in the fields, and they knew when—roughly—it had to be cut, and what the fields looked like afterwards. But as for grinding the corn—that was a closed book. No one had seen that, ever. In any case, the type of flour mill in commercial use before the plague was completely inappropriate for their current needs, because there was no electricity to power it: and although they'd all seen windmills and water-mills from the outside, not one of the community had ever watched one at work, never mind learned anything about how to control the process. The problem reared nightmare-like in front of them, a totally alien concept, unknown in size, unknown in complexity, unknown in danger.

They had, of course, postponed the problem for as long as possible, using the same mechanisms and excuses that apply to everyone when faced with an unpalatable job. They had—they rationalised—to wait as long as possible before milling the grain, because it would probably last longer in the husk. They occupied themselves with anything else but the task of grinding corn until they could wait no longer. The evil day had come: the supplies of flour that they'd been able to acquire from the shops and supermarkets was starting to run out and they needed to replenish their stocks.

'We'll *have* to get started in the next few weeks, Derek,' Paul confided to him. 'We really must. I know we're all scared of it but the longer we wait the more trouble we'll have if things go wrong.'

'Why are you asking me?'

'You're the engineer. We need your expertise. I don't think I'll be able to get a mill going without help.'

'I thought you'd got all the information you wanted from the archive.'

'Yes, I have—but there's no real substitute for hands-on experience, is there?'

Derek gave a sigh. It was just another thing on his plate, something he could do without, especially as the practice seemed to be occupying so much of his mental energy. 'All right. When?'

'Tomorrow.'

'*Tomorrow*?'

'Come on, Derek, bite the bullet. Tomorrow.'

Derek sighed again. 'All right. Let's look at your archive again first.'

It was then that Derek started to have real doubts. As an ex-engineer the principles of water-milling were obvious to him: the mill-wheel was powered by the gravitational effect of water falling from the millpond and this power was delivered by a variety of shafts, axles and bevel gears to two millstones placed one above the other. The top millstone rotated on the bottom stone and grain was fed between the two: the action of the millstones was to rub the grain in such a way that it split apart, releasing the flour within it.

So much for the theory—that bit was easy. It was at this point that Derek's problems started. It was all very well knowing how the mill worked in theory, but actually getting it to work in practice was a completely different problem. How far apart were the millstones supposed to be? How quickly should they rotate? How would he know whether they had ground the corn correctly? The information Paul had gleaned from the library at Foulislea Cottage was accurate and detailed—but only up to a point. The overall theory was there, but all the detailed practical information seemed to have been left out.

If he'd been uncertain and reluctant to start milling before, now Derek began to feel even more uneasy, the more so because he knew that everybody would be depending upon his engineering abilities to get the mill working properly, and while he was sure that he could get the machinery moving, whether he could make it do the job it was intended to do was a different matter entirely, not unlike the difference between building a bicycle as opposed to the neat and delicate art of riding it without falling off.

*   *   *

Mention 'mill' to most people and (other than the dark satanic variety) they usually think of windmills, with water-mills coming a definite second. However, very few working windmills remain: the wind is a very variable beast, and windmills are not the easiest things to control. Windmills are beautiful, classic, and very dangerous because they can get out of control so quickly: they are designed to face into the wind at all times, and if the wind suddenly shifts to come from behind—being 'tail-winded'—it can blow the sails right off, wrecking the mill in a few short moments. If the wind gets too strong, the mill can shake itself to pieces; or else catch fire from the excess friction of the grinding wheels.

By comparison, water-mills are just as powerful, but much more controllable. They don't require the miller to work high up on the sails in blustery conditions, with all the risks of falling off, being tail-winded, or having the mill get out of control in a gale. Simply shutting off the water supply to the mill-wheel is enough to stop the mill—much safer than the wind-powered variety! Not only is a water-mill safer, a water-mill is a much more dependable tool in a wet country like England where the water supply is more or less constant.

A water-mill works by converting the gravitational energy of water into energy of movement, as the water drops from one level to another, pushing the water-wheel round as it goes. Again, here lies a misconception. Most people think that a sizeable drop in water from the top to the bottom of the wheel is going to power it very efficiently. An overshot wheel like this is probably quite useful in high mountainous areas where the volume of water isn't great, whereas an undershot or breast-shot wheel—which is what most English mills use—only needs a good quantity of water from the stream to drop through a foot or two to provide very ample power indeed.

Nor does the mill have to be placed directly on a fast-flowing stream. Streams vary in the intensity with which they run, especially after a period of drought, or a time of especially heavy rain, and millers soon found that the best way to create a regular, constant and controllable supply of water was to dam the stream, diverting it into a millpond. From here the water could be let out into a sluice which ran to the water-wheel. In this way the millpond collected water during drier periods, as well as enabling replenishment of supplies during the night, when the mill wasn't working. At times of flood and excess rain, each millpond would have a weir over which excess water would run. In other words, the millpond was simply a device to store stream- or river-water ready for the mill to use, leaving the rest of the water to flow onwards down the stream.

The whole system was of course exceptionally environmentally friendly. All the water in the stream above the mill flowed into the millpond, and from there either overflowed back into the stream over the weir, continuing on its way, or else stayed in the millpond for a time, returning to the stream after it had worked the water-wheel. A mile downstream another miller could use all the stream water to work a second mill, and downstream of him another miller could use all the water of the stream yet again.

A combination of Paul's burrowings into the library at Foulislea Cottage and Henry and Neil's local knowledge showed that the nearest working mill was at Bromham: only a few working mills remained in the county, but fortunately Bromham was only about ten miles distant, to the west of Bedford. Like many old water-mills, Bromham mill was a tall wooden structure, with its own millpond and an undershot water-wheel. Before the plague it had been used as a visitors' centre, demonstrating how milling used to be done, and it actually had a small output of flour, most of which would go for animal feed.

After some thought Derek decided to do a trial run, taking along Alan and Paul. They would bring a couple of bags of grain, purely to experiment with. As a treat—and also because the community didn't want Derek to be out of the way for too long—they all piled into Paul's red Porsche with its personalised number plates— PIG 1—and shot off at speed for Bromham. To get there they had to negotiate the outskirts of Kempston: they had quite a debate about whether this was sensible or not, but eventually concluded that bodies in the streets would almost certainly have decayed completely, no longer posing any threat of infection.

It was a bright and breezy autumn day when they set off on the Bedford road, passing through the edges of Kempston and on through hamlets and little clusters of houses until they reached

Bromham itself. The mill was easy to find—having been a tourist attraction it was well sign-posted: had it not been for this they might have found it rather difficult, for it was tucked out of the way at the western end of the long, medieval-looking bridge that spans the River Ouse at this point.

The mill itself was picturesque, with many outhouses of old black-painted barns, and surrounded by sand-coloured shingle which had once formed the visitors' car parks. The main mill building was one of those wonderful old creations that had, like Topsy, just growed, with additions being put on as and when they were needed, in whatever vernacular style seemed appropriate, using whatever building materials were available at the time. In one place the bottom few feet were of stone: the next storey was of brick, and the storey above that was 'black and white' architecture—except that the white areas were filled with bricks. Despite this apparently higgledy-piggledy method of planning, the building had a curious wholeness about it, a sense of being totally integrated within itself, even though on the surface it appeared to be the architectural equivalent of a patchwork quilt.

The front door yielded quickly to Paul's wrecking bar and immediately they found themselves in the foyer of the visitor centre, with its till, sweets and racks of books. Paul went to these like a shot, searching for the official Guide Book and rapidly finding the pages describing how the mill worked. The three of them stood there looking at the diagram at the back which showed how everything was linked together. At first Paul almost panicked at its complexity, but Derek, who knew how to read mechanical diagrams slowly and carefully, worked through the layout of the wheels, axles and cogs, determining how and why each part of the structure needed to be in place. Satisfied, he walked to the back of the building where wooden duckboards had been laid in front of a large glass window which looked out on to the millpond itself. Through the cracks in the duckboards he could see the water beneath. He turned round to find, behind him, a huge water-wheel, its rusty red six-foot-wide vanes still and quiet.

On the left of the water-wheel was a low room, dominated by

two open structures of massive oak timbers, inside which Paul could see huge spindles and cogs made out of cast iron. For all the world it looked like a hugely magnified model of a child's construction in Meccano: but instead of tidy little cogs and thin angle iron, the structure was made of massive oak beams.

One of the oak cages backed on to the wall adjacent to the water-wheel that they had just seen. Against the far wall there was a similar cage, but the mechanism inside it was obviously derelict.

Plan in hand, Derek set about establishing the function of the various parts of the apparatus. At first sight it looked incredibly complex, but once he had mentally dissected it into its different components it was actually very simple.

'Look, Paul,' said Derek, pointing at a cast-iron ship's wheel on the wall backing on to the water-wheel assembly, 'that wheel controls the whole thing. It opens the sluice which regulates the amount of water that hits the water-wheel.'

Picking up a telescopic pipe on the floor nearby he fitted it onto the end of one of the spokes and levered the wheel round. There was a sudden rushing sound on the other side of the wall as the sluice opened, and with a shudder that could be felt throughout the structure of the whole building the water-wheel slowly began to turn.

Once everything began to move, Paul suddenly realised how everything worked. As Derek had said, in principle it was quite simple. The water-wheel itself was like the right-hand back wheel of a child's toy cart: as it turned it rotated the axle, which caused the left-hand wheel—the large vertical one inside the oak cage—to rotate also. By an ingenious sequence of bevels and cogs the movement of this vertical wheel was transferred to a large horizontal wheel at head height—the great spur wheel—which was now spinning round at an alarming rate.

Derek levered the sluice shut again: the water-wheel ground to a halt and the huge cogs stopped rotating.

'Is that all there is to it?' asked Paul.

'Nearly,' said Derek and he showed them how two further smaller cogs could be positioned against the great spur wheel so that the spur-wheel's motion could be transmitted upstairs, using another axle, to the millstones themselves. Putting down the plans Derek scrambled up the wooden ladder at the side of the great oak cage, which lead to the floor above.

He emerged into a large, airy, open room, quite unlike the confines of the control room below. Behind him were three sets of exposed millstones, without their driving assembly, but what was far more interesting was the apparatus in front of him: two flat, circular wooden vats sitting on the floor, each with a chute above for delivering corn slowly into a hole in the centre.

'Look down through the hole,' he said. Dimly, Alan could see a rough-hewn stone-coloured object.

'That's the top millstone,' said Derek. 'There's another one beneath it. The wooden casing around them stops the milled flour from flying everywhere. The wheels and cogs downstairs transmit the rotation of the mill-wheel into the rotation of the vertical axle we saw a few minutes ago. This axle goes up through the ceiling, through the lower millstone and is attached to the upper millstone, so when it rotates it turns the top millstone anticlockwise. The bottom millstone remains fixed. The grains of wheat in the chute are slowly dropped into the central area between the two stones and gradually work their way out to the edges, being crushed between the stones in the process. The flour and ground husk eventually come out at the edge of the stones and drop down a second chute into the floor below.'

'So where does the wheat that's going to be ground come from?' asked Alan. Derek pointed at the roof.

'From the floor above.' They found their way up yet another flight of wooden stairs and stood looking at a wooden hopper from which a vertical pipe dropped through the floor, terminating in the apparatus over the millstone. 'The corn goes in this hopper here,' said Derek. 'It drops down one floor, where it's fed in slowly into the centre of the pair of millstones. Once the flour is ground it drops down through yet another floor to the control room at the bottom.'

'Have we got to lift the corn up all those stairs?' asked Alan, paling at the thought. 'It'll be a nightmare.'

Derek looked at him and grinned. 'No, the old millers were

much more canny than that,' he said. 'Look here,' and pointed to a trapdoor in the floor through which a rope passed. Above it was yet another gigantic oak axle. 'When the water-wheel's turning, that axle also rotates, working a hoist which pulls up sacks of corn through the trapdoors in the floor.'

Alan's eyes widened, realising how cleverly it had all been put together. 'They certainly knew a thing or two, didn't they?'

'Ah,' said Derek, 'the best bit's still to come. All that massive machinery hurtling round—ten-foot-high mill-wheels and foot-thick axles—generally rather heavy and crude, wouldn't you think?'

Paul turned round to look at him. 'Well, yes, I suppose it is really. Mind you, what would you expect for the technology of a couple of centuries ago?'

'How far apart do you think the two millstones are when they're grinding?' said Derek.

'Oh, I don't know. A quarter of an inch, perhaps.'

'A *hundredth* of an inch,' said Derek. 'And there's a control to raise or lower the top stone off the bottom stone in order to change the degree of grinding, so as to produce either fine or coarse-ground flour. How accurate do you think that is?'

'Try me,' said Paul, suddenly very interested.

'Something like a ten-thousandth of an inch.'

'*You what?*'

'About a ten-thousandth of an inch.'

'You mean they could control a pair of millstones weighing a ton each with antiquated-looking machinery like this and do it to a tolerance of a ten-thousandth of an inch?'

Derek nodded. Alan let out a low whistle. 'Makes you see the old-timers in a different light, doesn't it?'

'Well,' said Derek, 'all we've got to do now is see if it all works.' They went downstairs to the control room on the bottom floor. Alan brought in two sacks of corn from *PIG 1*. Derek started the mill again and showed Alan how to attach each sack to the hoist chain running up through the trapdoors to the roof. He pulled on the control lanyard and the half-hundredweight sack was lifted effortlessly

through the trapdoor in the ceiling and on through the second trap-
door in the room above. He let go of the lanyard, and the sack
gently descended on to the now closed trapdoor in the top storey.
Alan went upstairs again, and found it was easy to undo the sack
from the chain. Then all he had to do was pull the sack across and
empty it into the hopper. The grain rushed down the tube connecting the hopper to the feeding device of the millstones. 'All we have
to do now,' said Derek, 'is link in the mechanism to make the millstones themselves rotate.'

'I see,' said Paul pointing to two smaller cogs near to the great
spur wheel. 'Bring those cogs down until they touch the teeth of the
spur wheel and we transmit the rotation of the spur wheel into the
rotation of the axle which moves the millstones above us.'

'Correct,' said Derek. The mill was up to speed now. Above him
the great spur wheel was thundering round and in the distance they
could hear the swoosh, swoosh, swoosh as the water hit each vane
of the water-wheel in turn. Paul was suddenly seized with a fit of
enthusiasm.

'I see,' he said craning his neck and studying the arrangement of
cogs under the millstone axle. 'All I have to do is rotate this control
wheel here and it'll drop this smaller cog down until it meets the
spur wheel cogs. It's really rather like a slow motion gearbox, isn't
it?' and without more ado he bent down and started working furiously at a wheel underneath the vertical axle. The cog to start the
millstones moving dropped slowly down to engage with the rotating great spur wheel.

'*Stop!*' yelled Derek in his ear. Paul started, jumped up and hit
his head on one of the big beams.

'What do you do that for?' he said, holding his head and screw-
ing up his eyes with the pain.

'Because you were just about to ruin the whole thing.'

'I was what?'

'What do you think will happen as soon as you drop that stationary cog with a ton of millstone above it against the rapidly moving spur wheel?'

'It'll start moving round, won't it?'

'More like it'll strip all the teeth off it.'

Paul went pale. 'Are you sure?'

'*Of course I'm sure*,' said Derek angrily. 'I'm an engineer, remember? You nearly ruined everything. This isn't a toy. It's big, bad and dangerous.' He shut the sluice gate again and the whole mechanism shuddered to a halt. '*Now* you can do it.' Paul twisted away at the cast iron control wheel, bringing the cog slowly down until it meshed with the huge spur wheel.

'Right, *now* we'll start it up,' said Derek, and he opened the sluice to its former position.

Nothing happened.

'What's the matter?' asked Alan who by now had returned from the third floor. 'Why won't it work?'

'I don't know,' said Derek. 'Maybe it needs a bit more force. There's more friction now that the millstones have to be rotated,' and with that he opened the sluice gate twice as far as before. With an enormous grunt the wheels starting rolling again. The noise was louder this time, until it seemed as though the whole building was vibrating. The power involved was enormous. Paul stood for a moment watching the water rush down the sluice as the wheels grumbled into life. Above them the millstones started turning.

'Now what?' said Alan after watching for half a minute.

'Look,' said Derek pointing to a square wooden chute at the front of the oak cage. In front of their eyes a thin trickle of white powder came out of the chute into the container underneath it. 'There you are. Flour.'

*　　　　　　　　*　　　　　　　　*

They had a number of surprises that day. Paul, who had never seen archaic equipment working before, was amazed by the power that the water-wheel developed: and not a little frightened by the machinery whizzing round. There was no brake, Derek had told him—no way of stopping the machinery other than by shutting the sluice off and letting the mill 'grind to a halt' (which was, as Paul was quick to point out, the origin of the phrase). But there were any number of places where an incautious finger could become trapped, or a hand get jammed between two cogs, and there was no way, no way at all, that the mill could be stopped before the finger or hand—if not the whole arm—was dragged inexorably into the machine. There just weren't such things as safety switches or cut-outs on water-wheels.

Most dangerous of all, and yet apparently so innocuous, was the damsel, a hooped contrivance that sat just above the millstones, rotating once a second, as it knocked the corn slowly and steadily from the feed chute and into the centre area of the millstones. It looked harmless, but the fine control of this feed was done by a device next door to it and if while adjusting it the miller got his finger caught in the damsel itself—an easy thing to do—it would wind the finger round and round until something broke or was torn off: and there would be no way of stopping it if the miller was working on his own, because the sluice control was situated on the storey below.

Alan was amazed at the accuracy with which the millstones could be set when grinding the corn: and Derek was overwhelmed by the fact that they had actually made it work first time, but slightly startled at the slowness with which the flour came out. He tried to increase the output of the mill using the various controls—such as increasing the feed, speeding up the mill and so on—but bumping and banging noises from above him, followed shortly after by pellets of unground wheat grains in the flour chute, soon convinced him that speed wasn't necessarily a virtue and that getting things correct but slow was more important.

On another occasion, when trying to adjust the fineness of the flour, he brought the stones too close together, and reduced the level of feed too much, until there was a sudden smell of burning. Paul reminded him that his archives recalled how many a mill had burned down when the stones got too close together or rotated too quickly, and the wooden vat surrounding them had caught fire from the excess friction. Derek hastily levered the stones apart!

It was nearly all controlled from the ground floor. Milling, it turned out, was a fine balance between controlling the speed at which the stones rotated, the distance the stones were apart, and the amount of corn fed in between them. The miller's job was constantly to monitor the fineness of the flour as it trickled out of the wooden chute, and to make any adjustments until everything was working correctly—until it really was all 'run of the mill'.

After a time they had the mill running smoothly, and at this point Derek measured how long it took to grind a bag of wheat. Then they put the flour in bags to take back.

They got home in the middle of the afternoon, amid much excitement. Many of the residents came out to see this most wondrous of things that they had at last created, the end product of all their endeavours in the fields, this beige-coloured powder. Derek proudly presented Anne with their first bagful of flour. Excitedly, she took it away and made it into dough, kneading it with water and yeast and leaving it to rise next to the fire, finally baking it in the oven on the range. The smell of new bread floated through the house and all of them agreed it was one of the most pleasant smells they'd experienced for some time.

Later that evening the first loaf was ready and the Jones' family clustered round the table, with Martin, Alan and Paul looking on.

'You first, Derek,' said Alan. 'This is your day.'

'That's very kind of you,' said Derek, slicing a piece off the loaf and applying a liberal spreading of butter. 'I wonder what it tastes like. We'll soon see,' and with a satisfied look on his face he bit into the bread.

There was a crack and a grimace, followed by a howl of pain. Derek's left hand flew to his mouth. Sweat appeared on his cheeks and his eyes narrowed.

'What's the matter?' said Anne in alarm. Gingerly Derek opened his mouth.

'I think I've just broken a filling,' he said, feeling gingerly round the inside of his teeth with his tongue. Going to the bathroom, he spat out the bread, rinsed his mouth out and felt around again. 'No,' he said with a sigh of relief, 'It's all right.'

'What on earth's the matter?' said Paul.

'The bread,' said Derek, pointing to it. 'It's disgusting. It's awful. It's like rock cake made with real rocks.'

'Are you criticising my cooking again?' asked Anne, huffily, breaking it and sniffing at it suspiciously. She put a small piece in her mouth, and cautiously chewed it. 'Oh. I see what you mean.'

They all tried a bit, gingerly. It *tasted* like bread—and very pleasant bread at that—but the texture was as though a liberal helping of sand had been added to the mixture.

'What on earth have we done wrong?' asked Alan.

'I didn't like to say at the time,' said Anne, 'but that flour felt awfully rough.'

'I must have ground it too coarse,' said Derek. 'We can grind it more finely, only it doesn't come out all that quickly.'

'I think you'll have to,' said Anne. 'Have you got any of the fine stuff?'

'Have we?' asked Derek looking at Alan.

'I think so. I kept a bit.' He went out to the Porsche and retrieved a small bag. 'This any better?'

Anne dipped her fingers into it. 'Oh yes, *much* better.'

Derek went very quiet. 'Teeth all right?' asked Paul. 'You look worried.'

'I am,' said Derek. 'I was just thinking how long it'll take us to grind flour if we've got to get it that fine.'

'I can tell you without looking,' said Paul. 'You can do about a ton a day with each pair of millstones. I read it somewhere.'

'That's not a lot,' said Derek.

'Sounds a lot to me,' said Alan.

'Not when you think about it,' replied Paul. 'How many people are there in the community?'

'About four hundred.'

'Let's say they all eat a pound loaf of bread a day. Do you think that's a fair guess?'

'I suppose so.'

'That's four hundred loaves. Four hundred pounds of flour. A ton is two thousand two hundred and forty pounds—or in other words, six days' supply. So to keep ourselves supplied we'll have to operate that mill one day a week at the very least, for ever.'

'Oh,' said Alan. 'I see what you mean.'

*   *   *

In the dimness of the twilight the watcher silently melted into the gloom. The time was getting near.

*   *   *

For a time Martin tried to keep up with all his physical work on the farm as well as fitting in pastoral visits, but he soon recognised that he couldn't do both jobs at the same time—at least, not with the same hundred per cent intensity that he would like to have applied to each.

It had been Derek who had raised the issue at the next council meeting. Martin was touched to feel that Derek should be so concerned for him when in fact Derek was probably under more pressure himself. He was even more touched because he knew Derek had no particular beliefs of his own, yet was positively encouraging Martin to increase his pastoral work. Yet Derek was adamant in insisting that if the community wanted to avail themselves of Martin's time as a pastoral worker and spiritual guide, then, just as they'd agreed to do Derek's communal work for him so that he could become their doctor, so they ought to recognise the importance of Martin's work and provide him with the time in which to do it. Derek explained this very amicably, expecting to have it passed almost on the nod, and was surprised at the heated response he received. Paul was the first to jump in.

'I don't see the need for this, Derek,' he said. 'I've always thought of ministers and social workers as being parasites—looking beatific, wasting a lot of time and not actually producing very much at the end. I've always felt these were two unnecessary overheads society could have done without.'

With that the meeting erupted. Whatever they felt about ministers of religion as parasites, social workers were a completely different matter. Susan—who was now well enough to come back for council meetings—was particularly incensed.

'I really don't know how you can say that, Paul,' she said acidly. 'I used to be a teacher, and there were many occasions when we found social workers to be of immense value.'

'But were they cost-effective?' asked Paul.

'How can you ask a question like that?' retorted Susan. 'How do you put someone's emotional stability on a balance sheet? In any case, you can't measure it simply in the here and now. You don't know what good you're doing for the future. For all you know, sorting somebody out early on may have huge repercussions later.'

'And for all you know, it may not,' said Paul pointedly. 'How do you know if it helps anybody? Has anyone worked out the statistics? How do we know it isn't one gigantic con? A huge placebo response, foisted on us by social workers, ministers and other do-gooders?'

'Paul, you're getting quite obnoxious,' replied Susan. 'I'd have thought with your background and the problems you had with drugs—'

Chris interjected. 'Susan! We've already stated as a principle that we won't go back to what's happened in the past. A clean slate—remember?'

'I wasn't going to criticise,' said Susan, trying desperately to keep calm and almost succeeding. 'I was just trying to point out that when somebody has emotional problems they need space, people to talk to, counselling, advice, pastoral support.'

'I didn't need that,' said Paul, his eyes flaring. 'I got out of it myself. Nobody helped me, thank you.'

'All right, so you're made of sterner stuff,' said Susan. 'Others wouldn't have found it so easy.'

'I don't agree with you, Paul,' said Martin quietly from the end of the table. ' I know I'm arguing in my own defence in this case, but I have to say I couldn't have done without the support of Anne and Derek in the past year, and I value it highly. I know just how much time they took to care for me—and others of you, of course. But I needed it then, and without support I might have drunk myself to death, or committed suicide. And yes, you are right in one sense in that you were able to get out of *your* problems with sheer grit and determination. All of us here applaud you for that. But just because you can doesn't mean that others are able to sort out their problems without outside assistance.'

He looked first at Paul and then at Susan. 'In a way you're both right. Let's not get angry because we take one side or another—because there aren't sides. There are different needs for different situations. It isn't an *either/or*, it's a *both/and*.'

Wisdom has a surprising way of deflating anger. The meeting suddenly halted, as if stunned by Martin's gently measured observations. Then Alan Rogers spoke, anxious to help defuse the situation. 'I agree entirely. The real problem is whether Martin should be used purely for counselling, and for what in past times would have been called social work, or whether we include spiritual work as well. Some of us don't agree with his religious point of view—I say that cordially, by the way—' Martin smiled and nodded, '—and it may not be appropriate to ask the rest of us to do extra work in order to free up his time to proselytise in a way we don't agree with. It does smack a little bit of the Middle Ages, when everybody had to pay tithes to keep the church going. A tenth of what you earned, just to keep the Rector in the style to which he was accustomed.'

'I take that point entirely,' interjected Derek, 'especially as it was I who proposed it in the first place. I certainly agree that we need someone like Martin to help with pastoral work, irrespective of their religious beliefs, but I'm not sure I agree entirely with you Alan, about the unimportance of the religious side. Like you I have no particular religious beliefs, but I know...' and he turned, slightly uncertainly to look at Martin, '...if Martin won't mind me saying this?...'

Martin nodded. 'Go on, Derek.'

'I'm sure he won't mind me telling you that the reason why he got better was largely because he managed to sort his own life out.'

'I told you it was possible to do it on your own,' muttered Paul. Chris turned to glare at him.

Derek continued, 'And though I don't really agree with his particular religious point of view, I do feel that sorting out his religious beliefs was what helped Martin most. I'm sure there are others in our community who would be helped by that type of approach.'

'Martin, can't you just do the pastoral work, without any religious input?' asked Alan.

'That's very difficult,' replied Martin. 'These things are often inextricably tied up together. After all, if I visit somebody who's gradually dying, do I have to say "I can't talk to you about anything to do with religion. I can just check to see whether you've got enough food and whether you're feeling comfortable?" '

'Life's a little more holistic than that,' said Derek. 'I must emphasise once again that I don't see eye to eye with Martin over the religious side of his beliefs, but we all need a creed to live by. Whether or not it's the Christian religion is a different matter. The one thing I am sure about is that if you don't know what you believe because you've never thought about it properly, then you're in the worse situation of the lot. After all, the one thing that distinguishes humans from other animals is that we have an idea about who we are and why we're here: we know we're going to die, and we have a need to make sure that we know what we're doing with our lives. Animals don't have this—and if we don't address this need then surely we're not addressing the most important part of our life on earth?'

'I still don't like the idea of using my effort to support Martin in promoting a set of beliefs that I don't believe in,' said Alan.

'Well, I think it's a very good idea,' interjected the Major, slightly crustily. 'It's a good idea to have a priest in the community. After all, we do live in a Christian country.'

'Christian country?' said Alan incredulously. 'If you remember, before the plague there were more Muslims attending the mosque each Friday than there were church attenders on Sunday. So why do you think we're a Christian country?'

'All our traditions are Christian. All our secular life is based round Christian values. I don't see any problem with Martin taking up his old role.'

'No, no, no,' said Alan, patently annoyed at the Major's apparent inability to see the point. 'I'm not arguing that Martin shouldn't do these things: I just don't want *my* time to be used to pay for *him* to do it.'

'This is where we need to go back to using money again,' said Paul.

'What on earth has that got to do with it?' asked Alan aggressively. 'Really Paul, Susan's right: you *are* being awkward today.'

Chris turned to Paul, irritation showing all over her face. 'Why did you have to bring that hoary old chestnut up again?'

'I'm not being awkward,' said Paul angrily. 'Just listen to me for a moment, will you, instead of prattling on? At the moment we've all got to do what everybody's agreed. Right? We can't plant a field or use a piece of equipment unless everybody agrees that it's the right thing to do. Well, it's getting to the point where we won't be able to govern ourselves. In the past I've talked about rewarding those who work hard, and leaving those who don't work with less— and I don't want to go into that now,' he said, glaring at Mary who'd just opened her mouth to object. 'But it would cut through the whole of this problem if we went back to having money, because then those who wanted Martin to spend time on his pastoral work— including the religious side—could give him money to buy the things he needs without having to spend time earning it himself.

'I'm sure the Major would want to contribute'—the Major nodded—'and I'm sure that you, Alan, would prefer not to. Fine. You're welcome to refrain from giving, if that's what you choose. And it would give Martin a completely clear conscience because he'd know that whatever he was doing he wasn't offending anyone.

'I agree with Derek—how can Martin possibly work as a priest if he feels he's offending against the beliefs of those who are doing his work for him? I agree with you, Alan—I have no religious beliefs at all, and I don't particularly want to work to support Martin's religious work either, but it's a free country: I certainly don't think we ought to stop him, providing there are those who are prepared to value what he does to the extent of paying him.

'Don't forget this is all in addition to why I said we needed to go back to using money. We can't go on as we are doing because some people are working hard and not getting a fair reward, and others are still doing only a minimal amount. Why don't we give everybody the freedom that having money confers on us?'

There was a silence. It had never been put like that before. Chris looked thoughtful.

'You've got a very good point there, Paul. I'm sorry I criticised you earlier. It wasn't appropriate.' Unexpectedly, Paul graciously nodded in acceptance. 'I don't think we can take a decision on this now,' she continued. 'We ought to take soundings, come back to the next meeting and see what we think then.'

*   *   *

New ideas are often unwelcome and often seen as a threat. The old order often works in a comfortable way, even when it doesn't work very well. Although Paul had not received any great support in the council during the meeting, there were many who went away, mulled over what he'd said and began to see the wisdom of it. It was true, there were those who did the bare minimum of work—'Kevin' was the main name that sprang to people's lips on these occasions, but even he was pulling his weight a bit more. It was also true that some people seemed to have got a really rough deal—like Derek, having to turn out at all hours of the day or night; or the shepherds, who had to work, freezing cold, in the fields in the depths of winter during lambing time; or those who had turned to the heavier jobs, and were constantly being injured.

It was also correct that their current system, in which all decisions had first to go through the council, meant that they had a sluggish, centralised, almost bureaucratic way of life. There was somehow not quite the same spontaneity as they had known when first they had come to Ampthill. The 'look what I've thought of and let's see whether it'll work' approach was becoming noticeable by its absence—the attitude that says, 'I don't mind putting a lot of effort into this because I believe in what I'm doing. If it works, it works and I'll benefit: and if it doesn't then I'm the one who loses out.'

Unfortunately, everyone was so concerned with working for the community as a whole that individual ventures tended to get stultified. In fact, outrage was frequently voiced if an individual took time away from his main task in order to do something else, however laudable, and however useful it eventually turned out to be. Concentrating on the stated needs of the community had had a subtly depressing effect on individual ideas and individual ways forward.

So when the council met again two weeks later the mood had changed completely. Yes, there was inequality about the work that people were doing: no, they were not being adequately recompensed for it. Eventually the system was going to break down, because ultimately it depended upon the goodwill of so many people to make it run, and goodwill can sometimes be a sparse commodity. As Martin had recently become aware, self-interest and selfishness would eventually put paid to it, even though it might take weeks, months or years to surface.

It was, of all people, Alan who started off the debate. 'On reflection, Paul, I think you're right. I do think we need to have some form of monetary system.'

Paul said nothing and just grinned inwardly. One down, nine to go.

Then Mary chipped in. 'I agree with Paul as well.'

I say, thought Chris, Mary's agreeing with somebody. This *is* a turn-up for the books, but she said nothing out loud and just smiled benignly.

'It will give more freedom to those of us who are vegetarian, too. I've never liked the feeling that we're all pooling our resources to rear and kill those defenceless sheep and cows. If we all get paid for what we do, then we can choose not to support some areas, and not to have any part in them.'

'I never thought I'd hear you saying that you'd welcome the use of money,' said Susan. 'I thought you were all for a golden age in which money, keys and locks weren't necessary.'

'Well, we're not in a golden age,' replied Mary tartly, her bun of grey hair bobbing as she spoke. 'If we were we wouldn't be killing to eat.'

'And it does get rid of the Kevin problem,' murmured Alan, almost under his breath. 'He can only use what he pays for and he can only pay for things if he earns the money.'

'And what if he doesn't work?' asked Chris.

'Then he doesn't eat,' snapped back Paul. 'It's his choice. He'll know the odds beforehand. It's not as if we're springing something on him without his knowing about it. He can make a choice. If he works he'll eat: if he doesn't, he won't.'

'And you'd really carry that out?' asked Derek.

'Not half,' said Paul with relish.

'I agree entirely,' said the Major. 'Little whippersnapper. Teach him a lesson.'

'What about those who can't work?' asked Anne of Paul. 'Mrs Summerfield for example, Susan's next-door neighbour. She's seventy-eight if she's a day.'

There was a pause. Obviously Mrs Summerfield couldn't be left to starve. And then a whole host of problems suddenly reared up in front of them: ugly words like social security, benefit payments, and—worst of the lot—*taxes*. It was one of those moments in a meeting where everyone knows what is being thought, but nobody really wants to be the first to bring up the problem on the grounds that, later on, when life gets difficult, everybody will blame them for drawing people's attention to it. It was Chris who eventually grasped the nettle.

'I can see some... er... er... *problems*... in this,' she said, turning to Paul who, as usual was sitting on her left. 'How are we going to deal with those who can't work because they are too old or too ill?'

'I certainly don't want *them* to starve,' Paul replied. 'That's not the idea at all.'

'Then we'll have to give them money to tide them over?'

'Yes.'

'Which means that we have to have some system of deciding who should and who shouldn't receive any benefits?'

'Yes...' said Paul, slowly and uneasily.

'Which means somebody has to decide who has a right to these payments and who hasn't. How do we go about that? More to the point, where's the money going to come from?'

'Can't we just give them some?' asked Mary innocently, and then wished she hadn't opened her mouth.

'Where's it going to come from?' asked Chris. 'The only way we can give any benefits out is if we collect money from those who are earning. You just can't print it.'

'Why not?' said Mary. 'If we used tokens in place of money, then if someone who was sick or too old to work we could make some more tokens and give them to that person.'

A chorus of '*No*'s ran round the room, *sotto voce*.

'Sorry Mary, you can't do that,' said Paul. 'Quick way to inflation. Too much money chasing not enough goods.'

'I don't follow.'

'Here,' said Paul, fishing out a piece of paper from inside his hip pocket, and writing 'One pound' on it. 'Here's a pound. Give me twenty eggs, would you?'

Mary looked down at the paper, then up at Paul in disbelief. 'No, of course I won't. This isn't worth anything.'

'Precisely. Just because I've made some "money" doesn't mean that money's worth anything. 'No, the only way we can get this whole thing to work with any degree of sensibility is if we all chip in out of our earnings and use those savings to give to those who can't work.'

'This is starting to look very unwieldy,' said Susan. 'Maybe we ought to try for a bit longer without money. It's working quite well at the moment.'

'Actually, it's not,' said Derek. 'We've had a sort of honeymoon period. We all had to club together because we were all fighting the common enemy of starvation—whether we would get through the first year or not. But now we've got through that first year, people aren't as likely to want to work for everyone when they know that some of the people in the community aren't working well—or aren't working at all. And I don't mean Mrs Summerfield. Everybody understands that she's got to be fed. No: now we've got through the first year people will start to say "Why should I work so hard when so and so isn't? Why should the shepherds be out in the biting cold of a February night during the lambing season when everybody else is tucked up in their beds?" '

'So what are you going to do about taxation?' asked Peter. 'We've got to get the money for the Mrs Summerfields of this world from somewhere.'

Alan interrupted with, 'Why doesn't everybody pay a standard amount into the general kitty?' There was a general nodding round the table.

'You mean a Poll Tax?' said Paul, innocently.

Mary erupted. 'We will *not* have a Poll Tax,' she shrieked. 'It's iniquitous.'

'Ah,' said Paul, looking her straight in the eye. 'You *are* awake. All right. We'll have a gradation. Those who earn more can pay more money. Is that fair?'

'Much better,' said Mary subsiding her face slightly less red.

'Then that means we're going to tax the shepherds more for their pains of being out in the middle of the night, are we? I thought the general idea was to reward those who worked and give disincentives to those who didn't. Now you're saying that because somebody earns more he ought to contribute more to the general kitty. Make up your mind—which do you want?'

'I... er... well, I'd like... um...' Mary spluttered, all too aware of the cleft stick that she'd got herself into.

'I'm quite neutral,' said Paul calmly, 'but you can't have it both ways. Money can't be both an incentive and a weapon at the same time. You can't use money as a reward and then at the same time penalise those who use it successfully. Next thing you'll be saying that those who've worked hard or have been prudent or haven't bought much oughtn't to have the extra benefits their savings give them, and that their money ought to be taken away from them and given to those who haven't got as much—like the Kevins of this world. Now make up your mind. You can't have it both ways. Incentive or weapon? Which is it to be? If you try to have it both ways you'll just get people neurotic.'

'How you do you mean, neurotic?' asked Alan.

'Because they won't know how to treat their money,' said Paul incisively. 'On the one hand they're being told that they're welcome to work hard and earn more, and on the other hand they're told that if they've managed to acquire more than the average that they shouldn't have it, that they're depriving others, or that they're leeching off people. In other words is it a good or a bad thing to be rich?

Is it a good or a bad thing to be poor?'

'If Kevin doesn't work he deserves to be poor,' said Alan firmly, wondering quite where the conversation was going.

'Precisely,' said Paul. 'And because he's poor are you going to give him money in order to live?'

'No... Yes... Er... Ah.'

'So we're back to this horrid Victorian concept of the "deserving poor"?' asked Derek.

'Are we?' asked Paul.

Mary murmured something under her breath in which the words 'Smart Alec' seemed prominent.

'What was that? What was that, Mary?' asked Chris angrily.

'Nothing,' said Mary sullenly.

'I think it was,' said Chris. 'And I think it was very derogatory.'

'Oh, very well,' said Mary. 'I just said I think Paul's a Smart Alec.'

'I'm not at all,' said Paul, looking her straight in the eye. 'I'm just giving you the options. You can all decide if you want, and I won't vote. All I'm trying to do is make sure that you understand the issues.'

'You're just showing your right-wing preconceptions,' hissed Mary.

'I'm not,' said Paul, quite gently for him. 'Really Mary I'm not. I know *you* see it that way. We're just resurrecting the problem that nobody had solved before we had the plague, which hinges on whether having lots of money is a good or a bad thing. So tell me, Mary, is it a good thing to have lots of money?'

'It depends how you got it.'

'So what is a good way to get money?'

'By earning an honest wage.'

'Therefore somebody who works more can earn more money. And somebody who works harder or in more difficult conditions can earn more money?'

'Yes.'

'And when is it bad to have a lot of money?'

'When you came by it in the wrong way.'

'Such as when you didn't work for it?'

'Yes,' said Mary. 'Speculators for example.'

'Or those who wouldn't work and were given it anyway,' said Paul pointedly, thinking of Kevin.

'As long as you don't include those who *can't* work or those with no job to go to... not a problem now, of course. And yes, you're right, I don't like the idea of people amassing a fortune out of the misery of others.'

'So now we're into the undeserving *rich* are we?' asked Paul. 'When the Victorians talked about the "deserving poor" we vilify them, but now when we talk about the undeserving rich we're doing something which is good? So it's all right to be poor, but not to be rich, even though some of those who are rich got there because they worked exceptionally hard, or didn't spend as much as others?'

'Er... Yes... Um... No... Um.' Suddenly Mary's preconceptions burst all over her like a wet bag of flour. She went very quiet as the logic of it all came home.

Paul continued his relentless exposition. 'So can we start off with some sense about money, so that we don't get hung up about it in the future? Because I seem to remember that in the past we all got bogged down with it.' He was aware that everybody in the room was looking at him intently. 'Money is simply a means of exchange—nothing more, nothing less. It's a measure of the work you do, the hardships you endure and the risks you take. It's really nothing more than a token for the amount of time you spend on a job. Money makes things much easier because instead of having to barter—you know, the "anybody got change for two hamsters?" routine—instead we translate our efforts into a common set of units—money—and then use those units to buy somebody else's time, expertise or produce. And that's all money is—nothing more, nothing less.

'Money *of itself* isn't evil or wrong. Riches aren't wrong in themselves. Nor for that matter is poverty—because it isn't what you've got but how you got it that makes all the difference. And yes, Mary, I do agree that those who make a quick buck for all the wrong reasons shouldn't be allowed to do it but that doesn't mean that people who are rich necessarily got rich by doing down someone else. So you're right, there are the "deserving" and the "undeserving" poor and, yes, there are the "deserving" and "undeserving" rich, but you can't use simple taxes to penalise those who are rich because when you do it you'll penalise the ones who got rich in the right way, just as much as you'll penalise the ones who got rich in the wrong way. And in the same way if you hand out money left, right and centre just because somebody is "poor" you'll feed the "undeserving poor" just as much as you'll feed the "deserving poor". Agreed?'

The attentive looks and the nodding heads said it all.

'So what I propose is this: we set up a simple system of money, and at the same time we arrange for all able-bodied people to make some form of contribution so that those who really can't earn don't suffer in any way—in fact they shouldn't notice any difference before and after we make the change-over. But we *must*'—and here he looked pointedly at Mary—'we *must* make sure that we don't use the amount of money someone has amassed as a measure of whether it should be taken away from them. You can only do that by looking into how they got it. Money is quite neutral. It's how you got it and how you use it that's the important thing.'

From the end of the table Martin at last spoke, steepling his long fingers together and throwing back the lock of hair from his forehead with a flick of his hand. 'Can I say, Paul, that I think you have expressed the whole matter very succinctly.'

Susan turned round to face him. 'I don't see how you can say that, as a man of the cloth. After all it says in the Bible that money is the root of all evil.'

'No,' said Martin gently, turning to her. 'No, it doesn't say that at all. It says that the *love* of money is the root of all evil. Quite a different thing, and one over which Paul and I, for once, are in total agreement.'

'But doesn't the Bible talk about people giving away their money and how difficult it is for the rich to get into heaven?'

'Yes,' said Martin quietly, 'but that's a matter of how you use the money you have, not of riches themselves. Don't forget it also says in the Bible that those who don't work shouldn't eat.'

'I never thought I'd hear you say that,' said Paul mischievously. 'I quoted that to you about nine months ago. You didn't seem to like it very much then.'

'No,' said Martin, 'I didn't, but I've had time to think more deeply since then. I agree with you, money is quite neutral. It's how you get it and what you do with it that is the measure of you.'

'Can't we do without it?' said Anne. 'It sounds as though we're going to create a complex system for no great benefit. We've already made a Department of Social Security and a Treasury today. Why don't we make a Department of Defence and a Minister for Employment at the same time?'

'It may come to that,' said Paul.

Prophets don't always realise what they're saying. Paul certainly didn't.

'Oh, don't be silly,' said Chris.

'It's true,' said Paul, realising that he might have just gone too far, even for him. 'What happens if we need people to keep the peace, or to defend us? We'll have to exact taxes and pay for them out of the money those taxes raise.'

'But it would be far simpler if we just all mucked in together and shared,' said Susan. 'Wouldn't it?'

A five-letter word occurred in eleven people's minds almost simultaneously. Kevin.

No, it wouldn't work any other way.

*   *   *

The members of the council went home that day deep in thought, and in some cases not a little unnerved. Life in their new situation was turning out uncomfortably like life had been previously. There was a horrible sense of *déjà vu*, a sense of recreating the past with all its problems—and yet there seemed to be no alternative.

Surprisingly the one person who had no problems at all with this was Martin, who reflected as he strode up Holly Walk to the Old Rectory that it was only because people were intrinsically selfish that any of the discussions that afternoon had taken place: not that the council members were particularly selfish in talking about it, but that in a perfect world where unselfishness abounded there would be no need for money at all, nor would there be any need for locks and keys. The reason Martin agreed with Paul about money was simply that Paul was putting forward a pragmatic response to the reality of selfishness and—in Martin's terms—to the effects of original sin on people's attitude to their own work.

By contrast, Mary went back to her bungalow and to her chickens deeply troubled. What Paul had said seemed so foreign to her, so completely wrong, so completely against the grain, that she couldn't stomach it. And yet, inside her she knew that there was an appallingly forceful logic about what Paul had said. She would think about it, she decided, awful though it was to contemplate.

Indeed, she did think about it. Tossing and turning that night, she was unable to get to sleep, disturbed because her previously deeply held convictions had in a trice been totally disrupted. It was like being bereaved—knowing that something dreadful has happened, yet paradoxically hoping that it won't be true, hoping that in the morning all will be well and that everything will be back to normal with the dead person alive again and life as it always was. In her heart of hearts she knew that she had just buried some of her most treasured beliefs. Yet she still hoped that in the morning they would still be there, undead.

- 5 -

*T*wo days later a small convoy moved out from Maulden towards Bromham. They didn't use the trucks any more because fuel was too precious: they'd found a couple of four-wheel farm wagons and had hitched up two pairs of the shire horses. Some of the farm workers loaded up the wagons with bags of grain until the horses, straining, could only just move them.

At the head of the convoy were Peter and Paul with, behind

them, Alan and the burly Trevor Smith. 'Walk on,' said Peter from his seat at the front of the first cart, flicking his crop near the ears of the cart horse which obligingly moved forwards. The first two horses, which for some unknown reason had been rechristened Portia and Shylock—lumbered slowly up to their normal running speed of two miles an hour and the convoy started out of the yard opposite King's Farm. Peter, white-knuckled, was hanging on to the whip and to the cart, and Paul suddenly started to get concerned. 'You don't look very comfortable,' he observed.

'No, couldn't be better,' said Peter giving him a sidelong glance, and then hurriedly looking to the front. 'I've just never done this before.'

'Yes, you have—you've driven horses and carts. I've seen you.'

'Only two-wheelers, not four-wheelers. And not with a load like this on board I haven't.'

'Ah.'

'I hope Shylock will stop when I ask him.'

'Well, why don't you try?'

'All right then. Whoa! Whoa!' Peter pulled on the reins and obediently the horses stopped. Paul could feel the momentum of the cart continuing to push the animals forward in a rather ungainly fashion, but the wagon eventually came to a halt, causing consternation behind as Trevor had suddenly to try to halt his team too.

'What have you stopped for?' he shouted.

'Just testing the brakes,' said Paul, looking over his shoulder. Trevor let out a hiss of irritation.

'Walk on,' said Peter, flicking the crop again and they went out of the gate and turned left to go towards Maulden.

It was at this point that things started to go wrong. And it was at this point that Alan suddenly found out why cobbled streets had cobbles. Shylock and Portia turned out into the Brache, a humpback road with a smoothly metalled surface, not bad for a minor rural side road—if you're in a car, that is. Shylock began snorting uneasily, clip-clopping down the road. Almost immediately the road started to fall away into a natural dip and Shylock started to walk more quickly. 'Whoa, whoa,' said Peter, his knuckles even whiter.

The horses tried to obey, but the weight of the wagon behind was too great. Shylock tried to do his best to stop, straightening his legs until they locked, but horses' hooves, even when shod with horseshoes, weren't designed to work on smooth surfaces. Hooves work best on rough surfaces, and the cobbled streets of so many northern towns weren't there for the sake of being picturesque. The cobbles provide a roughened surface upon which the shoes on horses' hooves can get a purchase. Shylock and Portia tried their best, but they couldn't get any purchase at all on the smooth road, and with the immense weight of the laden wagon behind them, started to be pushed bodily down towards the bottom of the dip.

Gravity did the rest.

Static friction and sliding friction are two quite different things. Static friction is the amount of sticking force that two objects exert when they are stationary and about to start moving. Sliding friction is the resistance to movement of two objects that are already sliding. Sliding friction is very much less than static friction—so once an object has started to slide it needs far less energy to *keep* it sliding than was needed to *start* it sliding—which is why, once the balance is lost on ice, it's very much harder to retain it, and why, once a car starts skidding, it's much harder to stop it.

Poor Shylock didn't know anything about static or sliding friction. Nor for that matter did Peter or Paul. They were all just about to find out. For the first few seconds, static friction worked, keeping Shylock's hooves firmly on the ground, but at the point where the static friction was overcome by the thrust of gravity and the momentum of the laden dray, Shylock and Portia started to slide. Once started, they just couldn't stop, and for a heart-stopping few seconds did an extraordinarily good imitation of a skier on a downhill run, fully laden wagon behind them and all. Fortunately the road was straight. Even more fortunately the dip wasn't great, and soon led into a rise. Shylock and Portia skied down the first part of the drop, legs straight, desperately trying to brake themselves against the combined force of gravity and the momentum of the wagon behind him, but with the cart going faster and faster they eventually gave up and started to trot, then to canter, and finally to gallop, but at the speed they were going their hooves didn't get a good purchase on the road. Shylock stumbled, hooves sliding everywhere. It was a good job he didn't fall, because the momentum of the wagon would have taken it over the top of the horses, throwing Peter and Paul off in the process. Downward they went, faster and faster, the horses slipping and sliding all over the place, obviously totally out of control, and Peter and Paul hanging on for dear life even though they probably weren't doing more than seven miles an hour.

Eventually they reached the bottom of the dip with poor Shylock—eyes staring wildly at the road ahead, head twisting and turning, and legs going everywhere—trying desperately to regain his balance. Eventually he did so as the pace slowed, but not before he'd slithered across to the side of the road, and at the last minute fell, dragging Portia down with him and giving the shafts of the cart a sudden lurch to the left. Momentum did the rest. The weight of the cart was so great that the shafts broke, followed shortly after by the dislocation of the whole of the front wheel assembly on its mobile turntable. The front of the cart dropped, flinging Peter and Paul off into the hedgerow as with a crash of splintering wood the dray turned over, spilling its precious load of wheat onto the road. By some miracle Shylock wasn't injured. He just picked himself up, snorted, whinnied, shook himself down and with the shafts still attached on each side, tried to canter off, only to be stopped by the traces that were still intact.

It was a sorry sight—a broken wagon, its contents strewn all over the place, and two bruised, sore, cut, bleeding and extremely sorry waggoners staggering up from the side of the road. Behind them Alan and Trevor had just managed to stop their pair before they had turned out on to the slippery part of the Brache.

Trevor got down and ran to where Peter and Paul were picking themselves up. 'Are you all right?' he said anxiously. Peter had a cut lip and a grazed face, and his sweater had experienced a pretty terminal event: Paul had a bruised hand but fortunately little else.

'What happened?' asked Paul, still dazed by the speed with which it had all happened.

'Never mind that,' said Trevor, 'let's sort out the horses first. There, there, my beauty, there there.' For all his burliness and lack of learning Trevor had a way with animals, and Shylock was immediately soothed by hearing his voice. Even so he still raised his head, showed the whites of his eyes and whinnied again. Trevor quickly undid the shafts and the traces and led both of them back to the stables at King's Farm.

'I thought you said the brakes were all right,' said Alan. Paul looked at him sideways.

'I was only joking,' he said. 'The horses couldn't hold the weight of the dray as we went downhill.'

'Well, why didn't you brake?' said Alan.

'Shylock was trying... What do you mean, brake?'

'You've got a brake on the dray. Two-wheelers don't but all four-wheelers do. Didn't you know?'

'Have we? Where?'

Alan showed him the lever.

'You put it on when you're going downhill so the horse doesn't get the full weight of the vehicle. Didn't you know that?'

For once Paul was nonplussed.

'Well, you've just managed to ruin a cart, haven't you?' continued Alan. 'And spill a lot of our precious grain—remember the stuff that you said we ought to keep carefully just in case, and you didn't want to waste any. Oh, come on, let's get it cleared up.'

But it took them a long time, even though they called in a lot of extra help. They manhandled the intact bags of grain back to the farm, and scooped up much of the rest. The cart looked as though it was beyond repair, but after a thorough inspection Alan declared that it was probably not too difficult to mend, but would take some time and would need the skills of a very good carpenter, and what were they going to do in the meantime? The four of them retired to King's Farm to mull over the problem.

'What bothers me,' said Paul, 'is that even if we'd remembered to use the brakes, Shylock still wouldn't have kept his feet.'

'I'm sure you could have managed the short distance up and down the Brache,' said Trevor.

'Yes, I'm sure about that too,' said Paul, 'but I'm not thinking of that. I'm thinking of the road out north. In fact I'm thinking of *all* roads north.'

'Why?' said Trevor. 'I don't see... Oh yes. Ampthill's on a high ridge, isn't it?'

'Not that high,' said Paul, 'but all the roads north are all very steep at some point. The main Bedford road's got a dreadful hill at Hazlewood Lane. The animals won't get down easily—not with a wagon behind. They might have done if the roads were cobbled but as they're not, there's no way they'll get down that hill fully laden.'

'What about taking another route—through Millbrook, perhaps?'

'There are still some pretty steep parts there—going into Millbrook, and coming out on the far side.'

'The back road to Houghton Conquest?'

'Don't be silly. That's even worse than Hazlewood Lane.'

'Well, what can we do?'

'We could try the A6 at Clophill. That's got a much gentler sweep as it goes down towards Wilstead.'

'It's blocked just north of the Clophill roundabout.'

There was an awkward, baffled silence

'I know,' said Trevor, 'we could go out on the back road towards Houghton, and then join the A6 just beyond Haynes West End. That would get us past the blockage at the Flying Horse. Then you'd be able to go down slowly towards Wilstead. Mind you, going north the Brache is just about as bad as any of the other routes.'

'But at least it's only little humps and bumps,' said Peter. 'What's really dangerous is if we have a continuous long drop. I think you're right, Trevor, that route's easiest—but we'll need a bit of practice with the animals first.'

'But we need the flour *now*,' interjected Paul. 'We haven't got time to practise.'

'I'd forgotten that,' said Peter. 'Tell you what—why don't we go in a vehicle for once and load it up properly? Let's get a really big batch of flour made up. That'll give us time to mend the wagon and learn to drive it a bit better. I never realised that driving a big farm wagon needed so much skill—nor that what was done to the roads stops us using farm wagons easily. Smooth roads and cart horses definitely don't go together.'

'OK,' said Paul, getting to his feet, 'let's load up a lorry.'

*   *   *

Martin watched in rapt attention as Anne, who had just cut the last white rose of the year, placed it in a long-necked vase and arranged it neatly on the side-table in the hall of the Old Rectory, turning it this way and that until she was satisfied that she had it exactly right. 'You know this house does look a lot better for having a woman's touch around.'

Anne looked over her shoulder at him and smiled. 'Sexist remark! I bet you're just as good as I am at arranging flowers. It's just that you haven't bothered, that's all.'

'It isn't that I don't do them, it's that I don't *think* of doing them. Anyway you've got that special sort of touch... It livens things up, makes the house come alive. Gives it... personality, somehow.'

'You'll get the hang of it soon enough.'

'I don't know,' he said straightening out a chair against the table in the corner. 'The place really does seem to have come alive since you and the family all came up here. Quite different from when I was on my own.'

For a second his mind went back to that dreadful time—when was it? not six months earlier, though it seemed like four years ago—when Anne had first come up to the Old Rectory with a bundle of music as a present, and found him in the depths of depression and despair. He shuddered inwardly. Things were so different now, but yet... The strength of the memory shocked him with its intensity. It must have showed on his face. Anne suddenly looked up at him.

'What's the matter, Martin?'

'Nothing...'

'I don't believe you.'

'No. Well... Well, yes... I was just remembering the first time you came up here, and what a mess it was in and what a mess I was in.'

His voice tailed away. He shuddered. A little thought crossed Anne's mind, a horrible thought, one that she almost dared not acknowledge. Martin wasn't going back into the abyss again, was he? Oh God, no, not again. It would break him. She came round the table and put her hand on his.

'It's the past, Martin. It's all in the past now.'

'I know,' he said brightening up slightly—but the far off mistiness was still in his eyes as he silently contemplated that dreadful day when he'd been too tired and too dispirited even to think about making food for himself or doing the washing up or keeping the place tidy; and how he'd burst into tears in front of her. Suddenly the memory rolled over him like a bank of fog, enveloping him, choking him. Although the sun was shining strongly outside it seemed to have gone two degrees colder in the house, and a great deal dimmer, as the memories came flooding back. The chaos of the place with dirty dishes everywhere... on the table, on the floor, books spread everywhere, where he'd started to read but where his concentration had dwindled after the second page and he'd left them there, open, where he'd stopped reading.

'I don't... think... that I want to be in here any longer,' he said, rushing through the kitchen, out of the back door, into the court-yard, and into the warmth of the sun. He was choking with emotion, staring blankly out in front of him. Anne came up and almost unconsciously put her arm round his shoulder. He stared out at the sky, unseeing, chewing his upper lip in anguish. 'I thought this was all over,' he said. 'I thought this was all gone. It can't come back now, it *can't*.'

'It won't, Martin,' said Anne, hoping her voice didn't seem as unconvincing as she felt. 'It's just a flashback, a memory.' She took her hand from round his shoulder and put it on his arm again. 'It'll go.'

'It was just... seeing you there tidying the place up like that brought it all back to me. How awful it was. How grey and drab and *empty*.'

'It's full of people now,' said Anne.

'I didn't mean the house, I meant me. Life.'

'Oh.'

He brightened up a bit. 'I'll be all right. It just took me by surprise, that's all. Took the wind out of my sails. The memories are so
overwhelmingly strong... There, it's all right. I'll go back into the
dining room.'

'Are you sure?' she said, tailing behind him.

'I'm sure,' and he strode through the dark hallway into the dining room and stood for a moment in the doorway, surveying the
scene.

'Do you often have bouts like that?' asked Anne, following
behind and still shaking from the sudden intensity of it all.

'No,' said Martin, 'not like that. At least, not as strong.' He
chewed absent-mindedly at the side of his lower lip. 'No, just a
flashback... a very powerful one. I was just reminded of what it was
like... that day... and how kind you've been. You helped me a lot.
Did you know?'

'I didn't do anything special, just tidied up a bit, washed a few
dishes.'

'Did you know what I was just about to do?'

'No.'

'Oh.' He gave a sigh.

'You weren't...? How?'

'I was going to do a Captain Oates—go out into the snow, lie
down and go to sleep. Then you came along. And smiled at me,
cared about me, cleaned up after me, and told me I was important.'

'I don't remember saying anything like that.'

'You didn't say it, at least not in words. You and Derek said it by
what you did, time and again. That spoke volumes. You went all the
way to London to pick up belongings from your own house and
even then you managed to have enough thought to find some music
that you thought I'd like to play. Now that's what I call kindness.'

'It was nothing Martin, it really was nothing. Just a few scraps of
paper that I happened to pass in one of the shops.'

'Yes, but you still thought about it. You actually went in and
picked it up. And you chose carefully as well.'

'Well...'

'You did. You seemed to know exactly what I like. It was very kind of you. Have I ever told you how much it meant at the time?'

'Not in so many words, but as you said, actions speak louder than words. You played one of the pieces at the concert, didn't you? And very effectively too.' She looked at him. His eyes seemed to have rekindled something of their original sparkle and the pale lock of hair had fallen down across his forehead again in a way that made him look deceptively young and vulnerable.

'You're very perceptive, Anne,' he said finally. 'Derek's a lucky man. It's nice to feel understood. Sort of... comforting somehow.'

'A return to mother's knee,' she said, looking at him in a coquettish sort of fashion.

'I suppose so.' Then the brooding intensity swept over him again and his face took on that deep far-away look. He fell silent.

'You must have felt very lonely in that first year.'

'I always had the feeling that nobody else really understood the problems I was trying to face up to, that they didn't really see why it was causing me so much trouble. But you're right—it is a help to be understood, to know that there's somebody who's really with you, who understands you enough to give you just the right sort of music to echo what you're feeling, and help you get on with working through it. Yes, it does help. Lots.' He paused. 'Hey, we ought to be getting on.'

'We can still talk while we're doing the washing up, can't we? What was it that you were worrying about?'

'When I was first here at Ampthill, you mean? Just about everything. I told Derek all about it. Doesn't he talk to you?'

'Yes... and no. Sometimes he doesn't think he ought to tell me what's going on because it's medical and confidential and at other times he may not say if he doesn't think I'll be interested. So I don't always pick up all of what other people tell him. What was bugging you?'

'Lots of things really,' said Martin, stacking the dirty plates. 'I didn't see how things fitted together with what I'd been teaching people and what I'd been taught in church. And then the isolation after the plague had passed.' He shuddered. 'That was dreadful.'

'No one left to understand you,' said Anne in a matter-of-fact way, scrubbing away at a recalcitrant mark on a dish. 'This water's getting cold.'

'I'll get some more,' said Martin and fetched the kettle from the side of the range. 'Yes, maybe. It isn't just enough to *be*, is it? We need to feel loved, as well as to love.'

'Now you *are* getting deep,' said Anne scrubbing away furiously again, elbows moving in all directions. 'Stop hanging around like that. Grab a cloth and dry something.'

'Does Derek get this treatment?' he asked wryly.

'Always,' she said, turning to him and planting a mock kiss on his right cheek, 'so you'd better get used to it. Oh, look, you forgot to fill up the kettle before you put it back on the range.'

Sheepishly, Martin went to the rain barrel to refill it.

*   *   *

Paul was sitting at the desk in the coldness of the study of Foulislea Cottage, scribbling furiously on a pad in front of him and pausing to blow on his fingers to stop them freezing solid. Not one to miss a chance, and having had his eyes opened for him, he'd quickly realised the enormous potential of the library they'd stumbled on. Mary's enthusiasm had somehow rubbed off on him, in the way that enthusiasm often does: but more than that, Mary had shown him how to use the library to look up items. It hadn't take long to learn, and given time he could easily have done it himself, but somehow being shown directly how to do it had given him a start. There's something about being shown at first hand by someone who knows what they're doing that gives confidence and impetus, letting the novice know that the job in hand is actually quite simple and—to put no finer point upon it—very obvious.

Once he'd got the hang of it he was away. From his previous experience as a stockbroker he knew all too well what effect tiny snippets of information could have on the value of the stocks and shares. Just a whisper, just a hint of anxiety about possible side-effects of a new drug being developed by a pharmaceutical company could send that company's shares plummeting; or there might be a change in trade barriers that made another company much more profitable; or a spate of bad weather in the American mid-West that sent the futures market in grain soaring. Little things could mean such a lot—such as the five-day electricity blackout in New York which sent the birth-rate up nine months later as, deprived of means of entertainment such as the television, couples turned to other methods of whiling away the time. Insignificant events could blow up out of almost all proportion. It was just a matter of spotting it, seeking the important thing, the lynch-pin, that tiny nugget of information that made all the difference. Sometimes it was easy to see what was happening; on other occasions it was difficult. Occasionally it almost needed a sixth sense. He knew people who'd got it—those who could look at company reports and tease out of them the one nugget of information that meant so much. His mind went back to the years before the plague and how some investors and analysts had become legendary—those who months before it happened had predicted the crash of Rolls Royce, brought down because of problems with the RB-211 engine, or those who somehow always managed to get out of shares that were about to drop and into ones that were going to rise—which always gave rise to the suspicion that they were indulging in insider dealing, which so often they weren't. They too were just piecing together tiny pieces of information, making sense of them, creating a unified picture out of them where others saw nothing.

In this frame of mind Paul had set to work to devour the information in Foulislea Cottage. Before he began on the archives themselves, he made a point of reading the books from cover to cover—five times each at least, all the while making copious notes. Then he started on the individual papers. By the time he'd finished he could have written a history of Ampthill without needing to glance at a reference book. He knew where every well was, where every old house had been and who had owned them, the names of the brewers and the hotel keepers and the butchers; where the village pond had been, where the sewers were.

As well as the interesting but inconsequential historical information, his mound of useful information grew and grew: how to build ploughs; how to butcher sheep; the best way to keep carp in ponds; how to make soap out of horse-chestnut leaves.

Perhaps the most important discovery was the location of the ice house. To his disappointment he found that the inhabitants of Ampthill of two hundred years ago hadn't known how to make refrigerators—they were not as well versed in science as that—so their ice houses were not places to make ice as much as to store it, until it was needed during the summer. They did this simply by creating a cool place where air, heat and sunlight couldn't reach, where in the depth of winter ice cut from river and pond could be stored, packed away in insulating straw, deep in the recesses of the pit. His first reaction, which had lasted all of half a second, was that this was going to an awful lot of trouble to get ice for the whisky; his second—and much more important—realisation was that ice could be used to help preserve food; to keep it fresh during the heat of the summer; to extend the time meat could be stored safely. The practical problems of keeping enough food available for each season of the year were bad enough—it helped knowing how to extend the length of time it could be stored.

The more Paul studied the more he began to realise just how clever the inhabitants of old had been, and how, working with little in the way of technology, and an even smaller knowledge of science, they had managed to solve problems that with hindsight might have seemed impossible. But perhaps the thing which astounded Paul most was the sheer variety of food that used to be eaten, and yet how limited the subsequent modern diet had become in the years prior to the plague, despite the advent of global travel. He could count almost on his fingers and toes the staple foods of a year and a quarter earlier and a very sorry and mediocre lot they now seemed: wheat, oats, rice, potatoes, peas, carrots, beef, lamb, chicken, eggs, milk, cabbage, cauliflower, beans... He searched around mentally for any more. Oh yes, tomatoes, apples, peaches and pears... bananas, though that was a bit foreign. Oranges... Things were starting to get a bit exotic. Kiwi fruit... Yes, a rather restricted diet, all things considered—especially when his records showed that two hundred years earlier it seemed as though every flower, tree, nut, shoot and living thing could be used for food in some way or another. Rabbit and hare, deer, geese as well as pork, beef and mutton, chicken, quail, pigeon, even hedgehog. Ah, hedgehog. He remembered that from Boy Scout days. Question: how to eat a hedgehog without getting your mouth full of spines? Answer, get all the unmentionable innards out, then knead some clay, encase the whole animal in it and bake it in the fire. When it's ready, tap the baked clay, which will fall open like· a walnut shell, taking all the spines with it, revealing the flesh inside which is now cooked and ready to eat. Easy when you know how.

His list of new foods spread across four pages. He knew the next step would be to go to Neil. The beauty of it was that with so many different foods to choose from, their diet would be that much more varied and that much more interesting—and if one of their mini-harvests failed—such as the apples—it wouldn't matter; there would be many more alternatives available as replacements.

And so many of the foods were simply there for the taking—they didn't even have to be sown or tended! He picked up a book entitled *Food for Free* which was all about edible plants in the hedgerows and other places, and began studying it again. The possibilities were enormous.

He put the book down again and stared out of the window, thinking, absent-mindedly chewing his pencil. Geese. Now there was a thought. Big birds with quite a lot of meat on: not as much as a turkey, of course, but the advantage of geese is that they can just wander all over the place picking up food wherever it's available. Suddenly he realised why there always seemed to be geese in the pictures of rustic villages that were so common in the early nineteenth century. There were geese everywhere in those pictures— because, in reality, there *were* geese everywhere, rummaging around, ferreting out morsels of food. Then when you wanted a feast you got one on its own and quietly wrung its neck. He shuddered. He still hadn't got used to that part of it.

He stopped staring out of the window and looked down again at the pad on his desk. Yes, he really would have to talk with Neil.

*   *   *

Kevin had a surprise for them all, as usual. Kevin had a habit of surprising people, not always pleasantly. He also had an innate craftiness about him, greater even than Paul's, and when he realised that all the wheat was stored at King's Farm, made a point of buttonholing Chris. 'Why do we keep all the corn over in Maulden?' he asked.

'It's convenient,' said Chris. 'What's the problem?'

'Nah, I didn't mean that. I said, why do we keep *all* the corn in Maulden?'

'Because it's convenient,' repeated Chris, puzzled.

'*All.* I said *all.* What if you have a fire, or rats, or thieves?'

'Why should we have thieves?'

'Why shouldn't we have thieves?'

'Everybody has enough to eat.'

'If you don't wanna take my advice you don't 'ave to take my advice. Just don't say I didn't warn you,' and Kevin stumped off back over the hill to his house at the northern edge of the town.

The difficulty with Kevin was, brash, loud and ignorant though he often was, that behind those sullen eyes and dark locks lurked a brain of immense cunning.

No, thought Chris to herself, watching his back recede. No, it doesn't matter. He's wrong. There won't be a fire, or rats. And as she went back to Foulislea Cottage she dismissed the idea from her mind.

Or so she thought. Her subconscious thought differently, as she found later that night when she woke in a sweat, dreaming of Kevin stealing the wheat, spoonful by spoonful, shovelling it into the never-ending tank of his Harley-Davidson, until the granaries were empty, and just as he was roaring off into the distance with their entire year's wheat supply she woke, suddenly alert, listening. How the night magnifies terror! She went to the window, rubbed the condensation off it and stared out into the street outside. It was quiet as the grave. In the moonlight she could see Brandreth House, opposite Dynevor House in Church Square, then gave a start as, in the cold white light of the moon, a shape detached itself from the shadows at the bottom of the wall and silently crossed the road towards her. Her heart beating, she rubbed away at the condensation again and then relaxed. It was a Muntjac deer of the kind common around the area: originally from the estate at Woburn Abbey, one or two had got out, and were now a common occurrence in the countryside around. Her heart still thumping from the adrenaline the shock had given her, she lay back in bed and shut her eyes. Immediately pictures of Kevin spooning wheat into the Harley-Davidson's tank rose back up again in front of her. No, not fire, nor rats, she hadn't been worried about those really. *Thieves.* But why? Why should Kevin worry about thieves? And now, of all times. Yes, there had been the looters when first the plague occurred, but gradually looting had died away as people recognised that there was enough for everybody.

No there wasn't, she suddenly realised. In the past the looters had gone for expensive items like jewellery and cameras. But the real need now was for food. What was different now was that they'd had a harvest. They'd assumed that everybody around them had probably got their own harvest in as well, *but that was an assumption.*

Good old Kevin, thought Chris, turning over in bed. Her subconscious settled down to sleep too. Having done its job of activating its mistress to recognise the hidden danger, and knowing that the hidden danger had been acknowledged, it too could rest, but just to be sure, for the rest of the night Chris dreamed about Kevin unloading *half* the grain, spoonful by spoonful, from the tank of his Harley-Davidson into a barn on the opposite side of Ampthill from King's Farm.

*   *   *

Meanwhile Derek was just about to start a living nightmare all of his own. Like all the best nightmares—or all the best horror movies—this one began innocuously, even gently, and quietly worked itself up into a frenzy.

The November morning was bright, though cold. Derek had just finished lighting the fire before morning surgery in the Dickensianwindowed shop on the south side of Market Square when there was a creak and a clang as the door opened, and in came a tiny woman of about five feet nothing, silver-haired, aged about sixty-five with a gentle smiling face, dressed neatly in a dress and a shawl. 'Halloo,' she purred in a soft lilting Western Isles accent. 'Halloo, I'm Janet MacKenzie. And you must be...'

'Derek Jones.'

'Ah yes. Derek Jones.' The voice purred over the words making it sound surprisingly like a melody. *I've seen you somewhere before,* thought Derek, feverishly racking his brain: *something to do with medicine.* You've not been a patient before, have you, he thought to himself. No, you can't be. I don't know anybody with an accent like that. But yet it seemed so familiar.

'I don't think we've met before,' she said as if to confirm his thoughts. 'I've only just moved down here. We used to live in Shefford,' she purred, 'when I was a girl. Then after the plague I stayed in Harpenden for a while, but I found that my good friend Dorothy Summerfield had survived so I've travelled here to be with her.'

The penny suddenly dropped. She was *exactly* like the TV version of the character of Janet in *Doctor Finlay's Casebook*. He felt better for knowing—the unease disappeared.

It shouldn't have.

'And what can I do for you, Mrs MacKenzie?'

'Ah, well, doctor—'

'I'm not a proper doctor, you know,' interjected Derek, anxious to make sure that she didn't start off with any misconceptions.

'Oh, I know that,' said Janet, 'but I've heard such good things about you that I'm sure everybody ought to be *calling* you doctor by now. Well, doctor, I've got this pain in my stomach.'

'Which part?'

'Just here,' she said, pointing to the middle of the abdomen on the left side. 'And... sometimes it moves across to the other side.' She pointed to the right-hand side of the abdomen but this time just a little lower. 'And it's so painful that when I get it I sometimes have to stop what I'm doing and hang on to whatever's near until it goes away again. And I *do* try to get over it, but it is just so painful.'

'Is it related to food?'

'No... I don't think so. Sometimes, but not often.'

'Your bowels all right?'

'Mostly. Sometimes I'm a little... bound... if you know what I mean.'

'Waterworks all right?'

'Oh, yes.'

'Periods?'

'Oh, doctor, I haven't seen those for many a year. Oh, no, no, no... there's no trouble there.'

'I'd better examine you then. Perhaps you'd like to undress.' Mrs MacKenzie walked primly behind the screens, took off some of her outer clothes and lifted herself up on to the couch.

'Ready, doctor.' Coyly she pulled up her clothes to reveal about an inch of bare flesh around her waist.

'I need to see a lot more than that,' said Derek. 'Keyhole medicine isn't in my style.'

'Oh dear,' said Janet flushing with embarrassment. 'Still I suppose if I must, I must.' She hitched her top up another two inches. 'There, will that do?'

'Just about,' said Derek, feeling her abdomen. There was nothing obvious at all. No lumps, no masses and, when he listened with his stethoscope, no extra noises either. He put his hand on her stomach again. 'Not tender there?' he said.

'No, no. *Ooh.*' She recoiled with the shock of he pain.

What on earth was that, thought Derek. 'I'm sorry to have hurt you,' he said, somewhat taken aback, and not a little flustered.

'No, no, doctor, you continue; you've got your job to do.' Derek's fingers felt gingerly round the area that had given the trouble. There was nothing. He prodded her again in a slightly different place. 'No, that's not the... *Oh.*'

'Hmm,' said Derek in a reassuring tone. He'd read somewhere that budding doctors in one medical school had been taught to make comforting noises like 'Hmm' and 'Yes' and 'Um' and so forth when examining their patients. Apparently it soothed the patients wonderfully. 'Hmm,' he said again for good effect, trying desperately to cover up the fact that he hadn't the vaguest idea what was going on. 'I think we ought to do one or two tests: perhaps a sample of your water and a specimen of blood.'

'Do you do the tests yourself?' she asked, her eyes open in wonderment. 'Oh, you *are* clever.'

'I don't do anything special,' said Derek, flattered, washing his hands, using shredded horse-chestnut leaves for soap. 'Just a thin film of blood on a slide to look at under the microscope—I can usually tell a few things from that. And it's easy to measure the ESR.'

'What's that, doctor?' said Janet. 'Do tell me.'

'It stands for Erythrocyte Sedimentation Rate,' replied Derek, rather grandly, flattered by the attention. 'There are two parts to the blood: firstly the cells, and secondly the fluid—the plasma—in which they're suspended. In a healthy person the blood stays much as it is when it's left in a tube, but in someone who's not too well the cells drop down very quickly, leaving the clear plasma in the tube above them. What I'm going to do is suck up a bit of your blood into a long thin pipette, and measure how quickly the cells drop down in the next hour. If there's twenty or thirty millimetres of clear fluid between the top of the cells and the top of the fluid then everything's normal, but if the cells have fallen more than this it usually means there's something going on like an infection, or rheumatism, or even something much worse. I'll take a blood sample.'

He did so, and immediately set up the ESR tube. After that he placed a further drop of her blood on a microscope slide and with the end of another microscope slide wiped the blood along the length of the first slide, spreading out the drop into an infinitesimally thin sheet. Then he clipped the slide into the microscope on the table beside him. 'That looks all right to me,' he said, peering down through the eyepiece. 'It'll take some time before the ESR result's ready. Why don't you come back next week? In the meantime I'll give you something that ought to help the pain.'

'What do you think it is, doctor?' purred Janet, her eyes looking up at him sweetly. 'I hope it's nothing serious.'

'Oh no, I don't think it is,' said Derek, trying to hide his uncertainty. 'You've probably got a bit of spasm in the gut. Maybe a diverticulum.'

'A diverticulum?'

'A little balloon-like area that sometimes occurs off the side of the large bowel. They can swell and become painful, and sometimes they get infected. They're quite common as a cause of pain in those who are—' He checked himself. He had been going to say "elderly" but decided against it. '...a little older. I'm sure the medicines will help.'

'Thank you very much, doctor,' said Janet, dressing herself. 'You've been *most* kind. Good day to you.' The doorbell clanged as she went out.

What a nice person, thought Derek.

*   *   *

With their stocks of flour running low, Paul and Alan drove a large load of wheat to Bromham Mill, together with a couple of the farm hands to do the heavy manhandling.

It was dusk by the time they'd finished. The four of them were covered in flour from head to foot. None of them had had an accident or tripped and fallen into any of the flour hoppers—but they couldn't have got any whiter if they'd tried. The fine ground flour was everywhere, hanging like mist in the still air inside the mill. No wonder the nickname for anyone called miller was 'Dusty', reflected Paul as he closed the door behind them and got up into the lorry, throwing off little clouds of flour with each movement. Behind them on the back of the lorry lay the precious sacks of flour—flour which had been created from wheat in almost the same miraculous way in which a dark wintry countryside is turned into a light airy one by the arrival of snow.

Alan started the engine, and they began the journey back to Ampthill, the headlights picking out the dark roads in the dusk. How familiar it looked—how eerily familiar, to be sitting in a lorry cab watching as the headlights blazed out into the night. Real lights powered by electricity. It was just like being back in the normal times before the plague, he thought as the headlights picked out the trees and hedges by the side of the road. It could so easily have been two years earlier... and then as they swept through the outskirts of Bedford the dead town reared up in front of them, houses with their windows eyeless and black, the street lights unlit, debris of all sorts starting to clutter the road ahead—tree branches, twigs, the occasional slate, leaves and bits of plastic. In many places the weeds had started to reclaim the road, filling up the gutters and spilling out into the carriageway.

By the time they got back to Ampthill it was dark, and in the absence of decent lighting they threw a tarpaulin over the precious flour, ready to unload it the following morning.

*   *   *

Over in the woods to the south of the town the watcher looked through his field glasses yet again, and then put them down. It wasn't time yet. Not quite.

- 6 -

*G*ood morning, doctor,' said Mrs MacKenzie as she came through the door.

Back already, thought Derek, a concerned frown on his brow. 'How are the pains?'

'They're no better, I'm afraid,' she said, her soft Scottish voice purring almost soporifically across the room. 'It's just there,' she said, pointing nebulously on the left side of her abdomen at a slightly different position to the site she'd indicated the day before. Derek examined her carefully. Again he could find nothing.

'And the medicines I gave you yesterday didn't help?'

'Not at all doctor, I'm sorry to say, not at all. Isn't there anything else you could prescribe for the pain?' Derek furrowed his brow, racking his brains to think what else might be useful. Maybe anti-spasmodics weren't the answer after all. I wonder whether she's got diverticulitis, he thought. That's always difficult to spot. No temperature though. I don't really want to use our precious antibiotics if she doesn't really need them.

'Perhaps we can try something different,' he said out loud. 'Another anti-spasmodic perhaps,' and went to get one from the shelf behind him. 'Try these.'

'Do you really think they'll work?' said Janet, looking at them dubiously.

'I'm sure they will,' said Derek with a nice, warm, practised smile which totally hid the gnawing uncertainty that was quietly developing within him.

'Well, I'm sure you're right, doctor,' she said, getting up. 'Good day.'

*   *   *

In Gates House, across the road from Foulislea Cottage, the Major was starting to turn his favour colour—beetroot. He'd called Chris over. The Major, being the Major, wouldn't go across the road to see Chris—*she* had to come to *him*.

And to be harangued.

Being Chris—and being amenable, up to a point—she'd complied: after all, he was one of the council. He was used to leadership, and ordering people about, and despite his somewhat fuddyduddy approach was not entirely unwise.

'I really object to this Courtauld fella coming in like this and demanding rent for my house.' There was ever such a slight accent on the word 'my', as though Gates House had been in his family for generations.

'But it *is* his,' replied Chris. 'We always said we wouldn't take anything from a living person, you know.'

'Bah. Why should we pay him, anyway? We're sharing everything, or hadn't you noticed?'

'It's his house.'

'It's not. Dynevor House is his house.'

'*And* Gates House,' said Chris thinking that the conversation was beginning to get a little boring.

'And I really don't like the way that he barges in after a year and suddenly thinks that he can be back to ruling the place like he used to.'

'Who said he used to rule the place?'

'It's obvious he did. Family's been in the town for centuries. JP. It stands to reason. But I still don't like the idea of paying him rent. That really rankles. Are we really sure he's genuine?'

'I've just taken him to meet Neil,' replied Chris patiently.

'And?'

'They fell about like two old buddies at a class reunion. Of course Henry's genuine.'

'Well, maybe Neil's in league with him to get a share of the proceeds.'

'Oh, don't be silly,' said Chris scornfully. 'Now you're being stupid.'

'Me being stupid?' retorted the Major.

'Well... Not quite stupid. I mean... just a bit over the top.'

The Major snorted and went silent. Chris looked at him intently. How he'd gone downhill in the past twelve months! From being a sprightly, dapper, wiry man of seventy, he'd suddenly started to look his age, with tremulous hands and a face that didn't seem to register emotion as it used to in the past—apart from the colour, that was.

And it was from that moment on that Chris suddenly began to understand the Major as she'd never understood him before. It was his *age* that did it—now he looked like what he really was, a product of the pre-second world war era, not a man of the post-*glasnost*, nuclear age. The Major belonged to a different age altogether—a time when honour was one of the most important attributes, and dishonour a matter for disgrace and even suicide: a time when fighting and dying for King and Country was a matter of honour too; when laying down one's life for the next man in the regiment was an honour, and sometimes a duty. The Major was one of the last to grow up in a house with servants, at a time when the structure of society was more rigid: when newcomers (and especially youngsters) were suspected of being upstarts if they became upwardly mobile. And suddenly, Chris at last saw through the

Major's eyes the extreme annoyance of having served his time pro-
gressing through the ranks of life—which in the Major's terms simply implied getting older—only to find, as he became a septuage-
narian, that what he had thought of as his natural standing as senior
figure and leader was simply being ignored by this *younger* and
more affable *newcomer*, Henry Courtauld—at least, a newcomer as
far as their new society was concerned.

With understanding, her sympathy increased rather than de-
creased: compassion rather than pity. Her voice lost its initial irritation and dropped down a fraction in volume. 'Don't you remember
the first thing that Neil said when he discovered Derek living in
Dynevor House? He said, "Where's Henry Courtauld then? The
chap who used to live here." At least, that's what Derek said he said.
At first Neil was really put out that Derek was living in Henry's
house. He's *got* to be genuine, it's *got* to be above board. Henry's
the one who owns Dynevor House.'

'Neil didn't say anything about Gates House, did he?' The
Major's body might be starting to fail but his brain certainly wasn't.

There was a pause.

'No,' said Chris, 'come to think of it, he didn't. I'll go and ask
him again.'

*   *   *

'Oh, *doctor*,' said Mrs MacKenzie as she came into the surgery
two days later. Derek's heart sank. Three times in four days.

'No better then?'

'Oh, no, doctor. If anything, I think it's a little worse.' With a
feeling of total despair Derek invited her yet again to lie down on
the examination couch.

*   *   *

Chris caught up with Neil the following evening when he'd come
home exhausted from supervising the sowing of the winter wheat.
'Hello, Chris,' he said as he took off his gumboots and wiggled his
toes in front of the fire. 'Ah, that feels good. Now what can I do for
you?'

'It's about Henry....'

*   *   *

After the millers had returned from Bromham there had been some argument about where to store the flour. Neil didn't mind where it was put, but emphasised the importance of keeping away rats, mice and insects; Alan wanted it stored back in the barns at King's Farm, along with the grain; Paul, practical to a fault, said that it needed to be stored in the centre of the town, where everyone could get to it easily, but Susan—as always at loggerheads with her husband Alan—was adamant that if they were now to sell the stuff, the main supply should be locked up somewhere far away with only enough for each week being brought to one of the shops in the centre of the town, for sale.

Chris, mindful of what Kevin had said to her several weeks earlier, was equally insistent that as precious a commodity as a large supply of flour—with all the added value of the work put into it, like harvesting and milling, to say nothing of the effort required to transport it—should be kept very securely indeed, somewhere in the middle of the community, where everyone could keep an eye on it, just in case.

'Just in case of what?' asked Alan testily. 'We haven't had any problems since we saw off Lew and his gang.'

Chris noted the use of the royal 'we', but remembered instead how much Kevin had been responsible for their despatch: and thinking of Kevin reminded her yet again of the need to protect the food.

'I still think we ought to keep it all in Ampthill,' she said finally, 'but maybe not all in the same place. Why don't we split it? Let's have the main store in the old car showroom by the garage on Bedford Street. It's got a big open floor area; we're not using it for anything else; it's dry; we've got easy access for a lorry or a wagon so that unloading and loading will be easy; it's near the centre of the town—well, sort of—and we can lock it up, too.'

'You mean the old school?' said Paul, who'd been diligently absorbing the contents of the archives.

'Was it?' said Chris. 'I didn't know.'

'It used to be the National School, until 1954 I believe. There's a commemorative window to it in the north wall of the church.'

'Quite the local historian, aren't you?' replied Chris, secretly thrilled that Paul had at last expressed an interest in something that wasn't just for financial gain.

'Come to think of it, it does look like a school building,' said Alan. 'You said you want *two* stores, Chris. Where would you put the second one?'

'How about the old carpet shop in Dunstable Street?' she mused, thinking out loud. 'Again the access is easy: it's right on the street, so we can unload a lorry or wagon straight into it, and it's not being used for anything else. Mind you, it doesn't have to be there. It could be any of the shops along that road. Most of them aren't being used at the moment.'

'I think you'll find that a lot of them soon will be,' said Paul, 'now that we're using money again. I wouldn't mind betting that a lot of people decide that they'll set up cottage industries of one sort or another. Like the old days—you know, the leather merchant selling goods from the front of the shop, and making them at the back. We'll see a lot of that now.'

'You're probably right,' said Alan. 'I must admit I was thinking of doing something in leatherwork. Funny you should mention it.'

Susan glared at him. 'You should stick to what you're good at,' she said tartly.

'Any other ideas?' said Chris, anxious to change the subject.

'I think you've got it right, Chris,' said Derek. 'We need two depots in case of an accident—a fire, a flood or something like that. Why don't we use the carpet shop to sell the flour, and the old school to keep the other half of the flour dry and secure?' There was a murmur of assent.

'All right, let's go to it,' said Paul.

As a result of their deliberations Trevor, Alan and Peter spent the next few days splitting up the grain stores, clearing out the old carpet salesroom and bringing in the first load of flour. It was a lot of work, but, they thought, very worthwhile. Even if there were no bandits around, they would at least be better protected against fire or flood.

*   *   *

In the safety of the woods the man with the field glasses raised them and put them down again. The time was definitely getting near. He would report back.

*   *   *

'Good morning, doctor.'

Not again! Five times in seven days. It's not as if she looked ill. Derek remembered how pale and drawn Susan had been with her gallstones. Mrs MacKenzie didn't look like that at all. In fact Mrs MacKenzie looked very well indeed. Derek was strongly beginning to believe that there wasn't very much wrong at all with Mrs MacKenzie: but perhaps that was putting things too strongly. *Half* of Derek was beginning to believe that there wasn't anything wrong with Mrs MacKenzie, but the other half of him was absolutely sure there *was* something wrong, if nothing else because Mrs MacKenzie kept on telling him.

'The pain... it's no better,' she said. 'It's moved slightly,' and she indicated a spot to the right of the abdomen instead of the left.

'Oh, it's moved, has it?' said Derek, for want of anything better to say. 'I'd better have another look.'

But as usual there was nothing. And having given her yet another medicine to try, Derek sat watching her departing back, wondering what he'd done to deserve someone like this. At least with Susan he'd felt rewarded by the gratified look she'd given him when he'd managed to relieve her pain. But with Mrs MacKenzie he had the constant feeling of being sucked dry; or alternatively that he was the captain of a ship approaching a whirlpool that would inevitably suck him under.

What he didn't know—because he hadn't got the experience— was that behind that soft, purring Western Isles accent lay a full-blown hysteric. Now hysteria is not what the layman is inclined to think it is. Hysterics 'put' their unsolvable psychological problems 'into' part of their anatomy, and then experience their emotional discomfort as real pain, localised into that organ. And it *is* real pain: although of psychological origin, hysterics feel real pain at the point they say they're getting it. So a hysteric isn't making it up—far from it—but the source of the trouble isn't the anatomical site of the symptoms.

Which is half the point. Simply because the apparent physical symptoms are such a way from the real source of the problem (their personality), hysterics usually find it almost impossible to believe that the cause of their pain is psychological. In any case they have a vested interest in not addressing their emotional problems—after all, it's because they can't cope with those very problems that they are 'put' into a different organ. In psychological terms, their problems are so unpleasant and unapproachable that hysterical patients distance themselves from these problems by 'putting them into' another bit of their anatomy. And—most importantly—because the cause isn't physically related to its apparent site, every attempt to relieve the pain by treating the organ the pain appears to be in, is doomed to failure.

And that failure is also part of the game—and it is a game. Quite simply Janet was playing games with Derek; but they were lethal games, just as children play games which sometimes get out of hand and end up in fights with fists and sticks and heavy blunt instruments; or adult children play games with guns and armies; or fight in court for possession of their children... Games can be fun; but they can sometimes be lethal, and Janet's games were more lethal than most. Hers was one of the most lethal of all—domination.

Contrary to common belief, hysterics doesn't rush around in a panic. Instead they make *other people* run round in a panic. In Janet's case it was a left-over from her childhood. Long experience of losing at home year after year to her domineering mother and her weak and compliant father taught her that she couldn't beat her parents by strength of character, and that the only way she could have any hold over them was by deviousness and subterfuge. She found early on that a good way to get out of school was to complain of a stomach-ache; and because her mother couldn't be completely sure whether or not the pain was genuine, as likely as not she would end up in bed, with a day off school, after which she would recover miraculously. Now, most children do this at some time or other, but unconsciously Janet learned that this technique could have wider application, and soon learned to produce it as a defence against her overdemanding parents.

It was so convenient to adopt the sick role instead of having to meet her horrible Auntie Jean; and she noticed also that the only time she really got attention from her parents was when there appeared to be something wrong with her: when she was well they didn't seem to notice her as much. Gradually she learned, unconsciously, to associate 'being ill' with 'getting more attention', and 'being ill' with a means of escape from problems that she didn't want to face. This deviousness was entirely unconscious: she herself didn't even know that she was doing it.

Seen from a distance it was quite a natural development. Janet had a personality like a gerbil—small, furry and innocuous. Her parents had personalities like cats. Cats and gerbils don't get on very well together, or at least, the gerbil doesn't. So Janet quietly developed an *alter ego* which was more like a lion. Lions and cats don't get on together very well, either...

And so Janet played games with all and sundry, being meek, mild and gerbil-like on the occasions when it suited her, leading on her opponent—they were all opponents—until they were in too deeply to escape, and then the lion pounced.

'Good morning, doctor,' says the gerbil. 'I've got a pain in my side...' which of course the doctor can't easily fathom out because it's a mental pain, not a physical one. Eventually, three months later, the doctor gives up entirely. 'Gotcha,' says the lion, chewing avariciously.

And so Janet played games with Derek.

'Good morning,' said the gerbil. 'I'm no better.' The more Derek saw her the more desperate he got. *Nothing* seemed to help her—which of course, it wouldn't. Derek began to feel drained, exhausted, emasculated—which of course, he was, mentally speaking.

He would look down the street before venturing out, to make sure she wasn't there to buttonhole him. He *dreaded* her coming through the door, dreaded her Scottish accent in the waiting room, dreaded the failure that always seemed to await him whenever they met. He was also beginning to be uncomfortably aware of something else in him—something that he'd never before experienced; something which frightened the life out of him. *He was really angry with her.* Increasingly he wanted to slap her silly Scots face really hard, and this confusing feeling of anger and fear troubled him greatly. He'd never felt like this before. He shouldn't feel *angry* with a patient! Patients were there to be helped, not hated; so when he felt angry he felt guilty, which made him want to try harder to help her, but then he failed, so he felt angry with that. And then he had to put up with her stupid, silly, smiling face saying sweetly to him, 'It's no better, doctor,' and he wanted to *HIT HER*!

Within two weeks Janet had him wound round her little finger, rendering him helpless and impotent. And didn't Derek know it! Every time he tried to help her she would find a reason why it wouldn't work; or else she'd want to go back to the medicine he'd used the time but one before, a medicine that she was now adamant had worked, even though it said on Derek's notes at the time that she was no better.

'Oh yes, doctor,' she said, 'I really did feel a little better on those other tablets you gave me. You know, the little blue ones... I would like to try them again—if you don't mind that is. After all, you are the one in charge...'

Yet again, Derek resisted the temptation to slap her and, fuming and impotent, gave her what she wanted.

Had he but known it, the instillation of rage into him was all part and parcel of the whole hysterical process. In fact, if a patient makes an otherwise patient carer angry it's a good indication that there may be a hysterical process going on.

What had happened was that Janet had transferred her own anger on to Derek. In reality the sweet, soft-talking Janet MacKenzie was blazing mad, angry primarily with her parents for what they had done to her and how they had treated her when she was young.

Simply by manipulating the situation, she transferred her anger on to other people as the only way she could deal with it, and then watched as they got angry. But, being the hysteric she was, she gave no opportunity for them to hand this anger back to her. Whenever anybody made a sensible suggestion she would counter it. *'Yes, but...* was a phrase that came to her lips all too readily as a way of annihilating or rendering impotent any sensible suggestion that anyone else might make.

'Why don't you try eating your food a little more slowly?' said Derek.

'Yes, but if I do that I get...'

'Well, what about using the blue pills again?'

'Yes, but when I did that last time I found that...' It was always said sweetly, with a little simpering smile that brooked no argument, rendered Derek impotent again, and made him want to *HIT HER!* She was the sort of person who, given a seat in the royal box, would complain pleasantly that she was still unable to see stage left. Nothing pleased her. Nothing worked. And meanwhile the anger, that deep burning anger that she couldn't contain and couldn't control, was pushed out of her brain and into her abdomen—and some of it spilled over onto Derek.

The cure for Janet was for her to face up to her psychological problems, but it would have needed a far more experienced man than Derek even to begin to approach this particular subject. It was bad enough failing to treat her abdomen—led up the garden path by a gerbil, and devoured by a lion. Had Derek tried to attack her psyche, he would have met not one lion but a whole pride of them, all on guard and very, very hungry.

And so Janet and Derek floundered away, day after day, week after week, both caught up in Janet's defence mechanism. Anything Derek suggested was immediately countered by the sweet smiling Mrs MacKenzie who still addressed him as doctor, though he knew that she didn't really mean it. And Janet knew that she didn't really mean it either, but said it anyway because it kept him in his place. All while Derek felt as though he were quietly being sucked dry, like a spider that has paralysed its prey, injected its digestive juices into it and is sucking out the nutrients while the victim, immobilised, can only sit and wait for the whole macabre experience to end.

And so they did a psychological dance of death around one another. But it wasn't as if it stopped at Mrs MacKenzie. The experience seemed to enervate Derek totally; he lost his confidence completely and because he couldn't understand what was going on, and because he kept thinking that there must be something physical to account for this woman's gnawing, unrelenting pain, something which he'd missed, he felt a fraud himself, incompetent, a quack, so much so that when patients with real physical problems came to him he felt uneasy, less capable and less competent—and the other patients spotted it. No longer did consulting Derek give them the same sort of boost that it had in the past. He didn't seem to have the same sort of bedside manner any more, that gentle, laid-back, caring effectiveness that had so attracted Chris and the others to him in the first place. In two short weeks Mrs MacKenzie had done as good a job of emasculation on Derek as if she had attacked him with a knife.

And that was probably the point at which it all started to go wrong for him.

- 7 -

So the idea is,' said Paul to the council, 'that we gather together whatever existing money we can find and use that.'

'There must be thousands of pounds lying around,' said Alan.

'No,' said Paul, 'there isn't.'

'I don't believe you,' replied Alan.

'It's true. I've looked.'

'What about the tills in the shops, the purses in the houses; the banks, the building societies?'

Paul looked at him and shook his head. 'No, it's all gone.'

'Where?'

'Where do you think? What would you do if you were running away? You don't just leave the place empty. At the very least you'd lock up the till.'

'Or take the money with you,' interjected Chris.

'And if you're the manager of a bank you don't just go out of the door and leave everything open, even if you do want to leave in a hurry. The built-in reflexes of years will make you slam the safe door and give the knobs and dials a little twiddle before you go. I tell you, there's not much cash around. Look, I've been into all the shops I can find within a radius of about ten miles and I've found just over three thousand pounds altogether.'

'That's a lot,' said Peter.

'Not between five hundred people, it isn't.'

'No, I suppose it isn't,' said Alan with a sigh. 'Six pounds each. No, it isn't much is it? How are we going to work with that? Six pounds won't buy you anything.'

Paul grinned. 'You've got the wrong mind-set on, Alan,' he said, grinning superiorly.

'Oh, come off it Paul,' said Alan, finally losing his temper with the grinning clever-mick sitting opposite him. 'If you're so smart tell us how we work it.'

'I was just about to actually,' replied Paul. For a second all the muscles round Alan's eyes and mouth went taut and Chris began to fear that he would finally respond to Paul's verbal goading and hit out physically. But he didn't, and the moment passed. 'The trick is not to think of money like we used to. Six pounds—what would that buy you in the past? Yes, you're quite right—not a lot. But if instead we were in the reign of George III, how much would six pounds buy? It would be a good wage for a year.'

'But that was before we got inflation,' said Susan, angry with Paul for getting her husband so cross.

'That's the point. Stop thinking of the small amount each pound was worth just before the plague: think of it in terms of what it would buy a couple of hundred years ago before the intervening two hundred years of inflation. All we need to recognise is—that's how we exchange goods. Maybe we say that a fair day's work now is worth 5p—and so long as everybody knows that this is the way we look at it then everybody will use it at the same rate. It's only a medium of exchange, for goodness' sake.'

'I see your point,' said Derek, 'but won't it be a bit difficult to get accustomed to it at first?'

'It may. But we'll all get used to it, eventually. Money's not a thing by itself. It's just a token, a way of saying "I value your work this much and now you can use this token of your work to buy something on which somebody's worked the same amount".'

'I can see a practical problem here,' said Mary. 'What if other people come in from outside with their own money? Aren't they going to have their own money and want different things for it.'

'I've thought of that,' said Paul.

'You've always thought of everything,' said Alan bitterly between his still-clenched teeth.

'We'll arrange for one of us to sign all the existing bank notes so that we know they're "our" legal tender.'

'Oh, that's nice,' said Mary. 'I like that. It's just like they did in the old days. "I promise to pay the bearer on demand the sum of One Pound—signed, Chief Cashier." '

'That's right,' said Paul. 'Why don't we get Chris to sign all the bank notes, and we'll agree only to use as legal tender those bank notes that have been signed: then if anybody comes in from outside they can't use their own. Fair?'

Alan opened his mouth and then shut it again, goldfish-like. 'I suppose so.'

'Any objections?' Paul looked round the table. Half of them seemed bemused by what was going on and the other half, seeing what had happened to Alan, didn't want to rock the boat.

'Are we agreed, then?' said Chris, looking round, slightly worried by the lack of comment. 'OK, I'll sign the notes. In a week's time we'll share them out equally to start everyone off on the same footing, then we'll start using them.'

'At least it'll sort Kevin out,' said the Major under his breath.

'And it'll deal with the problem of how to pay Henry,' said Chris.

'Why's that?' asked the Major.

'If we're *sharing* everything, including all our food, then how can we give one person any extra? There's no point in giving double the amount of food when each person can only eat one share. Having more food than you can eat, when everyone else has enough anyway, doesn't make you feel any richer or even make you any richer. When you share everything, everybody is equally wealthy. It's only when you have the means to accumulate other things that you get any idea of what it means to be rich or poor.'

'I told you it wasn't a good idea,' said Mary. Chris pretended not to hear.

'So what sort of exchange rate were you thinking of?' asked Derek of Paul. 'How much is a week's work worth?'

'How about a pound a day?' said Paul.

'A pound,' said Alan caustically. 'That means each of us has only got the equivalent of slightly more than a week's wages.'

'That's all right,' said Paul.

'How is it all right?'

'We'll just keep using the money, and it'll go round in circles. Say, Peter, you get paid a pound for a day's work transporting grain—so you go and buy food from Neil. With your pound Neil buys some engineering goods from someone else; he uses that pound to pay you, Peter, for transporting something else. It all goes round in a circle. It's not how much money you've got in the system that matters, it's how quickly it goes round.'

'I don't believe you,' said Alan.

'It'll work, you'll see.'

'So what are we going to pay Henry for Gates House?' asked Paul. There was a chorus of mutterings arising around the table. Somehow Gates House rankled, and not just with the Major either. 'Five pounds a year,' suggested Susan.

'Don't be silly. For Gates House?' said Mary.

'But we're talking about the new rates, not the old rates.'

'Five pounds isn't much. It's only a week's wages.'

'What would Gates House be worth in the old days to rent—as a proportion of the salary of the person who lived in it?'

'Difficult to say,' said Alan, 'because that depends how much the person living in it earned. Ten, fifteen thousand a year, a third of their salary maybe.'

'Twenty weeks' wages then. OK, Henry gets a hundred pounds a year while we continue to use Gates House. Backdated, of course.'

'That suddenly seems a lot of money,' said Mary, 'that is, if you're only earning five pounds a week.'

'You're getting the idea,' said Paul, genuinely for once.

'Idea of what?' said Mary.

'Exchange rates. It doesn't matter what you call the money, it's how much you can exchange for it that matters. You can... *could* do the same with Mars bars.'

'You what?' said Alan.

'Yep,' said Paul insouciantly. 'Measure the cost of something in terms of the number of Mars bars that have the same face value at the current price of the time. The cost of Mars bars has gone up almost exactly in line with inflation. So what you want to do is find out how many Mars bars you need to buy for a particular item and you've got its absolute value. Except, the large numbers of Mars bars are a bit unwieldy when trying to price a house. Much easier to do it in terms of weeks of work.'

'Yes,' said Alan, totally out of his depth.

And so it was agreed. Henry would receive one hundred pounds from the community for the past year of use of Gates House, one hundred for Dynevor House, and a further hundred for every year that Gates House continued to be occupied. The money would be raised by taxing everybody in the community a little bit. It had to be said, however, that not everybody in the community was happy about this arrangement, especially as just one person—the Major— got Gates House, and one other person—Henry—got the money.

Money, reflected Susan as the council members dispersed, appeared to be a very two-edged sword.

*   *   *

'We've agreed about the rent for your house,' said Chris, having been invited into the morning room at Dynevor House by the dapper Henry. She was even sipping his coffee—real coffee, too. How *did* he do it, she wondered. He always seemed to be able to come up trumps, to have contacts, to be able to acquire things that no one else could.

'And...?' Henry asked, quizzically.

Chris explained the arrangements. She thought she'd have difficulty explaining about the new value of the Ampthill Pound, but Henry took it all in immediately.

'Sounds about right to me. I'll accept that. More coffee?'

'Er... yes, please.' What was it about Henry that always made others feel inferior and at his beck and call? Yet he was always very correct, very likeable, very charming: very public school, she thought. Very.

'It's good to know that it's all been settled amicably, isn't it?' he continued. Chris chose to say nothing. She knew the undercurrents from the council meeting, but there was no point in resurrecting them now.

'How are things going generally?'

'With the community? About the same as last year, I think.' She paused, aware that she was actually nearly too hot: the log fire was blazing in the grate. Why was it that Henry seemed to live in such ease and comfort? The unaccustomed heat in the depth of winter began to make her feel drowsy, despite the coffee.

'No problems then? Of course, I've been out of circulation for a year—it takes time to pick up the traces... all the in-fighting that one gets on small councils.'

How does he know? she thought, and then reflected that years of wheeling and dealing would have taught him that wherever two or three are gathered together, there's usually an argument.

'Anything I can do to help?' he continued breezily and with total self-confidence, as though he were, in reality, sitting by the telephone waiting for the call from the Queen to become Prime Minister.

'I don't think so, thank you: not at the moment, that is.'

'Well, I'm here if I can be of any service. Just ask.'

'That's very kind.'
'Don't mention it. More coffee?'

*   *   *

Chris emerged from the meeting feeling that somehow she'd been summoned to his presence rather than the other way round. It was a curious feeling. She didn't like it, but she couldn't put her finger on just why it happened. A few days earlier the Major had commanded her to come to him at Gates House—but she had felt under no obligation. On the other hand, Henry had only to incline his head slightly and everyone seemed to be running about in his service. Yet, under it all Henry seemed genuine enough—genuinely ready to help if needed, genuinely willing to put his abilities and knowledge at the disposal of the council. It was this ease that attracted others to him, his openness and warmth that was so appealing, so despite the initial antagonism engendered by his financial claims, Henry soon acquired something of a following.

He knew the area like the back of his hand. What's more he had that difficult-to-quantify attribute known as 'leadership'—the peculiar ability to motivate others. It's always said that the worst leaders lead from behind, driving their troops on to the slaughter; better leaders lead from the front, sharing in the risks, but getting the glory: but the very best leaders make the people think that they did it themselves. Henry wasn't quite in that category, but he didn't fall far short of it. With a magnetic personality, and an undoubted—and totally genuine—air of authority, he was a source of great comfort to those he led. He was paternal in the very best sense—paternal rather than patronising, genuinely concerned for the good of the community. But also, reflected Chris, also concerned for his own standing within the community—which is perhaps why he never quite made the very highest grade of leader, because he wanted others to recognise and respect his attributes. This apart, as a leader, Henry was among the best.

All of which made the Major livid. He too had once been in command of men, but somehow had never acquired the effortless sense of authority that Henry possessed. Perhaps it was all due to height.

Henry was tall: the Major was small, and had tried to adopt a bigger personality for himself to make up for his lack of physical stature. Physically people had to look up to Henry, and perhaps metaphorically that was why they looked up to him for leadership, too. People had to look down on the Major—perhaps they looked down on him metaphorically as well.

In fact, it wasn't like that at all: the Major simply hadn't the right temperament: a small organiser, yes—a great leader, no. The fact that he had only achieved the rank of Major after an extremely long career in the army was testament that his leadership abilities weren't such as to allow him to be promoted further. The Peter principle says that the cream rises until it sours, so that in time everyone gets promoted to a job one step above his or her own level of competence. So it was with the Major who, his senior officers eventually realised, should really have remained a Captain, a job at which he was actually very good. However, Major he was, and Major he stayed, but always with that little chip on his shoulder that said, 'I should have been a Brigadier,' and a continuing need to establish his authority on those around him, even though, once out of the army, that official authority had vanished. Hence his need to refer to himself by his rank, even as a civilian, and why he was so put out by the arrival of Henry.

Another way of looking at the Major was by the type of mind he possessed. People seem to divide themselves into three categories according to their willingness to be open-minded. First-class minds think for themselves, untrammelled by what anyone else might think, say or believe. These are the people who come up with novel ways of doing things, the ones who make great contributions to science, art and literature, the ones who can see a need, an opportunity, or a discovery, and home in on it.

Second-class minds are not as gifted or free-thinking (and it is this that marks out a first-class mind, not necessarily intelligence). The hallmark of the second-class mind is that he can't stand anyone else telling him that he is wrong or behind in his thinking; so he detests the first-class mind, and out of jealousy or revenge seeks to undermine the first-class minds whenever he can. There are more second-class minds than first-class minds, so the really brilliant minds are usually outnumbered.

And the third-class minds? They don't think at all. They just go with the majority, which in this case happens to be the view of the second-class minds. Hence government by majority decree is nearly always dull, staid and dependably boring because the first-class minds are outvoted: whereas government by the first-class minds—who tend to do it as a sort of *bravura* performance—is much more interesting: though they can sometimes get extremely egotistical about it, as witness the behaviour of many an Oxbridge don.

The best way to decide what kind of a mind an individual has is to look, not at his abilities, but how *he* looks at the abilities of others. Those with first-class minds try to surround themselves with other first-class minds (or better, if that could ever be arranged) whereas second-class minds prefer to surround themselves with third-class minds (or worse).

The Major was definitely one of life's second-class minds. It didn't make him any the less of a person though! At heart he was a genuinely nice Christian man, with decent standards, a decent life behind him, a decent wife, and—before the plague—a decent family with decent schooling and decent jobs which they held down conscientiously. Nevertheless, although an honest, upright, pillar-of-the-church, establishment personality, he hadn't got the verve, dynamism, leadership, foresight or lateral thinking that people like Henry and Paul possessed, and the knowledge of this made him spitting mad—hence his overwhelmingly bitter reaction to Paul once Paul had proved to be fallible. And hence his reaction to Henry. The Major felt usurped, denuded and deprived of his 'rightful'—as he saw it—position in society.

Pillar of the church and establishment that he was, nevertheless he didn't always exhibit as many of the Christian virtues as he might; and because he always roundly condemned the type of vices that those listening *didn't* possess—such as sexual problems, or grand larceny—his opinions often acquired a spurious patina of virtue as his audience usually agreed with him. After all, it's so much easier to condemn others for sins *we* are not involved in.

It's surprising how the church can sometimes seem to grade sins on a league table, with sexual misdemeanours, murder and theft way out at the top, hypocrisy a little further down, and envy and jealousy at the bottom. In reality their roles should perhaps be reversed: sexual misdemeanours are, after all, a good deal more understandable (being more biological) than more cerebral misdeeds such as envy or greed.

Over at the Old Rectory, Martin had just got to the point where he was reading through the Gospels—with his new non-rose-coloured spectacles on—and was suddenly and forcefully struck by the way in which Jesus was relatively light on those who were caught *in flagrante*, those who knew they were wrong, but extremely hard on those who were hypocrites, those who should have known better, but didn't put it into practice. And yet the Pharisees and hypocrites were actually the church establishment of the day! Perhaps nothing had changed in two thousand years after all, he reflected ruefully. Those who don't learn their history really *are* condemned to repeat it, and churchmen who don't learn their Bible are condemned to make the same mistakes as their forebears.

He was to reflect upon this vividly in the months to come.

All of which goes to explain how and why the Major could at one and the same time be a pillar of the church, and so unutterably envious. Sociologists would doubtless have put it all down to the fact that the Major was vertically challenged, but it just wasn't as simple as that.

*   *   *

That evening Martin was practising in the Old Rectory. The piano was an antique Bechstein, fitted with brackets on the front that had originally been used for the very purpose for which Martin was now using them—holding candles. He was concentrating hard and almost didn't notice the door open behind him, except that the movement of the air made the candles flicker. He stopped in mid-bar.

'That was nice,' said Anne from the doorway. 'What was it?'

'Beethoven. The *Pathétique Sonata*, middle movement.'

'It's very beautiful. Can I stay and listen?'

'If you want,' replied Martin, 'but I'm just practising: it's not up to standard yet.'

She drew up a chair and sat down.

'Most of it's not too difficult,' said Martin, almost as though Anne hadn't spoken. 'Except for this bar here in the middle. There's an awkward turn in it and I can't quite get my fingers round it.' He played it a few times, slowly, and with a slight hesitation at the difficult part. 'The rest of it's quite easy. It's just this one bar...' He looked up. 'Isn't Derek in?'

'No,' said Anne slightly tight-lipped. 'He's out seeing someone *again*. Mrs Summerfield in Woburn Street. She's taken a turn for the worse. Derek thinks she's dying, poor soul.'

'It happens to us all, unfortunately,' said Martin, sympathetically. He paused. 'And Sarah and David?'

'Sarah's in bed. David's down in the town somewhere with a couple of his friends. Do play for me.'

Martin started off the slow, contemplative theme, got to the bar with the turn and to his surprise managed it—almost—when out of the corner of his eye he noticed a tear rolling down Anne's left cheek. He stopped and turned to face her.

'Trouble?' She gave a little shake of the head and a slight gasp as she tried to pull herself together.

'It's just a year...' she began.

'Since what?'

'Since Alison first became ill. November 18th. She'd been unwell for a few days before, and that day she went unconscious... and Derek and Paul went to the Health Centre to try to find out what to do.' She gave out a loud sigh. 'I know they pulled her round that time, but it was really the beginning of the end...' Her voice tailed off and another tear rolled down her cheek.

Martin put his hand on her arm. 'I remember. I'm sorry.'

She tossed her head, trying to remove the tears and get back in control. 'It's very difficult losing your daughter. Mothers and daughters do seem to have a special sort of bond, you know.'

'I know.'

She gave out another big sigh. 'When things like that happen it all seems so... pointless... We sow, we reap, we work, we sleep and then we die. What's the point?' She stood up, went across to the window and pulled the curtains open. Outside it was pitch black. The occasional star became visible, then disappeared again as the dark clouds scurried past. She clasped her hands round her as if hugging herself to keep warm, then pulled the curtains to and turned to face Martin. 'If there's a God out there, then why does he allow it? Why did he allow Alison to die? Why does he allow all this...?' She sat down into the chair with a bump, eyes staring vacantly forward.

'You know you're saying almost exactly what I thought a year ago.'

'Am I?'

'More or less. Mind you, I hadn't lost one of my children..... But I do understand. The bleakness... the sense that nothing matters... the sense of emptiness and lostness, of being purposeless and hopeless...'

'...and alone.'

'And alone. Mind you, at least you've got Derek and David. I didn't have anyone at all.'

'I don't really have anyone,' replied Anne, somewhat tartly. 'Not any more. I never see Derek. He's always out looking after somebody else. When he *is* there I don't really seem to be able to communicate with him any more. He's either too tired or too wrapped up in the problems of his job. And as for David... well, he's always off with his friends: Darren Rogers, Trevor and that brat Kevin. There's Sarah, I suppose, but Sarah's mine by accident rather than design. So perhaps I'm just as lonely as you were.'

'I'm sorry to hear that. Is there anything I can do?'

'Not much. About the only thing that would help would be if somebody else was to be the town's doctor, then I could have Derek, my *engineer* husband, back.' She suddenly raised her voice in anger. 'Oh, I do wish he'd spend as much mental energy on me as he does on his patients.' She stood up again, kicking the chair back, stamped over to the window and looked out, arms down by her sides, hands clenching and unclenching. 'It just seems that there's... Oh, I don't know.'

Martin stared up at her from the piano stool, the yellow candle-light glinting off the side of his face, the lock of hair falling over his forehead as usual. 'You sound very bleak...' Anne turned to face him. 'Lonely, neglected and angry...'

'And lost...'

'Been there, done it, got the T-shirt...'

'All right,' said Anne, turning round to face him, 'if you're so sure, you get me out of it.'

'I can't.'

'Well, shut up then.' She turned to face the blackness outside.

'I didn't say the problem couldn't be solved.'

'What *did* you say then?'

'I said *I* couldn't solve it. Only *you* can do that.'

'What do you mean?'

'Only you can solve it for yourself. It's only when we understand what's happening at first hand that it makes any difference to us.'

Anne turned round to him. 'You're sounding just like a priest.'

'Well, I *am* a p— I'm sorry... Am I? I didn't mean to be.'

'You're being patronising.'

'I'm not trying to be. I'm just trying to put across something that's rather difficult to convey, that's all.'

'Like what?' she spat out.

'Like that very difficult lesson that we really only learn things properly when we experience them ourselves, and we really only learn how to get out of situations when we've experienced them at first hand.' He got up from the stool and went across to her, picked up her hand, and looked directly at her. 'Anne, I'm sorry if I've upset you by what I've said, and I'm sorry if it comes out as being patronising. There is a way out, but I can't find it for you. You've got to find it for yourself. I can point you in the right direction, but you've got to be the one to do the exploring. I can show the way, but you won't see anything or find anything unless you work it out for yourself.

'I said I'd got the T-shirt, didn't I...? It took me a year. At the end of it I actually found only what I'd been taught in theological college, but I found it out in a way that I'd never understood before and in a way that actually meant something to me, for once.'

'What *did* you find?'

'A tiny simple little truth, if you must know. One that was standing staring at me all the time and I missed it. That people were selfish and that it was built into them in such a deep way that they couldn't get away from it. I mean, it's only written in the Bible from stem to stern and it's only taught in theological college from day one. I just managed to miss it. I had my own interpretations. I didn't like the implications, so I ignored it and got myself into a mess and it took me a whole year plus a lot of whisky to get out.'

The intensity of the memory suddenly hit him: the emptiness, the pile of bottles outside the front door, the despair. His eyes took on that faraway look again and he shuddered. It was Anne's turn to grip his hand more tightly.

'But it's over, Martin.'

'Is it?' he said pulling his free hand through his hair and pushing the curl back above his forehead. 'Is it? Sometimes I'm not sure. Sometimes it comes back to haunt me. The memories....of how I was.' He shuddered again. 'They're still too real. Too fresh.'

He let go of her hand and sat down at the piano again, surprised both by his sudden vulnerability and his inability to communicate what he really wanted to say to her. He stared at the music in front of him, then turned back to face her. 'What are you *really* looking for... deep down, I mean?'

Anne stared out, sightless, into the night, then turned to face him.

'I suppose,' she began slowly, 'the bottom line is that I'm lonely. And no,' she continued quickly, 'I don't mean lonely in a human way—not lonely for Derek, or for any other form of company for that matter. No, I mean a sort of cosmic loneliness. The feeling that there's nothing out there, or at least nothing that cares.'

'That's a very special kind of loneliness. A deep, hopeless loneliness. A feeling that whatever you do is tinged with gloom and despair and pointlessness and hopelessness. So... did you ever believe in God?'

'Oh yes. Standard C. of E., Sunday school, confirmation classes: the usual thing—conveyor-belt Christianity. It didn't mean much at the time, and it means less now.'

She returned to staring out into the night. From deep within himself Martin wanted—*longed*—to tell Anne about the God he now believed in: a God who was warm and caring and considerate and kind—but something seemed to stop him. It would come out wrong; he would sound stupid, immature, childish.

Unnerved by the sudden silence he turned back to the piano and started playing. The lush, warm tones filled the air once more. Half-way through he got to the bar with the turn in and made a passable shot at it. He looked up briefly at Anne and grinned—and found to his surprise that she was staring at him, and had been doing so all the time he had been playing. Coming to the end of the piece, he finished off with the three quiet chords in the bass register, then let the sound hang in the air as it faded away, and let the silence speak. It was a warm silence; a full silence, redolent with the calm, persuasive tones of the music. Anne turned to him.

'You don't mince words, do you?' she said. Martin opened his mouth with the surprise of a man who's just been bowled a googly and has heard the crash of the stumps behind him.

'I haven't said a word.'

'You didn't need to,' said Anne. 'The music did it just as well. It's so beautiful. Tell me, is He really there. Does He really care?' Martin looked round at her, his pale green eyes looking directly at hers. He said nothing.

'I mean, aren't you going to *evangelise* me, or something?'

'Do you mean, am I going to convince you that God is actually there and that your idea of God really is OK?'

'Something like that.'

Martin shrugged.

Anne was taken aback. 'I thought you'd be bursting to tell me all about it.'

'I'd like you to know about it if that's what you mean. I'd like you to understand it, to feel it.'

Inside, Anne was at screaming pitch. Why wouldn't he comfort her? Tell her that God was there, that Alison hadn't gone into black oblivion. '*Why won't you tell me?*'

'It depends whether you're ready to listen or not.'

'I'm listening, I'm listening.'

'No, *really* listening. Listening so intently that you'd be prepared to change your mind and throw away your preconceptions.'

'Like you did?'

'Like I did. I had to. I'd got to that stage already. The sheer emptiness when nothing fits together. The point where you can safely tear down the wreckage and the rubble of what you once believed without any fear or loss of face because there's nothing left to lose. And then you can start building it up again in a different order, like a Lego house that you've broken up because you've built it wrongly, and now you've got all the pieces, and you've got to fit them together in a different order and suddenly you can see how it all *does* fit. Only it'll never fit together correctly unless you start at the right place on the right foundations.'

'Please tell me. Please tell me.'

She was looking at him intently, almost begging him to get on with it. He shrugged slightly, turned back to the piano and began to play again.

- 8 -

On the Sunday two weeks later, Derek decided he just must have some time out with his family. It was a perfect day, oddly warm for December, and they'd decided to go on a general exploration on their bicycles. That'll be good for Sarah, thought Anne, because we can show her the motorway: she'll like that. David, who had developed a practical hobby—a passion for rabbiting—packed his Black Widow catapult into his back pocket against the possibility that as dusk approached he might manage to produce the source of their next evening meal, literally by a pot shot.

Although there wasn't much happening medically speaking, nevertheless Derek left instructions as to where he could be found in case of emergency and the four of them set out down the Flitwick road and on towards Westoning and Toddington. For some reason Derek had never really explored that area before. Of course Paul had scoured the area for provisions, but they'd never explored it in a recreational fashion, to enjoy the scenery.

They weren't going particularly quickly—after all they had to go at the pace of the slowest, which was Sarah, but she was enjoying herself pedalling along on her next-size-up bicycle that David had just acquired for her. It was getting towards midday as they passed through Westoning out on the flat, fast road which links to the M1, and stopped at the motorway junction.

The connection with the M1 is very ordinary; the road between Westoning and Toddington continues straight on over the motorway. There isn't even a roundabout to enable traffic to get on and off smoothly, merely an exit and entrance road on either side of the motorway. But Sarah was intrigued by it, forgetting—as children do—that just a few moments earlier she had been complaining of being tired. Suddenly she developed a second wind and started rushing about the junction, eyes wide, staring about her in amazement.

After a few minutes more, trying to make sense of it all, she turned round. 'Auntie Anne, what was this for?'

'It's where two roads join. One's a very big one. It goes underneath us. Look, I'll show you,' and she led Sarah to the parapet of the bridge and held her up so that she could see the three-lane dual carriageway running beneath her. The carriageway from the south was completely blocked, with traffic nose to tail as far as the eye could see: no car could get off the motorway at the junction because there had been a pile-up on the exit road, so although the Westoning/Toddington road was free of traffic, no one could have got on to it from the north-bound carriageway. For a moment Sarah surveyed the lines of vehicles, stationary in the bright winter sunlight. She turned and looked again at the road they were on, and then up at the traffic lights standing silent and motionless, dead in the air.

'What were these for, Auntie Anne?'

'These had lights in them. There was a red light at the top and a green light at the bottom. When the red light showed you had to stop your car. When the green light showed you could start off again. The lights were linked so that they would always show red on one road and green on the other and then it would change round.'

'Why?'

'If the road was busy and we didn't have traffic lights, all the cars used to get muddled and jumbled and jammed, and we found that if they went in turns they could get to where they wanted to go to much more quickly.'

'How does stopping a car make you get there faster?'

Anne smiled.

'It stopped one group of cars getting in the way of the other group of cars.'

Sarah looked round, uncomprehending. Anne was puzzled. Why was Sarah so confused by a simple crossroads and two pairs of traffic lights?

And then the penny dropped. *She couldn't remember traffic!* For Sarah, who in the past year had never seen more than three cars moving at the same time, the thought of a traffic jam must be quite impossible and with that curious effect of memory which all children exhibit, she couldn't really remember things that had happened more than a year or so beforehand. *Sarah couldn't remember traffic!* And suddenly Anne saw that simple junction through Sarah's eyes, not just a junction but a flattened layer of asphalt laid on the ground—never mind twenty yards *long*, twenty yards *wide*—with four sets of sticks with lights on top to regulate what appeared to be absolutely nothing. Anne suddenly had a surrealist image of the traffic lights still active all these months later, winking away, carefully regulating the movement of... nothing at all.

Looking out southwards again at the two carriageways of the M1, Anne suddenly realised how vast they were. She walked down the slip road, which a car would have traversed in a matter of seconds, and realised that it was nearly an eighth of a mile long. Then she stood where so few people had ever stood before—in the middle of the southbound carriageway. It took her several seconds to walk out into the middle of the carriageway and several more seconds to walk onward to the central reservation, lost in thought. With a start she realised that she was only a few yards away from the crashed cars on the other side, and inside those cars were... She shuddered and backed away, then thought again. Surely the bodies wouldn't still be infectious? She peered through the windows. In most cases the cars were empty, their inhabitants having left and continued on foot when they realised that their way was irrevocably blocked. But in others there were the shrivelled remnants of travellers, shrunken down inside the collapsed remains of their clothes. She shuddered and looked away again.

Behind her the grey concrete bridge carrying the Toddington-Westoning road arched overhead, casting a deep shadow over the whole motorway and suddenly the enormity, the total enormity of it, hit her. Much as the size of an ocean liner is only apparent in all its vastness when the observer is standing on the quayside looking up, so Anne saw the motorway through Sarah's eyes—a vast swathe of flattened earth covered with tarmac and concrete, bridges with huge concrete spans; ribbons of corrugated steel crash barriers... *going on for mile after mile.* Even the markings on the roads were enormous. She'd never realised that the arrows painted on the road surfaces were nine feet long and three feet wide: that the signboards were twenty feet high, or that the 'portable' men-at-work signs were six feet high. In that instant she felt overwhelmed and diminished by it all, like a traveller staring at the Pyramids, wondering how it was ever done, and why.

Suddenly its colossal size threatened to overwhelm her, telling her that she wasn't important, that she was only a small microcosm in a huge universe, and in that instant it dawned on her that this was how civil engineering projects had always been, how so often they dwarfed the people they served, demeaning them in the process. To be sure, they did the job effectively: roads and bridges carried hun-

dreds of thousands of people efficiently through large distances of
the country in a manner, and at a speed, that could never have been
envisaged even two hundred years earlier, let alone in the Stone
Age. But they still demeaned people in the process.

And in that instant she saw something else about civilisation that
not even the perceptive Martin had realised—that in building arte-
facts that were overwhelmingly bigger than man, man had been
subjugated by his own designs. *I've read that before somewhere*,
she thought to herself as she stared up once again at the huge bridge,
and walked yet again across the enormous width of the carriageway.
Who had said it? Suddenly she remembered. Albert Speer, Hitler's
architect, who had deliberately built Nazi architecture three times
too big so that it dwarfed the ordinary people, to make them feel
subservient to the state. His Chancellery had eighteen-foot-high
doors to overwhelm visitors, and slippery floors inside to make visiting diplomats feel literally wrong-footed before they ever came
into the presence of the Führer, putting them at an instant (and subconscious) psychological disadvantage.

Even Hitler hadn't started it. Louis XIV, the Sun King, had deliberately built his palace at Versailles large in order to overwhelm foreign dignitaries and ambassadors, impressing upon them his power,
wealth and influence. Buildings can so easily overwhelm the
humans that they should be serving...

Dejected by the experience, Anne walked back up the hill of the
slip road.

'What *have* you been doing?' asked Derek and then saw her face.
'What's the matter?'

'I just feel a bit... overawed... The size of it all. I've got so accustomed to the human scale of Ampthill that it's quite a shock to come
back to something as gargantuan as this.'

'This isn't gargantuan,' said Derek. 'This is a tiny junction.'

'It's gargantuan compared to us,' said Anne. 'Look at it. Look at
it through Sarah's eyes. It's huge.'

'I suppose it is,' said Derek in an abstract and rather uncomprehending sort of way. 'It's not very pretty, is it?'

'No,' said Anne, 'not pretty at all.'

'Come on you three,' shouted David from the far side of the bridge. 'I've been waiting for ages.' They picked up their bikes and pedalled off in the direction of Toddington, but the road began to rise steeply and soon they had to get off and push. Fifteen minutes later, out of breath, they arrived in the centre of Toddington and found a good place to eat their packed lunch, sitting on a bench at the far corner of the large diamond of grass in the centre of the village, looking out over the church.

Toddington is a pleasant old village but with slightly less immediate appeal than Ampthill, as the architecture changes more quickly from the old to the modern. But the centre is gracious and friendly in the manner of so many old English villages, and it has a large village green bordered by an interesting variety of houses, shops and old taverns. Sitting on the bench eating his sandwiches, Derek automatically began to count the chimneys: it was a habit ingrained in him, because where there was a chimney there was a flue, and where there was a flue there was a hearth, and a house with an open fire was one that could be lived in. There were a lot of chimneys. Toddington would be an obvious place for the Ampthill community to expand into, should their numbers outgrow their available useful houses.

David gobbled down his food, and then spent an interesting twenty minutes rushing up and down all the various side roads on his bike. Then without warning he disappeared for a considerable time, to the point where Anne and Derek were starting to get concerned that he might have either got himself lost or else had an accident. When their anxiety was just starting to rise to a fever pitch and they were looking at each other as if to say 'Where on earth do we start looking for him?' David came hurtling back, his face red as beetroot. He was shouting before he got within thirty yards of them.

'Dad, you *must* come!'

'Why, what, what's happened?' said Derek, dropping immediately into his 'don't worry, I'm a doctor' mode and then realising rather foolishly that this was unlikely to be the current problem, seeing as there probably wasn't another soul for miles.

'You've just *got* to see this. Come *on*.'

'What is it?' said Derek.

'I'm not going to tell you. You've got to come and see it for yourself. Come on, Sarah.'

'I *am* coming,' said Sarah huffily, pedalling away as fast as her little legs would take her, 'it's just that my legs aren't quite as long as yours.'

David, leading, rounded a corner and then stopped at the entrance to an ordinary-looking house.

'Come on,' shouted David, waving his arms. 'It's in here.'

'What *has* he found?' murmured Derek as they went into an oversized garage, past a sign saying 'Toddington Power Company'.

'There you are, Dad,' said David, waving his hand proudly. 'It's what you always wanted. Your own electricity generator.'

'What the...' said Derek looking at the packing cases and pylons and vanes and batteries and terminals that seemed strewn around the building.

'Dad! Plug yourself in! Switch yourself on!'

David rushed over to an office area in the corner. Derek followed behind him. On the walls were picture after picture of generators of the sort that could be seen on farms, small and not-so-small windmills which worked a small turbine or a pump. 'Now do you see?' said David, his round cheery face grinning at his father in the way that sons do when they know they've managed to score off their parents.

Derek looked round, stunned. Wordlessly he moved back from the office area to the front part of the garage, seeing the materials there in an entirely different light, and making sense of it all, casting a professional eye over the rotor arms, transformers and pylons in various stages of production. Suddenly, without saying a word he rushed out of the door into the sunlight, and sat down on a large stone in the garden. Sarah and Anne walked out of the factory more slowly, but Anne was concerned to see that her husband looked quite ashen.

'Oh, what a fool I've been,' said Derek, sitting there like an oversized garden gnome, his eyes staring unseeing into space. 'What a fool I've been! Why, why didn't I think of this before? Oh, what an *idiot* I've been!' He started pummelling his right fist into the palm of his left hand and shaking his head. 'What a fool...'

'What *are* you on about?' said Anne, catching up with him.

'What's the matter Uncle Derek?' said Sarah, reaching out her hand. 'I don't like you sad. I want to make you better.' There was a shout as David shot out of the factory door.

'Hey, wait for me. What's the matter with you all, going off like that?' He caught sight of his father's face and stopped in mid-sentence. 'Dad, what's up?'

Derek looked at him. And then at Anne.

'Out of the mouths of babes and sucklings...'

'What do you mean?' asked Anne.

'Nothing,' said Derek. 'It's just that David here has made the biggest discovery of the year. On the scale of Archimedes and his bath.'

'I don't understand,' said Anne. 'What's so special about a garage?'

'It's not the garage that's special, it's what it's making,' said Derek. 'Tell her, David.' David pulled himself up to his full five foot six, pleased as punch with what he'd done.

'Windmills, mum. They're windmills, portable windmills.'

'So?'

'They make electricity, Mum.'

'And it's been staring me in the face all this time,' said Derek, 'and I've missed it, and I'm supposed to be an engineer. What an idiot...'

'You mean we'll be able to make electricity, run power tools and vacuum cleaners and lights and heaters?'

'No,' said Derek, 'no, Anne. Not like that. We won't be able to be able to do any of the heavy stuff but we'll be able to use these to provide us with a bit of electricity—enough to power things like a few electric lights, computers, CDs, amplifiers.'

'Vacuum cleaners?' said Anne hopefully.

'Nothing like that. They take too much power.'

'It can't be much use if it doesn't power vacuum cleaners,' she said, deadpan. Derek fell for it. He was too busy kicking himself to see the twinkle in Anne's eye.

'No, no, there'll be lots of things we can use it for. I mean, think of all the lights...' Anne gave him a playful shove, and Derek almost fell off his stone.

'Oh, stop being so serious, Derek. I was only joking.'

'Were you?'

'Yes.'

'Oh... Sorry... I'm not really in the mood for jokes at the moment, I'm just thinking of what we've all missed for the past year simply because I'm too asinine to think straight.'

'Oh come off it Dad, you weren't to know,' said David, somewhat chastened.

'We could have built one of these ourselves if only we'd thought about it,' replied Derek, shaking his head again.

'I'm still not really with it,' said Anne. 'Now tell me, in words of one syllable, and without pausing to kick yourself, what is it you've discovered, and why is it so important?'

'They're windmills,' said Derek. 'Not the big sort that people once ground corn with, but little ones with vanes about four to six feet in diameter at the top. They sit on tall poles or on an open lattice-work scaffolding, about twenty-five feet high so as to catch more wind. When the windmill turns it drives an electric generator which makes electricity...'

'... which we use directly to power light bulbs. Great,' said Anne.

'No,' said Derek, 'if we did that then the lights would go bright or dim with each gust of wind. No, we use the turbine to charge a battery, and then we use the battery as the source of energy. Judging by the size of the batteries they've got in the factory, and the information on the display board, we should be able to get quite a lot of current.'

'So we *can* use it for vacuum cleaners?' persisted Anne.

'No, no,' said Derek, 'windmills like these just aren't big enough. They produce the right number of volts but not enough current. It will power things that require mains voltages but only if they don't consume much power—things like light bulbs; but nothing big, no machines or motors.'

'So why are you so upset at not having discovered it before? If it can't power tools then what's the use?'

'Because the sort of things that we can use electricity for are enormous. It'll give us control of things. You wait—even if it won't make us much power, this is going to change our lives. It'll be like the industrial revolution all over again.'

* * *

Early the next day Paul, Alan and Trevor brought the lorry out to pick up three of the windmills, complete with controllers, inverters, metering panels and batteries. Paul had seen the possibilities immediately while Anne still wasn't so sure that his discovery meant anything other than a different sort of night-time illumination. Before noon that day they'd begun erecting the first windmill—a small one—in the triangle of land between Kevin's house and the Old Rectory, on top of the Greensand Ridge, in an open area of land. It was a windy day—the weather was back to its old tricks—and Paul, Alan and Derek had picked the site carefully to get the maximum breeze. Then they began to erect the open tower piece by piece, like an oversized jigsaw puzzle.

Two days later they'd finished. Above them the windmill rotated in the breeze, with the rest of the equipment beneath it in a large closed box, protected from the rain. It wasn't just a matter of making the windmill produce current directly: as Derek had said, that would mean power would only be available when the wind was blowing. So they needed batteries. However, alternating current—the sort that domestic circuits supplied in the past, and which the generator on the windmill produced—can't be stored, so the output of the wind turbine had first to be converted into direct current, which was then stored in a bank of lead-acid accumulators, which looked like large car batteries. When electricity was needed, direct current from these batteries was first changed back into alternating current, then, using an inverter, transformed up to the familiar 240-volt output with which they were all familiar.

Finally, they had constructed a trip to avoid the circuit being overloaded: if the demand at any one moment were to rise to too high a level the trip would activate, cutting off the supply rather than the allowing the equipment to be damaged by too great a load in a short space of time. Too great a demand for electricity over a period of time was a completely different problem: the batteries could only supply power for a limited period before needing recharging. If the weather were windy, then all well and good, but more than twenty-four hours of calm and they'd be back to mutton-fat candles again.

To the outside observer little of this was apparent—all they saw was a vane rotating in the breeze at the top of an open-work tower. At the base of the tower was a cupboard containing all the electrical equipment and batteries, from which a pair of wires led towards the Old Rectory, snaking along the field, their position carefully marked out by poles to ensure they weren't trampled on or cut.

The revolution was about to begin.

*   *   *

'Good morning doctor,' said Mrs MacKenzie as she walked in through the surgery door at the beginning of evening surgery.

Oh no, thought Derek, not again. He forced a jagged smile. 'And how are we today?'

'Not so good doctor, not so good. The pain—it's no better. In fact, do you know, I think it's worse. I've also noticed that when I get the pain I get a little sort of trembly feeling up high, beneath my rib cage.'

'Have you got it now?'

'Well, no, but it does come from time to time.'

'I'll have a look then.' Derek's fingers probed the upper right side of her abdomen and a dreadful thought occurred to him. What if it were gallstones, as Susan had had. Not again! The thought of all those call-outs in the middle of the night, the repeated injections of pethidine, the feeling that he could never get away from the patient and always had to be on hand for the next attack, until Nicholas the surgeon returned—whenever that might be. But his probing fingers found nothing. He tried to reassure her, but inside he knew that he didn't feel reassured himself. Maybe Mrs

MacKenzie had gallstones after all. Maybe antibiotics would help her if the gall bladder was becoming infected. He pulled down some of the precious remaining antibiotics from the shelf and gave her five days supply. In the absence of a temperature he thought maybe he *was* clutching at straws a little, but so far nothing he'd done had helped at all. He added an anti-spasmodic for good measure, and a painkiller. 'Try these. I think perhaps these will help. Maybe we've put our finger on the problem at long last.'

'Oh, thank you, doctor, I do hope so.'

The gerbil in her gazed at him adoringly, while in the background the lion snarled.

*   *   *

With the cable Alan had found at the industrial site at Elstow he soon finished connecting the output from the windmill to the nearest house, which just happened to be the Old Rectory. A few minutes' work with a Stanley knife, wires, and a few clips, and the electricity supply from the windmill was bolted firmly onto the incoming mains cable at the fuse box.

'So all we have to do now,' said Derek, 'is switch on.' It was a breezy afternoon outside and the windmill was running swiftly.

'Let's see what it'll do,' said Alan, reaching up to switch on one of the standard lamps in the room. He clicked the switch. There was a definite and distinct sensation of nothing happening.

'Maybe it's not plugged in at the wall,' said Derek, checking. But it was. 'Perhaps the bulb's gone. I'll try the main room light.' He switched it on. Still nothing happened. 'This is daft... The windmill is producing power, isn't it?'

'Yes,' said Alan. 'I checked that a couple of minutes ago. That end's definitely working all right.'

'Well, we'd better check it again. Maybe we've forgotten to connect up a cable somewhere, or we've got a dry joint or something.' Puzzled, they went back to the windmill to check.

'Aha,' said Alan, bending over the inverter at the bottom. 'The trip's gone. It's overloaded itself.' He switched off the inverter, swung the trip back into place, and then switched on again.

Immediately the trip activated, shutting down the power.

'We've got a short in the system,' said Derek. 'That's what's happened.'

'Can't be,' said Alan. 'It's a single wire all the way down to the Rectory. And I know I didn't create a short where I joined it in with the mains cable because I checked very carefully.'

And then they looked at each other and burst out laughing.

'You know what we've done, don't you?' said Alan. Derek nodded, then shook his head at his own stupidity. Maybe he had better stick to medicine, he thought.

'We're trying to supply the whole of Ampthill with power. I've forgotten to isolate the house from everyone else. All we need to do is pull the mains fuse and stop the current going backwards, into the town.'

By the time he'd re-vamped the wiring at the Old Rectory it was after four and the light was beginning to fade. Alan went back to the windmill, put the cut-out back into the correct position, then holding his breath, switched on the current, his eyes glued to the cut-out. This time it didn't move. He hurried down to the Old Rectory.

'How're we doing?' said Derek.

'Fine. The cut-out stayed in its place.'

'All right,' said Derek, 'here's hoping,' and flicked the light switch on the wall.

In the hall the light came on.

*   *   *

Alan and Derek stood transfixed by the tiny 60-watt bulb hanging in front of them, illuminating them with its dim yellow light. Two years earlier, they would have said it was underpowered. Now they almost winced with the unaccustomed brightness.

They looked at each other. 'We did it,' said Alan, grinning. 'Nice work, Derek.'

Derek said nothing but moved his gaze back to the light bulb. There was a long, long, pause. 'Ah well,' he said, 'civilisation, here we come. This is the first moment of the road back.'

*   *   *

Martin returned half an hour later, and on hearing the news soon connected up the CD system that the previous owners had left. By then it was completely dark. Reaching out his hand to the amplifier he switched on. There was a satisfying clunk from the speakers as they sprang to life. Looking around him he sorted through the CDs until he found what he wanted, his hands trembling, rushing in his urge to get the music on.

What would he put on first? There was such a choice. Suddenly from having no music at all he had hours of it available to him. It seemed appropriate to choose the first item carefully, and so with hands still shaking, he found a recording of Mahler's second symphony, put it in the CD player, pressed the play button, and then sat back in his favourite chair as the music filled the room, music that he knew like the back of his hand, yet which seemed so fresh for not having been heard for so very many months. And then he called Anne, who had only just come in, to come and share it with him.

- 9 -

*I*n the weeks following the Harvest Festival, Martin had thrown himself afresh into the religious life of the community. Perhaps 'thrown' is the wrong word because he hadn't gone at it with the unsubtle enthusiasm of a recent convert, but had come to it instead with the wisdom and maturity that his year 'in the wilderness' had engendered in him.

He'd had a hard time in his own personal wilderness. For a lay-man to lose his faith is bad enough, but when it happens to a cler-gyman the effects are inordinately painful, involving as they do the loss not just only of personal faith but of the reason for being in their chosen calling. Martin had had an emotionally traumatic time: and in many ways was not fully able to realise the good it had done him, benefits that wouldn't have been available to him by any other route: there were many of these, but he was still too near to the event to be able to view dispassionately what had happened.

He'd learned a lot on the way—some deep truths, such as the real nature of man—but he'd also learned a whole clutch of other things too. While giving the sermon at the Harvest Festival—his first since the recovery of his faith—he'd been aware of how much the congregation was listening to him and concentrating on what he was saying. In the distant past, before the plague, he'd told his parishioners what he'd thought they ought to hear and what he thought they ought to believe—in practice, as it turned out, little more than Christianised pacifism. And although the members of the congregation had always nodded politely and thanked him afterwards, he'd always had the feeling that he wasn't quite getting through to them.

On that Harvest Festival morning he'd noticed a completely different atmosphere: how those looking up at him from the pews were *really* listening to him, absorbing what he had to say, enjoying it and feeling how relevant it was to their own lives. The experience had been so profound that, even in the space of time that it took to descend the few steps from the pulpit he had resolved that never again would he preach *at* his congregation but that instead he would preach to them or, better, share *with* them. He intended to carry this principle into practice from then on.

With this in mind he'd immediately asked the regular church attenders if they would be interested in meeting more frequently. The Major, of course, was delighted that Martin was once again willing to lead the worship on a regular basis and immediately asked if Martin could celebrate the Eucharist each Sunday morning.

Yet Martin didn't feel satisfied by this: although he didn't want to preach *at* his congregation, nevertheless he'd learned many profound lessons in his year in the wilderness, and he was sure it wouldn't be possible to convey these deeper truths in the short time allotted for the normal Anglican sermon. In any case, having lost his previous intellectual arrogance he was just as anxious to learn from the others as he was to teach them: he wanted to go with them to learn about God. So, tentatively, he'd suggested that they might all meet on a more informal, relaxed basis—perhaps on a weekday evening, simply to talk, study the Bible, and pray.

Not surprisingly, the number of his flock who were interested was even lower than the number who wanted to attend church regularly. It is a curious feature of many English people that they wish to keep their religious and private lives quite separate—not that there was necessarily any great disjunction or schism between the two, but perhaps that the stiff upper lip of formalism and slight emotional sterility that so characterises the English spilled over into matters of religion, so that there was a place for everything, and everything in its place, and the place for religion was on Sunday, and Sunday alone, and that religious activity on any other day of the week would somehow be... inappropriate.

Nevertheless Martin persisted, and eventually, during the first few weeks of the autumn, a group of four or five churchgoers began to meet regularly in the dining room at the Old Rectory. The Major was there, of course; the other two regulars were Edna and Fred Higginbottom, a couple in their late sixties who now lived down Dunstable Street, next door to Janet MacKenzie. A handful of other people came from time to time, but none on a regular basis. Martin wasn't in the least dismayed by the small size of the group, and enjoyed sharing with them the lessons that they had all learned in the past year.

However, it had come as a profound shock to the Major to be meeting in that way. In the past he'd been accustomed to a very formal High Church style of worship, and the thought of private devotions and Bible study, or even—whisper it quietly—discussion, whilst not actually anathema to him, wasn't far off it. To be honest, Martin had been surprised that the Major had come at all, bearing in mind his background; and was delighted when he turned up on that first Wednesday.

If Martin was surprised then the Major was even more surprised. He didn't even know why he'd turned up. He had just somehow felt that it was a good idea, had gone along, and having started, found the experience most enjoyable. He also found it quite challenging, and not a little unnerving. From his point of view, he could recite everything in *Hymns Ancient and Modern*, and virtually every one of the Prayer Book services off by heart: he knew the Bible readings appointed for each Sunday and the Psalms that were sung each week—but he didn't really know the bits in between. He knew about the garden of Eden, but not much of the genealogy of the patriarchs; about the Exodus, but nothing of the Tabernacle; of the Ten Commandments but little of Leviticus; of David but not of Solomon; of the major prophets such as Elijah but little of Amos or Habakkuk; of Daniel in the lions' den, but nothing of Daniel's prophecies. He knew the Gospels of course, but had never realised that the Acts of the Apostles, taken in one piece, reads like a thriller. He knew many excerpts from the epistles of Paul—especially of course the splendid passage about love in 1 Corinthians 13—but he'd never realised that on either side of it in chapters 12 and 14 was the most explosive stuff about supernatural power and the gifts of the Holy Spirit.

As for Revelation he knew only excerpts from the first few chapters—the four horseman of the Apocalypse, and Laodicea, the church that was neither hot nor cold—but nothing of the rest. He'd never studied the Song of Songs, read the details of the Old Testament prophecies about Jesus, or studied the symbolism of the Old Testament in prophesying what Jesus would be like.

After two weeks, the Major started to realise that his understanding and knowledge of Christianity had barely scratched the surface—even after a lifetime of regular church attendance! He was, to put it mildly, amazed, but also began to be infected by Martin's enthusiasm, and because Martin was no longer trying to speak *ex cathedra* but was simply sharing and discussing with everyone, the Major didn't feel threatened by what was going on and, to be truthful, really began to enjoy it. It was very different from what he'd been accustomed to; but it was very rewarding, deep, and comforting as well.

And so, without fuss, the church in Ampthill—meaning the people, not the buildings—started up again, and a different kind of light also began to come out of the Old Rectory.

- 10 -

*L*ooking back they could see that it wasn't a coincidence, but at the time it seemed just serendipity that the three strangers came when they did. If ever there was an undignified entrance, this was it. Ambassadors are supposed to ride in the best conveyances available: Rolls Royces, Bentleys, Daimlers, Mercedes, Zils—but these three came from the west on battered bicycles. On a cold, damp, January morning the three of them stood shivering in the market square, looking lost and forlorn, gaunt, half-starved, dirty, and with that slightly haunted, large-eyed look of people who haven't really eaten well for the past three weeks. They were relatively young—in their late teens or early twenties—but their sufferings had put years on their appearance. The prim and proper Janet MacKenzie was the first to meet them, as she was walking back to her house from visiting Mary. In the time-honoured phrase of comics and bad science fiction they uttered the immortal words 'Take me to your leader,' or something similar, so Janet ushered them a further hundred yards along Church Street to Foulislea Cottage. Chris answered the knock on the door, with the ever-present Paul, pencil and a sheaf of papers in hand, behind her.

Chris looked at the strangers in surprise, amazement and then concern. 'Do come in,' she said, beckoning them inside, 'You look frozen.'

'We are,' they said, enviously eyeing the fireplace with its grate of blazing logs.

'Can I get you a drink?' asked Chris and watched as three pairs of eyes lit up. After half a second's hesitation she added, 'and something to eat?' Their eyes lit up even further. As she opened the door into the kitchen the aroma of newly baked bread filled the air. The three visitors positively drooled. 'Herb tea or acorn coffee?' asked Chris, popping her head round the door.

'Anything,' the three of them chorused.

'Biscuits all right?'

'Biscuits would be fine,' said the first of them, who looked as if biscuits, followed by at least a loaf and a half of the bread they could smell, followed by another plate of biscuits, followed by another loaf and a half of bread, might be more the order of the day. While Chris was occupied in the kitchen Paul introduced himself and asked their names.

The first one spoke again. 'I'm Vince Andrews, this is Jason Harbury, and Shaun McCluskey.' They shook hands, slightly awkwardly.

'We haven't seen you around here before,' said Paul pleasantly.

'No,' said Vince, 'we've come from some way away.'

'We live in Buckingham,' interjected Jason.

'Really?' said Paul. 'I didn't know there was a community there. How many people are there?'

'About two or three hundred,' said Shaun, looking at Jason, who nodded. 'Yes, about that.'

'How are things going for you?' asked Paul, knowing instinctively what the answer was going to be.

'Not very well,' said Vince, still shivering, and surreptitiously edging more closely to the fire.

'Why so?'

'There's nothing to eat,' said Shaun. 'We've run out. We've scavenged food from as far as we can, but there's none left. All the shops are empty. There's nothing within forty miles now—apart from you here in Ampthill.'

'But what about your crops?' asked Paul.

'Crops,' snarled Vince. 'What crops?'

'Well... didn't you gather in the wheat? What about milk and beef and mutton? Potatoes, fruit?' Vince shot back a look that could have killed Paul.

Shaun, who seemed much the uneasiest of the three, chipped in. 'You see we didn't know what we were doing. None of us knew. We ate the food in the shops, and when that finished we killed any animals we could find, but there weren't many left.'

'But what about the crops?' asked Paul as Chris returned with the drinks and a plate piled high with biscuits. Ignoring the question the three of them made a grab for the pile and only succeeded in knocking half of them on the floor. Shaun stuffed the first biscuit he could lay his hands on in his mouth, then grabbed for all the rest that were rolling round his feet and put them back on the table.

'Sorry about that,' he said, spluttering crumbs. 'You must think we're...' his voice tailed off as he concentrated on chewing as quickly as he could in order to make room in his mouth for the next biscuit before the other two had finished and could grab them. Paul and Chris exchanged glances.

'I still don't get this,' said Paul 'Why are there no crops?'

'Because we don't know how to farm,' said Vince angrily. 'Nobody does. We never knew when to do things or what to do and either we did them too early, or too late.'

'We tried to get the wheat cut,' said Jason 'but it was all green and decayed and we didn't know what to do with it. And when we'd stored it, it all went rotten and the rats got it.'

'Hang on a minute,' said Paul. 'Do you mean to say you haven't got any flour at all?'

'That's right,' said Vince.

'Potatoes?'

'No. When we tried to pull them up they were rotten. We think we left them too long.'

'So what are you living on?' said Chris.

'I've told you,' said Shaun. 'Anything we can get our hands on and kill—rabbits if we can get them, dogs if we can't.'

'But what about all the farm animals?' said Chris. 'Surely you can't have eaten your way through all of those?'

'I tell you there's none left,' said Vince truculently. 'None at all. The ones that didn't die of starvation or thirst we ate. There wasn't anything else, you see.'

Gradually the awful tale unfolded. Just as survivors had gathered in Ampthill, so another group found themselves together in Buckingham. Although Buckingham is a country town, like Ampthill, it's not overly large. Like Ampthill, it has an old centre with a market place, in the middle of which is an old prison. The town is built on the side of a hill, and is surrounded by countryside, acre upon acre of fields: a town marooned in a sea of green. Despite this, by design, accident, laziness, sheer ineptitude, bad luck or a combination of all five the survivors in Buckingham had got it just about as wrong as it was possible to get, and their story contrasted sharply with what had happened in Ampthill. The more that the three starving wretches in front of them told their tale, the more Chris realised how much they had to thank Paul and Neil for; Neil for his farming experience and Paul for his meticulous planning. Listening to the refugees talking she shuddered involuntarily as she realised that the same things could so easily have happened to them.

The Buckingham group had gone about it exactly the wrong way round. Instead of planning for the future as Paul had insisted, they had lived for the present. At first they'd lived like lords off the tinned produce in the shops and supermarkets, and because it had been autumn when the plague struck, the frozen foods had remained edible for a long time. According to Shaun, the first month had been one glorious free feast. But they'd had no farming advice and hadn't had the foresight to seek out cattle, sheep or chicken to provide meat, milk or eggs. Instead of carefully husbanding their resources, making sure that they never butchered more animals than the flocks and herds could sustain, they'd given no thought to the future and had simply lived for the present. They hadn't conserved their supplies of petrol. They hadn't planted anything—firstly because they didn't know how to use the machinery, secondly because they didn't know where to get any of the seeds from, thirdly—Paul suspected inwardly—because they were too lazy, and fourthly, because they didn't know when to do it, nor what to do afterwards. Gradually a wasteland had developed around Buckingham, and it had become progressively harder to find animals to kill, or produce to eat.

The final straw for them had been the terrible summer. With no farmer to advise them they had tried to get the wheat in, but did it too early. Timing with wheat is essential. Get it in too early and there will be little flour in the grain. Bring it in when it's too damp and it will moulder, fungus will grow and the whole year's produce will turn into a festering stinking mess that not only won't produce much in the way of flour, but will provide a lot in the way of dangerous fungi and toxins. Wait too long to bring the harvest in, and it will be rotting on the stalk or else crushed flat by the autumnal gales and incapable of being harvested easily.

In short, the Buckingham residents had progressively spread devastation in an expanding circle around Buckingham, leaving the farms and the land fit for nothing, denuding them of what they had and creating nothing for the future. Gradually the picture emerged of a miserable, frightened group of people who were slowly starving to death with not the vaguest idea of how to change their situation for the better.

'You haven't got any more of those biscuits?' asked Vince after another few minutes.

'I'll see what I can find,' said Chris. 'I'm a bit low at the moment. I was just cooking.' The smell of the bread wafted across the kitchen.

'What we wanted to know,' said Jason between mouthfuls, 'is, can you let us have some food?'

'We're doing just that,' said Paul.

'No,' said Jason, 'I don't mean for the three of us, I mean for all of us.'

'What, *all* of you?'

Chris came back from the kitchen, her face a picture of total concern.

'For all of you?' she asked. 'How many did you say?'

'Two hundred,' said Shaun, looking down and shuffling his feet.

'More like three,' said Vince.

'What will you pay us?' said Paul. Chris shot an angry glance at him, but out of view of the refugees he glared at her, motioning her to be quiet.

'Pay?' said Vince, looking up at him with the daggers in his eyes again. 'Pay? We can't pay you for anything. We haven't got anything. We're starving. Haven't we made that clear?'

'I'm sure you've got something,' purred Paul.

I don't believe this, thought Chris. He's reverted to type. The little so and so's going to do them for all he can get out of them.

She opened her mouth to protest and Paul shot her the most furious glance he had ever given anyone. The words died in her throat and instead she gave a curious spluttering cough, and made out that she'd choked on a crumb.

Paul looked Vince squarely in the eye. 'Now hear this. There's no way that we can support three hundred people. No way at all. We've only just got enough for ourselves. We haven't had it easy either.'

'Maybe not,' said Vince, 'but you've had it better than we have.'

'Only by luck and hard work. Now don't get me wrong. I'm not saying we won't help, I'm just saying that I don't think we can help you to the extent you're hoping for. If we try to help you it may be a noose around our own necks; we may not survive ourselves, and that won't help anybody. Anyway I can't make any decisions on my own, I've got to ask the rest of the council.'

'Well, couldn't you let us have some of your new supply of flour that you've just ground? That would help us out for a bit.'

'How did you know we've just ground flour?' asked Paul, suddenly very alert.

'Your wife told us,' said Vince glancing at Chris.

'She's not my wife. We're not married...' He stared at Vince. 'I've told you, I can't make any decisions myself. As I said, you'll have to wait until the rest of the council have met.'

'Well, can you ask them?' said Vince. 'This afternoon?'

'The council isn't due to meet for another week,' said Paul. 'Why don't you come back then?'

Vince shot daggers at him again. 'Because we're starving, that's why,' he shouted angrily.

'All right, all right,' said Paul. 'Calm down. I'll see if I can get them together this afternoon. Just stay there a minute. I need to have a word with Chris, privately.' They went out into the kitchen and closed the door.

'Why were you trying to shut me up?' whispered Chris angrily.

'Because I don't believe a word of it,' said Paul. 'You didn't tell them that we'd just ground our first lot of corn, did you?' Chris opened her mouth to speak, and then shut it again.

'No,' she said. 'I don't think so.'

'Well, neither did I,' said Paul, 'so how did they know?'

'Maybe they knew because of the bread. Didn't I say something about baking?'

'We didn't say anything about it being the first lot of flour, so how did they know? I smell a rat and a very big one too. I think we ought to be very careful about these three here until we know what's going on.'

'Are you sure?' said Chris. 'They look genuine to me. They're starving, for goodness' sake. I think you're trying to read too much into the situation. We'd better call an emergency meeting for this afternoon.'

'Where are we going to keep them in the meantime?'

'We can't "keep" them anywhere—at least not against their will.'

'Why don't we park them off with someone else for a bit: Peter—or Henry? Send them across the road to Dynevor House.'

'Why can't they stay here?'

'We've got the archives here, remember? I don't want to risk anything happening to them.'

'You're paranoid.'

'I'm not paranoid. I need the archives. They're valuable. Right?'

Shaken by his demeanour, Chris nodded her head. 'All right. You were right before, weren't you?'

'Over what?'

'Planning to keep us all alive. I kept on thinking all the time they were talking how much we owe you. All of us.' She put her hands round his neck, pulled his head down and gave him a long lingering kiss. 'So I am very grateful to you, my big, handsome, arrogant friend. Very grateful indeed. I just hope you've got it right this time, that's all.' She rubbed her nose against his.

'I tell you somebody else I want in on this conversation,' said Paul. 'Kevin.'

'*Kevin*?' Chris looked at him with incredulity, knowing that Kevin and Paul were like chalk and cheese, only worse.

'I know,' said Paul. 'I know just what you're thinking. I don't like the little rat. I don't think you do either, but he's a jolly good strate-

gist and I just have the feeling that we may need his help. He may
be able to "read" them better than I can. They're more his ilk, I suspect.'

'That serious?'

'That serious. I might be wrong. I hope I am... Mind you, I don't
know. If I *am* wrong then we've got another three hundred people
to feed and that's not going to be easy.'

'Well, you got it right before, and you planned it all out and
we're doing well now so I'll trust you planning for the future,' said
Chris, giving him a quick hug. 'You take them across the road to
Henry. I'll call a meeting.'

            *   *   *

Kevin was beginning to look a little bit like the three refugees,
thought Paul as he knocked on the door of his house at the northern
end of the town. What a mess, he mused, looking at the debris
strewn everywhere. Kevin came to the door and looked up inso-
lently at Paul. The relationship between them had never been the
same since Paul had tried to put the blame for his theft of the pethidine onto Kevin.

'Whaddya want?' In the background, Paul could see the huge
bulk of Trevor lumbering around. David, Derek's son, was there as
well, together with Alan and Susan's son Darren, working on some
metal contraption which Paul couldn't see clearly.

'We'd like you attend the next council meeting,' he began. Kevin
looked up suspiciously.

'Whaddya trying to pin on me this time?'

'We're not trying to pin anything,' said Paul in his most unctuous
manner. 'We need your help.'

'*You* need *my* help? Why?' Paul explained. Kevin looked up at
him again.

'It'll cost.'

'What will?'

'My time. Time is money. That's right, isn't it?' He looked back
at Trevor who sniggered. 'Yer, it'll cost.'

'But this is for the whole community, which includes you.'

Although accustomed to rooking other people in a completely imperturbable fashion, Paul was never happy if anybody else was doing the same thing to him. Kevin eyed him.

'Six pounds.'

'You what?'

'Six pounds.'

'What for?'

'Going and talking to the council, or whatever it is you want me to do.'

'But that's a whole week's work.'

'So what?'

'You can't charge that amount just for two hours of talking.'

Kevin eyed Paul with a particular look of malevolent insolence. 'Why not?'

'Because it's too much, that's why.'

'Too much for who? I think my services are well worth it.'

'Out of the question,' snapped Paul.

'Suit yourself,' said Kevin and turning round, began to shut the door. Paul thought better of it and put his foot in the jamb.

'On second thoughts...'

'Oh, so you *are* going to pay?'

'I never said that.'

'Yer, but you mean it. So why shouldn't *I* charge for *my* services—at the going rate?' He put on a sing-song voice. 'We've got this nice little economic community, haven't we, where everybody gets paid for *working*...' he said the word with a particularly disdainful curl of the lip '... we sell our labour or our skills. Well, I'm selling mine, and that's my price. OK?'

He had a point, Paul had to admit to himself. In fact he had a very good point. It was one that he, Paul, would have used on many an occasion in the past. It was just that, coming from Kevin, it rankled. Not so much class distinction as class disdain. Kevin looked up at Paul, his eyes grinning from underneath his unkempt hair. He'd won, of course. He knew he'd won. What's worse, Paul knew that Kevin knew that he'd won. *Why is it*, he thought to himself, *that I can never manage to get the better of this little upstart*? But the community needed Kevin's innate sense of cunning, and both Kevin and Paul knew it. Behind Kevin, David and Trevor had stopped working at the metallic contraption, had put their tools down and were standing, grinning at Paul.

'All right then, six pounds,' said Paul, irascibly.

'I told you you'd have to pay,' said Kevin, slamming the door on Paul about a tenth of a second after he'd withdrawn his foot.

*   *   *

It would have been trite to say that the council was not amused by the discovery of the Buckingham community. As they trouped into the courtroom, each of them knew that something was afoot, but none of them was prepared for the scale of the problem that Chris and Paul outlined to them. In the space of a few hours their situation had turned from the relatively comfortable to the extremely precarious. After the first harvest they'd congratulated themselves on how well they'd done—they'd probably got enough grain for two or even three years, and it would tide them over if there were to be a lean harvest or two. Whilst they hadn't exactly been flush with goods and food, nevertheless they had enough to be going on with and, where food is concerned, there is no great virtue in having too much because it's impossible to consume more than a certain amount. The only value of their extra food was as a buffer against future problems. But now they were faced with another group of hungry mouths to feed, and what by all accounts sounded like a very large number of people indeed.

When Chris had finished there was a long pause, broken only by the sound of the wind whistling in the trees outside and the rain battering on the window.

'Well,' said Mary brightly and totally inappropriately, 'this is a turn-up for the books.'

'Too right,' said Paul menacingly.

'Why, what's the problem?' asked Mary innocently. 'All we do is share our food. We've got enough, haven't we?' She turned to look at the rest of the councile. 'Why can't we just share it and let everybody have what they need? We've got enough.'

'That's all very well,' said Alan, 'but we worked for it. Why should we just give away what we've slaved for? You know yourself how hard we all had to work last year. And Neil, what about Neil? He's had to take all that responsibility and then instead of being able to relax, he finds that all these people do is ask for food and we give it away.'

At the other end of the table Martin watched and waited.

'How much food do we have, Neil?' asked Chris. Neil coughed, jotted a few notes in pencil on the pad in front of him and then looked up again, sucking his teeth. 'It all depends...' he began slowly. 'On the face of it we've got quite enough, as Mary's just said. We probably gathered twice or maybe three times what we need in the last harvest, so we could support a community that was two or three times our size until next year, *but*...' and he looked round the council to emphasise the seriousness of what he was about to say '...we're unlikely to get a harvest of the same size next year. For a start, there are nothing like the number of fields planted. Last year everywhere was wheat, because all the farmers had sown it just before the plague struck. This year we've only sown what we thought we needed. And I know I've underestimated the crop we can get, but I've done that quite deliberately, so I've overestimated the number of fields we had to sow—but that was just to keep *us* alive, not us and another group which is at least the same size as ourselves if not bigger. As I said in the meeting just after the harvest, I can't guarantee what's going to happen this season. I'm sure our yields will be a great deal lower without pesticides and without fertilisers. I really don't know how the land is going to respond—I really don't.'

'Can't we sow more fields?' asked Alan. 'After all wheat doesn't have to be sown in the winter. It can always be sown in the spring, can't it?'

'There is that,' said Neil, 'but the more of the grain you sow, the less there is to eat.'

A bit like casting your bread on the waters, thought Martin, but still remained silent.

'You haven't really answered the question,' said Paul.

'Haven't I?' said Neil affably. 'I thought I had. Ask it me again.'

'Can we afford to feed them?'

'You mean can we feed them or can we *afford* to feed them?'

'Both really.'

'All right. "Can we feed them?" Yes, we can—just—but it will be tight and there won't be any leeway for subsequent years. If I've overestimated the yield then we're *all* going to starve or at least, go a bit hungry. As to the second question, "Can we afford it?" I think that's up to the community to decide.'

'I hope that by that you don't mean you're prepared to let them starve,' said Mary, her colour rising.

'Why not?' said Paul. 'It's not our fault that they haven't got any food.' There was a chorus of disapproval from the others at the table.

'It's not their fault either,' said Susan. 'After all, there but for the grace of God—' she turned round to Martin '—sorry Vicar—go we. It's only because we've got people like Neil, Paul and Derek that we've got this far.'

'That's kind of you,' said Paul, 'but we wouldn't have been much use if no one had turned up to help with the hoeing, the weeding, the milking, the reaping and the calving. It's *everybody's* harvest, not just ours. Everyone in the community helped.' He looked at Kevin.

'Yes, I did as well,' said Kevin truculently. 'Don't you remember?' and he turned to Martin who was sitting on his right-hand side. 'I *was* there. Remember?'

Martin nodded.

'Why should we give away everything that we've got?' said Susan.

'Nobody said about giving everything away,' said Chris. 'Just giving them enough to live on.'

'Do you mean live on comfortably, or live on just to avoid starving?' asked Susan. Chris opened her mouth to say something and swiftly realised that she hadn't got anything to say because she didn't know the answer.

'To put it in a nutshell,' said Alan, holding up a hand and extending the fingers one by one as he ticked off the points, 'One, are we going to stop them starving? Two, are we going to share everything that we've got or just let them have enough to keep body and soul together? Three, what are we going to do next year—or are they going to play the same trick on us again?'

Another murmur of disapproval ran round the table, but several council members were shifting uneasily in their seats, torn between a desire to keep what they had quite fairly earned for themselves, and the need to make sure that their fellow men and women didn't suffer. Yes, the people in Buckingham were human beings. Yes, they did deserve to live life to the full like everybody else, but, no, there wasn't an overall reason why everyone should suddenly give up their more comfortable style of living just because somebody else had made a mess of it.

At the far end of the table Martin winced. He could have predicted every word of the conversation, of the selfishness that suggested that others less fortunate than themselves should be condemned to a life on the breadline—or less—simply because they wished to hang on to what they already had. There was, he recognised also, some truth in the feeling that perhaps the people in Buckingham deserved what they'd got because underneath it all they'd probably been lazy as well as stupid. So maybe they shouldn't expect to get as much as those who had worked. But most of all he could see in the eyes and the minds of the council members that selfish streak that seemed to permeate everybody in society, that selfish streak that he'd only really first noticed properly in Nicholas, a streak that most of the time was hidden but sometimes came to the fore in no uncertain manner. A year ago they would willingly have shared everything among themselves—when they had nothing. Now, when they did have something to share, they didn't want to share it. What is it about mankind, he thought, where people are generous when there is little to be generous with, then get progressively more selfish the more they have—which by definition means when they have more to share, and more that they could give away without hurting themselves?

He caught himself just in time, as he suddenly became aware that he was sitting in judgement on everybody else, while forgetting that the same selfish streak applied to him. And *how* it applied to him! When he'd had life and health he hadn't prepared to share that out too, as the dying had flocked past his vicarage window when the plague first struck. How he'd hidden away so that those in need couldn't get near him and couldn't infect him. Suddenly Martin was aware that he'd gone bright pink and he hoped—oh, how he hoped—that nobody was looking in his direction.

He needn't have worried—the argument, intransigence, self-satisfaction and general indignation rose to a crescendo with every-one talking excitedly to everyone else. Mary was puce—again—her tight grey bob bouncing up and down animatedly. Alan seemed to be having a slanging match with Paul, which made a change from his having a slanging match with his wife; Chris and Neil were exchanging points and even Peter was joining in agitatedly.

As the arguments raged back and forward Kevin sat silently at the end of the table thinking to himself that this was the easiest six quid he'd ever earned.

'Stop. Stop! STOP,' shouted Chris above the row. 'Come on everyone, this is ridiculous. We'll never make any decisions like this. Now, *one at a time*, what are we going to do?'

'Wait a minute,' said Derek. 'We haven't explored all the possi-bilities yet.'

'Such as what?' said Paul.

'Such as whether we can help the Buckingham group to help themselves.' The table fell silent.

'Well, you *hadn't* thought about it, had you? And the honest truth is, we don't know all that much about them. We don't know what they *could* do, and we don't know whether the tale these three have told us is true, and I think that before we do anything else we ought to find out a little bit more about them.'

Kevin suddenly became uncomfortably aware that everyone had stopped talking and was turning to look at him. 'And what do you think, Kevin?' asked Chris from the other end of the table.

'About what?' said Kevin, slightly lost, his mind coming back to the matter in hand, having been otherwise engaged elsewhere, largely with the machine that he, David and Trevor had been creating. He sniffed. It seemed the appropriate thing to do, and anyway it gave him a few seconds more to think. 'Whaddya want me to say?'

'What do you think about the Buckingham set?' asked Chris.

'Whaddya mean?'

'I mean,' said Chris in an exasperated tone. 'Do you think they're what they say they are? What's their game? Why haven't we heard about them before?'

'Yer. Well... there is that. How do I know? I've only talked to them for a bit.'

'Do you think they're telling the truth?' said Chris, trying hard not to lose her temper.

Kevin shrugged and then went silent, his mouth tight. 'Nah... Nah... They're not telling the truth. They're a bunch of liars.'

'Why?' said Paul, his eyes narrowed, staring hard at Kevin. He had his own ideas, of course, but first he wanted to hear what Kevin had to say.

'It's too easy, innit? They come round here just after we've done our first lot of corn—made it into flour, like. Bit of a coincidence that, don't you think?' Paul did think. He'd thought it first, but he didn't want to let on. 'And they seemed... *frightened* somehow... Maybe there's a big geezer somewhere, leaning on 'em.'

'Ping' went a connection inside Paul's brain. That was it. That was what didn't fit. They didn't have a haunted look, they had a *hunted* look—an unease, as though each was wary of what the others were saying, as though each was being monitored by the others, just as soldiers in the former communist bloc were always sent off in twos or threes to make sure that each kept an eye on the others.

That being Kevin's sole contribution to the meeting he reckoned he'd been paid at something around seven pence a word. Not bad going, he thought. At the other end of the table Paul was thinking similar thoughts—but with a slightly different emphasis, on the lines of 'that was six pounds well spent'. Somehow Kevin, as always, had put his finger on the tactical situation in a way that

others never did. Inside himself, Paul had always known that there
was something wrong about the refugees' looks and behaviour, but
he just couldn't work out what it was. It had made him uneasy, nothing more. He knew that nothing fitted, but he didn't know why it
didn't fit. And now Kevin had made conscious that which previously had been subconscious, and for the first time since meeting the
refugees Paul relaxed.

'I like that idea of Derek's,' said Alan, 'of seeing if we can teach
them to fend for themselves.'

'We'll have to go about it in a completely different way,' said
Paul, back in his comfortable role of being the strategist. Kevin
might be the tactician, but Paul could always see the wider viewpoint. 'The first thing we need to do is make a reconnaissance—to
see what they're like. See what the land's like. See how bad it is—
or how good for that matter. Then we need to count how many
people we're trying to feed. We may even have to make a list of
them to make sure that we're not being conned, and if we're right'
—Kevin noticed the use of the royal 'we'—'then perhaps we'll
manage to find out whether they're acting under some sort of
duress.'

'Who's going to go?' said Alan.

'Me, I think—one of the women, too. Susan, would you come?
Alan. And... Kevin.'

'Only if you pay me,' grunted Kevin.

*   *   *

Three more square meals later, a convoy of just two vehicles left
Ampthill by the Woburn road and headed for Buckingham. They
could have gone by bicycle or horse, but Paul was insistent that they
cover a lot of ground and go speedily so that there was no chance
that news of their coming could be sent to other groups within
Buckinghamshire. Quite deliberately, Paul wanted to arrive like a
whirlwind to see what there was to see, then disappear with the
same quick ferocity. They went—somewhat unfortunately as it
turned out—in Derek's big Peugeot and Paul's blood-red Porsche,
PIG 1, having first made sure that they had an adequate supply of

food and a lot of extra petrol on board.

Just for good measure Paul also included a gun that he'd found in one of the houses along Dunstable Street. But he wasn't going to tell anyone. It wouldn't do to make out that he was scared.

In the Peugeot Alan also had a gun... which no one else knew about. It wouldn't do to let anyone else think that he was scared, he reasoned.

Quite deliberately, Paul split up the three refugees between the two vehicles, with strict instructions to Alan to pump for information, surreptitiously, whilst exchanging pleasantries. It would be particularly important, he said, to try to get incidental information out of them as they were starting to enter the area they knew best. Kevin and Alan would be the eyes and ears in the Peugeot, with two of the refugees. Paul and Shaun McCluskey would go in the Porsche, with Susan in the back.

At first light they roared off, the birds and wild animals in the hedgerows and the domesticated animals in the fields starting at the unaccustomed and devastatingly loud sound. Paul enjoyed the sensation of speed as the engine of the Porsche crackled. The thrill of driving it had never left him, and his only sadness was that petrol was now so scarce that he hardly ever had the chance to take his beloved car out. He'd always been cross with Kevin for burning up and down the roads on his bike, wasting petrol, but when it came to it he was a good example of the psychological adage that one hates in others what one cannot stand in oneself. Paul loved every minute of the journey. Alan, driving the Peugeot, was totally left behind as Paul put his foot down and the Porsche disappeared over the horizon in a cloud of spray and mud. The roads were treacherous—a year of no traffic, blown dust, grass seeds, blocked drains and a wet week had seen to that—and more than once Paul had to correct a slide. After the first five miles he looked round to see Susan sitting in the seat behind whimpering slightly, her eyes tight shut, her hand in front of them. 'I'm sorry,' he said blandly. 'Am I going too fast for you?'

'Just a little,' she said wanly. Perhaps he'd better slow down a bit, he thought, if only to allow the Peugeot to catch up.

The roads were relatively unblocked, with not much in the way
of crashed cars, though the junction with the A5 was difficult near
Bow Brickhill and the short distance up towards the centre of
Bletchley needed caution; but then they were out on the western
side of Bletchley, past the station and heading almost due west for
Buckingham. The countryside was deserted, open and green, looking as untouched and as normal as it had been in the days before the
plague started. Nine miles out from Buckingham, Paul quietly but
deliberately began to drive less aggressively until they were simply
coasting along. Although he didn't seem to be particularly interested in the countryside, and his head seemed to be looking mainly
straight ahead, his eyes were constantly darting about, watching for
signs of life, or tell-tale signs of buildings that were inhabited: but
there was nothing, nothing at all—a totally dead landscape as far as
the eye could see.

Until he looked in his mirror. It was strange, but on more than
one occasion he thought he saw a figure by the roadside at a place
where he was sure no one had been when he went past. After a few
minutes he made a special point of looking. The Peugeot was right
behind him now and he could see in the mirror that as they passed
a clump of trees or a small spinney, from time to time a figure
seemed to detach itself and stand up and look at them as they reced-
ed into the distance. Paul had the horrid sensation that something or
someone was spying on their every movement. But it was only a
sensation. Perhaps he was wrong.

When he came round the next bend and saw something move he
jammed on the brakes and screeched to a halt. Alan wasn't looking
properly, and very nearly piled into the back of him. Paul jumped
out of the Porsche, stood up quickly and looked behind him—to
find a lone black and white cow staring soulfully at him from the
corner of a very large field, chewing the cud in an amiably contented manner. With heart beating, and Alan's angry shouts ringing
in his ears, Paul got back into the Porsche, slammed the door, and
spun the wheels in fury as he drove off.

*   *   *

'Good morning, doctor,' said Janet as she came through the door. *Not again*! screamed Derek to himself, trying desperately not to let his emotions reach his face. He smiled a wan smile.

'Good morning, Mrs MacKenzie. And what can I do for you today?'

*   *   *

Eventually they reached the outskirts of Buckingham. For the last few miles they'd gone at a snail's pace—ostensibly, as Paul pointed out to Shaun, to make sure they didn't come round a bend and knock anybody over. After all, after a year without petrol nobody would be expecting the red blur of the Porsche suddenly to come around the corner at eighty miles an hour. Shaun agreed entirely that this was a wise and sensible move so, gently and carefully, Paul steered the Porsche into Buckingham at the best possible speed for seeing things, and while on the surface he and Susan appeared nonchalantly to be surveying the scenery, in fact they were making detailed mental notes which they would compare later on.

It didn't look good. As they got nearer to the centre of the town they began to come across people—but not the jaunty, healthy-looking, well-fed community members they'd been accustomed to see in Ampthill. These people were quite different. They were thin, they were dirty, their clothes were grubby and frequently in tatters, they looked cold and half-starved. And they all had that same hunted look about them that Vince, Jason and Shaun so obviously carried.

But there was something else about them. Susan couldn't quite put her finger on it, until finally, as they swept into the main square from the east, past the castle-like building in the centre, and parked at the west end, she realised what it was. Despite the fact that out of the blue two cars had appeared, one of which was rather prominent and quite rare even before the plague, those present in the square took little notice. They just sat where they were and stared listlessly as though it was the most common-place thing in the world to see a red Porsche and a beige Peugeot pull into the centre of their town when there had been no road traffic for a year.

Paul switched off the engine and looked round. There was a moment's silence, during which nothing very much happened. 'They don't seem very pleased to see us,' he observed tartly.

'No,' said Susan, 'they don't, do they?' Gradually one or two people detached themselves from the huddled groups and came over, slowly, to look at the newcomers. Shaun extricated himself from the Porsche and stretched himself, looking round at—to him—the familiar surroundings. It was a disheartening sight. To put it bluntly, the place was in a mess, as if it had been ransacked by a marauding army. The windows of the shops were smashed, their contents often strewn about into the pavement outside. No smoke came from any of the chimneys; no one moved around in any purposeful way. There was no activity, no business, no conversation—nothing. Just a hundred listless eyes, staring—or not even bothering to stare—from the sides of the square. Why are they all in the square? thought Susan to herself. It's not a particularly warm day. Why should they all come out? And then she realised. Because it's warmer in the square, in the sun, that's why. Involuntarily she shivered, thinking of what it must be like at night. From time to time, as the sun moved round in the sky, and shadows blotted out the end of a group of people, those in the shadowed area would shamble across to where the sun was still shining, to sit down again.

There was an unnatural stillness about the place—no chatter, no conversation, no purposeful behaviour, no sounds of footsteps, bicycles, horses' hooves, carts; no hammering, banging, machinery, shouts of workers one to the other, no noise of cattle, pigs, sheep, geese—just a dead, flat silence, broken only by the sound of a curtain flapping in the wind on the outside of a smashed window.

Behind them, Alan had brought the Peugeot up into the square and parked alongside the Porsche. He and his three passengers got out and looked around, and *still* no one came near. Little fingers started running up and down Susan's spine. This was really eerie.

Paul turned to Alan and grunted under his breath. 'So who do we go and see now?'

Alan turned round to Vince and Jason who were just behind him. 'Who's your leader?'

'Dave. Dave Wittering.'

'Where can we find him?'

'He's got a cottage down on the north side of the Square, the warm side.' He pointed beyond the squat bulk of the ancient prison to an area of cottages basking in the sunlight.

'Well, shall we go and find him?' said Alan to Paul, starting to walk away.

'You can if you want,' said Paul. 'Someone must stay with the cars.'

'What?'

'Someone must stay here with the cars,' repeated Paul quietly under his breath so that no one else could hear. 'I am not, repeat *not*, leaving them unguarded.'

'But we can lock them up,' protested Alan.'

'And a lot of good that would do when faced with a brick through the side window.' Looking round the square Alan surveyed the debris of the houses and the shops.

'I see what you mean. You, Kevin and Susan go. I'll stay here.'

'OK, but be careful.' Paul moved even closer to Alan. 'There's a gun in my car if you want, underneath the front seat.'

Alan looked at him and smiled a thin smile.

'It's all right, Paul, there's one under my front seat too.'

'OK, Vince,' shouted Paul, grinning to himself. '*Take me to your leader.*' In his youth, in his wildest dreams he'd never ever thought that he would get to say that! But it was a bitter smile that was soon wiped off his face as he followed Vince and Jason toward the eastern end of the Square.

Buckingham is built on a hill and the main street runs roughly east to west, rising as it does so. At the top there are shops, banks, a chemist, hardware shops and the like. Halfway down the main square there is a curious castellated building, which divides the central area into two oblong shapes. Below the castellated building— the old prison—is another oblong square, open at the eastern end, and with many cottages on the northern side. It was to these that Vince and Jason escorted Paul and Susan. They had to tread gingerly because there was debris all around—broken glass, empty tins, old squelchy cardboard boxes, wrappers, packing—all had been strewn without any regard for tidiness or order. Glass crunched underfoot as they walked near one of the shops which had been opened some considerable time ago—with a brick. It looked, thought Paul, like a vision of hell without the flames, a desolate, god-forsaken, exhausting, exhausted place, a town with no life, no spontaneity, no joy and no purpose. And no peace and no beauty either.

Ducking his head Vince bent under one of the low eaves on the cottages and knocked on the door. It opened. Inside, the sun was just starting to fill the room, and sitting right in the middle of the sunlit patch was a wizened old man—or at least he seemed to be old until he spoke, and then Susan realised with a shock that he was probably just into his fifties. A thin, grey, gaunt man with grey stubble on his cheeks, a thin face, thin hair and those same eyes, with their mixture of lassitude and anxiety.

'Dave, we've finally made contact with someone else,' said Vince by way of introduction. 'Quite some way away, though. They live in Ampthill. In Bedfordshire.' The eyes flickered from Paul to Susan and back again to Paul... and then back to Susan whose corpulent figure seemed as grotesque as the thinness of the man sitting in the sun. Dave looked her up and down as though she were a turkey, being selected for roasting.

'Dave's the name, Dave Wittering.' The voice was curiously tight, gravel-like and croaking as though at any moment its owner would pause to cough and clear his throat.

'Paul Greatorex. And this is Susan Rogers.'

'Pleased to meet you,' said the tight harsh voice and the lined face looked up at them both with what could actually have been a little less lassitude. 'Come in. Sit down.' The economy of words mirrored the economy of action of the people in the square.

'You've obviously got... food,' said Dave, surveying Susan yet again. In the past Susan had gone through several stages when people had looked at her. When she was young and much thinner she had rather enjoyed it when the boys had looked her up and down. She'd enjoyed being sexually attractive. Then, shortly after she'd married she'd gone through a phase when she couldn't stand men looking at her. She felt reviled, repulsed, exploited, mentally raped. This even included her husband. But now she was fat and gross, and no one looked at her sexily any more, not even her husband who had long ceased to want to anyway—not that she would let him, but now that she was so fat, not that he wanted to. So it was a strange sensation to her to be looked at again in a possessive way; but she had never *ever* been surveyed for what she perceived as her eating potential, and it gave her a most unpleasant feeling.

'Yes, we do have food,' said Paul finally.

'Much?' said Dave who couldn't keep his eyes off Susan.

'Enough.'

'*We* haven't got any,' said Dave.

'Nothing?'

'Nothing,' said Dave. 'We ran out last week. Completely.' He paused to let the words sink in. 'Can you help us?'

'Oh yes,' said Vince enthusiastically. 'They've got a lot—' Dave silenced him with a fierce glare.

'Can you?'

Paul gazed down at him, his piercing grey eyes trying to read what was going on in his mind, trying to fathom out why the Buckingham community had had such a different time to their own. There was still something at the back of his mind that was bothering him. Something that didn't fit in, something that was disturbing him. Perhaps it was just a feeling, he thought, maybe brought on by the sudden strangeness of the situation. He turned his mind back to the task in hand.

'Can you help us?' repeated Dave.

'We might. How many people are there in your community?'

With some effort Dave lifted his right hand. 'About three hundred.'

'What age range?'

'Pretty much evenly spread, I suppose. Not many in the 20 to 35 age group—not men. We've got quite a few women and some children. There aren't many of the young strong workers, if that's what you mean.'

'We heard what had happened to you from Vince and his two friends,' said Susan. 'We've come here to see what the situation is and what we can do to help.' She stopped, realising that Paul was staring at her. 'That is,' she continued, 'if we *can* help. We wanted to see what the situation was at first hand.'

Paul turned his eyes off her and back on to Dave. 'We're considering what we can do to help you,' said Paul, 'and I've been asked by the leaders of our group to give them a report about the state of things here—what you need, whether you've got any food at all, what provisions there are for the future, that sort of thing.'

'There's nothing,' said Dave, the tight reedy voice suddenly strong with emotion and anger. 'Everything we tried to do went wrong. We didn't know what to do, we didn't know where to start. I mean, how could we?'

'You don't have any farmers then?'

'Farmers?' said Dave. 'You're joking. We haven't got any.'

'You just said you'd got three hundred people,' said Susan.

'Yes, but they couldn't do anything to help. We just didn't know where to begin.'

'*Did* you start?' said Paul suddenly, thinking of the shattered glass and the way in which they'd obviously gone through the place pillaging rather than conserving.

Dave looked down at the ground. 'We did try,' he mumbled unconvincingly.

Paul and Susan exchanged glances. 'Well, what have you got?' said Paul. 'Let's run through it. Food?'

'Nothing.'

'Crops planted?'

'No.'

'No stores of anything edible at all?'

'No. We ate the last of the tins last week. We'd got some apples but they've all gone rotten.'

'Grain?'

'That went rotten as well.' Again Paul looked at Susan in a mixture of disbelief and annoyance.

'Petrol?'

'Some—but much good will it do us. You can't eat petrol, or hadn't you noticed?'

'Don't you get shirty with me,' said Paul angrily. 'I'm only asking. Do you want help or not?' Dave looked down at the floor again. 'Any industry?'

'What do you mean, industry?'

'You make things that other people can buy off you or exchange for food.'

'Like what?'

'I don't know. Anything. Metalwork, leatherwork, bricks, thread, needles, clothing materials.' There was a blank look on Dave's face. Paul knew that he was prodding a dead horse. 'So there really is nothing apart from the petrol.'

'That's right.'

'Can we have a look around?'

The anxious haunted eyes suddenly flickered up, glancing quickly at Vince and Jason, and then down at the floor again. 'I suppose so.'

It's like battering your head against a brick wall, thought Paul. 'What I mean is will *you* take us round?'

'Yes.'

'Now?' said Paul.

'If you want.' With a great effort Dave levered himself out of the chair and wrapped his coat around him. The way it hung, Paul thought, he'd obviously once been quite a large man. Slowly and with a stumbling gait he led them out of the door.

They walked the hundred yards up the hill to the cars. Paul and Susan got there first, but had to wait for a full two minutes before Dave caught them up. He wasn't fighting for breath as much as fighting for energy. Kevin and Alan were there surveying the scene, and still no one had come near them.

'No point in wasting petrol,' said Paul. 'Kevin, will you stay here with the Porsche? Sit in it and lock the doors if you want. And don't hesitate to use the gun if you need.'

'What, against this lot?' said Kevin. 'I could take them out with my bare hands.'

'I doubt if you'll need to,' said Paul smoothly, 'but... just in case.'

'OK boss,' said Kevin, not meaning a word of it.

The remainder of the party got into the Peugeot with Alan driving. Dave sat in the front seat. Susan and Vince were in the back and Paul occupied the rearmost seat of all. It wasn't chivalry—he wanted to get a good back view. The movement in his wing mirrors still haunted him.

Under Dave's instructions, Alan did a quick tour of the area. It was exactly as Dave and Vince had described. There was nothing. No animals, no signs of fields being ploughed. All the farms they came to were silent and still. There were no farmyard animals, but at each farm or hamlet there were isolated groups of people with the same dull stare, observing them as they went on their way. Dave guided them on a quick tour of the immediate area around the town. In the back of the car Paul's eyes scanned the retreating horizon but didn't see anything untoward. Yet there was still something in the back of his mind, bothering him.

It was starting to get late when they came back into the centre of Buckingham again. Alan pulled up by the Porsche, which was now the other way round. 'Have you had trouble?' said Paul. Kevin wound the window down.

'No,' he said in a surly voice. 'Should I have?'

'You've moved the car.'

'I borrowed it. Nothing was happening here so I decided to go for a quick spin.' Paul looked daggers at him.

'You needn't worry,' said Kevin, 'drivers don't have to be insured any more.'

'This is my car, and *you* don't drive it,' said Paul.

Kevin took his hands off the wheel. 'I'm not driving it. You can have it back.'

For a minute Alan thought that Paul was going to hit Kevin. Paul pulled the door of the car open, grabbed Kevin by the scruff of his neck, yanked him out of the seat, and pushed him until he fell on his knees in the roadway.

'Now, now, children,' said Susan.

Alan turned to Dave. 'Thanks. We'll be off now. We've got to report back.'

The anxious eyes turned on Alan. 'You haven't by any chance got any... food...?' said the croaky voice.

'A little,' replied Alan thinking of the food they'd packed for the journey and hadn't yet eaten. He could share it with Dave, he thought. And then pulled himself up. *Share it*? he thought. *Alan Rogers, you callous brute. You've got a full meal waiting for you when you get back home and all you can think about is part sharing the food you **have** got with this half-starved creature in front of you.* 'Here you are,' he said, reaching for his parcel of sandwiches. Dave moved like lightening, grabbing the food and jamming bits into his mouth before he'd even had a chance to say thank you: but the anxious eyes said it all, leaving Susan to ponder on the vagaries of human behaviour when two people fight over who should drive a car in the presence of another human being who was just about to starve to death.

*   *   *

They were silent on the journey back. Kevin of course had to ride with Alan—given the chance Paul would probably have set him down just outside Buckingham and told him to hitch-hike back, so they went in the same cars in which they'd come.

Susan was still smarting from being looked up and down like a fatted calf. Kevin was feigning his usual uninvolved insolence. Paul was still bothered, but because he couldn't work out what he was bothered about he couldn't talk about it. He just had a vague but complete sense of total unease. It was, he rationalised, probably related to the awful state in which the survivors in Buckingham were living. Survivors, he thought to himself grimly, that's hardly survival: and there won't be many of them left if we don't do something quickly.

But it was Alan in the Peugeot who was most affected. Afterwards he didn't remember anything about the ride home. He just hung on to the rear-lights of the Porsche, letting Paul do the navigating, tailing him passively like one boat being towed by another. All he could see, endlessly, were the people around the square, emaciated, exhausted, staring at him dully. Sometimes the mind cannot take in the horrors of what the eyes see. He tried first to make sense of it, and then finally the enormity of the horror washed over him as it had washed over Martin a year earlier. The pain and suffering, the waste of life, the waste of resources, the sadness, the desolation, the hopelessness of it all battered into his senses like the waves of a storm breaking against a headland until, when they got back to Ampthill, all he could do was stagger back to his house in Woburn Street, crash out on a bed and fall fast asleep.

Ironically, he didn't even stop to have his supper.

*   *   *

The landscape flashed by in Paul's mind. Dark trees and shapes scudding past, haunted eyes staring at him at every turn, eyes which lined the road at hundred-yard intervals, each person standing straight like a lamp, and with both feet in a bucket of cement. And then he was in the square at Buckingham again and the dust and debris and paper was blowing around, rolling about like tiny footballs which then changed into a hundred versions of Planet earth, each with the continents printed on in black and white, rolling around, bouncing towards him and over the car. And then he was out again on the road back to Ampthill, and these patterns and shapes were bouncing over the car, bouncing, bouncing, bouncing, each threatening to hit the windscreen and knock him off the road. 'What is the world coming to?' he thought, looking at each version of the earth spinning in front of him. We were so nearly like they were. What can we do to save the world? And in front of him the earths turned, bouncing like giant hailstones off the bonnet of the car, the continents clearly showing up black and white, just like the markings on the side of a cow. And then there were cows skating along the road in front of him. They had their feet in buckets of cement too. Skating past the people who were still standing upright, lighting the way, using their lives to light his way. And still the cows skated in front of him...

THE COWS...!

Caked in perspiration, Paul shot upright in his bed. In front of him he could dimly see the outline of the window against the night sky. *The cows!* That was it. He *knew* there was something. The dream had been so vivid that in the blackness he could still see earth-shaped balls with Friesian markings bouncing towards him and it took another ten seconds before they disappeared. *The cow!* That was it. *Why hadn't they eaten the cow?* Now wide awake, and cooling down rapidly because of the sweat, he got up, put on his dressing gown, went to the bowl in the corner of the room, and rinsed his face, shuddering at the cold of the water. Swiftly he dressed and in the dim light of the moon walked out of his thatched cottage on Woburn Street towards the centre of the town, then out on to Church Street to where Chris' cottage lay quiet and white in the gloom. As he passed through the square the clock on the Moot Hall, standing gaunt and slightly eerie high above him, read eighteen minutes past two, as it had done for the past year. He reached Foulislea Cottage and tapped on the door. No answer. He tapped more loudly. Above him there was a sudden noise as the window opened and Chris looked down at him in surprise.

'It's me,' he hissed.

'What do you want at this hour?'

'I want to talk to you.' There was something in his voice that pulled her up short. Quickly she shut the window, pulled on a dressing gown and went downstairs. There was a rattle as the door was unbolted. Paul looked at her in the dim light. 'What on earth's the matter?'

'I couldn't sleep. Can I come in?'

'I've told you...' said Chris with a wink, '...not before we're married,' and then, seeing Paul's face, decided that that might not have been the best thing to say. Paul banged his hands against his upper arms, trying to dispel the raw cold of the winter night.

'I had a nightmare,' began Paul.

'Oh you poor thing,' said Chris. 'Do you want me to come and kiss it better? Tuck you up in bed,' and then she caught the look in his eye. 'I don't blame you. Buckingham must have been awful.'

'No, no, it wasn't that,' said Paul. 'You know how I said that there was something that made me uneasy.'

'Yes.'

'And that I couldn't work it out.'

'Yes.'

'Well, I dreamt about it. And suddenly it all clicked into place.'

'And it was...?'

'It was the cow.'

'The cow?'

'The one I saw in my mirror when I thought we were being observed..... Well, go on Chris. You work it out. You're just as bright as I am.'

She sat down in the chair opposite him, by the long-dead fire, which surprisingly was still exuding warmth from the heat stored in the surrounding bricks. Her eyes peered through the gloom of the room, trying to make out Paul's face.

'I can't work it out. You'll have to tell me.'

'*Why was the cow there?*'

'What do you mean why was the cow—? Oh yes, so we were right. All is not what it seems to be over in Buckingham. Maybe they just missed it.'

'Don't be silly. How do you miss a cow? It wasn't that far out and it was in a field, for goodness' sake. It wasn't as if it was wandering along the road. It was there. A cow. Uneaten, and yet they're all starving.'

'Or maybe they just missed it. How far out were you?'

'Oh, about eight miles out perhaps.'

'Well there you are, one cow lost amid—how many square miles? Area of a circle πr^2, about two hundred square miles.'

'Yes, it is a lot, isn't it?' He paused, absent-mindedly gnawing at his upper lip. 'I suppose you could lose one cow. Just not notice it was there. Eight miles is a long way out, isn't it? Almost the distance from here to Bedford.' He sighed. 'Yes, I suppose you're right. I was probably just upset by what I'd just seen. But I knew there was something that didn't fit.' He shivered.

'Are you still cold?'

'No, not physically. I'm still shaken from the dream, though. It was so intense... I don't remember having one like that for years. Quite scaring.'

She came across to him and felt his hands. 'You *are* cold you know—absolutely freezing.'

'I'm more upset than cold.'

She sat down on his lap and threw her arms around him. 'Maybe this will warm you up. Perhaps I can kiss it better.'

'And then...?' said Paul, hopefully.

'And then,' she said, 'you can go home.'

Part II

- 11 -

*T*wo days later Mrs Summerfield died. The occupant of Lime View, the house next door to Wisteria House on Woburn Street—and hence Alan and Susan Rogers' next-door neighbour—she had been causing concern to Derek, who had never had to care for an elderly dying person before. If the truth were told, he had coped with it extremely well. She'd been old and frail for a long time, though mentally bright as a button, but when she started to lose weight, Derek surmised—quite correctly, as it turned out—that she had cancer. It hadn't taken that much expertise to notice the emaciated look on her face, her jaundiced complexion, and the gradually increasing size of her liver. To be honest, Derek had thought that she would die many weeks earlier and had been surprised by the tenacity with which she'd clung to life. Perhaps that's why she'd managed to get to the grand old age of eighty-three, he thought.

He'd called in to see her every day, watching as she quietly went downhill. Quite appropriately he'd treated her pain with morphine, but soon noticed that the discomfort in her arms and chest—which, again correctly, he took to be bone secondaries—seemed to be resistant to morphine however high a dose he used. Having consulted the books he found to his surprise that pain relief isn't concerned so much with the intensity of pain as with its type. Pain from bone secondaries can sometimes be better alleviated with—of all things—aspirin, and to his delight he found that with a regular dose of this her discomfort vanished, leaving her needing only a minimal dose of morphine by comparison with what she had previously been having.

Gradually, however, she grew weaker, and Derek watched helplessly as her life gradually started to slide away. For the first time he experienced that exhausting feeling that all doctors have when confronted with a dying patient—that if only medical science knew more they could make the patient better, and that there *must* be a way to cure cancer, if only someone could establish what it was.

As day by day she became weaker, Dorothy Summerfield valued Derek's visits greatly, though it has to be said that Derek didn't think he was achieving much: he just felt frustrated, unable to provide anything that she really wanted or needed, beyond pain relief. Mrs Summerfield, on the other hand, was greatly comforted by his presence and the touch of his hand on her arm. Chris had been right those many months ago when she'd first led the delegation to Derek to ask him to become their doctor: he did have a good bedside manner, a reassuring, comfortable way of talking with people in a way that lifted their spirits, all the while disguising the inner pain that he felt at the hopelessness of the situation. Yet again Derek took on board the pain and anguish of someone else, whilst outwardly remaining calm and unruffled.

Dorothy Summerfield was his first terminal case. Over the last weeks of December—over Christmas, just to make it worse—he'd watched her slide slowly and imperceptibly into her final decline. By stages he watched, waited, sympathised, empathised and gradually became totally frustrated and angry with the sadness of it all. Now, in late January, he could only wait and watch as the cancer took its final hold on her and her strength and physical substance ebbed in front of his eyes.

He let none of his feelings out to anyone—not even to Anne, whom he was gradually discovering couldn't quite understand the enormity of the emotions that he was experiencing. Dear Anne, she was so kind and loving and supportive, but she'd never gone through what he was going through and although she said all the right things and nodded in all the right places, he *knew* that she didn't really understand what was hitting him—not in its full intensity, anyway. He couldn't talk to anyone else about it of course, because he now felt constrained by the Hippocratic oath—not that he'd taken it formally, but he certainly couldn't discuss the problem with, say, Paul, as he might have done for any other situation. Swallowing his sadness, daily he visited Mrs Summerfield, bringing light and peace in with him, and each day leaving with some of her pain and sadness—though he would never, *ever* have breathed a word to Mrs Summerfield, for whose gentle and kind life cancer seemed such an inappropriate end.

As ever, he was there when he was needed, on that last Friday in January, with the wind whistling outside and the rain battering on the windows in a frenzy. But what she said that evening made a profound difference to him. Weakly, and with many pauses for breath she had held on to Derek's hand and with long gaps between the phrases and sentences thanked him for everything he'd done.

'I want you to know how grateful I am to you, Derek. I don't know what you think of your abilities, but I certainly think of you as a doctor.' And she meant it, unlike Mrs MacKenzie.

There was a long pause while Derek tried to smile comfortingly back at her.

'It was a shame that you had to leave Dynevor House,' she said slowly. 'When I die'—Derek didn't like the word and felt the squeeze of her hand as she said it—'I'd like you to have this house—for you and your family. It's not fair that you have to share with anyone else. Not fair at all, especially as you've been so... kind...' Her voice trailed away into silence. Derek waited for a moment in case she wanted to say more.

'That's very kind of you. I don't really feel I deserve it.'

'Of course you do, *doctor*,' she said, smiling at her use of the word, 'and I do mean it about the house.' Edna Higginbottom and Janet MacKenzie, sitting by her, looked at Derek and nodded.

'We all agree,' they said. 'We were talking about it before you came. We all said it was quite wrong that you should have been thrown out by Henry, and Dorothy was quite insistent that you should have her house after she'd gone.'

Derek didn't know what to say. Mrs Summerfield could sense his unease. After all, here he was, watching while she died, with the knowledge that he was supposed to move in with his family once his patient had moved out. What would the others think? That he'd hastened her death so that he could provide a better place for himself? Or that he'd used his influence unfairly, suggesting to her that she should leave him her house in this way? She squeezed his hand again softly. 'I really do want you to have the house. I know what you're thinking; that you shouldn't benefit by the death of one of your patients. Well, it isn't really my house to give—is it? I've only got it on loan. Come to think of it my body's not mine either—I've only got *that* on loan.' She smiled—a gentle mischievous smile, her personality undimmed even through the haze of morphine. 'Even Henry'—she paused to cough—'even Henry, although he actually owns Dynevor House, has only got that on loan... Until he dies, if you see what I mean.'

Derek smiled again, wondering, lost for words. Then he said the only thing that he could say. 'Thank you.'

'Don't mention it. Or rather, do mention it. I'm glad that you and Anne and the children are going to have it, so enjoy it. Look, I'm just a temporary inhabitant of it. It's been here for generations and there must have been many different families who've lived here—maybe ten or twenty of them. We've only got it on loan after all, so enjoy it. You deserve it.' She smiled up at him, squeezed his hand again, and then sank back on the pillow, exhausted with the effort of her little speech.

That evening, with Derek in attendance, she died.

Unlike the past where a body could lie in a refrigerated compartment for days or even weeks before burial or cremation, there were no longer the same facilities, and for decency and to avoid the odours that so quickly erupt from a recently deceased body Martin conducted the funeral service as soon as a grave could be dug.

Two days after her death Martin conducted the funeral, on a crisp, bright February morning, a day when the air sparkled and the breath of the mourners formed clouds. They buried her by the side of Alison and Jane: and again Derek was left to think about the loss of his daughter, and his inability to save Jane; and once again another piece of his life was eroded from him. Although, in the standard words of the funeral service, Martin began with 'I am the resurrection and the life, saith the Lord,' nevertheless Derek didn't believe it, couldn't take it in, and felt an increasingly overwhelming sense of hopelessness and despair at the waste of it all, the transience of life, the sadness and the pain of it all, when a good, kind, alert lady like Dorothy Summerfield had to die, and die slowly and painfully at that.

*   *   *

Mrs Summerfield had undoubtedly had all her wits about her, even at the very end. She *knew* that Derek wouldn't want to take up her offer—so she'd briefed Edna and Janet appropriately. They waited a week, then made a point of telling Chris of Dorothy's dying wish. Shortly afterwards, Chris approached Derek and asked when he was moving in.

Derek, rather embarrassed, went red. 'I feel very uneasy about it,' he confided to her. 'I'd hate anyone to think I'd... bumped her off, if you see what I mean.'

'Nonsense,' said Chris firmly, looking him straight in the eye. 'No one feels that at all. If you must know, most people are still very embarrassed that you've had to share with Martin. They think you deserve better than that.'

'Martin's a very nice chap,' replied Derek immediately. 'I like him immensely.'

'Oh, no, I didn't mean that,' said Chris, laughing at the misunderstanding. 'I meant the fact that you've had to *share*. They think... We think... that you've done sterling work for the community and quite frankly, at the very least you deserve your own house to yourself...'

'...*even if you're in it a lot less than other people,*' they both chorused together, thinking of the night visits. Derek smiled—sadly, an increasingly rare event, thought Chris, watching him. The last year had certainly taken its toll.

'So when are you moving in?' she continued, and the slightly sheepish look returned.

'I suppose in the next week or so. I've not really thought about it.'

'Well, you must,' said Chris. 'We all want you to and no one will say anything against you.'

'That's very kind of you,' said Derek, not really quite believing it.

*   *   *

The Old Rectory was still the only building with electricity: the first windmill was only tiny and wouldn't supply much power, but Alan was working hard on erecting a much bigger version, which he hoped would be ready soon. It was strange for Derek and his family to move yet again from a world with electricity to one without it. Even more strangely, he himself hadn't really comprehended the fact until they were halfway through the move, when the strictures of not being able to read by a decent light came back to him again. On the other hand, it wouldn't have stopped him moving. Fond though he was of Martin, and fond though Martin was of the whole family, friendship isn't quite the same when two families have to share a single dwelling, and it was nice to take up residence once again in the middle of the town, rather than at its edge.

Like Wisteria House next door, Lime View had been built on two levels, dug into the side of a hill. The front door led out to Woburn Street, but upstairs the landing led directly out to the back garden, at the same level. It was a friendly house, with a strangely warm atmosphere to it—as though its walls had somehow been used to the resonance of laughter, humour, kindness and goodness over the centuries, had stored it and had radiated it back to later inhabitants, much as bricks store the heat of the sun on a hot day and radiate it out again in the evening.

As soon as the front door opened Sarah and David ran upstairs each to make claim to his or her own bedroom. As Derek and the ever-present Peter pulled the last of their belongings off the horse and cart that Trevor had kindly made available to them, Anne plopped down in one of the chairs in the lounge, and looked round. The sun was illuminating the room full on, its yellow mid-day rays picking out the wisps of dust in the air. 'Do you know, Derek, I think we'll be really happy here,' she said.

Later on Anne would remember that day, and her words, and wince.

*　　　　　*　　　　　*

Once again Martin was alone in the Old Rectory but unlike previous times, he was alone in the positive sense, not a negative one. Even though he had now come to terms with the problems of the past year, Martin was still essentially a solitary creature. In previous ages he might have earned a living as a hermit (which paid employment was actually available in a few stately homes a couple of centuries earlier). There was something about the rush and bustle of ordinary life that in an odd way almost repelled him and he found the silence of solitude strangely clean and comforting—like the stillness of a still-life painting, or the economy of style of the minimalist artists. Now that he had come to terms with the universe and no longer thought of it as a threat he welcomed the space in which to be solitary, the freedom it gave him to think and contemplate, and for him the solitude became rich and warm. Now he could think deep thoughts, thoughts that took many minutes to get into, without interruption. It gave him time to meditate on the universe, and why it was like it was, and who had made it. It allowed him the opportunity to delve into the meaning of that curious word 'life' and the purpose of existence. Now, when he stood outside his front door he could gaze up at the heavens in awe and wonder instead of in fear, as he had in the past. He was still amazed by the vastness of it all, but the difference now was that he no longer felt alone in it nor threatened by it.

On the other hand he no longer had the need to cut himself off from his fellow man. Rather, his ability to be quiet and enjoy his solitude gave him a greater and deeper wish to get to know others, to respond to their needs, and to reach out to them.

That was on the good days. Unfortunately the good days didn't always come and then it was back to the old routine of standing outside the front door looking at the stars in screaming agony, feeling totally lost and alone, with a desperate need for human company and yet paradoxically at the same time a desperate need *not* to be in company because it hurt too much. At times like this there was within him an inner, aching loneliness that screamed out that he was unlovable and that that was why he was on his own.

By and large the good days outnumbered the bad: but the bad days—although not as bad as they had been in the past—were still awful by comparison with the good days: so in some ways he felt his lonely periods that much more, simply because of the contrast.

The day on which the Jones family left was a good day—not, it must be said *because* they were leaving: it was more that the unfathomable balance of pros and cons that fluttered round in his subconscious came down more on the side of the pros on that occasion. In many ways he was extremely sorry to see them go; he and Derek had had many deep conversations in the past and enjoyed mulling over philosophical problems together. But Derek didn't always have the time to stop and chat, nor, increasingly, did he have the energy —his work was seeing to that.

Being a fatherly type of person, Martin also missed the exuberant fun of the teenage David, and the simple, trusting approach of Sarah. And he missed Anne, not for any improper reason but simply because she was a kindred spirit. Apart from the obvious similarities of a love of music, they had many attributes in common—a common way of looking at the world, some similar experiences, together with a certain brittle vulnerability and sensitivity. And though Martin would not have recognised, let alone agreed with, the proposition, there was also a maternal aspect of Anne to which he responded. Anne seemed secure, somehow—a great attribute in an insecure world.

So it was to his surprise, that first evening after the Jones family had departed to Lime View, that Martin found himself wistfully remembering and missing Anne more than any of the others—an entirely innocent, and non-sexually charged memory. It wouldn't have mattered what sex Anne had been—apart from the maternal aspect. There was not a hint, not a whiff, of underhandedness in his attraction for her: they could, quite genuinely, have been brother and sister—but he missed her, and missed her abundantly.

Perhaps the one thing more than anything else for which Martin missed Anne was the music. To Martin, music was the next best thing after God. Music spoke to him in a way that languages could not: in an untranslatable, unsummarisable fashion, a language which couldn't be described in words, yet gave a totally vivid description of reality. Music spoke to both of them as nothing else did, and more than anything else Martin missed the ability to share with Anne the music that he discovered from time to time.

Right at the beginning, of course, it had been piano music, those items he had played so sensitively and in some cases so devastatingly; but with the advent of electricity his musical interests could enlarge according to which CDs he could lay his hands on. Now he could explore all the beauties of symphonic works, string quartets, operas, jazz, musicals. When he had the time, he systematically searched the unused houses in Ampthill for CDs and tapes, in this way coming upon many a treasure that he might never have stumbled on in the past. Anne had done the same—and because their tastes were so different and yet complemented one another, they would both bring their discoveries to each other to share and enjoy.

In this way they shared some amazing musical finds: Martin was able to show Anne the beauties of some of the more abstruse works that, from their names, simply sounded boring—some of Beethoven's sonatas that were simply called by their opus numbers: works by Poulenc, Richard Strauss, and Benjamin Britten, chamber music by Brahms, symphonies by Bruckner, and Bax, works by Delius, Debussy and Ravel. In turn Anne introduced Martin to vibrant music from the operettas and musicals such as *A Chorus Line* and *Man of La Mancha*, from the soundtracks of Fred Astaire's films; Glenn Miller, scores by Bernstein and Lloyd Webber; film music by John Williams: and they both learned to take the best of each genre and enjoy it for what it was, in its context, without pretensions, taking in the emotion and the logic of the music in the way the composer had wanted and listening to it in the way the composer had originally intended.

And so it was that night, alone again in the Old Rectory, with a single candle on the table beside him (the windmill could give him music or light, but not both together at the same time), that Martin put on a CD of Bernstein's *Candide* and sat back, mellowly, to enjoy it.

*   *   *

It was a sombre council meeting in the courtroom. The sky was grey with the leftovers of the winter afternoon, cold and bleak, the sparseness of winter all around. The atmosphere inside was cold

and bleak too. Paul, Susan and Alan all presented their reports.
Kevin was there too—but only after production of his six pound fee.
He was doing well out of this, he thought to himself. The others on
the council—if they knew about the fee—didn't care. Their attention was riveted on the three speakers who described in graphic
detail the horrors that were occurring just forty miles away. Most
pertinent of all was their description of the apathy of the inhabitants: how most hadn't the energy even to get up to investigate the
two cars that had arrived in the square.

'But why?' asked Mary. 'Why wouldn't they run forward?
Surely they knew that you might be able to provide food or help. It
sounds totally bizarre.'

'It sounds bizarre to me as well,' said Chris. 'Are you sure they
weren't putting it on?'

'Nobody could put that on,' said Susan. 'I don't believe anyone
could make themselves look that ill or that thin.'

'It looked perfectly genuine to me, too,' said Paul.

'I think you must be right,' said Derek. 'I read somewhere about
this happening in the concentration camps: even at the point when
they were rescued, most of the inmates were so weak they couldn't
show interest in anything—especially the children. They didn't
even have the energy to play. And that's what convinces me that it's
totally genuine. I don't think they could possibly be making it up.'

'Well, *you* knew about the lethargy,' said Neil. 'Why shouldn't
they, and fake it?'

'I only know it because I read about it in a textbook on nutrition,'
replied Derek. 'It would need a pretty elaborate deception to go to
those lengths.'

'You're right, Derek,' said Paul. 'I must say I didn't know previously what you've just said. Anyone else here know?' He looked
round the table. No one moved or spoke.

'All right,' said Chris, 'what are we going to do about it?' The
sixty-four-thousand-dollar question or, to put it better, the 'work for
six months of the year, and then give it all away' question. Because
that's what they were being faced with.

'I don't see that we've got any option,' said the Major. 'We'll just have to feed them.' There was a murmur of assent, from everyone except Paul.

'Are we all agreed?' asked Chris. 'Martin, Susan, Alan, Mary, Derek?' She turned to Paul and Paul shook his head. From the opposite side of the table Mary let out a long hissing noise followed by a rather rude word, *sotto voce*, that up until then even she didn't know she was capable of uttering.

'Paul, you can't be serious?' said Chris.

Paul looked at her. There was a silence as he gathered his thoughts.

'I want you to listen to me, all of you. I want you to listen very carefully and not prejudge what I'm going to say because once you understand the truth about the situation I think you will see things in a different light.

'Firstly, can I remind you that if *we* don't succeed then nobody is going to succeed. If *they* succeed in bringing *us* down then we all starve. I think it is probably better that half of us survive than that none of us do.'

Again the same in-drawn hiss from the other side of the table.

'If we give them the food that they want we will feed them for the moment. They will survive. They may even increase in numbers and at the end of another year we'll have to feed them the same amount, or more, again.

'However, last October Neil told us that we may have difficulty this year in growing enough food for ourselves, so in the years to come we may not be in a position to feed ourselves properly, never mind anyone else. How are we going to cope with that? How are we going to cope if we share our food, get them through the first year, and then have to say no, we can't give them any more? What are we going to say to our own people who have loyally worked hard throughout the year if we then give their food away, and at the end of the year they haven't got enough?'

Mary was getting angry. Chris motioned to her to keep quiet.

'Understand this,' said Paul, looking especially at Mary, 'I'm only asking this rhetorically. I haven't told you what I believe yet.

'Let me put another scenario to you. We can *sell* them our grain.'

'What on earth can they buy it with?' Alan expostulated. 'Use your head, Paul.'

'Petrol?' said Paul looking at him. 'They've got a little bit left and they can't use it. We can. We can sell them grain for the petrol.'

'A bit mercenary, isn't it?' said Susan.

'At least our people will feel they've got something in return for their hard work: we could do with the petrol; and the Buckinghamshire lot will be fed.'

'But that's not the only way,' interjected Martin. 'How about us teaching them to look after themselves?'

'I was coming to that. We can show them what to do. We can go in there and organise them, because obviously they can't do it themselves at the moment. They need leading. Once they've got some food inside them they can probably work, as long as they know what to do.'

'But it's going to be a bit of an uphill struggle,' said Neil. 'They'll need someone on the spot most of the time. Can we afford to lose our key people for that length of time?'

'Again, maybe they can pay us for our expertise,' said Paul. 'They can start off by paying us in petrol: and when the crops come in they can give us a proportion of what they have grown—as a sort of tax, if you like.'

'Well, I vote we just give them what they need,' said Mary. 'We can afford it.'

'Can we?' said Paul, his grey eyes staring at her. 'I hope you're right. What if you're wrong? Who's going to break the news to our people if there's not enough food to go round. What are we going to say to Sarah? "You can't eat because your daddy gave away your food"? It's all very well for now. We've got food to spare—but what's going to happen next year, the year after that, and the year after that?'

'I think you're too pessimistic,' said Martin, entering the fray at last. 'If we teach them how to look after themselves they'll soon become self-sufficient. After all, the countryside round Buckingham is very fertile, isn't it?'

'That's true,' replied Paul, 'but so far they haven't managed to use it very well, have they?'

'Isn't that because they haven't had the right sort of guidance?'

'I don't know, perhaps it is.'

'If that's the case then all they need to enable them to get back on their feet is a bit of knowledge, some food to tide them over the immediate next few months and soon they'll be self-sufficient. *We* won't have a problem, *they* won't have a problem—and if in future years we have a bad harvest maybe they won't have quite so bad a harvest and will be able to supply us when in turn we're in need. Agreed?' There was a series of nods. Paul half-nodded.

'You look unsure. Why?'

Paul wasn't sure. He couldn't quite say why. Part of it was selfish—not wanting to give away the hard-won food: nor did he like the fact that his careful planning for the future for everyone at Ampthill had been undermined by the behaviour of other people, so that the Ampthill community would no longer be able to enjoy the fruits of his particular labours.

Even taking this into account, he was still uneasy. The only thing he could put his finger on was the cow. And the cow was worrying him immensely. No matter what Chris had said logically to comfort him, there was still a big question mark over that cow. As if a starving group of people would allow something as large as a cow to escape their attentions. Beef on the hoof—no, of course they couldn't have missed it.

Unless... Unless...

'What do *you* think, Kevin?' Paul asked finally. Kevin jerked into action: his mind had only been half on the matter in hand. He'd been thinking of other things, other plans.

'About what?' he said, eyeing Paul.

'Do you think everything's above board over there?'

Kevin sniffed. 'They're scared of something.'

'What?'

'Dunno.'

'Come on, you must have some ideas.'

'*I dunno.* I just told you that. I dunno *why* they're scared. I know they *are* scared. I just dunno *why* they're scared, that's all. What do you take me for—a fortune teller? How should I know what they're scared about?'

'But they are scared?'

'Yer.'

Paul's mind began to race, scouring his memory banks for significant pointers.

And all he could come up with was the cow. No one would be afraid of a cow. But Kevin was right, they had looked scared. And from the time that Kevin had confirmed what Paul and Chris had suspected when they first met the three refugees, Paul had been even more troubled. He let out a long sigh through his nose.

'You look worried,' said Alan.

Paul chewed on his lower lip. 'I'm very uneasy. There's something about this that doesn't fit, and I don't know what it is. I don't think we've got enough information to find out, either. And I suppose all I would say is that if we *are* going to help them, then we've got to go very carefully indeed.'

'I think you're making a mountain out of a molehill,' said the Major gruffly. He'd never trusted Paul, and trusted Kevin even less. He also didn't care much for emotional judgements, which was mainly what Paul and Kevin seemed to be going on. 'You'd be scared if you didn't have enough food. You'd look hunted if you hadn't got enough to eat.'

'Would you?' said Paul. 'Scared, yes. Hunted? I'm not so sure.'

'What do you think they're scared of?' Derek asked Kevin.

'I've just told you, haven't I? I dunno.'

'No, I didn't mean it like that,' said Derek. 'Are they scared of some*thing* or some*one*?'

Kevin merely shrugged. 'Well, I'd be scared if I didn't have any food. It's what I felt like when everyone in London started dying.'

'Has anyone got anything else to offer?' asked Chris, looking round the table. 'No? Well, in the absence of any other concrete ideas, are we agreed that we'll give them food and try to teach them how to look after themselves? Right, then let's get on with it.'

- *12* -

*T*o his great delight Martin acquired a new recruit to his next mid-week Bible study group—Anne. Unlike her husband she'd always had a residuum of belief and as with many in the community the imminence of death and the ever-present spectre of disaster had concentrated her mind wonderfully. Like being hanged on the mor-row, living a hand-to-mouth existence with no safety net, far from pushing philosophical and religious thoughts into the background, actually makes them more real. Before the plague it had been easy to dismiss thoughts of death as being something that could be faced twenty, thirty or forty years hence: 'live now, pay later' was the order of the day. But the collapse of society and the knife-edge nature of their existence—coupled with the normally preventable deaths of her daughter Alison and her friend Jane—had served to bring back to Anne's full consciousness the age old questions—'Why am I here?' 'What happens afterwards?' and 'What am I sup-posed to do about it?' Like many of the others, Anne had offered up occasional prayers for the harvest, just when everything seemed to be going wrong: crisis theology. And although many had used prayer as a religious talisman, as a port of last resort, or as some-thing to do when all else had failed, Anne had had reawakened in her an inexplicable sense of the numinous, a feeling—for it was probably no more than that—that there was someone else Out There and that someone Out There might actually have a watching brief over them, even if that watching brief didn't seem to accommodate saving the lives of Alison and Jane. Like so many women Anne had a religious nature to her, and found it easier to slip back into the pat-terns she had been taught early in her life, starting with her routine confirmation at the age of fourteen that had at the time meant so little to her.

In short, Anne had a simple—and moderately simplistic—belief in the presence of a loving God and, not being the sort to want to live a lie, began to be increasingly aware that perhaps she ought to do something about this belief, and that perhaps her beliefs ought to result in different actions in her life.

In any case, she was bored living in Lime View on her own, bereft of adult company when Derek was out helping others, as so often he was, and as she genuinely enjoyed the company of the others in the midweek group, it seemed quite natural for her to begin attending the meetings at the Old Rectory.

Once she had taken the plunge and begun to attend regularly, Martin and the rest of the group enjoyed sharing their faith with her, gradually leading her into deeper theological territory. Anne was a ready learner with an uncomplicated view of Christianity. As she started to study the Bible again, reading the stories and digging into the Epistles, the others watched in delight as her understanding of her faith grew in front of their eyes. It wasn't just Martin who assisted her: frequently the other members of the group helped by explaining those things she found she didn't understand. In turn, this helped the Major, because his view of Christianity had been quite severely blinkered by the straight-jacket of his previously more formal religious observances, and the freedom with which the gospel was expounded by the others allowed *him* to understand while she *was* being taught.

Anne didn't convert as much as deepen. There wasn't a point at which she had a big revelation, visions, dreams, or a conversion experience. Looking back she couldn't put her finger on the moment when she decided she was going to follow Jesus, but she knew now that this was what she intended, whereas in the past she hadn't been as aware of it.

Despite never having had a conversion experience to identify the exact beginnings of her Christian life she certainly had some very identifiable deepening experiences while in the tiny group that met midweek. The first came when they were studying the Tabernacle, largely at the request of the Major, who had been intrigued by something Mrs Higginbottom had said. Quite nonchalantly she'd referred to the Tabernacle in the desert during the period just after the Exodus from Egypt, and in that instant the Major realised that he hadn't even the vaguest idea of what she was talking about—

and said so. (And he a churchman too!)

'You don't know what the Tabernacle was?' said Mrs Higgin-bottom, folding her hands across her rather portly stomach. 'Well, I *am* surprised,' and looked across at her husband Fred.

'Now, Edna, don't be unfair,' said Fred. 'If the Major hasn't had the opportunity to learn about it, it's not up to us to criticise. After all he probably knows a lot about things that we don't know about.'

'Well, I don't know about that,' said the Major, sounding as though he was simply trying to be humble, but actually agreeing with Fred. 'But do tell me.'

And so Edna did. Over the next two hours—which afterwards felt as though it had only lasted ten minutes—Edna described the Tabernacle in detail, and the Major and Anne listened agog. To the Major it was merely an interesting interlude, one that he found quite enlightening, but no more. To Anne it was a revelation of the highest order—as though she had suddenly found a secret passage in a house she'd known all her life, a passage that led into a garden of the sort of elegance and beauty that she had never dreamed could exist.

Edna, of course, loved talking about the subject, but not in a self-ish way—she loved talking about it because she herself found it fascinating. And in the same way that those who love their subject inspire others simply through their own joy when discussing it, so Edna enthused everyone in the room.

At first Anne had thought it was going to be boring: when she realised what the subject was going to be, she started to wish fervently that she had chosen to do something completely different that evening—something really interesting, like the ironing. After all, what was the Tabernacle? Just a tent with a few furnishings, carried around by the Children of Israel as they wandered for forty years in the Sinai Desert. The Tabernacle was simply a portable church. 'Really,' thought Anne, thinking of the ironing. 'How interesting' (the ironing, not the Tabernacle).

'You see,' continued Edna, now unstoppable, 'the Tabernacle was surrounded by a rectangular fence-like screen made of cloth, with a single entrance at the front. In the middle of this area was a tent—the Tabernacle itself. In front of this tent was an altar for sacrifices.

'Inside, the tent was divided into two areas by an opaque screen called the veil, which was more like tapestry than gossamer. On the near side of the tent—the Holy Place, where the priests could go— was an altar for incense; and on the other side of the veil, hidden from view, was the Holy of Holies, the place where God resided. Inside the Holy of Holies was the Ark of the Covenant—the receptacle, inlaid with gold, containing the actual stone tablets on which Moses had written the Ten Commandments.'

I could have been doing the ironing, thought Anne as Edna droned on in her flat, unmodulating voice. But something made her continue to listen. It was as if, unknowing, she was walking down a boring old passage in her old house and had just got to the place where the secret door lay hidden.

'But the really interesting thing,' said Edna, her eyes lighting up, 'isn't what it was built of, but what it all means.'

'Means?' said Anne, 'what do you mean "what it means"? How can a tent "mean" anything?'

'Ah well,' said Edna, looking at her husband, 'this is the really interesting bit. The whole thing is a Type of Christ.'

'A what?' said the Major.

'A Type. Oh, I see, you don't understand. It's a sort of picture, a parable, a model, something like that. A reflection.'

'Oh, I see,' said the Major, definitely not seeing. But Anne saw— or at least started to see.

'So how is the Tabernacle a Type of Jesus?' she said, leaning forward in her chair, suddenly interested. Edna looked at her husband again, wondering if she'd said too much or overstepped the mark. He nodded to her to go on.

'When the Tabernacle was set up in the desert, God came and inhabited it. Do you remember reading the story from your schooldays about "the fire by night and the pillar of cloud by day"...?'

'Oh yes,' said Anne. 'Wasn't that supposed to be God leading the Israelites and when the pillar or cloud stopped they set up camp there?'

'That's right,' said Edna. 'There's a special name for it—the Shekinah Glory of God. Well, when they were in the desert and the Tabernacle was set up, the Shekinah presence of God inhabited the innermost recess of the Tabernacle, the Holy of Holies.'

'You mean where they all came to worship?'

'Oh no,' said Edna. 'Ordinary people couldn't get near. They weren't allowed to go anywhere near the presence of God. It was too holy—too dangerous.'

'Strange,' thought Anne. 'I thought God was supposed to be very approachable.'

'I know what just you're thinking,' said Edna. 'You're thinking that God is supposed to be very loving, warm and approachable.'

'Something like that.'

'Ah, well, you've got a bit of rethinking to do—don't forget, this was long before Jesus. At that time only one man—the high priest—was allowed to go into the Holy of Holies, to the Shekinah presence and even *he* was only allowed in on one day of the year, the Day of Atonement: and even then he could only meet with God if first he brought the blood of a sacrificed animal, and poured it out on top of the Ark of the Covenant that contained the Ten Commandments.'

'It was so terrifying going into God's holy presence,' said Fred, 'that the high priest even had bells on the hem of his robe so that the priests on the other side of the veil could hear he was still alive. And he could only remain in the presence of God because there had been a sacrifice and the blood of the sacrifice had been used to cover up the law.'

'I still don't understand,' said Anne. 'I thought God was supposed to be kind and loving and forgiving.'

'Oh, he is that,' said Edna. 'But he's also perfect and pure and holy and terrifying—he can't stand wrong-doing, and the only way that those who have done wrong can be in his presence is if their wrong-doing has been paid for—through the sacrifice.'

And the door into the secret passageway swung open.

'I think you've got to go back in a sort of timewarp,' said Martin, sensing Anne's puzzlement. 'You've got to imagine what life was like before Jesus came.'

'But isn't it the same God?' said the Major, echoing just the
thoughts that Anne was about to utter.

'Oh yes,' said Martin, 'and he hasn't changed.'

'Well, why the difference?' said Anne.

'The difference,' said Martin, 'is that in the meantime Jesus
came. Do you remember that Edna said there was only one way in
through the entrance to the Tabernacle area? Only the Children of
Israel were allowed in: the hangings that made up the doors were of
gold, blue and scarlet: gold for royalty, blue for heaven, scarlet for
sacrifice. Once inside the courtyard an Israelite who wasn't a priest
could only offer an animal in sacrifice on the outer altar. He wasn't
allowed to go any nearer. Only the priests could go into the outer
part of the Tabernacle—the Holy Place—as near as they were
allowed to get to the presence of God. But only the high priest could
go in to the real presence of God, and only then if he took the blood
of the sacrificed animal.

'The veil outside the Holy of Holies was there to keep sinful men
away from holy God, and the veil had pictures of the seraphim and
cherubim on it. Do you remember the creatures that God put outside the Garden of Eden after Adam and Eve had sinned, to keep
them out, to keep them away from a holy and perfect God?'

Something kept coming up into Anne's mind, something from
her past, something odd, a set of words, a phrase. She couldn't identify it and it troubled her. There was something she knew, something
that bothered her. Something that made the back of her hair stand
on end.

And then she remembered. 'The veil of the temple was torn in
two...' Where did that come from? And then she knew. *Just after the
crucifixion.* And suddenly she was through the passage and into the
secret garden beyond, and in that instant understood that the
Tabernacle itself was a parable about Jesus. There was only one
way into the presence of God and the doorway was gold, blue and
scarlet—royalty, heaven and sacrifice—a symbol of Jesus. And the
only way that men could approach God was through the blood of a
sacrifice; and after that heaven-sent Sacrifice had died outside

Jerusalem on the first ever Good Friday, the veil of the temple was torn in two permanently; and from that moment on God and man could meet once again in harmony over the blood of the permanently offered Saviour.

For Anne it was like watching television in black and white, and suddenly finding there was a button that could turn up colour. Suddenly all those bits of the Bible that she didn't understand and had never managed to fit together came together. In the past, she'd never really understood why Jesus had to be crucified, and had thought of his death on the cross as being little more than just a symbol of the extent to which one should go to express love and pacifism. Now she viewed it in a different manner—as the supreme sacrifice foreshadowed by the Tabernacle, and one which now superseded the Tabernacle, because there was no longer any need for the sacrifice of animals once the real Sacrifice had been made.

The effect on Anne was incredible. It didn't produce any form of emotional release: there were no angels dancing around in front of her eyes, no amazing emotional religious experience, but merely a quiet contentment that everything had at last slotted itself into place, and that the whole core of Christianity stood in front of her complete, whole, and sparkling like a diamond. It was like putting the last piece in the jigsaw puzzle, with its sense of fulfilment, of satisfaction, and its sense of finality: and as with a jigsaw puzzle, which before completion seems to be just a selection of pieces of cardboard of various shapes and sizes, once the final piece was in place she was aware only of the overall picture, and not of the lines in between the pieces that made up the picture.

She didn't say anything but continued listening in rapt attention to the final details. It was an hour past their usual ending time when Edna had finished, but no one noticed. Anne just drank it all in, in amazement.

'Well, thank you very much,' said the Major to Edna. 'That was most interesting. I'd never realised that.'

Anne nodded. It wasn't that she was speechless, it was just that she couldn't find the right words to convey what she had just experienced: superlatives sound silly under such circumstances. And besides, she didn't want to break the spell, the magical feeling of completeness that had just overwhelmed her. Smiling briefly at Martin, she said goodnight to the others, put on her coat and went back to the town.

'You don't think I went on a bit much, do you dear?' said Edna to Fred. 'Anne didn't say much.'

'No, dear,' said her husband. 'Though you did go on a bit. But I wouldn't worry—she could have left if she didn't like it that much.'

*   *   *

'Good morning doctor,' said Janet MacKenzie, coming through the door.

Aaaaaaargghhhh... went the silent scream inside Derek's head.

- 13 -

*T*he campaign to improve the lot of the Buckingham group was getting under way with tolerable speed. Paul had been adamant that the Ampthill community should'nt simply give their hard-earned flour away but should sell it for the only thing the Buckingham community could give them in return—petrol. He struck a hard bargain too, insisting that for each consignment of flour that went west, a tankerful of petrol came East. Soon the Buckingham community had flour and other foodstuffs and to their great delight the Ampthill community acquired a large amount of fuel that otherwise they would never have possessed. Whether it was an equitable bargain or not didn't cross Paul's mind. A deal was a deal, and that was that. Certainly Martin had his doubts as to the price that the Buckingham set were paying: surely they too would have need of fuel in the future? But he had to acquiesce in the general feeling within the council that as the Buckingham set could pay for the food they were using, then they should.

As the weeks passed the Buckingham dwellers seemed to gain in weight—but somehow they never seemed to lose that hunted look. And although they were given more than enough food to keep body and soul together, for some reason none of them seemed to get fat on it.

Within a few days of the original foray by Paul, Alan, Susan and Kevin the first lorry-load of flour had gone across, together with equipment to help make the flour into bread. Peter Abrahams volunteered to be in charge of the operation, and an excellent job he did of it. To his horror, he found that there was hardly anywhere to bake bread. It had somehow not occurred to the members of the Buckingham set that they needed to seek out the old-style houses and use the old-style implements—the ones that had first been used long before the days of gas, to say nothing of electricity. For some reason the Buckingham residents just couldn't seem to work out what to do. They would work long and hard, but behaved like a chicken with its head chopped off—totally clueless as to how they should use their efforts, husband their resources and organise their abilities. In short, they seemed entirely incapable of getting themselves out of the twentieth-century way of life and back into the eighteenth—at least, as far as common domestic activities were concerned. This type of organisation had seemed so obvious to the Ampthill community, and by now was almost second nature—but the Buckingham group seemed to need leading over everything, as if the whole society needed kick-starting.

One of the first things Peter did was to scavenge the antique shops for old implements: using these they soon learned to cook all types of food on open fires and on ranges. They even built items especially for the purpose, such as beehive ovens.

Thinking about it, Peter began to recognise to what extent the Ampthill survivors had depended upon Paul's analytical and organisational abilities. It was only when he saw how disastrously the Buckingham set had functioned that Peter understood just what strength of leadership Paul had given them. He'd taught them, in essence, that they *could* make a go of it: that there *was* a way out, and that they *would* be able to find a solution to the various problems that faced them. Peter had to teach the Buckingham set how to think in this way and, like so many inventions which are obvious afterwards, the methods Peter taught them seemed so obvious to the Buckingham dwellers—but only once they'd been shown.

There were many such ideas—such as the installation of a fireplace crane to hold a kettle in the fire, keeping it constantly on the boil yet instantly manoeuvrable; or the use of a skillet—a pan with three legs—that could be put in amongst the ash and embers of a fire to cook without overbalancing. The trick that always surprised everyone was the way to bake bread. Following the old tradition, they built a cone of brick, inside which they lit a fire: when the fire had gone out, the still glowing ashes were raked out and the dough put in, to be heated solely by the warmth emanating from the bricks. *And it worked!* It proved an excellent way to bake bread—the exact reverse of what Peter would have expected, because he'd always thought of an oven as something that one heated from the outside, constantly. Yet there were also ways of making ovens like that: a metal plate with a cupola of iron over the top, suspended over a fire, formed an excellent closed space in which to cook bread, bake scones or even roast meat. Peter took great delight in showing the Buckingham set all the tricks the Ampthill group had learned over the past year, and watched with delight as one by one they changed from being entirely dependent on food brought in from outside to being self-sufficient.

But they still didn't lose that hunted look. Not at all.

*   *   *

Whatever Susan might have thought about his leatherwork, under Derek's tutelage Alan was gradually developing into a first-class engineer. Although really a teacher—having graduated in chemistry—like anyone with basic scientific knowledge, he could focus his training on to any of the many branches of science or technology with appropriate success and so had found it easy to learn the intricacies of the strengths of materials, ways of joining metal, and electrical engineering. With Derek he had been instrumental in helping to assemble the first windmill which was only big enough to supply enough power for a single house. But now Alan had got the big windmill up and working, and it was time to connect up the rest of Ampthill. He soon had a makeshift power-line rigged up in the trees down Holly Walk, running towards the centre of the town.

First they had wondered how they were going to connect the cables up, and whether simply to have overhead wires going from house to house, but it seemed such a complicated way to do things, and as Derek said, what happens when there's a storm? Was it all going to be waterproof and windproof?

Alan scratched his head, his thin bony fingers contrasting with his shock of curly grey hair. 'It's so complicated,' he said. 'There *must* be a much better way. At this rate I'm going to use miles of cable—quite literally. What happens when we get it into the inside of the houses? What do we do then? We've got to use even more cable.'

'It's a pity we can't use the existing electrical system,' said Derek, tightening up a bolt.

'Why can't we?' said Alan, his face lighting up. Derek stopped tightening and winced. He put the spanner down.

'Do you know, Alan, when I'm doing medicine I think I'm out of my depth and it's great to come back to engineering: and I was just thinking "at least this is something that I know how to do". And then I find that I'm just as inept at engineering as I seem to be at medicine.'

Alan stared at him. 'What brought that on?'

'Well, it's yet another thing that's been staring me in the face—like this windmill here.' They both looked up to where the vanes were circling against the bright blue of the sky. 'Here am I, an engineer and I'd forgotten about the possibility of using windmills to generate power. Here am I, an engineer, and I'd forgotten that we've already got a nice infrastructure of electrical wires all laid in, ready to be used. All we've got to do is connect the leads from our windmill to the mains system and we're there.'

'Where's the transformer?'

'In the windmill.'

'No, I don't mean that one. Where's the Electricity Board's transformer—the one that steps down the power from the National

Grid into the 240-volt variety.'

'Why?'

'Well, won't we need to connect our wires at that point so it feeds the whole of the town?'

Derek grinned. 'It's not like water, you know.'

'Eh?'

'It doesn't flow downhill.'

'I know that.'

'But don't you see? All you have to do is tap into the electrical system *at any point* and you'll supply the whole of the local system with energy.'

Alan's eyes lit up. 'So all this cabling...?'

'... is practically useless. What we need to do is take a cable to the house nearest to the windmill, plug it in there and the whole of Ampthill gets a power supply... or does it? Hang on a minute let me think... No... We can't plug it into an ordinary wall socket because the wiring won't take the load. Remember the wiring in the house is a bit like the branches of a tree. The mains comes in at the bottom like the trunk and spreads out into areas of the house each of which can't take more than a certain amount of current. So what we really need to do is to tap our windmill onto the mains supply to the house and that will provide us with a high enough rated cable to take the electricity we provide in all directions safely—mainly down to the town—and then we're home and dry. Bingo.'

It all seemed too easy.

And then the awful truth dawned on Derek, and he began to think that maybe he'd better stick to medicine after all. He looked up at Alan in a slightly hazy way. 'I think I must be going senile. Maybe the country air does things to you. Lowers your IQ or something... We've forgotten something, haven't we?'

'What?'

'Three things. Firstly we're sending electricity into the whole of Ampthill, aren't we? So that we can switch lights on. And we're trying to flood the whole of the mains system with electricity.'

'Yes...,' said Alan slowly.

'But we've forgotten that when the original inhabitants fled they wouldn't necessarily have switched everything off.'

'You mean there's a lot of lights already switched on?'

'Worse than that. What about all the automatic stuff that will still be on—fridges, central heating pumps—for example? Think of the amount of power they'll take.

'Oh dear,' said Alan. '*Oh dear*.'

'And more than that—the transformer that you mentioned.'

'Yes...'

'I should have listened to you. You weren't so stupid after all. You can transform electricity up as well as down.'

'Yes...'

'So electricity from our windmill is flooding into the electrical sub-station which is automatically transforming it *up* into 11,000 volts or more. In fact what we're actually trying to do is feed the whole of the National Grid from this tiny little windmill of ours behind us. I really do think I'd better stick to medicine...'

Alan grinned. 'Don't worry yourself about it, Derek. It's an easy enough mistake to make. Nobody's never tried to do this sort of thing before—feeding the electricity system backwards. You only learn things like this when you try it out after all. What was the third thing?'

'I'd forgotten to allow for the phases...'

'The what?'

'Too technical to explain easily... but we'll definitely have to feed the transformer directly from the windmill, and I'll have to do some alterations to the circuitry there.'

After a search, they found the transformer at the bottom of Fallowfield, and scaled the protective outside wall with a ladder. Alan surveyed the massive metal object in front of him with considerable caution. Notices saying encouraging things like *Danger of Death—Keep Out* were plastered on every surface. 'What happens if it's still working?' said Alan.

Derek looked up at him. 'There's hope for me yet,' he said.

'Why?'

'If it was still working we'd get electricity when we switched lights on, wouldn't we?'

It was Alan's turn to feel stupid.

'Oh, yes,' he said, casting his eyes heavenwards. 'Isn't thinking difficult when you've got to do it from a new perspective?'

'I suppose it is. It's a bit like writing a computer program. It looks great on paper and then you put it into the computer and it tells you 'No such variable' or something helpful like that. And you look at the program and suddenly realise what you've done, and how logically obvious your mistake is... Except that you didn't see it *beforehand*. And *that* is why practical experience wins hands down over theoretical knowledge, any day. You can create a nice self-consistent theory that on paper looks as though it's going to work, but when you put it into practice it doesn't work at all, simply because you've left out something very obvious.'

Derek surveyed the grey transformer in front of him, trying to work out which part did what. Finally he decided which cables to disconnect and which to reconnect. The cables were big and the work was hard. Sweating, he sat back on his haunches. 'You'll never guess what this reminds me of.'

'Try me.'

'A lock on a canal.'

'A *what*? Why?'

'Because it sits there waiting to work, and it doesn't need any complex control mechanism or power supply of its own. A lock on a canal stops the run-off of water until you choose to let some of the water out, and this transformer here,' he said, tapping the big metal rings, 'has no moving parts at all and will work for ever and a day, whenever current comes in through one side of it. The only thing that will stop it is if rust breaks the electrical circuit. There,' he said, straightening up, 'I think that's done it.'

For the next two days Alan and Peter went round the whole of the town finding the fuse boxes in each unoccupied house and switching off the mains supply. Then the occupants of each inhabited house checked that everything in their own house was unplugged—fridges, freezers, fires, fan heaters, videos, televisions, radios, central heating systems, door chimes, the lot.

It was late on the second afternoon when the job was finished. 'I wonder whether anything really will work, down in the town?' asked Alan, making the final adjustments and checks on the new windmill.

'We'd better go and try. Don't put on too many lights, in case we overload the system and the trips go out again. It'll be impossible to see what we're doing if we want to put them back again at this time of night.'

Alan didn't walk as much as run helter-skelter down Holly Walk, as fast as he dared in the twilight. Rushing past Dynevor House—because he would never announce something like this to Henry—he banged furiously on the door of Foulislea Cottage. Chris answered the door, with Paul in the distance behind her.

'Good evening, Alan,' said Chris. 'You look a little excited. What's happened?'

Wordlessly Alan reached out for the light switch and switched it on. The room was flooded with light.

'Not bad, eh?' he said.

'Congratulations,' said Paul, blinking in the sudden blast of light.

'It wasn't just me,' said Alan, 'it was mainly Derek. After a few false starts, mind you. We don't want too many people to switch on yet, so can we pass the word around not to try it?'

But it was too late. There were enough passers-by to see the light in Chris's lounge, and there was only one thing that could give an intense blaze of light like that—electricity! Each passer-by rushed back to his own house and experimented with the light switches, and each told his neighbour, and they too told *their* neighbours and, like grains of rice on a Chinese chessboard or bacteria multiplying in nutrient broth, or contacts dying from Legionnaires' disease, the light spread out into the town... until about half an hour later, when some of the last people to hear of the event went back to their houses and switched their own lights on, whereupon, without warning, the whole system finally overloaded, and everything went off again. A communal groan went up from each and every dwelling.

'I told you so,' said Alan to Chris as he passed Foulislea Cottage on the way back up Holly Walk and the windmill. 'I *told* you how important it was not to have too much load on the system at once.

We'll all just have to wait until tomorrow. We can't switch it on again easily tonight.'

*   *   *

Half an hour later it was as if the harvest had come home again. The White Hart was thronged with excited gabbling people. No matter that they were still working by the light and smell of mutton-fat candles, there was only one topic of conversation on everyone's lips. Electricity had arrived! It was galvanic, to quote a pun. Everyone's eyes lit up when they were talking about it. To see a light bulb working again after over a year! Instead of peering at things, they could see properly in the dark, into every corner of the room! Instead of hurting their eyes trying to read in the long winter nights they would be to able to see easily. They would be able to use CDs, they would be able to use TVs... No, they were *not* going to be able to use TVs, nor the radio. It took some time for that fact to sink in. Just as Derek had had difficulty working out how to construct an electrical supply system backwards, so the inhabitants of the community had difficulty in remembering the limitations on their use of electricity now that the outside world was no longer in existence.

The proprietor of the White Hart was delighted with the news—sales of his home-made beer rocketed that evening and discussion went on long into the night, long after he had normally closed up, damped down the fire and gone to bed.

In the morning Alan and Derek met with the rest of the council. They'd calculated earlier that the windmill could supply enough electricity for every house to have one low-powered electrical item on at a time, but it seemed in the enthusiasm of the discovery that certain of the community had gone from room to room exuberantly switching on every light they could find, and had overloaded the system in the process.

In the cold, natural, light of day, Derek and Alan checked their calculations again and said that they could still supply electricity to everybody—provided there was a wind. If there wasn't a wind it might be more difficult, because the storage batteries weren't that large. There was certainly no question of using any electrical power equipment such as drills, pumps, vacuum cleaners, electric irons, washing machines or fridges. If there were no other demands for electricity then there was easily enough power to work a few of these items, but no way that the whole town could be supplied with electricity to light the houses and at the same time supply any further power needs. The council agreed there and then that should there be any urgent communal need for electrical power tools to be used, then everybody else would just have to be switched off, and that was that.

But then they reached an awkward point. Despite the council having issued an edict that each house could have either one light or one low-powered electrical appliance working at any one time, *and no more*, no one obeyed. Everybody assumed that everyone else would be expected to keep their use of power down to a minimum but nobody was prepared to do it themselves. There was always someone who would be selfish and put on more than their fair share of equipment—and each time this happened the whole system overloaded and *everyone* lost out. There was always somebody who would 'just try' a vacuum cleaner, or a power drill, or an electric heater to take the winter cold out of an upstairs bedroom (where, perhaps, someone was lying ill). Like motorists caught speeding, there was always a good excuse. And each and every time the whole system tripped out.

The culprits were never found, of course, because after the system had crashed they simply switched off, unplugged and kept quiet. Mary was incensed. 'It's exactly like it was before the plague,' she said bitterly to the council, after the power had gone off for the tenth time that week. 'It's just like the way everybody selfishly polluted the planet or cut down the forest, insisting that their little bit of effluent wouldn't make any difference—but it always did, together with everybody else's. It was always somebody else's fault, never their own. And we've got it again.' She glared at Paul. 'And I think it's all because of the way you've introduced money. It's made people selfish again.'

'Oh, don't start that again,' snapped back Paul. 'It's nothing to do with money. In fact it's precisely *because* it's nothing to do with money that everybody's abusing it so much. It's just like it was before the plague: the things that were polluted most were the things that apparently came free, like rivers and the air and the seas. The minute you start charging, people are much more cautious about the way they look after their resources.'

'He's right, you know,' said Chris gently.

'You would support him, wouldn't you,' rapped back Mary tartly, 'you two lovebirds.'

Chris coloured. 'My private life has nothing to do with what we decide in the council, Mary, and you should know that.'

Martin interjected. 'I think Chris is right, Mary. It's what I've been saying for the past few months—people are basically selfish and they think of themselves first, irrespective of what it does to others.'

'Well, it shouldn't be like that,' said Mary.

'Maybe it shouldn't,' said Martin, 'but no matter how much we'd like it to be different that's the way people are built.'

'Can't we do something about it?' said Mary.

'What do you suggest?' said Martin. 'You can't alter human nature. And if you try and build our community on any other assumption than that everyone is selfish, then it's just not going to work. You're asking for the impossible. The only way you can really get to grips with this is to understand that people will be selfish, and won't think of the effects that their decisions have on others—and then see if you can change things so that they have a good *selfish* reason for doing what everybody else wants them to do.'

'I don't follow,' said Alan. 'Like what?'

'You've got two alternatives—either you make rules to prevent people doing something, backing them up with punishments if necessary, or else you make them pay for what they're using in such a way that they have a great disincentive to use more than their fair share.'

'So what do we do about the electricity?' said Mary, pointedly looking at Martin.

'Well, we've got two alternatives—three if you like, but the third one's not too brilliant. The first is to say that people aren't allowed to use more than a certain amount of electricity, and that we'll punish them if they're caught; but you'll never catch them, and you'll never prove it, unless you fit every house with a fuse which blows if their consumption rises too high. But that's not very practical.

'Next, we could make people pay for the electricity they use.'

'But that would mean meters in every house,' said Susan, 'just like installing trips.'

'But there *are* meters in every house,' said Alan.

'Who asked you?' retorted Susan, and then went red. 'Oh yes, there are, aren't there?'

'Or,' continued Martin, trying to ignore the angry glances passing between Alan and his wife, 'we could simply turn off the supply to certain areas in turn, so that people *couldn't* overload the system. That might not be too difficult to do but it certainly means that everybody suffers because everybody's selfish.'

'Why should everybody suffer just because some are selfish?' said Mary. 'Why can't we all live agreeably and peaceably and think of everyone else?'

'I only wish we could,' said Martin, 'but I'm not responsible for human nature.'

'Look at him,' said Mary. 'A man of God and he says he's not responsible for human nature. Well, it's God's fault then. He made us like this.'

Martin sighed. It really was very difficult to get through to her.

'No, Mary. God didn't make people like this. God made people with freedom to choose, and we chose wrongly. That's why we're like we are. And I wish it were different, but it isn't, and unless you come to terms with how people really work then you've no business trying to lay down the laws for the community because you'll get it all wrong.' Mary's colour rose even more.

'You're insufferable,' she said under her breath.

'Let's not get too worked up,' said Neil. 'Why don't we issue a warning that if the electricity isn't used properly then we'll have to ration it in some way, and that'll be awkward for everybody.'

'We can try,' said Martin. 'I'm not sure if it will work for long, but we can try.'

'And,' said Chris, 'maybe we can fix up another windmill so that we can double the amount of power we can use.'

'Technically a bit difficult,' said Derek. 'Getting them to synchronise their power output isn't as easy as you think—but we can look into it.'

'And in the meantime we'll tell everybody that unless they really restrict their own use of electricity then everybody's going to suffer,' said Chris, 'and we'll see if that works.'

*   *   *

The arrival of electricity had a profound effect upon the Ampthill community. On the evening of the big switch-on there was no one— just no one—in the streets: they were all inside, playing with the lights. It was so strange, so amazing, to go to a little plastic box on the wall and with one flick of the switch throw the whole room into brilliant lighting. Even a single 60-watt bulb was immensely bright by comparison with the tiny mutton-fat candle flames they'd been using. Sarah, whose memory didn't really extend back much beyond a year, spent the whole evening experimenting—switching a light on and off, then going to the next room to play with the light there, just to see what happened. Over the next hour she made it her business to find the location of all the light switches in the house, discovering to her delight that the hall and landing lights could be switched on and off from either end: it took her some time to realise that sometimes a switch would be up and sometimes down and the light could still be on, depending on which way the other switch was pointing.

And the brightness of it all! They could actually see. No more peering at books: they could even read the small print. There was no squinting, or angling the page to the candlelight, tilting it this way and that to get more light so as to work out what a particular word was. No straining of the eyes, none of the dreadful smell of burning mutton fat, none of the fear of fire if a candle was left unattended or fell over while its owner's back was turned. No trimming of wicks, none of that dreadful feeling that there were no more candles left until the morning now that the last one had gone out. No problems in the middle of the night over getting a light when a child was ill with earache. No worries about leaving a light on all night for a child frightened by the dark, with the constant fear either that a draught might put it out or that it might topple over and set fire to the whole house. No problems lighting the candle in the first place (because matches were now a thing of the far distant past). They had *light!*—light that illuminated everything, that threw harsh shadows, that showed up dirt, that penetrated into the far corners of the furthest recess of the innermost cupboard.

And the light didn't run out! There was no longer any danger of running out of candles, or of having to eke them out until the morning.

So in house after house the children experimented, running up and down stairs, switching lights on one after the other, with strict injunctions from their parents ringing in their ears not to have more than one light on at once, in case they fused the whole system.

Alan had made it very plain that no one was to use equipment that required any quantity of power, so motors, vacuum cleaners, drills, electric fires, washing machines, microwaves and ovens were all completely forbidden. Even so, there were many other electrical items that could still be switched on, utilised and enjoyed. At long last they could charge the rechargeable batteries, so torches, children's games, calculators and Dictaphones were all now usable (not that anybody had any cause to dictate a letter).

To his delight, Derek realised that medical equipment with batteries—such as the instruments for looking in eyes and ears—would all work, now that he could recharge the batteries that powered them.

Martin had had light for some time—in the dining room—so he wasn't quite so fascinated by it: that night he put a CD on, but mindful of the fact that he had to keep his use of electricity low he didn't dare put the electric light on as well, so he lit a candle—and in doing so was probably the only house in Ampthill that evening that *wasn't* lit by electric light.

After the first hour of playing with the lights, others in the town had similar ideas. Anne, who had been thinking about what to do once they all had electricity, knew precisely what she would do: and it would be especially for Sarah. Going across to the previously defunct television and video recorder in the corner of the room she switched it on, and with Sarah watching open-mouthed, popped in a tape of *Oliver* that she had found in the video shop. Sarah's eyes opened even wider. Anne, of course, knew *Oliver* from the past, but even she suddenly saw it through new eyes as she watched the joy in Sarah's face as she listened to the songs and watched the dancing.

After the big number in Covent Garden with the last crane shot pulling back and back to reveal the hundreds of dancers, Sarah turned round to her. 'What a lot of people, Auntie Anne. Where did they all come from?'

Suddenly Anne was in floods of tears, looking at the actors and the massed ranks of dancers in the market scene, hundreds upon hundreds of them—and they were all dead, almost certainly, every last one of them; and the heartbreak and waste of it all washed over Anne as it had never done before. All those people! All gone.

'Why are you crying, Auntie Anne?' said Sarah suddenly. 'It's very pretty, isn't it?'

'I know, darling,' said Anne, putting her hand on Sarah's. 'Yes it is, isn't it? I don't think you'd quite understand even if I told you.'

'Can we see that bit again?'

'Yes, let's,' said Anne and watched with a mixture of fascination and silent misery as the film unfolded.

All gone! The people, the society they lived in, those who made the film, all the backstage crew, all dead. And London, instead of being the live vibrant community portrayed on the film, was dead too. Twenty minutes later Sarah spoke again.

'I'm bored with this one. Can we have something different?'

'Yes, dear,' said Anne wiping away a tear in the darkness, for they too hadn't turned on the lights while the video was working. 'Yes, let's. I wonder what there is.' She held up the candle to the small rack of video cassettes on the shelf. None of them was pre-recorded: all had been used for taping odd television programmes in the past. Selecting one at random she put it in the video recorder and used the fast forward button to find out what was on the tape. It was the usual assorted mixture of items that families record, part of a series here, a nature programme there, a comedy special, a couple of episodes of *Neighbours*. She reached the end of the episode, but left her finger on the button just slightly too long and there on the screen was the familiar BBC logo for the six o'clock news, with the news-reader telling of the rise of an infection that had started in south-west London, where they thought it had come from and what they thought it was. And suddenly she found herself reliving the last days of civilisation before the plague struck.

'Why are you so sad, Auntie Anne?' asked Sarah. 'I don't understand. This is lovely. I haven't seen one of these before, have I?'

'No dear, you haven't,' said Anne, gently caressing Sarah's face. 'Well, you probably did when you were a lot younger, but you won't remember.'

'I think I remember something like it,' said Sarah. 'A long time ago.'

'Shall we look at *Oliver* again?' asked Anne.

'Oh, yes please,' said Sarah.

And as the flickering light from the screen dimly illuminated the pair of them in the room that evening, Anne silently wept inside for everything that had gone, everything that had been destroyed, everything that once had been built up and was now no more, for a civilisation that—for good or bad—would never come again in their lifetimes.

*   *   *

Up and down the town various members of the community had discovered and rediscovered uses of electricity. Soon most of them had tried putting on records or CDs: a lot of them had reflexly switched on the television only to realise with some irritation that of course there wouldn't be a picture, because nothing was being broadcast.

Everybody had something special to remember about that night:

the first piece of recorded music they'd heard for nearly a year and a half; the first film; the first book they could read with ease. After Sarah had gone to bed, David commandeered the television and plugged in a Sega game. Derek, however, was nowhere to be seen— he'd been called out just as they'd started to put on *Oliver* and didn't come back until way after David's bedtime. But he knew what he was going to do with the electricity: and slipped into the video recorder one of the pre-recorded medical programmes he'd found so many months ago in the Health Centre and had been keeping ever since. He was tired, but he didn't notice it—because for the first time in his life he sat down to be taught directly by real doctors, talking on programmes that were made specifically for other doctors, and he was *fascinated*. They showed computer-animated diagrams of anatomy and physiology, explained how various diseases happened and what could be done about them, how drugs worked through being targeted on receptors in body cells. He saw X-rays being taken, and watched a cardiac catheterisation; listened to discussions about the best treatment for the depressed, or the psychotic; and watched enthralled as key-hole surgery was explained. Suddenly a whole new world had opened up in front of him. He didn't go to bed until three o'clock that morning, and even then didn't get to sleep for another hour and a half, so great was the effect on him.

* * *

Kevin too was up late. He also had a video recorder, and he and his friends were using it in just as fascinated a manner as all the others in the community. He too had been into the video shop and spent the evening watching three pornographic films, one after the other.

* * *

The next day most of Ampthill awoke late, struggling to get up, bleary-eyed. There was but one topic of conversation. 'What did you use the electricity for?' With many people it devolved to 'what records did you listen to?' or 'what film did you watch?' There was an excited buzz of conversation as people swapped stories.

There was the first injury too when next morning Derek treated a small electrical burn in a child who had touched the exposed terminal of a lamp that hadn't got a bulb in. Fortunately the effect of the electricity on the child's muscles had been so quick and in such a manner as to cause him to pull his hand away, so the burn was only small, but it left Derek ruefully contemplating the principle that any advance usually has a corresponding problem attached to it. Like money, electricity was neither good nor bad: it was how it was used that was the crux of the matter.

*   *   *

The following evening in Foulislea Cottage, Paul was unusually quiet. Chris had made them both some food as the sun went down, but for a long time he sat staring into the fire, watching the flames dance and flicker. Chris knew better than to interrupt him when he was in one of these states because she knew that he was thinking, and thinking very deeply indeed. Finally, without even touching his tea, he stood up, said, 'I'm just going out, I'll be back in a minute,' and without another word whisked out of the front door.

With a mixture of puzzlement and slight anger that he'd not touched the food she'd made, and shaking her head because that was what she'd come to expect from him, she covered his plate and awaited his return.

Five minutes later he was back, together with Alan and Derek. Chris wondered how he'd managed to find both of them so quickly and then realised of course that, now Derek had moved from the Old Rectory they were next-door neighbours, in Woburn Street.

Paul was obviously concentrating but he also looked agitated at the same time, so much so that Chris wondered if there was some big problem that she hadn't thought about.

'What's the matter?' she asked, crossing to him and holding his hand.

'Nothing particularly,' said Paul. 'Just a lot of opportunities, and I don't know what to do—which is why I wanted Derek and Alan here.'

'What, medical opportunities?'

'No,' said Derek. 'I'm reverting to type. Engineering ones.'

'What I want to know,' said Paul, 'is, can we use electricity in other ways? We can't use it to provide lots of power because the windmill isn't up to it: but we can provide electricity for things that don't use up a lot of energy. I've just had some thoughts, and I want you two to tell me whether you think I'm off my rocker.'

'You two,' said Chris indignantly. 'What about me?'

'Well, I meant you,' said Paul, abjectly. 'It's just that Derek and Alan are...'

'...men?' finished off Chris, acidly.

'No, no,' said Paul. 'Well... not entirely, they're engineers and they know about electricity.'

'And I suppose I don't know anything about electricity, even though I did help run a radio station,' said Chris tartly. 'All right, I know my place. I'll go and get some more food. And do the washing up. I'll just be the servant for the evening, if that's all right with everyone. Will that be all, master?'

Paul flushed. 'I didn't mean it like that, Chris,' he said.

'Are you sure?' said Chris, flouncing out of the room. 'Just because something's mechanical or electrical doesn't mean I can't understand it.'

'I didn't mean it like that,' repeated Paul, looking as though the sky had just fallen in.

'I don't think he meant it, Chris,' said Alan. 'I really don't. But face it, Derek did use to be an engineer, and I'm supposed to be trying to look after the engineering side of things, so it is going to be rather obvious that he is going to talk to us about it. He didn't mean to exclude you, though.'

'Didn't he?' said Chris, subsiding slightly. Paul stared at Chris and then suddenly decided that might not be a good idea and promptly looked away through the window before continuing.

'What I wanted to consider—all of us to consider—is how we can use electricity best. I'm no engineer, so you'll need to advise me. Are there things that we can do now that we couldn't do last year because we didn't have electricity?'

'Let's go through the things we *can't* do,' said Derek. 'Quite simply, anything that uses lots of power is out. So we can't use anything that works in an effortful way.'

'So there are no labour-saving devices?' asked Paul.

'That's right.'

'But where we *can* use electricity,' said Alan, 'is where you've got controls, tiny motors, things that need lots of volts but not much current.'

'Such as?' asked Chris. ·

I told you you didn't understand, thought Paul, smiling sweetly at her.

'You mean like computers, radios and communications equipment?' she continued.

The smile disappeared from Paul's face.

'Yes, that sort of thing,' said Alan.

'Could we power a computer?' asked Paul.

'Easily,' said Derek, 'so long as you don't want it to control anything that uses a lot of power, like a lathe. As long as you only want it to calculate things...'

'A computer printer?'

'Ye...e...es,' said Derek hesitatingly. 'Though that needs a bit more power.'

'Well, that means we've got a printing press.'

'Until we run out of paper,' added Alan.

'Yes,' interjected Paul, 'but there'll be a lot of that around in offices. Tons of the stuff, if you only look. Still, you're right, we don't want to waste it. What else is there?'

'Radio?' said Chris.

'Don't be silly,' said Paul, still irked. 'Who will there be to listen to?'

'Who said anything about listening? I was thinking about transmitting.'

'You couldn't set up a radio station,' said Derek. 'It needs far too much power.'

'I didn't mean that,' said Chris. 'I was thinking about ham radio. We might be able to make contact with people further afield—that is, if there's anyone out there listening.'

'I don't see why there shouldn't be,' said Derek.

'How far away could we reach?' asked Alan.

'All round the world if you get the right conditions,' said Derek. 'Certain types of radio frequencies bounce off the Heaviside layer.'

'The what?' asked Paul.

'The Heaviside layer. The ionosphere. It's an area of the earth's atmosphere which acts like a mirror to radio waves. Radio waves rise up towards it, and are then reflected down again towards the ground, bounce up again off the ground, get reflected off the Heaviside layer again.'

'That doesn't get us very far, does it?'

'I don't follow you...' said Derek, '...oh I see. You're assuming that the radio waves are going straight up—think of the radio wave going along towards the horizon, but it misses the horizon, goes on, hits the Heaviside layer, bounces off it again, comes down again another few hundred miles further on, bounces up again... It ricochets all the way round the world like that. You could listen to someone in the outback of Australia if you had the right equipment, got the right weather conditions and found the right frequencies.'

'Assuming there *is* anyone in Australia,' muttered Alan gloomily.

'Yes, there is that,' said Derek with a sigh.

'Have we got any radio equipment?' asked Chris.

'Yep,' said Paul. 'There's a house in Marston with a huge radio mast. I bet there's a ham radio station there.'

'Can we dismantle it and bring it across here?' asked Alan.

'Might be difficult. It won't be easy getting the mast down, but we can try.'

'That would be useful,' said Chris. 'If we could communicate with other groups we could find out what was happening elsewhere.'

'How would that help us?' asked Derek.

'I just thought it might be a good idea...'

'Perhaps it would give us a better picture of what the weather was going to do if we knew the sort of weather other people were having.'

'No,' said Derek. 'That's wrong. It wouldn't help. Most of our weather comes in from the Atlantic so we get it first. I suppose we could help other people by telling them what sort of weather we'd got ourselves...' And then his jaw dropped.

'What on earth's the matter?' said Chris. 'You look as though you've seen a ghost.'

'Weather,' said Derek.

'Wouldn't it be nice if we could predict it?' said Chris.

'Well, of course it would,' said Paul. 'I'd know whether I needed to take my mac and brolly to work.'

'No,' said Derek, suddenly angry with Paul for his flippancy. 'I'm serious. It doesn't matter so much at the moment because it's winter, but what about in summer? What happened last year? What was the one thing that Neil had to worry about?'

'The harvest.'

'That's right.'

'And when he tried to get the wheat in, all he could do was look up at the sky and hope that he'd got it right. I remember him saying how much he missed the regular weather forecasts and the satellite pictures. So *we* can get the satellite pictures.'

'You what?' said Alan.

'We can get the satellite pictures.'

'Are you off your rocker or something?'

'While we're sitting down here in medieval misery there are still communications and weather satellites out there, on station, twenty-two thousand miles up, automatically keeping themselves locked on to the earth, regularly taking pictures which they then transmit back down to the earth. They're powered by solar energy, so they'll still be going strong, and they'll have fuel enough to keep themselves automatically in the right orientation to the earth for a long time to come. So all we have to do is find out where those satellites are, build a dish to receive the signal, decode the signal, and Hey Presto! we've got weather maps.'

'Are you sure we'll be able to do all that?' asked Chris. 'It sounds a pretty tall order to me.'

'We should be able to do it,' said Derek. 'Maybe if we explore what's on offer at this house in Marston—the one with the radio mast—we might find the right sort of information there—frequencies, decoding mechanisms, satellite positions and so on.'

*   *   *

The next fortnight was a culture shock for everyone. The initial elation of using lights, hearing music and seeing films took some time to subside. But then the defects started to become more obvious, like the day when David—it had to be David—discovered a guitar and a hundred-watt amplifier and married the two together. 'Yes,' he thought to himself, 'it works just like I remember.' The neighbours thought it worked just like they remembered as well, and came round banging on his door and telling him to stop, or preferably to find a field a long way away. Irritated, David observed testily that he didn't know of many fields that were wired for electricity. Eventually Derek and Anne prevailed upon him to turn the volume down and promise not to disturb the neighbours again.

But then the community noticed something else happening, not quite as violent as the electric guitar but almost as unpleasant. Although at first they had all sat down to *listen* to the music that was available to them, after a time people started to use it as they had before—something to shut out the silence. Although initially it stopped them thinking, and gave them something different and perhaps more pleasant to think about, soon it became like an auditory drug that was turned on at the beginning of the day until last thing at night, anaesthetising instead of heightening the senses. Gradually the hive of activity, bustle and intermittent sounds that had been the auditory signature of Ampthill degenerated into a background mush of music that seemed somehow to be all pervading, like an aural version of the plague. And although bright lights and loud music were enjoyable and fascinating at first, there were not a few who were sorry to see the silence and the quietness go.

There is something very positive and intense about silence. It's not just the absence of sound: silence isn't emptiness, silence is full of noise—the sound of the wind, the creak of branches, the clickings of a house settling and moving, the scurryings of little animals, the rustling of leaves, the drone of bees and flies, the creaking of cartwheels, the clunk of horses' hooves, the squeak of chairs and bicycle chains. All this was starting to fade with the ever-present musical wallpaper that sprang up everywhere, drifting out of open windows, polluting the silence of the street, or the garden door. Somehow the pace of life seemed to quicken and instead of living life a day or a half-day at a time, now there was something by which they could time themselves. All the clocks worked, for a start. Recorded programmes took half an hour, or fifty minutes, or an hour; CDs played for only an hour, records for thirty minutes a side. Unconsciously time was divided into smaller and smaller fragments, insistently undermining the sense of peace and slowness. Almost without realising it the inhabitants of Ampthill started measuring time in smaller and smaller units and noticing how quickly it seemed to pass. So although electricity brought with it great advantages, it also caused other effects which weren't quite so nice.

*   *   *

The excursion to the house in Marston went well. After looking at the roomful of radio equipment that it contained, Derek soon realised that they'd stumbled on a very powerful radio system indeed—but it was no use where it was, because they couldn't get electricity to it. So, led by Alan, a posse of five strong helpers was detailed off to dismantle the equipment, including the mast, load it carefully on to a lorry, bring it back to Ampthill and re-erect it at a suitable site. They chose a point not too far from the windmill—not because they needed immediate access to power but simply because that was the highest point around, and as Derek had explained to Alan, the taller the mast and the higher the take-off point for the radio waves, the further they would go.

It took some time to set up the equipment on its new site. They'd chosen the New Rectory for the radio station, a modern house situated on Holly Walk midway between the church and the Old Rectory. Alan set up the transmitter in one of the ground-floor rooms, with the mast and aerial on the lawn outside. He'd also had the sense to scour the house in Marston for all books, periodicals and other sources of information about how to operate the set, and which frequencies were best to listen on.

The equipment was finally set up, and everything was ready. His heart beating slightly more quickly than usual, Alan pulled up a chair, clasped the earphones on his head, and reached out his right hand to switch on the power.

Nothing happened. Even the tell-tale power lights on the transmitter refused to light up. He tried again. Nothing happened. Getting down from his chair, Alan crawled under the table to check the connections to the mains. They were all in working order. Methodically he went through the whole system checking lines, switches, circuit breakers, trips and fuses. He got nowhere. Nothing would induce the equipment to work. It wasn't even that he couldn't hear anybody on the airwaves—he couldn't even get the equipment itself working.

There was no heat in the room, either and Alan, who had been working in the starving cold of a house that hadn't been occupied for eighteen months and was now in the depths of winter, was frozen to the marrow. At the fourteenth attempt he thought he'd cracked it. He switched on again—and again nothing happened.

Cursing softly under his breath he stepped outside the house to think. Outside it was still and *very* cold, his breath hanging in front of him in clouds. *Why* couldn't he get the equipment to work? What was it that he'd done wrong? The electricity cables were intact—he'd checked the connections thee times already. So the power would be getting to the house, but now that he'd plugged everything in, nothing would work at all. The fuses were all right—he'd checked those three times too. He thought and thought and racked his brains; and the more he thought the more perplexed he became, and the problem seemed more and more like the cloud of vapour that formed in front of his face, hanging there in the still air. The more he breathed the bigger it got and the bigger it got the more it seemed to reflect his inability to crack the problem.

And then the penny dropped. No wonder the cloud was mocking him. It had every right to. 'Oh, *Alan*,' he said to himself looking at the condensation hanging there motionless, 'you *fool*...' The cloud hanging in front of his face meant still air. Still air means no wind. No wind means no windmill working. He walked on to the croquet lawn outside for confirmation and instead of the usual slow thrum of the windmill he heard... nothing. His own internal cloud lifted. At least he wasn't going totally bananas even if he had missed a rather obvious source for the problem. He'd just have to wait until the wind got up before he could attempt to communicate with anyone else.

*   *   *

Four hundred yards away, out on the fields at the back of Kevin's house Kevin, David and Trevor were crouched down in the grass, hoping that they were not too visible. In David's hand was the contraption that Paul had seen a few weeks earlier, a long T-shaped affair, with the old wishbone of a car suspension forming the T-piece, and a long lengthways furrow along the wood that made up the vertical part of the T. Quietly they waited. After about ten minutes a small brown shape detached itself from the hedgerow about a hundred yards away and came lolloping across the ground in front of them. Then it stopped. The hare cocked its head as though listening. It lolloped on another few feet and then started to nibble. Very quietly David swung the object in his hand until it was pointing at the animal.

'Go on,' whispered Kevin as quietly as he could. The hare heard something, stopped and stood on its back legs bolt upright.

'Shut up, Kevin,' hissed Trevor. David, unperturbed, sighted along the long arm of the T-piece and pulled the trigger underneath. There was a swish and twang. The hare leapt into the air and came to rest three feet from where it had been sitting, a quarrel transfixing it through the chest. Kevin and Trevor let out whoops of joy and rushed off to see the results of their actions. David, being more phlegmatic, slowly levered himself off the freezing ground, dusted himself off, shouldered the crossbow and marched off after them. It had worked brilliantly. Engineering was obviously a genetic trait in the Jones family, and Jugged Hare would be on the menu later that week.

*   *   *

In past years Alan had been quite a keen sailor, and many times in the past had been becalmed on the sea. He'd never been becalmed on land before, but after an hour spent looking up at the great brown blades of the windmill lying motionless in the still air he felt that same surge of frustration he'd known so often when trying to navigate his boat. Being becalmed on land seemed to be a bit of a misnomer, but there it was: no wind, no power. It was candles tonight for everyone. and no way of kicking the radio into life. Frustrated, he stamped his feet with a mixture of anger and cold and in the gathering gloom walked back down to the town.

*   *   *

Anne could stand it no longer. The videos had brought it all back to her so vividly that she couldn't cope, and stumbling up the path to the Old Rectory that evening, she had thankfully found Martin at home. It was dark of course—with no electricity he couldn't use the electric light. As she rounded the end of the drive she could see a candle burning in the window of the dining room, and in the still air could faintly hear the sound of the piano. She knocked on the door and heard his familiar steps walking briskly down the corridor towards her.

'Hello, Anne,' he said, opening the door and holding out the candle to see who it was. 'Do come in.'

'Thank you,' mumbled Anne as Martin closed the door behind her.

'You look upset. Has anything happened?' Wordlessly Anne shook her head.

'You're frozen. I'll get you a hot drink.' He ushered her into the dining room. It was warm, cosy and restful, so different from what it had been in the past. She heard the clank of cups in the kitchen and her mind went back to that time a year ago when things had been the other way round and it had been Martin who couldn't cope and Anne who'd been his comforter and support. And how the room had changed! Once it had looked cold and unfriendly, disorganised and chaotic. Now it looked cosy, warm and comfortable—a little

Spartan maybe, and still very much a bachelor pad, without the soft touches that go with a woman's presence in the house, but neat, tidy and organised for all that.

'Here we are,' said Martin, coming in with two steaming cups of soup and some oatmeal biscuits. 'Now what can I do for you?'

The soup tasted good, and it seemed to warm her as with shaking hands and a trembling voice she told him how she couldn't cope with the memories that the videos had brought back. All those people! All gone. That intricate, enmeshed society. All wiped out. That whole lively battling metropolis—all gone. And it would never, *ever* come back again. Suddenly Anne began to feel the loneliness that Martin had felt a year earlier, the utter, isolated, cold, loneliness of it all.

Martin listened, quietly and carefully sipping his soup, watching Anne by the light of the candle. She had a very pretty face, he thought, delicate and sensitive, and from the corner of those large dark eyes from time to time a rivulet of glistening liquid poured as she told him how lonely she suddenly felt.

'Is it just that?' asked Martin after the initial outpouring had ceased. 'Nothing else?'

'No. Why? Well, there's Alison of course.'

'Nothing else? You and Derek all right?'

'Oh yes,' she said in a tired sort of way. 'Yes. No problems there. Not that I ever see him, of course.'

'He's very busy, isn't he?'

'He never seems to stop. He's so worried about it all, you know. He's bothered that he's going to make a mistake and kill someone. I don't think he's really got over Jane's death.'

'He couldn't have done anything about that, could he? I thought we'd been into that.'

'We had. When he's logical he says he knows he couldn't have saved her, but it still hit him very hard. He was very fond of Jane.'

'Yes,' said Martin, 'she was a nice person, wasn't she? Very glamorous. You didn't suspect any sort of...?'

'Who, Derek? You must be joking.'

'Just asking. It's important, you know.'

'I know,' said Anne, then paused. 'No. There wasn't anything going on. Anyway, Paul wouldn't have let him. All the same, Derek doesn't seem to be the same person I married.'

'He's changed over the past year then?'

'Changed?' she said angrily. 'Of course he's changed.'

'Mind you, we all have,' said Martin. 'We've all been affected by it.'

'Derek's been affected more than most. I don't think he knew what he was taking on when he agreed to be a doctor. He didn't have the vaguest idea, not the slightest inkling of what it would mean.'

'Well, he does it very well,' replied Martin. 'You ought to hear the things I hear about him. I've never heard anybody say anything against him at all. Well, there was that Mrs Moody, but that all blew over. Mind you, she complains about anything.'

'I don't know,' said Anne flatly, almost as if she hadn't heard, 'I think he's just exhausted. He's certainly not home very much. I can't look to him for any form of support and when he does come in he's too tired to do anything. He barely has time to eat his food and then he falls asleep in a chair—that is, assuming that nobody calls him out again. And the amount of time he spends studying... yet he still doesn't think he's good enough, he doesn't know enough, and he wants to learn more. He's probably down in the house now, watching the medical videos he found in the Health Centre. For the fiftieth time. Or, he would be, if the electricity were on.'

'Oh, dear, dear,' said Martin, reaching forward and putting his hand on hers. 'You need a bit of support, don't you?'

She sniffed slightly. 'I suppose so... It's been a traumatic year for Derek, but it's been a bad year for me as well, and I haven't really had him there to support me. Everybody says how hard Derek works but they don't see what happens behind the scenes to his family—to us. And they don't see, when he's worried about something, that that worry overflows onto me; and when he's really got a problem either he gets very quiet, or gets irritable, or else he's just too tired to do either.'

Martin put his free hand on her other wrist and they sat there for a moment across the fire, motionless. He gave her hands a comforting squeeze. 'I'm sorry. I had no idea it was so difficult for you.'

'Don't get me wrong,' she said, brightening up slightly. 'I'm not upset with him, I've not fallen out of love and he's not fallen out of love with me. It's just that... Well, life's difficult. It's a strain, and it's a strain in a way neither of us could have foreseen.' She sat back in her chair then wiped away the remaining tears from her left eye.

'At least you've acknowledged the problem,' said Martin. 'It's the first step.'

She smiled a brief little smile, then her face lapsed into sad disappointment.

'I think you'll find things are easier now you've told someone.'

'Do you?' she said, her face brightening up again. 'I'd like to think you're right.'

'Well, it helped me in the past—when I was honest enough to tell Derek what was worrying me.'

'I hope you're right. You've been very helpful.'

'I don't feel I've done very much.'

'Oh you have, you've been a great help. I feel a lot better just from talking with you. Thank you,' she said, more firmly, 'you're a good friend!' and standing up she reached for both his hands and squeezed them. 'I'm very proud to have you as a friend, you know.'

'There's no need for that,' said Martin, colouring slightly, 'but I was going to say, why don't you come again in a few days when you've had time for things to settle down, and let me know how you're getting on?'

'I'd like that,' Anne replied. 'I'd like that.'

*   *   *

The next day Alan took up his seat in front of the transmitting equipment. This time there was a wind—a brisk one—and the thrum of the blades could be heard clearly from outside the door of the Rectory. He went to the equipment and switched it on as the instruction book had said. This time, to his delight, all the lights came on. Putting on the headphones, he listened to the crackle of

static with distinct pleasure. After satisfying himself that all was in
order, he selected a frequency band and patiently and carefully
began searching the ether for any signs of radio transmissions.

- 14 -

As requested, four days later Anne came back to see Martin. By
then she'd had time to digest some of the things that had surfaced
and had begun to understand some of the frustrations that were
bothering her so deeply. She was still upset by one of the videos
which David and his friend had insisted on watching. 'Upset' was
perhaps the wrong word—'unnerved' might have been a better one.
The ordinary videos had been bad enough, reminding her as they
did of a life that had now vanished, but to add insult to injury she
came in one day and found David watching a particularly bloodthirsty video which he'd acquired from the video shop. It was nothing special—it only had a 15 licence—but the more Anne watched
it the more appalled she was at the degree of violence portrayed. As
if it wasn't enough to be reminded of the demise of many millions
of people, here was a video that gloried in the imitation killing of
another few members of the human race in whatever gory manner
the director could devise. Not having seen anything similar for eighteen months, it was a real culture shock and it brought her up with
a start. Gore is all very well when it's imitation, but it's no fun when
you've just seen the real thing and are still coming to terms with it.
After the Second World War children in Germany didn't want to
play with tanks and guns.

Anne had sat there horrified, watching the way in which the
writer and director of the film had thought of ever more intriguing
ways to kill off, injure, hurt or maim members of the human race
until, totally disgusted, she ran out of the room and sat sobbing and
shaking in the kitchen. 'We watched *those* for fun?' she kept asking
herself over and over again. 'We thought it *entertaining*?' She'd

asked David to switch it off, but he wouldn't and as he'd got a couple of his friends in to watch it with him she didn't want to create an embarrassing scene for him, so she suffered in mute silence and then decided that maybe it was a good time to go and visit Martin again.

As it turned out, it was exactly the opposite.

She trudged up Holly Walk in the darkness, glad to have the use of her torch with its rechargeable batteries. It was a wild night and in the distance she could hear the pulsating throb of the windmill. From time to time on her left she could see the occasional light from houses in the town—the statutory one bulb and nothing more—or else she could see a room lit only by the blue-white light from a television. Then came the long, dark, dismal driveway up to the Old Rectory itself. She always hated going up there at night. Although she didn't fear any form of attack, nevertheless it was spooky in the extreme and she was always glad when she rounded the bend and saw the house ahead of her. As usual there was a light in the dining room—candle light. He must be listening to music, she thought, stepping under the porch with its long columns and knocking on the door.

No answer.

Strange, she thought. He must be in, surely. She knocked on the door again; then from the corridor she could hear Martin's footsteps shuffling along. He opened the door. It took a minute to recognise who she was in the gloom. 'Oh... hello, Anne...'

'Hello, Martin. Can I come in?'

'Oh.' He'd lost the sprightly step and his face looked anxious and worn. 'Am I interrupting anything?'

'Oh... No.'

Anne's heart went thump as she realised the signs. Martin was having one of his bad days. Far from him being able to help her with her problems he wasn't even able to help himself with his own.

She tried to make her excuses. 'It looks as though it's a bad time, Martin. I came to talk but...'

'No, no, Anne,' he said tiredly, making a great effort to be helpful. 'I can listen. Do come in.' They went into the dining room again. Oh dear, thought Anne, looking at the remains of the last three meals on the table. At least there was a fire burning in the stove.

'Do sit down.' She suddenly became aware that there was music playing.

'What's that?'

'Mahler. His fifth symphony. The slow movement. The Adagio.'

'I recognise it from somewhere.'

'It was the background music for *Death in Venice*.'

'Ah yes... Isn't it sad?... And beautiful...'

A wistful look came across Martin's face. He paused and sighed. 'Yes. I just felt like putting it on.'

'What's the matter? What's happened?'

'Oh, nothing. It just comes back again from time to time.'

'The depression?'

'Yes... A bit like flu—it lingers on afterwards.' He made an effort to pull himself together. 'Now, Anne, what can I do for you?'

'I suppose I feel like you, really.'

'No better?'

'No better, in fact worse.' She told him about the film. He listened carefully then leant forward and picked up her hand with his.

'Oh, dear Anne, you are having a bad time of it, aren't you? I wish I could make it better for you.' He gave her hand a squeeze then tried to let go. She clung on to him.

'I'm just finding it... very difficult...'

'Like before?'

'Just the same. Only worse... more raw. I think talking about it has made me realise just how hurt I've felt over Alison, for everything that we've lost...'

'And Derek?'

'I'm sorry for what's happening to him. How tired he's becoming. He can't support me emotionally any more.' She looked up at Martin's face. 'You know you're such a comfort to me, Martin, you really are.' He tried to draw away but she still clung on to his hand.

'I'm glad I can help you,' he said, waving his remaining free hand. In the background the Mahler continued on its way, softly and sadly, the furrowed look on Martin's brow reflecting the music as it played its gorgeous, sad lament. Anne looked at his eyes. They had a faraway look in them, half concentrating on the music, half thinking of other things.

'So why are *you* upset?' she rejoined.

'Me?' he said, staring at his feet. 'Nothing special. I just feel a bit lonely, I suppose. I haven't got a family around me like you have, and although it's nice to have the solitude, it's nice to have family and friends and to feel loved.'

'You *are* loved,' said Anne, squeezing his hand tightly. 'You *are*. We all love you.' Martin shrugged and went silent and Anne could see that in the corner of each eye a little glistening teardrop was beginning to form. She grabbed his other hand. 'Oh, Martin, you are loved you know, and it is good to be with you.' He smiled briefly at her.

'And I like being with you.'

She flung her arms around his shoulders and gave him a peck on the cheek. 'There you are, I told you you're loved.'

'I need a lot more than that,' said Martin sadly.

'Well, you shall have a lot more than that,' said Anne, hugging him again and putting her head on his shoulder. 'You've got to learn I'm very fond of you. We all love you.' She kissed him again on the cheek and then on the lips. Not the best thing to do under the circumstances. Martin had never had much interaction with the opposite sex before, largely because he'd been too shy, and suddenly, when at his lowest, to have an attractive woman cuddle and kiss him was just too much to bear. He knew he found her attractive but what surprised him was *how* attractive she was—everything about her, her voice, her looks, her scent, the way she touched him. It all helped to assuage the ache he felt inside, the aching void of loneliness. She kissed him again, more firmly and for longer.

'I really don't think,' he began—or tried to begin—but it was too late. Their combined need for company and affection and reassurance, their mutual understanding, their mutual sadness, drove them together like two magnets.

And then the natural human hormonal responses took over. The

logical part of Martin wanted to stop. The emotional part didn't, and
the vast gaping chasm of his emotional needs was quite sufficient to
swallow up and overwhelm whatever ideas his logical mind had
been thinking.

The same was true for Anne. The fuse had been lit and nothing
was going to put it out. Leaving the dining room, with the Mahler
continuing its sad and weary way, Martin led her upstairs to the bedroom.

Just as willingly, she followed.

*   *   *

The guilt set in before they'd even started to dress again. Their
emotional and physical hunger satisfied, all that was left was the
knowledge of what they had done. Like a black cloud, that knowledge and guilt descended on them both. Unlike a legitimate relationship in which physical consummation brings the two partners
closer together, more intimately entwined emotionally and psycho-
logically, all Martin and Anne's intimacy had done was drive them
apart in a curious, uneasy way, as if the magnet had reversed its
polarity, and repulsion had taken over. Each was aware of their
fondness for the other, yet each was aware that their fondness had
gone too far and had half destroyed itself in the process—to say
nothing of the betrayal of Derek by Anne his wife, and by Martin
his friend, and of God by them both.

'We shouldn't have done that,' said Anne, turning to Martin. 'It
was nice but it was... awful.'

'I know,' said Martin turning his head away from her, clouds of
guilt enveloping him like fog. 'Oh, don't I know it.' He was kicking
himself mentally. What had they said at his training college? 'Don't
counsel members of the opposite sex in circumstances which may
become intimate. Get out of the situation before it gets too
intense—and if you have to do one-to-one counselling in highly
charged emotional circumstances make sure there are other people
around, nearby, so you can't get intimate without being discovered.'

In the gloom, his mind dulled with the awfulness of what they
had just done, he reached out automatically to put on the light by

the bed. The light flicked on—but he'd forgotten that the CD was still playing downstairs. For a second the light went on—and then the system overloaded. One electrical item to each house had been the rule, and he'd just broken it: and the lights went out, not just in his house, but in the whole town.

It seemed very symbolic.

*   *   *

Afterwards Anne dressed carefully, making especially sure that she'd left nothing behind, no evidence of what had just transpired, making sure that her attire looked exactly the same as when she'd come, so that no one in her family could notice that she'd buttoned her blouse differently and wonder why.

She needn't have worried. The wind outside was still howling as she opened the door and slipped quietly and gratefully into the waiting gloom, her carefully combed hair blown to bits in the gale, her garments whipping around in the wind. No one could possibly make any accusations about her apparel after a journey outside in a night like that. As she trudged the long dark laurel- and holly-lined passage down to the town, over to her right was thick darkness. All the lights were off in the town.

She was glad of the dark. On the way up it had seemed a menace. Now it was a cover, a concealment, a disguise, a way of becoming anonymous. Even if she met someone, with a bit of luck they wouldn't even recognise who she was.

When she reached Lime View she found a single candle burning in the front room, with David on the doorstep saying goodbye to his friends, who were obviously most disgruntled because their video had been cut off in its prime. Anne smiled a bitter smile to herself. At least *some* good had come of their actions—but there were other and better ways in which that same happier result could have occurred. Mumbling something to David about being tired she went straight to bed.

Derek wasn't in, of course. Probably attending to some patient on the far side of Maulden, she thought bitterly, as she lay down and tried to sleep. But sleep didn't come easily. The more she tried, the more restless she became. The more she thought about what had happened that evening, the more she hated herself, and the more she wondered why and how she had ever allowed herself to get carried away so completely and so unstoppably.

She tossed and turned for an hour until she heard Derek come in. Thinking she was asleep he undressed quietly and slid gently into bed beside her, trying hard not to disturb her, and within minutes Anne could hear him snoring, exhaustion having taken over. She lay awake beside him, staring at the sky which dimly outlined the window, and listened to the wind buffeting the world.

Up in the Old Rectory Martin was in a similar situation. Like Anne he couldn't sleep, but unlike Anne he eventually got up and stood staring through the window in front of him. Mostly he could see very little. Just occasionally the clouds parted and a little gleam of moonlight illuminated the landscape: but just as quickly the clouds blew across the moon again and the light was extinguished.

Martin felt dreadful. He'd got a tension headache as the muscles in the back of his neck went into continuous spasm, a thick head from being overtired, depressed and miserable, and now also not a guilt complex but *real* guilt, guilt that weighed down on him as though he'd been buried in a landslide.

Which was roughly what he would like to have happened to him. He wanted to run away, to go somewhere where no one would see him: especially where *God* wouldn't see him, and as he looked out of his window at the occasional star that was revealed, at the same heavens he'd stared at during that other dreadful crisis in his previous vicarage where he'd lost his faith, he now experienced the same awful feeling, except this time it was more dreadful. At least when he lost his faith he'd felt that death would just mean annihilation. Now he knew all too clearly what he'd done. He knew that God knew; he knew that he could never go back in time and undo his actions; nor could he ever escape from the all-seeing eye of God who would always know how badly Martin had let him down.

He stayed at the window for an hour, lost, frightened, guilty and overwhelmed. From time to time the clouds parted to let him see the stars. Now that it was March a different view of the heavens appeared compared to that first dreadful October night. The darkness was the same but the stars were different. Then it had been the constellations of Pegasus, Aries and Taurus in front of him. Now the patterns were different, and the heavens seemed to be laughing at him. Even the constellations seemed to know what he had done: there was Cancer, the crab; Leo, the lion; and... Virgo. How spectacularly inappropriate... Next was Boötes, with—appropriately enough—Serpens, the snake, following on close behind.

But what he didn't see, because it was obscured by cloud, was Hercules, following shortly afterwards, rising in the east.

*   *   *

Next morning there was a knock on the door of the Old Rectory. Martin, bleary-eyed, dragged himself downstairs to find a beaming Chris and Paul. The look on their faces when they saw Martin, tousled, red-eyed and dishevelled, could almost have come from a comic strip. Rarely have two people's fun and joy been punctured so emphatically as in that second when the door opened.

'Oh,' said Chris. 'I'm sorry, we seem to have come at a bad time.'

'No, no,' said Martin trying to smooth down his hair. 'Do come in. I just had a bad night, that's all.'

'It must have been a *very* bad one,' said Paul. 'It's eleven o'clock.'

'Is it?' said Martin, his mind only half on the conversation. At least it hadn't been Derek knocking on the door. That was one doctor's house visit he would definitely prefer not to have. Very definitely.

'Do come in. Sit down. Make yourselves comfortable. I'll just go and smarten up.'

It only took him five minutes. When he came down again he walked in awkwardly, embarrassed. 'Sorry to keep you waiting.'

'It's all right,' said Chris.

'What can I do for you?'

'We want to get married.'

'Really?' said Martin, his mind still only half on the situation. 'Er... congratulations. Um. What do you want me to do?'

Chris and Paul exchanged glances. 'Why, marry us of course, in church. Weddings. Remember?' said Paul.

'Er... Um... er, yes,' said Martin. 'Sorry, it's just that it's been rather a long time since I last did one. I rather thought they'd gone out of fashion.'

Paul coloured slightly. After all, he hadn't actually been married to Jane...

'It's just that... well, with all the upheaval of the past eighteen months, nobody's thought about any regulations for getting married. I was beginning to think the whole thing was a bit superfluous.' He was about to say 'Why don't you two just shack up together like everybody else does?' then thought about Anne and decided that it wasn't a very appropriate thing to say anyway, but went red all the same. 'I'm sorry, Paul, it all just seems a little strange, that's all. So many rules and regulations have gone by the board that it feels as though it was a different century when people got married officially. Come to think of it, even before the plague the Solemnisation of Matrimony seemed to have gone out of fashion.'

He recovered, realised he was making an utter fool of himself, and forced himself to become composed again. 'I'm sorry Chris,' he said. 'I've only just woken up and you've caught me by surprise. It just feels strange, that's all. How nice. How nice that you want to get married. I'm sure you'll be very good for each other.'

'I'd have gone without a marriage ceremony...' began Paul in an off-hand manner.

'...but I wouldn't let him,' said Chris, looking firmly at Paul and then glancing at Martin and smiling. 'I have to keep my maidenly virtue and honour intact, you know.'

Martin hoped Chris hadn't noticed how red he was becoming.

'When's the happy day?'

'We thought in about three weeks,' replied Chris.

'That's not really long enough,' said Martin. 'You have to get the banns read and...'

Chris looked at him quizzically.

'No you don't, do you...' Martin continued, now even more flustered. 'Not any more... Well, I suppose you could if you wanted to, but there doesn't seem much point, does there? The reading of banns was only to make sure that everybody *did* know. We can tell everyone very quickly that you're going to get married. It'll be all round the town in five minutes, anyway. We don't need to read the banns officially. I'm sure that's one of the regulations that can go by the board. I'm sure three weeks will be fine. Which day of the week for the ceremony itself?'

'Saturday,' they both said together.

Normally at that point Martin would have enquired as to whether one of the engaged couple was a baptised member of the Anglican Church, and if they weren't regular attenders at the church, would have asked why they wanted a church wedding. This had always irritated him. It seemed so silly that people often didn't acknowledge the existence of God except for the three cardinal offices of the church—hatches, matches and despatches. It made him feel rather used. It often seemed that the only reason why a marriage was being conducted in church was that it looked prettier: after all, the Registry Office was such a bleak place for the ceremony. There was an antique solemnity in getting married in a church that had seen hundreds of years of history, with local residents being baptised, confirmed, married and finally buried via its portals. English parish churches could look so nice and friendly and reassuring on these occasions. Nothing wrong in that, he supposed, but he did feel that perhaps a little more enthusiasm for the spiritual side of things might not be a bad thing. Why weren't people honest about it? he asked himself. Why didn't they go the whole hog and say they didn't believe in God, they weren't going to get baptised in church, they weren't going to get married in church and they weren't going to get buried from church? Why not put your money where your mouth is? he thought. Churches should be for Christians for whom the faith means something. Not for non-Christians who are living a lie if they come to church.

And then he pulled himself up short. What had he been doing last evening but living a lie? Talking of chastity, and the sanctity of marriage, and then doing... He shuddered inwardly, and not for the first time that morning. Clumsily he forced himself back to the matter in hand, the implications of which by now had filled him with dismay. How could he act as God's representative to marry these two people, even if they didn't believe in God? How could he do anything other than just hang his head in shame, disappear off the face of the earth, and hope nobody ever came looking for him? He wanted to die, to find a large hole in the ground and cover himself up with earth; and to have Paul and Chris come so soon, with delight on their faces and joy in their hearts, to discuss the beginning of their own union, when his illicit union with Anne had occurred just the night before, caused him a great deal of distress. How was he going to conduct the service? How could he look anybody in the eye again? What if other people found out? What would they say? They'd just point the finger of accusation at him and murmur under their breath about hypocrites. And he'd deserve it....

Somehow he kept this inner turmoil away from his face, and for the last time that morning, with a great effort, made himself— *forced* himself—to contemplate the matter in hand. Perhaps it was habit or professionalism but he'd learned what to say and how to say it, and knew how to give the confidence that the engaged couple needed over the procedures of the ceremony itself.

He sat back. 'Can I offer you a drink? I'd certainly like to make some for myself, seeing as I've not yet had breakfast,' and he smiled that warm smile. Chris and Paul, who had actually been slightly unnerved by Martin's uneasy approach, suddenly relaxed and nodded. Martin put a kettle on the stove and came back into the room. 'I think all we need to do is to announce the banns this Sunday and next Sunday. Everybody will know in ten minutes anyway. In any case I'm sure you'll want to tell everybody.'

Paul and Chris exchanged happy glances. 'May I ask why you want to get married in church?' He knew Paul had no belief in the supernatural—he'd known that already from the ribbing, not all of it good-natured, that he'd received at Paul's hands in the past; and as far as he could make out Chris had never exhibited any interest in religious things at all.

'It was my idea,' said Chris. 'To be honest, Paul wasn't even interested in getting married. You'd have been quite happy just to move in with me, wouldn't you?' Paul nodded. For once, Martin thought, Paul is subdued, and has been subdued by Chris. How interesting.

'I haven't got any particular beliefs,' continued Chris, 'but my family is... *was*... Roman Catholic on my mother's side, so I suppose it's been ingrained in me that good girls get married. And I really didn't want to risk getting pregnant without being officially wed. It didn't seem right. After all, contraceptives are in such short supply now, so I gather.'

Contraceptives.

Martin felt as though there had been an audible thud as his heart hit the floor. He'd not even thought about that. Probably Anne had, he thought: after all, David is fourteen...

'No,' he said sweetly, recovering himself. 'I gather Derek said he's got a few packets of the Pill left, but the stocks of sheaths have run out completely. I hadn't realised that chemists actually kept so few of them. Are you planning to have a family?'

'Oh yes,' said Chris. 'Eventually. Though we're not in any hurry.'

'It'll be nice to have some new lives around,' said Martin. 'We have so few couples of child-bearing age.'

'You won't need to worry about that for long,' said Paul. 'There are enough adolescents in the community—I should think they'll all be pairing off soon. We're just the first, that's all.'

Out in the kitchen the kettle started singing. Martin went out to make some acorn coffee and returned with three steaming cups.

'Now, what hymns had you thought of having?'

*   *   *

The community was set abuzz by the news of Paul and Chris's impending wedding, and the talk over the next three weeks was of little else. What sort of a wedding would it be? Would the bride wear white—and if so, where would she get it from? Where were they going on honeymoon—and if so, how? In the absence of hire car facilities, how were they going to get to and from the church? All they knew was that a banquet had been planned, and the White

Hart Hotel commissioned for the evening, but further than that Chris wasn't saying. It was all a Big Secret.

For three people in those next weeks, the time passed at completely different rates. Einstein taught us that time was a relative phenomenon. He certainly was the first to prove that time moved at different rates according to how quickly or slowly you were moving. Paul could have sworn that Einstein knew all about weddings.

For Paul, who couldn't wait to get Chris into bed with him and finally consummate their relationship, the three weeks seemed to stretch out to infinity: time passed like a snail.

For Chris, immersed in all the preparations, dresses, plans and food, there were just not enough hours in the day, and the hands on the clock in her lounge seemed to move round at an express pace.

For Martin, time seemed to have stopped still. Although on the surface he was still functioning normally, inside he had a lead weight where his heart ought to have been, and that same agonising, exhaustive, panic-stricken depression that he'd experienced when the plague first struck had returned to haunt him.

But it wasn't the same depression. The previous time he'd been in despair because the God whom he had once thought he knew seemed to have disappeared out of existence. Now he was an all-too real, ever-present, omniscient God and Martin was his particularly unfaithful acolyte. And Martin knew that God knew; and Martin felt that God would be *extremely* cross with him. Martin had of course prayed about what he'd done and asked for forgiveness—and for a moment the clouds seemed to lift. But then they returned, and it was like praying to a brazen sky, his inner cries unheard, his pleas for forgiveness and mercy unnoticed. He told God he was sorry for what he'd done. He told him that, given the same time over again, he'd do something entirely different. It wasn't as if it was a repetitive sin that he'd fallen into. He'd been caught on the hop just once and really, it was out of character and he wouldn't do it again...

Only it didn't make any difference. The prayers still seemed to bounce off the ceiling of his room and return to haunt him like a letter marked 'Return to sender, addressee unknown'. If ever a man kicked himself for his folly, Martin was that man. He didn't know where to put himself. After a time he couldn't even pray, he couldn't read the Bible, he didn't want to talk about God to anybody, he didn't want to meditate on Christian themes; all he could think about was that he had let God down in the most unbelievably crass and devastating way imaginable: and, not content with fouling up his own life, had managed to foul up someone else's in the process.

It is bad enough to sin oneself: but how much worse to induce someone else to sin also? And how much worse again when he was supposed to be in charge of that other person's spiritual growth and development? To say nothing about the effect that it would have on Derek and Anne's marriage if the truth got out. And if *that* happened, what would the effect be on the children...? Small things, small decisions, small events can sometimes have enormous consequences—like leaving broken air filters in hospital laboratories working with dangerous bacteria. Sometimes they can have a huge knock-on effect, causing devastation in ever-increasing quantities to those around; and sometimes—paradoxically—they have no effect whatsoever, and disappear as if they had never existed. Martin hoped fervently that his behaviour with Anne was of the latter variety.

The truth was that Martin desperately needed somebody to talk to, someone to whom he could unburden himself, somebody to hear his confession—not that the confessor could, of himself, rid Martin of what he had done, but by employing the biblical principle of confessing one's sins to a fellow Christian Martin would have been able to offload the burden: and as the saying goes, 'a trouble shared is a trouble halved'. Had he had a confessor to go to, he would have been told those things that he would have said to anyone else in the same situation—how everyone does wrong; that all sins are just as bad as (and no worse than) each other; how God is always ready to forgive, and does so readily; that the problem is all too often that the sinner has to learn to forgive himself; and that, now that Martin had confessed his sins to God, the real guilt was gone and that Martin's guilt *feelings* were just that—guilt feelings and human emotion, not real guilt, and certainly unrelated to what God was *really* like. But

Martin had no one to go to—and he certainly couldn't talk to anyone within the community. That would be just too appalling for
Anne. And so Martin stayed as he was, unable to move emotionally,
totally trapped—and wracked with an overwhelming sensation of
guilt.

- 15 -

*T*he snow came late that year. For many people—especially those
who live in towns—winter is the time of year when the nights are
longest. People like this feel that winter really should end by the
middle of February. Country people don't think like this, however!
It's no accident that on the calendar, winter extends from the 21st of
December until the 21st day of March. Even though the sun rises for
longer, the earth is gradually and progressively losing heat, and
March can sometimes be as cold as, if not colder than, January. So
it was that year, as the snow drifted down from a leaden sky, covering the earth in a blanket four inches deep, to the delight of the children, the fear of the elderly and the annoyance of those who had to
work in it.

Martin was one of the latter. Part of his job within the community was to help with the sheep which, during inclement weather,
were penned in a barn high up on the top of the Greensand Ridge
above Houghton House. It was Martin's job to bring them bales of
hay, as they were totally unable to get at the grass in the fields for
the thick layer of snow covering it.

That next afternoon he had to get up to the barn to do his chores.
As it happened he needed to go and see Mary first, and having left
her house on the Maulden road the obvious route was to go up Gas
House Lane and over the footpath up to the top of the ridge. He
trudged up the first part of the walk along the unmade lane with
hedges on either side. Then the country became more open and the
footpath, though indicated by signs, lay buried under a blanket of

virgin snow. Martin trudged up the track in the late afternoon, the dazzling whiteness of the snow around him. Surprisingly, it was a warm day, without the usual clammy coldness that one gets in snow. For anybody else other than Martin it would have been an exhilarating walk because the footpath offers one of the best views of Ampthill and the surrounding landscape. But Martin couldn't see anything. Blind to the world around him, conscious only of the trudge, trudge, trudge of his Wellingtons into the snow but really thinking only of the awfulness of what he had done, he wandered up the footpath.

From most parts of Ampthill the object most visible on the horizon, looking south, is the great water tower at Pulloxhill which appears to dominate the scene. It seems to be the most important and prestigious object around, lording it over the landscape, standing tall on top of the hill on which Pulloxhill sits. But a walker up that footpath to the top of the ridge under which Ampthill nestles finds that something quite strange happens as he ascends towards the summit, because that great water tower suddenly becomes reduced in significance. Standing on the ridge, looking back, the walker sees in front of him the town of Ampthill, nestling securely against the side of the Greensand Ridge, and then beyond it the vast bowl of the valley leading up to the Chilterns. From the top of the ridge, the hill of Pulloxhill appears quite puny—hardly a hill at all, more an overgrown lump—and the water tower itself appears to be almost at the bottom of a long shallow bowl of a valley, beyond which the Chiltern Hills rise in the distance, a much more magnificent range than the tiny hill upon which Pulloxhill is built. Had Martin bothered to stop, look and take notice, he would have seen the whole of the valley covered in pristine whiteness, with the drab greens and mud colours of the countryside in March covered by a shimmering, shining, glistening white garment that made the roughest, darkest, most unappetising areas scintillate. Had he looked. Martin might have been reminded of the verse in Isaiah which says 'Though your sins be as scarlet, they shall be as white as snow.' Had Martin realised it, he was actually walking through a living parable.

Had he had his eyes on the sky and the horizon he might have seen it, but looking downwards as he was, all he could see was the tips of his green Wellingtons plunging into the snowdrift, as with head bowed he walked towards the barn and the sheep. Behind him the great water tower had paled into insignificance: the dark, drab, sadness of the winter fields had become glitteringly beautiful in their new clothes. The town of Ampthill was snug and secure in the shelter of the Greensand Ridge and the sun was bathing the whole area in light.

But he missed it and continued to trudge towards the sheep thinking of only two things—what a fool he was, and how badly he had let God down.

*   *   *

The day before the wedding there was a knock on the door of the Old Rectory. Martin hurried from his study, to find Anne on the step. Almost by reflex he looked past her, and was relieved to find that Derek wasn't there.

'Hello,' he said, 'you better come in.'

It was the first time they'd met since their brief affair. Martin had been avoiding Anne like the plague. Anne hadn't been too keen on meeting Martin, either, but managed a weak smile.

'How are you?' he said.

'I've missed a period,' she said, without more ado.

Martin staggered as if sandbagged. 'You've what?'

'I've missed a period.'

'Are you sure?'

'Of course I'm sure.' The green eyes stared at Martin in a mixture of contempt, anger and fear. 'What do you take me for, a fool?'

'No, no it was... I mean... aren't women sometimes... late?'

'With a positive pregnancy test as well?'

'Oh.' Then the realisation dawned. 'You mean Derek knows?'

'No. I slipped into the chemist's while no one was looking.'

Martin still looked dazed, his mouth opening and shutting like a fish, without any sound coming out. The enormity of it all had only just started to sink in. Not only had they disobeyed God but the results didn't just stop there.

'Are you sure it's... mine?'

'Yes.'

'Couldn't it be... Derek's? I mean couldn't you go back and sleep with him and make sure that he doesn't realise...?' Fleeting memories of an Old Testament story came back to him—Bathsheba.

'It would make no difference.'

'Why not?'

'He's had a vasectomy.' In Martin's brain the last little glimmer of hope suddenly died.

'What about... doing away with it?'

'*Martin!* You, a priest, talk about things like that. How could you?' The tone in her voice had passed from fear, through anger to total disdain.

'I... well... it seemed... Well, it's different now, isn't it?'

'Different?' she said. 'So it was all very well for you to pontificate when it was someone else having an abortion, but when it's convenient for you, you think your bit on the side ought to have one.'

Martin reached out his hand to hold her arm. 'Anne, I didn't mean it like that.'

'*Get your hands off me,*' she snarled. 'How *dare* you touch me.'

Martin recoiled as if he'd received an electric shock, like a primitive amoeba, all the pseudopodia pulled in together into one little blob.

'Anyway, how do you think I could get one done? Who'd have to do it? Derek, of course.'

'Ah... Oh... Aren't there ways...? What did the old country people do... strips of willow bark or something? There's always knitting needles, I suppose.'

'*You are the pits,*' snarled Anne. 'You really are. You disgust me. You really do. You're quite content to pull me into bed with you but you don't exactly want to bear the consequences, do you?'

The thought did float through Martin's mind that her description was not a complete and full representation of what had actually happened on that fateful evening, but wisely he chose not to rise to the bait.

'All right,' said Anne, her eyes still blazing. 'I'll tell you what we'll do. I'm going to have the baby but you're not to tell anyone who the father is.'

Martin's jaw dropped.

'But Derek will know...'

'Derek won't know, and even if he does, you're not to tell anyone else. Have you got that? You're my priest, aren't you?'

All Martin could do was nod his head. 'And everything that passes between a priest and a parishioner is confidential, isn't it?'

Martin nodded again.

'Well then, the name of the father of my baby is confidential. Do you understand? You are to reveal it to no one. *No one.* Do you hear?' And having said that she spun on her heels and stormed off down the drive leaving Martin, still open-mouthed, staring after her retreating figure.

                    *   *   *

The following day was *the* day—the first wedding in the community. The snow had gone, to be replaced by a warm, slightly breezy April morning. The crocuses had been and gone, but the daffodils were out and Chris and her helpers had decorated the church with large bunches of them. Little else was available: no early flowers from the Scilly Islands or tulips from Holland any longer—just daffodils and narcissi in their yellow and white profusion.

The wedding had been set for midday and by eleven-thirty quite a crowd of townspeople had gathered outside Foulislea Cottage to watch the bride walk the short distance to the church. Their patience was eventually rewarded when at five minutes before noon Chris emerged in a gorgeous white wedding gown that she'd found in a dress shop in Woburn. There were three bridesmaids, of whom Sarah was the smallest and prettiest—and the proudest. Chris of course had no relatives, so Derek had agreed to stand in to give her away—but with two minutes to go it was a suddenly tearful Chris who realised with a certain sudden grim finality that her real father should have been there to do the honours, and would have been, had it not been for the plague.

It was with a mixture of tearfulness and joy that she finally stepped out over the threshold for the last time in her unmarried state. The little retinue slowly made its way to the church, surrounded by cheering well-wishers. The quiet and gentle Peter was one of the ushers: David had the job of pumping the organ again—for a suitable fee—and as Chris walked up the aisle on Derek's arm she could see the tall figure of Paul waiting for her at the chancel steps, with his best man, Neil, at his side.

Martin was at the chancel steps, too, standing, waiting, though his thoughts were very far away indeed. He announced the first hymn: the packed church echoed to the rafters as virtually everyone in the community had come to take part and the cheerful noise spread outwards to the open door, wafting over the now still and silent town outside.

The hymn ended and Martin began the wedding service. 'We have come together in the presence of God, to witness the marriage of Paul and Christine...' Everything went well until Martin reached the point where the couple make their vows to each other and suddenly, yet again, the enormity of what he'd done seemed to be displayed in front of his eyes and waved around publicly for everyone in the congregation to see.

At least it seemed that way to Martin. No one else realised what he was thinking—except Anne, who, standing in the first pew on Martin's right, was next to where Derek would sit once he had given away the bride. Studiously she avoided Martin's face. It was a good job that she did, for had she looked at him, he would probably have been able to bear it no longer and would have broken down.

First of all, there was the charge to Paul: 'Will you take Christine to be your wife? Will you love her, comfort her, honour and protect her, and, forsaking all others, be faithful to her as long as you both shall live?' to which Paul answered—surprisingly softly—'I will'.

Then Martin repeated the same question to Chris, which she answered in a similarly hesitant manner, obviously affected by her emotions. As always, the congregation strained their ears to hear.

Martin continued: 'Paul, will you repeat after me. I Paul Ignatius

Greatorex...'—he saw Paul wince at the mention of his second name—

'*I, Paul Ignatius Greatorex.*'

'...take you, Christine Mary Wilson.'

'*take you, Christine Mary Wilson.*'

'...to be my wife.'

'*to be my wife.*'

'...to have and to hold...' Martin felt his knees start to shake. With a desperate effort he pulled himself together.

'...to love and to cherish.'

'*to love and to cherish.*'

'...till death us do part.'

'*till death us do part.*'

'...according to God's holy law.'

'*according to God's holy law.*'

Oh God, thought Martin. He looked up at Anne. For one brief second their eyes met, and then she looked away again. *O God*, thought Martin, *what **have** I done*? I've cuckolded her husband, I've impregnated his wife, I've helped break these same marriage vows that *she* made before God; I can't undo it, there's no going back, and soon everyone will know about it. Nothing I can do will make any difference at all. And in that moment he wished that the stone floor beneath him would open and swallow him up, and wished—sincerely—that he had never been born.

Out of the corner of his eye he could see the yellow daffodils trembling in Chris's hand. At first he thought it was something that he'd said or done, that some hint of what had happened had been given away by an involuntary movement of his face. But then he realised that Chris was responding not to him, Martin, but to Paul.

He led Chris through the same promises. Pointedly she had said that she would not agree 'to obey' but nevertheless she also was obliged to recite the phrase 'to love and to cherish, till death us do part' and at that same moment Martin glanced up again at Anne, who was studiously regarding the interesting architecture of the floorboards at her feet.

The rest of the service was a blur to Martin. How he got through

it he would never know, but habit and professionalism took over—
after all he had performed the service so many times for so many
unbelieving parishioners he had had to marry that he could have got
through it blindfolded, backwards and asleep, had he needed to. But
he said the right things in the right way, at the right time, with the
right phrasing, and looked to the congregation as though he was
benignly pleased to be able to give the church's statutory pat on the
back—or was it the head?—for the couple choosing on just that one
occasion to bother to come.

And then it was over, and the wedding march sounded as the
beaming couple slowly processed down the aisle, followed by the
bridesmaids, including an excited Sarah who in her enthusiasm
nearly trod on the bride's train. Anne processed out on Derek's arm
with not a glance at Martin as the rest of the congregation poured
out of the church by all available exits to come round and act as a
human tunnel through which the couple passed on their way out of
the church door, under the lych gate, and into Church Square in
front of Dynevor House.

Martin was left alone in the chancel, staring at the receding congregation. They all seemed symbolically to have turned their backs
on him and though the light in the church was bright and golden in
the noonday sun and the flowers cheerful and bright, Martin could
see none of it. To him the world looked and felt the colour and the
weight of lead—grey-black, pressing down on him, burying him,
suffocating him. And there was no one to tell, no one at all. He
couldn't even share it with Anne, for Anne, he knew, had now totally disowned him.

The bridal party made their way to the White Hart Hotel, opposite the clock tower at the end of the Market Square, for the recep-
tion. For everyone else other than Martin and Anne there was something wonderful about that day, that burned itself irrevocably into
their memories. It was the first new day of the new age: the first day
of new life. It was a celebration, the first couple to be married since
the plague had destroyed nearly everything in its path, and now on
this brilliant and beautiful spring morning with the early flowers
coming out in their radiance, there was a sense at last that life was

going to continue, and that out of the union of these two people—
and many more to follow—would come new life, new hope, and a
new generation. Even though it was early April everyone knew that
it was the beginning of the New Year. And though the harvest of the
previous September had been an occasion for great rejoicing it was
the close of a year, not the opening of one. Now the old year had
gone, and as in the old days when the New Year was considered to
occur at the end of March, so the present-day inhabitants also felt a
new age had arrived.

The happy mood shone into everyone's hearts that day—except
two of them—and the laughing, bubbling, cheerful faces of the
townspeople who had come to celebrate with Chris and Paul were
glowing with exuberance. There was no forced merriment, none of
the false bonhomie induced by an excess of alcohol. Instead, there
was genuine happiness: a simple, carefree enthusiasm that welcomed what the day meant, that upheld what the two of them had
promised to each other, that rejoiced with them in their good fortune, and at long last looked forward with them to the future. There
was feasting and dancing and speeches and merriment and wine and
beer and food—and more food, and more food—until the inn which
seemed so much an extension of their existence and the centre of
the communal spirit seemed to burst with the celebration within,
and the people danced until they could dance no more, and ate until
they could eat no more, and talked until they could talk no more.

And then it was evening, and time for the bride and groom to
leave. Where were they going for their honeymoon? As Paul had
said, Jamaica's out this year. As in the old days, they didn't go on
honeymoon at all. Surrounded by the same horde of well-wishers,
Paul simply led Chris off, hand in hand up Woburn Street, until they
came to his thatched cottage on the far side of the hill. Stooping to
undo the gate, Paul walked up the short path to the door, unlatched
it, returned to pick up his bride, and to the 'Ooohs' of the onlookers, carried her over the threshold.

He closed the door behind them, then put his arms round Chris
and gave her a long passionate kiss. 'Not so fast, young sir,' she said
coyly, gently pushing him away in fun. 'You'll have to wait just a

little bit longer. I'm going upstairs to change.'

'Well, there's one good thing,' said Paul, relaxing on to the sofa. 'At least if we didn't go off in a car we didn't get a trail of Coke cans behind us. Not so much room for practical jokes, eh?'

By that time Chris had reached the top of the stairs and switched on the light in the bedroom. There was a white flash and a scream. Paul shot up the stairs to find a quivering Chris standing at the top, not sure whether to cry, scream, laugh, or hit someone. Outside there was a great guffaw from the crowd.

'I knew I'd find a use for that flashbulb one day,' said Trevor very loudly, to no one in particular. Grinning, Chris sagged into Paul's arms and then looked up at him.

'It was a good day, wasn't it?'

'It was a good day,' echoed Paul—then, putting on his most Machiavellian look—'but there's more to come.'

'Is there?' she said, letting him unbutton her dress, studying his face intently as it slipped to the floor.

'I've been waiting for this moment for a long time,' he said as he guided her towards the bed.

'And what makes you think *I* haven't been waiting for this for a long time, too?' she replied, looking at him with a glint in her eye.

'Well, you've been pretty restrained about it all.'

'That doesn't mean I'm not looking forward to it,' she said, deftly helping him out of his clothes.

'I love you.'

'Well, come on, then,' she said, pulling him on to the bed. 'Show me how much.'

- 16 -

*T*o Peter Abraham's relief the work with the Buckingham group seemed to be going well. There had been no time to find or train shire horses to plough their fields—but desperate times require desperate measures. Even after paying for the grain, there had been just enough fuel left in the Buckingham area to allow them to use the tractors, almost as one last despairing effort at the end of February. They'd used some of the seed corn that had been saved from the last year's crop in Ampthill and, with not too much time left, had managed to plough and harrow the fields, then drill and sow them with wheat. Neil hadn't enjoyed making the decision to use the diesel and petrol, but he was faced with little alternative. If they didn't set more fields to wheat then they definitely wouldn't have enough food for the next year, bearing in mind that the community had effectively doubled in size. He was acutely aware that the yields were going to be low: petrol there might be, fertiliser there certainly was not. Nor was there any weedkiller.

Once the Buckingham group had got food inside them they were much more capable of working, and as soon as Neil and Peter showed them what to do they cottoned on well. Even so, both men noted how little initiative they seemed to have. Whilst they were good at working, none of them seemed able to think ahead, and although they would respond by working willingly, thoroughly and effectively, they always responded to what Neil and Peter suggested, and never anticipated it. Still, by the end of March they had managed to plough and set a large number of the most fertile fields, and all that was needed was to wait to see if the wheat would grow well enough without extra fertiliser. It was going to be a bit of a race anyway, because the fields had been planted at the very last minute, and were far behind the wheat that had been sown in the autumn in Ampthill.

And Neil had started looking up at the sky again. Always an unnerving sight, thought Peter, remembering back to the previous year. The weather is so critical in farming, and so unpredictable. He just wished they could know more about it.

*   *   *

For the past two months Alan seemed to have disappeared off the scene entirely. Glad of any excuse to be away from his nagging wife, he turned her into a radio widow. Not that Schrödinger, the cat, noticed: within two days he'd managed to find where Alan was working, and turned the New Rectory into *his* second home, too.

While Susan had been busily engaged writing up her diary, and their son Darren loafing around with Kevin, David and Trevor, Alan had buried himself in his work with the radio up at the New Rectory. He could afford to spend time on it—he'd negotiated a very favourable rate with the council, telling them that he would use the radio equipment to the best of his ability, and then report to them on his findings. Paul wasn't particularly enamoured of this open-ended arrangement, but the others, who saw no need to distrust Alan's judgement, were content to see what he could produce. They recognised that it might take some time, not to say a little bit of pure serendipity, both for him to work out how to use the equipment and then have the luck to be listening in on one of the thousands of available frequencies at just the time when someone else was broadcasting on that same frequency—if indeed anybody *was* broadcasting.

By the end of March Alan had notched up a total of twenty-seven separate ham radio stations in various parts of the globe. From them he'd worked out that more or less precisely the same series of events had happened in the rest of the world as had occurred in England at the time the plague struck. In each nation there'd been initial disbelief and administrative inertia—until it was too late: then the altered Legionnaires' organism had gone on the rampage, infecting all and sundry in its path. As in England, the inhabitants of other countries had died in their millions, fleeing from the centres of outbreak which were universally the cities, and particularly the airports. Unlike the Black Death, which in the Middle Ages had spread at a rate of about three miles a week, courtesy of the movements of the black rat, modern-day transport systems had ensured that the plague of Legionnaires' disease had spread round the world almost instantaneously. Just as flu epidemics started off in the Far East, sweeping across the world, aided by air transport, so Legionnaires' disease spread across the world in the same way. A different deadly disease, malaria, is spread by a flying vector—the mosquito—which bites its victims and injects minute quantities of blood infected with the malaria parasite. So too did the Legionnaires' disease have a flying vector—but in this case it was encased in large aluminium cylinders many times bigger than a mosquito, with fixed alloy wings and screaming jet engines, and packed with people. It was still a flying vector though, and just as deadly. It was also faster than the mosquito.

During the last weeks of February and first two of March Alan had sat shivering, huddled over the transmitter, headphones clamped to his ears, hands carefully sweeping the dials, listening for any sound of a broadcast.

And he'd found them: not many, but they were there all right, transmitting erratically, and intermittently. Some of them were previous radio hams with a fluency of operating that was immediately obvious. Others were total amateurs, driven to the radio by pure necessity in the need to make contact, or get help or advice.

When from time to time Alan picked up another ham radio station he would always first make arrangements to talk with them again at a particular time on a particular frequency. The last thing he wanted was to contact someone by luck, and then not be able to find them again. The next thing he did was discover what had happened in that particular area. Many of the hams he conversed with could speak English, but some couldn't and so from time to time Alan would bring one of the Ampthill residents who could speak French or German or Spanish or Portuguese up to the New Rectory to see if a mutual language could be found, a ploy which often worked for stations in Europe, Africa and the Americas, but wasn't quite so good for Asia. Many of the Asian population did have a smattering of English, though, but even so there were many stations that he couldn't communicate with even though he could *speak* to them. The frustration was enormous—knowing that there was somebody there, yet not being able to communicate at all, other than to make noises in strange languages which, on both sides, were unintelligible.

By mid-March it was apparent that the epidemic of Legionnaires' disease which had begun in Richmond had spread throughout the whole of the globe and in each country the pattern of destruction was virtually the same as in England—cities desolate, piles of bodies on the streets, immovable traffic jams around the outskirts of towns, blocking the main roads. As had happened in England, groups of survivors in these other countries had come together, some because they were already immune to the disease, others because they'd had antibiotics that protected against it, or else—in solitary places, hill stations, isolated villages and the like—because the plague had simply passed them by.

Day after day and night after night—because he was talking to people on the other side of the world—Alan pored over his set, scribbling down the information he received: sheet after sheet of it, names of contacts, where they lived, the frequencies they were transmitting on, how many there were in their community, how they were faring,. what lessons they'd learned, what problems they'd had... In the manner of everyone thrown into a difficult situation they shared their ideas, swapped their stories and sometimes even solved each other's problems. Almost like a Newsgroup on the now defunct Internet, they helped each other out, suggesting answers to problems and ways of getting out of situations that the other groups had somehow not cottoned on to. More than once Alan called in Derek to try to help someone with an ill child or an injured relative, and just like the old Flying Doctor service in the past—where most of the consultation was done over the air and not face to face—so Derek was able to spread his practice to the far-flung corners of the earth.

His most spectacular success to date had been to help a small group in the wilds of Canada. One of them—a young lad—had fallen and given himself an obvious Colles' fracture of the left wrist. Derek, who a year earlier had had to treat Alan's son Darren with the same problem, gave step-by-step instructions over the air on how to reduce the fracture, manipulate the arm into its normal position, and then hold it in place.

The only problem was that the people in Canada had no anaesthetic, and no plaster of Paris either, and for an hour afterwards Alan could still hear the screams of the patient as the manipulator crunched the bones of the forearm back into their correct alignment, and then taped the arm against a convenient board to hold it steady for the next three weeks. But it worked, and a month later Derek heard to his delight that the arm was mending and, now out of its imitation plaster, was functioning normally with no sign of any nerve or muscle damage.

Alan's list of contacts grew longer by the day: he had now made contact with people on every continent. Australia seemed to have more than its fair share of radio hams, perhaps because the plague hadn't managed to penetrate into the wilds of the outback, and outback dwellers often had radios anyway. However, Alan found to his frustration that although he could often hear them, they couldn't hear him. This was because although his equipment was rigged up to listen on a wide variety of frequencies, it was constructed only to be able to transmit on a smaller range of frequencies, owing to the previous regulations under which ham radio stations worked before the plague. There were one or two people broadcasting in Europe, quite a number in South America—but not many in Africa; there were a few from the Far East, but nothing, just *nothing*, in the whole of the Indian sub-continent.

When he talked with his contacts in Europe Alan always asked about the weather, in case the information might help Neil—but it always seemed to him that he knew what their weather was going to be before they did, and not vice versa. That would fit of course, because in general weather fronts come in from the Atlantic and head out over Europe, so Alan would know first. What the people in Ampthill really needed was information from the Atlantic—from the Azores, perhaps, or else from some of the weather ships. Only there weren't any.

All this information Alan had assiduously been relating to the council: they considered that it was well worth the money he was being paid, and kept giving him a weekly fee for his trouble.

And then came the silence. It was as if Alan had gone into purdah. Hardly anybody saw him—except perhaps for Martin, on his way to and from the Old Rectory. The reports to the council dried up completely. Just occasionally Alan could be seen beavering away, fiddling with one of the antennae on the lawn outside, or else moving around inside the ground floor rooms of the New Rectory, but what he was doing, or how he was getting on with it—that remained a mystery. The only time he spoke to anyone was three days after Chris and Paul's wedding, when he came to find some chicken wire. Apart from that it was as if he had disappeared off the face of the earth.

Indeed it had got to such a stage that the members of the council were starting to ask awkward questions. Paul in particular was beginning to wonder if the money Alan was being paid was worth it, but Chris gently urged him to be patient, and Derek, who knew all too well how much time was needed before someone studying an unfamiliar subject could be even remotely proficient in it, agreed. If Alan was working on something, and Alan felt it was worth it, then as far as Derek was concerned, it was worth it too.

In the middle of April, Derek was sitting in the front room of Lime View house one lunch time studying a book on parasitology, when there was a sudden furious knocking on the front door. Putting the book down he hurried into the hall, thinking with a sinking heart that he wasn't going to get much peace before he had to go off on the rest of his rounds. He opened the door to find the excited face of Alan grinning at him. 'Have I got something to show you,' Alan began. 'Come and have a look.' Derek grabbed his coat and yelled to Anne that he was going up to the Rectory. Anne's heart missed a beat, as at first she'd thought he'd meant the Old Rectory —but then she realised that it was Alan with him, not Martin.

All the way up Holly Walk Alan talked about everything except the real purpose of his visit. He spoke about the crops and the flowers, questions about how the work at Buckingham was going, asking after Derek and the practice—anything but the reason why he had come down to Derek with such speed. By the time they had got to the Rectory Derek was both intrigued and infuriated, irritated he'd been disturbed, but certain that if Alan wanted him to come it would be worth it. Even so, Alan's continuing habit of not answering questions was proving frustrating.

Reaching the Rectory Derek could see all manner of poles, metal rods, radio dishes and other antennae dotted on the croquet lawn, attached to sundry parts of the roof, or tacked on to masts that had been hastily erected around the place. Ducking through the door Alan gestured Derek to sit in front of the mass of equipment that was spread out on the table in front of him. There were banks and banks of it. It had obviously grown by several factors since Derek had first seen it. On the left-hand side of the desk was the familiar shape of a computer, linked by numerous wires to the radio console.

'Where did you find all this?' asked Derek, waving a hand at the extra equipment.

'Oh that,' said Alan in a slightly dismissive way, obviously concentrating hard on setting everything up correctly. 'That's been there some time—ten days, I suppose. I found another house with ham radio equipment in it, in Flitwick. There, it's ready.' He sat down in the chair and rolled himself up to the desk.

'I should think this lot uses up a bit more than a hundred watts?'

'Not half. I had to get special dispensation from the council—oh, of course you weren't at the meeting, were you? You'd been called out... They agreed. They were all quite happy... Sit yourself down Derek, do.'

Reaching across, Alan switched on, first the computer, and then the radio station itself. 'Don't touch a thing,' he said, pointedly knocking away Derek's hand as he was about to touch a particular dial and ask what it did. The screen gradually faded up into life as the computer went through its start-up routines, then automatically switched into the program that Alan had prepared. On the screen, building up slowly, line by line over a period of about three minutes, a pale white disc appeared, surrounded by an intense black border. When it had got to the bottom the line began again at the top, overwriting what had previously been there.

Derek stared at it. At first it looked as though it was all the same shade of white but on closer inspection he could distinguish differences—faint nuances of light and dark, wispy strands that were lighter than other areas. It looked like a mottled light bulb viewed end on, from the top. After perusing it for another two minutes Derek turned to Alan, puzzled.

'So what's the big deal. What is it?'

'You don't know?' said Alan, staring at him in disbelief. 'You really don't know?'

'Try me.'

'You're looking at yourself.'

'I'm what?'

'You're looking at yourself.'

'I know I'm going bald but this is ridiculous.'

Alan grinned. 'You really don't know, do you?' He jabbed his finger at a point on the circle at about two o'clock, halfway from centre to edge. 'That's where we are.' Alan looked at Derek again, half spluttered and half laughed. 'You really don't know what this is, do you?'

'No...'

'It's a picture from the NOAA weather satellite. That's the Atlantic. That's us.'

And then Derek saw. When we don't know what we're looking at we often can't make head or tail of the picture, but once we understand what it is that is being viewed everything suddenly snaps into place. Suddenly Derek could see it all—the vague outlines of Europe and North Africa, the great whirlpools of cloud, far out in the Atlantic Ocean, heralding the arrival of weather fronts with their rain. He looked up at Alan, his eyes shadowy in the reflected glow from the screen.

'How on earth did you do that?'

'With a lot of hard work, a great deal of application, goodness knows how many reference books and a radio dish made of chicken wire.'

'So there really is a picture to be received?'

'Why shouldn't there be? The weather satellite's still out there broadcasting automatically just as it's been doing since it was first launched. It's above the equator, circling the earth once every twenty-four hours, so it keeps on station at exactly the same point all the time. It doesn't need activating by any form of ground control—it's powered by solar energy, and it just keeps on relaying back the pictures it sees, twenty-four hours a day, three hundred and sixty-five days a year, whether there's anyone on the ground to

receive them or not. So there you are. That's what I've been working on for the past two or three weeks. Worth it, do you think?'

Derek sat back in his chair dumbfounded. 'Have you shown this
to anybody else?'

'Not yet. I thought you'd be the one who'd be most interested.'

'You've not shown it to Neil?'

'He'll be the next. Be a good chap and go and get him for me
would you, while I fine-tune the aerial again? It's gone off slightly:
must be the wind...'

'I most certainly will,' said Derek levering himself up out of the
chair. 'I most certainly will.' It wasn't often that Derek was given
his marching orders in such a peremptory manner, but the cloud of
concentration had descended on Alan again, and Derek knew better
than to interrupt him in his thoughts.

Fortunately, Neil was in his house, diagonally opposite from
Dynevor House. On hearing what Derek had to say he just dropped
everything and ran up Holly Walk arriving breathless, a hundred
and fifty yards ahead of Derek. Neil rushed into the room with the
radio equipment and stood transfixed by the image glowing on the
computer screen in front of him.

'Well I never,' he said slowly. 'Alan, you're brilliant. I never, *ever*
believed that we could do this.'

'I have to say I'm a little surprised myself,' said Alan. 'I think it
was more by luck than good judgement.'

'Well I never,' said Neil again, not really listening to Alan's
answer, his mouth remaining open in a sort of perpetual gasp.
Suddenly he turned and looked at Alan in the gloom and quiet of the
darkened room, with the only sound the whistle of the TV screen.

'Do you know how to read these things?'

'No, I thought you might.'

'Not really. I mean... like everybody else, I used to see the satellite pictures on the television but the forecasters usually told us
what it all meant. And anyway, they had the outlines of the continents and the land drawn by hand. It's not quite so easy to see where
everything is, is it?'

'No.'

'But I think if you see up here...' Neil pointed to about three o'clock on the screen, '...you can see a vaguely lighter area. I think that's got to be at the western bulge of Africa.'

'Yes,' said Alan. 'Yes, it is.' By now Derek had joined them, three faces staring at a glowing white screen in the darkened room, like three witches over a cauldron. Appropriately enough, Schrödinger chose that moment to nestle up against Alan's legs in the hope of food, and was most displeased to get a peremptory shove out of the way.

'Look,' said Derek, pointing to the mid-Atlantic. 'Look at this whirlpool of cloud here. And this bit...' He pointed at a thicker band. '... I should think that's a front. Have we got any books on weather forecasting?'

'I'm sure there'll be some in the library,' said Alan.

'Why don't you turn the Rectory into a weather station as well?' continued Derek. 'See if we can find a maximum and minimum thermometer. We can make a rainfall gauge and measure the wind speed.'

'I know just how to get that done,' said Alan. 'There's weather equipment out at Silsoe at the Agricultural College. Do you remember that white box made out of slats with an anemometer on top of it? It's in the middle of the grass in front of the College. Let's get that and bring it across here. It'll probably have a sunshine recorder in it as well.'

'How does that work?' asked Neil.

'Very simply, as it happens,' said Alan. 'It's just a simple glass ball—the sort a fortune teller would use—which focuses the light of the sun onto a strip of paper surrounding it, so that when it's sunny it burns a hole in it, and when it's cloudy it doesn't. As the sun goes round the sky and as the day progresses, the amount of line burned on the paper indicates how long the sun has been out. All you have to do is remember to change the paper each day and label it with the date, and you've got a permanent record of the amount of sunshine each day.'

'So what I do is set up a weather station here, find out what the weather is like and correlate it with the weather patterns that I see relayed down from the satellite.'

'Got it in one,' said Derek. 'And that way, once we've learned what the weather patterns in the Atlantic mean, we'll be able to predict what the weather's going to do to us over the next few days.'

'Brilliant!' said Alan.

Neil turned to them both, his face wreathed in smiles.

'Do you realise what this means?'

'I think we have a rough idea,' said Alan.

'It'll take all the guesswork away,' said Neil. 'Thank goodness.'

*   *   *

True to his promise, over the next two months Alan copied down the pictures from the screen and made meticulous recordings of the weather outside. His leatherwork could wait, he told himself. Susan, of course, disagreed, but soon changed her mind when she heard what sort of retainer the council had finally agreed to pay him, so instead she simply confined herself to nagging Alan about not having a proper job, being out all the time, not spending enough time with Darren, and coming in at strange hours.

But Alan had long got past caring. He knew the value of what he was doing, and wasn't going to be deflected from his task. Soon he had learned to distinguish the various types of cloud and what each sort meant, and by comparing his observations with the patterns of the satellite photographs was increasingly able to predict the weather that Ampthill would experience the next day. In his years as a farmer Neil had already acquired a considerable feel for the weather, but only in a local way—until now he hadn't had to interpret the wider information that came directly from the satellite. He was on a learning curve, too, and regularly would go up to the Rectory with Alan to pore over the pictures on the computer screen, looking for the subtler details, trying to extract every possible bit of information from the picture. To make life easier, during good weather when everything was clear they'd drawn in the outlines of the continents on the screen with a Chinagraph, so they could always know where weather fronts were, even if the cloud was so dense as to cover the land outlines entirely.

During the next two months the pair of them became increasingly good at predicting the weather for the next few days, though, like the professional forecasters before them, they found that forecasts beyond this time were much less reliable, courtesy of chaos theory.

Their first major triumph came when Neil had to decide when to mow the hay. Looking directly at the sky in late May he'd thought that perhaps the next day would be a good time to start, but on going to the Rectory he saw on the satellite picture the ominous signs of a front moving in from the Atlantic. The mowing would have to wait. True to form the next day was dull and drizzling, but then the skies cleared and as expected the sun came out, the air grew hot and Neil finally gave the order for the hay to be cut and left to dry.

That the weather did exactly as they had predicted gave Neil enormous confidence and a much surer hold on the decisions that he, and only he, could make.

Over in Buckingham the hay had been mown too, followed shortly afterwards by the beginnings of the soft fruit harvest, the strawberries. As agreed, a proportion of the harvest—some ten per cent—was carted across to Ampthill to pay for the work, expertise and grain that had previously been shipped west.

It was then that the first real signs of stress began to show. There was a marked surliness on the part of the Buckingham group at any mention of paying their tithe, as it came to be known. No matter that they had been rescued from the brink of total starvation, no matter that they owed their very existence to the generosity and backing of the Ampthill residents, they were still very resentful of having to pay for what they had already consumed. For Peter, it spoiled what was otherwise a very satisfying and successful spring.

*   *   *

For Martin the summer became a dazed mixture of anxiety, panic, guilt and loneliness. At the purely human level he was all too aware of what he'd done: how he'd made someone else's wife pregnant, and the rift in the family that this was undoubtedly about to cause. At a religious level he suffered enormous guilt for what he'd done against God, deeply aware of the lack of trust that he'd displayed, and that he'd let down those who had depended upon him to keep his feelings under control in his work as pastor. And then there was the problem of his standing—and by implication God's standing—in the eyes of others, when knowledge of the origin of the pregnancy became public, as surely it must sooner or later.

And he had to face all of this alone, his misery made worse because Anne had so obviously cut herself off from him. He began to miss her dreadfully. It was only after she had severed herself from him that Martin began to realise how deep were his feelings for her, feelings that he'd not been aware of in any conscious way: not lascivious or sexual desires but a deep sense of affinity and unity with Anne, all she was, and all she stood for. The more he realised what he'd lost, the more insecure and unsupported he felt, and the more anxious it made him. Only when she'd finally gone out of his life did he realise how much he'd been depending upon her for his own source of stability.

Yet how was it, he wondered, that someone as sympathetic, perceptive, outgoing and relaxed as Anne could suddenly turn into an icicle? That such a warm and caring friendship could suddenly evaporate without trace? But in asking the question he instinctively knew the answer: the single word 'betrayal'. Even so, knowing the diagnosis only served to emphasise the finality of his condition.

He tried to bridge the gap—oh, how he tried!—but it was no good. Anne was resistant to all his approaches and entreaties—not that he wanted her as his lover, nor to take her away from Derek—but he did so much want to assuage the dreadful void that had opened up within him, a void where previously there had been understanding, acceptance, and common ground.

The truth was that Martin *needed* Anne, perhaps not so much as a lover as a friend; someone to talk to, someone to be succoured by, someone to confess to, someone with whom he could share his life—all the myriad little events, conflicts and decisions that go to make up each day. Now more than ever he needed her, to think through the situation he'd—*they'd*—got themselves into, and the possible solutions; not that there were many, and they all had dire disadvantages—but he needed to talk through the possibilities. Even more than this he needed just to *talk*: about anything—fishing even—just so that he could gain companionship and lose the feeling of being totally alone, one man against the universe, the rest of society, and God.

As if he hadn't enough to contend with at that time, life suddenly added an extra dimension of guilt to Martin. In the way in which some coincidences happen that aren't actually coincidences because they're nothing more than a self-fulfilling prophecy, whenever he opened his Bible or tried to study, Martin seemed to come across references to David and Bathsheba with unnerving regularity. *Everything* seemed to point towards that hideous episode in King David's life, the revered, god-fearing King of Israel, called to leadership by God, successful, dynamic and a true biblical hero, the man who through his many wives would give rise to the lines of descendants from whom both Mary, the mother of Jesus, and also her husband Joseph, would come.

And then this godly King David, with many wives and even more concubines, committed adultery with Bathsheba, the wife of one of his friends. She became pregnant—and nothing was ever the same afterwards. Nor could she disguise her adultery because her husband, Uriah, was away with the army at the time. It was just like Martin's situation: a man called by God, who then betrays the trust that has been placed in him, and through whom disaster comes as a result.

But in truth the parallels were not as great as Martin tried to make out: King David had many wives to comfort him—Martin had none. King David was secure and confident as the result of a long campaign doing God's will and seeing the results: Martin had little confidence in himself, and only a short experience of the benefits of following what God *really* wanted him to do. The truth was that because Martin was feeling guilty, he picked up every remote reference to the source of his guilt. And because he was in an emotionally unbalanced state he made an unbalanced assessment of the biblical story. He couldn't see—he *literally* couldn't see—anything relevant in the story other than the seriousness of David's adultery.

All he was aware of was the unpleasant parallel between King David and himself: both were in positions of responsibility, before God and before the people. Both of them had committed adultery and then found that their lover had become pregnant. Both had then discovered that there was no way of hiding the pregnancy and making out that it was actually the offspring of the husband.

There the existing parallel finished but in his mind's eye Martin could see the awful future that lay ahead for both David and himself: the disruption to the other person's marriage; the need for a cover-up: the fact that a cover-up couldn't be obtained; and finally and most gruesomely, the gradual public exposure of the true nature of events. In the biblical story, as Martin was acutely aware, after the adulterous liaison which made Bathsheba pregnant, King David compounded the felony by arranging for the murder of her husband, Uriah, who had once been one of David's closest friends. But somehow to Martin this seemed peripheral: the adultery was the real sin, not the murder, it seemed to him. And Martin was also acutely, incessantly, continuously aware of the way in which, after this event, the fury of God had descended upon David and Bathsheba; how the child that was born of their illicit relationship eventually died; and how the adultery and everything that followed set the seal on the eventual destruction of David's kingdom, as though from then on the face of God had been turned away from David and vengeance had been let loose.

The parallels were so fierce and so appalling that all Martin could do was descend into a hell of anxiety, guilt and mental torment; knowing what he'd done, but not being able to make amends or undo what had happened. He would dearly have liked to rewind time to the day of the adultery, and in his fantasy he would then have gone off for a very long walk, on his own; or visited one of the other communities—perhaps the one in Harpenden; or performed a twenty-four hour vigil and fast... or anything, *anything* not to have done what he had done. The enormity of his action, the way destruction was spreading outwards from just one little event, was too appalling to contemplate. Soon the whole community would know about it. It couldn't possibly be kept secret. Anne's pregnancy would soon be noticed, and then...

Then his mind turned to other things: the ways in which the old country people used to dispose of unwanted pregnancies. He was sure there were many folk 'remedies', probably all pretty dangerous, if not lethal, to the mother. He even started to look up the ways in which this could be done, until sense prevailed and he realised that this was going just too far.

He also thought about suicide. At least if he were dead people would know that he had atoned, that he was sorry and he would have no reason to fear the stares and glances, and the behind-the-back whispers. In the first weeks of Anne's pregnancy the prospect of suicide seemed to him almost welcoming. But something stopped him—he didn't know what. A sense of self-preservation perhaps, the hand of God? Who knows? Perhaps he was just a coward and couldn't finally have pulled the trigger, or hanged himself, or thrown himself down a quarry face. Perhaps in his heart of hearts he was still hoping that the pregnancy might be one of the ten per cent that miscarries before twelve weeks, and then everything could be hidden, disguised, forgotten.

But it didn't happen. Soon after their affair, whenever he and Anne had met—never by design, always by accident—he would try to greet her, but pointedly she would cross to the other side of the street, but not before he had glanced quickly at her abdomen to see if there were any tell-tale signs yet.

And there were.

*   *   *

It was on the first day of June that Anne eventually plucked up the courage to tell Derek of her pregnancy. She told him bluntly, matter-of-factly, apologised to him, and said that she hadn't seen Martin since, and didn't intend to. Derek and she had always been close, and she simply and quietly asked his forgiveness.

Derek had been in the garden of Lime View house, sitting on a deck chair in the warm summer evening, an evening that somehow had turned very chill and cold inside him. He didn't say much: he just sat and stared at the apples in the tree in front of him that were gently and relentlessly getting bigger by the day, and thought what an apt metaphor they were. The harvest would be so, so different this year.

Anne had told him in a flat, almost bored tone, bereft of emotion and—to those who could read the signs—dangerous in its lack of emotional content: but Derek was too shell-shocked to read the signs. Anne asked him one more time for his understanding and forgiveness, but he turned his face away from her and said nothing.

'One more thing, Derek,' she said. 'I've told you that I'm sorry—that I didn't mean it to happen, and that I wish it hadn't—but the past is the past. I can't do anything about it, and I can't undo anything. But I want to make this clear. You're my doctor, aren't you, as well as my husband?'

Derek nodded silently, tight-lipped and grim-faced.

'Well, as my doctor, I forbid you to tell anybody else—anybody—about where my pregnancy came from. Is that clear?'

Derek started forward in his deck chair, looked at her uncomprehendingly, and then when it began to sink in he sat back once again, his face a mixture of confusion and anger. 'I'm going to see Martin,' he said finally. 'I presume he knows? I suppose you don't mind me talking with *him* about it, do you? Or am I banned from doing that as well?'

His voice was sarcastic and hard. Anne tugged at his arm. 'Please don't do anything that you'll... regret.'

'You're a fine one to say that,' said Derek, angrily brushing away her arm.

'I've told him not to tell anyone else either, bearing in mind that he's my priest. And no one else knows,' she added firmly to emphasise the point. 'If anyone—*anyone*—learns of who the real father is then I'll know that one of you two has talked out of turn and betrayed your professional trust. Got it?'

Wordlessly Derek stared at her, then got up from the deck chair, went through the house, out of the front door, and in the golden sunlight of the evening strode off down Woburn Street, across the Market Square and up past the church to the Old Rectory, oblivious to the beauty of the evening light around him, the sounds of the birds in the trees, or the gentle waft of the evening air on his face. All he could think of was black, galling anger, betrayal and disillusionment. He stormed up the drive and hammered on the front door of the Old Rectory.

Martin knew who it was even before he'd opened the door. It was the moment he had been dreading. Fortunately, he thought, there was no one else there to witness the scene and he wondered what would happen once he'd opened the door. Would Derek go for him? Beat him up? Kill him? Who was to stop him? Tremulously, he opened the door to see Derek's face, suffused with rage, a mere two feet away from his. There wasn't much point in pleasantries. Wordlessly Martin indicated to Derek to come in and pointed towards a seat.

'I'll stand, thank you,' said Derek. Martin swallowed hard. Derek glared at him for what seemed like half an hour, though it was probably no more than thirty seconds and then in a voice that was surprisingly quiet brought the house down around Martin's ears. 'How could you? Martin, how could you? How could you—you who have known me so long—mistreat me in this way? You've abused our friendship, you've violated my wife, you've defiled my marriage and you are *supposed* to be a representative of the church.'

Martin's mouth moved but nothing came out. 'I'm sorry,' he eventually managed to say.

'Sorry is not enough,' said Derek. 'Sorry doesn't get rid of the legacy you've given me. Sorry doesn't put my marriage back together. It doesn't take away my wife's pregnancy. It doesn't do up what you have just undone—all our friendship, all the trust both Anne and myself placed in you. You've cheated us,' and before Martin could say anything else Derek turned on his heels and marched out of the room, leaving the front door open behind him as he strode back down Holly Walk.

It was just getting worse and worse, thought Martin, abjectly. Derek and Anne had both been his closest friends and now by his own stupidity he had turned both of them against him. Dazed, he went into the kitchen and proceeded to open the largest bottle of whisky he could lay his hands upon.

*   *   *

By the end of June the wheat was coming on fine in Ampthill. Despite the title 'flaming June', the month had started off quite cold and not a little wet, but towards the end of the month the sun came out with a vengeance and stayed that way for the next five weeks. The harvest could be early this year, thought Neil as he went among the fields rubbing the ears of wheat in his hands and chewing grains to find out whether it was ready for cutting or not. After all, whatever the state of the weather, if the wheat wasn't ready there was just no point in bringing in the harvest.

By the end of July he knew that the harvest was ready and, in a re-run of what had happened over the hay, had made up his mind to start the following day—until he looked at the satellite picture, whereupon he suddenly decided that a delay of three or four days might be a very good idea indeed. The rain, when it came, was light—but it would have made a great deal of difference to the harvest: wet grain doesn't survive for long and is prone to all sorts of disease. Dry grain needs little extra work, is easily threshed, and is much more proof against infection and fungus.

Two days later the skies were clear again and so was the satellite picture: and the prediction for the next four days was good. Out came the combine harvester, using up yet more of their precious diesel, and in came the harvest.

In Buckingham things were a little different, with no petrol or diesel to speak of. Peter had done a good job of reconnoitring the area, looking in farm outhouses and stables for horse-drawn farming equipment. He soon stumbled upon two of the old-style harvesters with windmill sails that cut the corn and tied it into sheaves. It was harder work than a combine harvester, and more labour-intensive, but it was horse-drawn and needed no petrol. One man and one horse drove the machine, with other workers walking behind, picking up the sheaves of corn and stacking them vertically, three or four at a time, into a stook so as to dry naturally. Afterwards, the stooks were transported by horse and cart to a barn. Outside the barn a wood-burning traction engine had become the power supply for an antique-looking threshing machine half the size of a house, and seemingly made entirely of duck-boarding. Yet despite its age and apparently dilapidated state, the threshing machine worked well—sheaves of wheat were put in one end, and, with a rumble of mechanical digestion, straw came out of one orifice, chaff out of another, and grain from a third.

It was hard work, but at least they were using renewable sources of energy. The horses could exist on grass, and occasionally fertilised the fields as they worked. The traction engines really should have used coal but managed quite happily·on wood, and on any other form of waste that could be made to burn.

Power from the traction engine was delivered to the threshing machine through a gigantic belt, what Peter thought of as being the largest rubber band in history. There was something faintly romantic about setting to work in the morning, firing up the traction engine, getting up steam and then switching in its great driving wheel to power the belt that drove the thresher. All that was needed, Peter thought to himself with a faint grin on that first day, was a couple of rustic types wearing smocks and they could be back in the nineteenth century.

Halfway through the day he didn't think himself to be quite so lucky. It was, to be frank, quite exhausting work. Sheaves of corn are not light, and certainly not when thrown around on the end of long pitch forks. A combine harvester would have been a much easier way to do the same job. Having the threshing machine meant they didn't have to batter the grain off the sheaves with flails—that would have made it even worse—but even so, by the time the sun was at its zenith the perspiration was running off Peter's brow and he was beginning to wonder whether he, or any of them, for that matter, would make it through to dusk without having to stop.

Nor was it so easy being downwind of the smoke from the traction engine, as often happened when the wind changed direction. The smell of wood smoke is lovely—for a time—in camp, or at the bottom of the garden on bonfire night. When it's a working hazard, when the smuts get in the eyes, when the stench of the smoke attaches to hair, moustache, beard and clothes then it's a different matter entirely.

During that harvest season Peter worked as he'd never worked before, with hands that were raw and blistered from levering sheaf after sheaf of corn into the threshing machine, glad when the sun went down and they could all stop.

Unfortunately he ended up with the lion's share of the work. The Buckingham men, though gradually filling out with the food that had been sent across to them, were nevertheless still very weak and their stamina left a lot to be desired. And *still*, for some reason they always seemed to be looking around, over their shoulders—that same hunted, haunted look that Paul, Kevin and Alan had noted so accurately earlier in the year.

Quite what they might have to fear Peter couldn't say. He'd seen no sign of predators nor of any threat whatsoever but the dark eyes, hollow cheeks and nervous, anxious movements told another story—one that didn't fit in, one that Peter couldn't work out. It intrigued him. As an ex-policeman he knew when people weren't telling the truth, or were afraid: he knew there was a problem, but that was as far as he could get. There was something wrong—he just didn't know what. He tried asking them but, as expected, they said nothing, shrugged their shoulders, and wouldn't comment further. There was nothing wrong, they said, nothing at all. At least, their voices said it—their body language didn't.

After a time their manner became quite contagious and from time to time Peter found himself looking over his own shoulder and around at the horizon, not quite sure what he was looking for. Perhaps it was just the after-effects of starvation, he thought to himself, as he saw nothing on the horizon for the hundredth time that day. Perhaps it's me who's going cuckoo, not them. I suppose I'd have an anxious, haunted look if I'd nearly starved to death and suddenly there in front of me was all the grain I needed for the next year. Yes, that would be it. *Wouldn't it...?*

*   *   *

They had the yearly voting for the council that June: to the Major's intense annoyance, to say nothing of Derek and Chris' irritation, Peter Abrahams had been voted off the council in favour of

Henry. To be honest, it was a bit of a foregone conclusion. Peter, who spent most of his time in Buckingham, was out of the public eye, whereas Henry was somehow always to be seen in all the right places at all the right times and with all the right people. In contrast to Peter's unassuming dedication, Henry had that affable arrogance of the born leader, and as such inspired trust and confidence in all around: moreover, as he was so intimately acquainted with the Ampthill of the past, and had such extensive knowledge of the area, he was immediately perceived as being a valuable asset to the community and a wise person to have among the leadership. Apart from Peter's departure and Henry's arrival, nothing changed: by common consent Chris was re-elected chairman.

*   *   *

Over the past few months Henry had been happily living in Dynevor House, and even more happily drawing rent for Gates House, much to the continuing fury of the Major, and to the annoyance of many others who had to pay for it in their taxes. By July there was such rumbling discontent about the money that the council were obliged to call a special meeting to discuss the matter, to be held as usual at the magistrates' court on Woburn Street. Henry had been invited—or rather, commanded—to attend.

Chief doubter, for once, was Mary. There was something about the situation that felt wrong. Something that didn't fit together—a general feeling of unease whenever Henry's name was mentioned—and she couldn't put her finger on it. Perhaps it was that the whole tale seemed too glib.

'Mr Courtauld,' she said, using the formal manner of address in the way so many people do when they want to be rude. 'Mr Courtauld, you say that you own both Dynevor House and Gates House.'

'That is correct.'

'Do you have the deeds?'

'I'm afraid not. They're with my solicitors. But Neil Rawsthorne will vouch for me as I've been in Dynevor House for many years, and my family before me.' They all looked to Neil, who nodded.

'That's perfectly correct. The Courtauld family has been in residence at Dynevor House for as long as I can remember.'

'And Gates House?' enquired Mary.

'No,' said Neil, after a short pause. 'That *was* a shock, I have to say. I didn't know Henry owned it.'

Henry seemed to be a little on edge. 'That's going to be a little harder to prove. As I said to Derek, I'd only just bought it. It was going to be a wedding present... for my daughter...' Uncharacteristically he bit his lip, and looked down. 'She... the plague...'

'Er... Yes...' said Chris considerately. 'We understand.'

'But I do assure you that I'd bought it—about three weeks before the plague struck. We were just getting the formalities sorted out.'

'So where are the deeds?' asked Mary again, refusing to be put off.

'With my solicitors. I told you.'

'Where are they?'

'Hallam Street, W1.'

'And it was a surprise present for your daughter?'

'That's right.'

'Are you normally in the habit of giving houses as surprise presents?'

'No, but then I only had the one daughter, and I'm not in the habit of seeing her get married very frequently,' spat back Henry, rattled.

And then the penny dropped. It wasn't any one person who had the answer. Neil knew something, and Derek knew something, and Martin knew something and it didn't fit, and all the meeting had to do was to realise it. But would they?

'You said that your daughter was an accountant... did she live with you?' asked Derek.

'She was in London most of the time.'

'No, no,' interrupted Neil, 'she told me she was a lawyer... When I last met her a couple of years ago I'm sure she said she was a lawyer. At Lloyd, Bloom and Rumark, or something like that.'

'I know that name,' said Martin from the far end of the table, 'I'm sure I do... Didn't you say they were *your* solicitors, Henry?'

Henry had gone pale.

'Er. That's right. They're my solicitors. My daughter works there.'

'But you said she was an accountant,' said Martin, suddenly *very* still, centred and very alert. The lock of hair had come down across his forehead but he made no move to brush it away. He had his hands steepled in front of him, the tips of his fingers coming up to his mouth, elbows leaning on the table. And the eyes... the eyes fixed Henry with a look of steel. After a moment Henry dropped his eyes and avoided his gaze.

'But you said she was an accountant,' repeated Mary, who had dropped her voice to a soft, gentle tone, which heightened the effect. There was no other noise in the room as everybody stared intently, first at Mary, and then at Henry. 'But now you say she was a lawyer.... And you also said that you wanted to buy Gates House as a wedding present for her... *as a surprise*. But if she were working at the same lawyers it would be rather difficult to keep it as a surprise, wouldn't it? Which is why you made out that she was an accountant. Which means that you never did buy Gates House, did you? Because it couldn't have been a surprise for her if the solicitors with whom she worked were handling the legal side of it: with the best will in the world it would have been difficult to keep everything away from her. So there never was a surprise gift, and you never did own Gates House, did you, Mr Courtauld?'

Henry said nothing, but his knuckles were white with the pressure.

'Is this true, Henry?' asked Neil.

Henry said nothing.

'I'm ashamed of you, Henry,' said Neil. 'To think that you've deceived us all in this way, especially as I've been the one to vouch for you all along, as a friend. I think you owe me an apology. In fact, you owe all of us an apology.'

Henry remained silent, and looked at the table.

'Alan,' said Chris. 'Would you like to escort Mr Courtauld to the cells here where he can stay until we've decided what to do with him?'

'With pleasure,' replied Alan who, although much less heavily-built than Henry, would have no difficulty in restraining him should Henry decide that the cell was a destination to which he didn't wish to go.

Henry stood up, and wordlessly left the room. His silence seemed to remain on the rest of the council even after he'd left. They all looked at each other, wondering what to say. Eventually Derek cleared his throat.

'We'd better not do anything until Alan returns. We can't leave him out of the discussion.'

'No...' said Chris, staring distantly into space. Alan returned and was struck by the silence, almost the lethargy, of the meeting. Groups of people can behave like individuals and can become anxious, depressed or even schizophrenic. The meeting had certainly become depressed and in the typical way of a depressed person who finds it hard to start sentences and gives long pauses before replying, nobody really wanted to be the first to speak, and when anyone did he or she spoke slowly, hesitantly and with difficulty.

It was Susan who eventually broke the silence. 'I think my first reaction is "Oh no, not again." Why is it that people on the council keep on doing this sort of thing? We're supposed to be showing a lead, for goodness' sake. What's the rest of the community going to think now?'

And then a most remarkable thing happened, because the next person to open his mouth was not Martin (who knew just why) but the Major. 'I seem to remember,' he said, stopping to clear his throat and with a slight sideways glance at Martin, almost as if to seek approval of what he was about to say, '...I seem to remember that that's what *I* used to think until Martin... put me right... for which I'm most grateful, I may say. He said we're all fallible... *all* of us. I suppose that means whether we're found out or not we're all still fallible—and we've all got things that perhaps we wish others didn't know about. And that goes for everyone—everyone here on the council, everyone in the community outside the council. And we've got to accept that it's a fact of life. Everybody makes mistakes, everybody's selfish, and so it's not appropriate for anyone to say, "You are low and miserable but I am high and mighty, I am virtuous, and I have the right to tell you off.' So it's not up to us to judge him as a person: and we should expect those on the council to be just as capable of doing wrong as anyone else. In other words, just because we're on the council doesn't make us virtuous.'

There was an instant interjection from Alan. 'But he's done wrong. Surely you're not saying he shouldn't be punished?'

'I didn't say that,' said the Major. 'What I said was, we mustn't judge him on the basis that we're virtuous and he's not. We've got to treat him as an equal, but as an equal who has done something against the laws that we all made. So, yes he must be punished—but not judged. *Of course* we have to punish him, and pretty firmly too, to make an example so that no one else is inclined to try and follow what he's just done. He's tried to steal from all of us and nearly got away with it. But we mustn't pass judgement on him as a person—he's still our equal.'

There was a buzz of conversation round the table and behind the steepled fingers that covered up his face Martin smiled a small, hidden smile. The Major had learned well, and Martin was delighted to see the change in his approach that the lesson had brought. 'So we *must* punish him,' said the Major, looking directly at Susan. 'Of course we must, but afterwards there must be no recriminations and he must remain on the council.'

I can't believe I'm hearing this, thought Martin gleefully. It was almost a re-run of what had happened with Paul—but on that occasion the Major had been taking the part of Susan and Martin had been taking the part of the Major.

Chris looked round the table. 'Anything more to be said?' The corporate depression had lifted. There was an instant shaking of heads, in agreement. 'Well, what's the punishment to be then?'

'I think we ought to fine him,' said Paul.

'What, no barbarism?' said Susan, acidly. 'Don't you want to flog him?'

'Now we use money we *can* fine him,' retorted Paul. 'If you remember, that wasn't available to us in the past.'

'I should think a very stiff fine might be appropriate,' said Derek, 'one that he'll have to spend a long time paying off.'

'We could always confiscate Dynevor House,' suggested Mary.

'No,' said Paul. 'We can leave that for later—tell him if he does-n't pay the fine we will confiscate the house. That'll give him a good reason to pay up.'

'Good point,' said Chris, 'I like that. So how much has he got from us in rent altogether for Gates House?'

'Including back payments, I reckon something like a hundred and seventy-five pounds,' said Paul, making a quick calculation.

'Then I suggest that he has to pay that money back, and we fine him double that amount as well. That'll keep him quiet for a very long time.'

'And if he doesn't pay, then we take Dynevor House away from him,' said Alan.

'Yes. Any comments?' They all looked at each other. It seemed a fair way to go about things. 'Very well then.' She nodded to Alan. 'Would you bring him back in again?'

*   *   *

By the beginning of August it was obvious to everyone that Anne was expecting and a little *frisson* of excitement ran round the community. A new baby! The first of the new generation after the plague! The first proof that mankind might after all survive, multiply and conquer the earth once again.

True to their vocations, both Derek and Martin kept their mouths shut and in the absence of any obvious evidence to the contrary everyone in the community assumed that Derek was the father. No one dared ask whether at Anne's age of thirty-nine the pregnancy had been intended, or whether Derek had just not yet got round to learning the chapter in the medical books about contraception. Accident or planned was the main topic of conversation related to Anne's pregnancy—but no one was impolite enough to ask directly! Most assumed that, with the death of Alison, Anne had wanted further additions to her family, and, bearing in mind her rel-atively recent bereavement, were quick to congratulate her on her pregnancy and make encouraging noises about it. They did so want to make her feel supported. They also wanted to make Derek feel supported as well, so they would frequently refer to Anne in glowing tones in front of him, unintentionally making matters worse.

Even Mrs MacKenzie commented, during one of what were now proving to be weekly visits to Derek. 'Good morning doctor,' she said brightly as her face came round the door and Derek's heart sank. 'And how is your dear wife getting on? I was so *delighted* to hear of your impending happy event.'

Derek smiled at her—or rather, his face adopted a certain fixed grin slightly related to the position normally adopted in smiling. Mrs MacKenzie was too wrapped up in herself to notice the signs— how the mouth was smiling, but the eyes weren't.

'You must be delighted and very proud,' she prattled on. 'We're all *so* looking forward to the event. You really must be thrilled. But I haven't come here to talk about you.'

Too right, thought Derek.

'I've come to talk about me...'

And so it went on... and on... and on...

*   *   *

To add insult to injury, Chris was the next patient in the waiting room. She'd come to tell Derek that she had missed two periods and was—very happily—pregnant. She looked very contented and Paul, who had accompanied her, was both supportive and relaxed. Somehow Derek managed to bring the portcullis down over his own personal feelings and forced himself to congratulate her as warmly as he could. When all was said and done, he was genuinely pleased for Chris and Paul, and genuinely happy that *they* were happy; and genuinely pleased that they were looking forward to the event. But the almost identical events in Chris and Anne had such a different meaning and such a different set of emotions attached to them that somehow he couldn't disentangle his own inner turmoil from them both.

It was probably Chris' happy pregnancy that caused his final resistance to snap. The anxiety of his job, the debilitating effects of long, uncertain hours and interrupted sleep, the snub to his man-

hood and the removal at a stroke of the completeness and sanctity
of his marriage, and of the trust and security he had in his wife,
finally proved too much. Like so many stressed people who find
themselves increasingly unable to cope, he forced himself more and
more into his work, hiding in it, enjoying it to some extent, but in
all honesty letting it overwhelm him to the point where he was
unable to think of anything else—which in subconscious terms was
actually the object of the exercise. Just as Martin was trying to turn
himself back into an alcoholic in order to forget, Derek was turning
himself into a workaholic: both were trying to erase the anguish of
the emotions each of them felt, though using different routes.

In some ways Martin did it better. Because his reaction was so
obviously inappropriate, unhelpful and wrong he could see the
wrong in what he was doing and managed to stop in time before the
alcohol took over yet again. With a huge effort of will he forced
himself not to drink—not an easy thing to do when it's the only support that's available. Derek, on the other hand, was already overworking himself and was too exhausted to summon up the reserves
he needed to force himself to stop. He wasn't helped by other
people, either. What Martin was doing was obviously unhelpful and
Martin knew his drinking would meet with general disapproval. But
because work is always approved of in Western societies, Derek's
extra diligence, though inappropriate and an escape from reality,
was heralded as a wonderful example of a general practitioner who
could never do enough for his patients—in fact, Derek was increasingly seen as little short of a saint. The motivation that drove him to
it was never seen nor understood, let alone questioned, by those
who applauded his behaviour. In fact, he was actively encouraged
on his descent by the congratulations of those who regularly
received far more than they really should have done from Derek—
far more attention, far more concern, far more empathy, far more
consideration: they too were involved in the conspiracy, albeit
unknowingly, because they too had been selfish; they too wallowed
in the attention that Derek had given, without thinking of what it
was costing him and without any awareness of how they were sucking him dry, leaving nothing either for himself nor for his family.

Not that he saw much of his family. When he wasn't trying to catch up on his sleep, having been called out in the middle of the night, he was off doing good somewhere or other, or else, when there weren't any patients to deal with, throwing himself into even more study, giving himself harder and harder targets. What he'd previously expected to do in a week he now wanted to do in four days. Knowledge that in the past would have taken him a fortnight to acquire he wanted to learn overnight, and he got angry and cross with himself when he couldn't do it in the time or else when he found he hadn't retained the information as well as he wanted to. And this failure only drove him on to further activity: he must be an idiot, he thought, if he couldn't learn at a faster rate. But the more tired he became the less he could remember, making the situation worse: he responded, not by resting, but by trying harder. He didn't deserve a rest, he told himself, not when he hadn't fulfilled the tasks he'd set himself. On and on he went, making increasingly impossible demands upon himself, exhausting himself totally, taking himself far beyond the point at which normal tiredness sets in, on into the realms of continuing debilitating exhaustion, blanking out his tiredness and his feelings from himself, and from others, and—in all this—smiling weakly when well-meaning patients and friends asked about Anne's condition, promising to give her their good wishes, and then changing the subject.

One important event loomed large: he was going to have to deliver his wife's baby, and this after the disaster of Jane's pregnancy. The thought filled him with horror because underneath it all he was so fond of Anne and regretted the estrangement: but Anne had gone icy on him too, and there seemed nothing for it but to accept the situation and wait until the bastard child was born. He dreaded the thought of looking after Anne during her confinement: as far as obstetrics was concerned Jane's delivery had knocked all the confidence out of him.

The worst thing of all would be to lose his wife into the bargain. No, he corrected himself, the worst of *all* would be to lose his wife, but save the baby, having to look after it day after day, watching it grow up, yet knowing that it wasn't his, having responsibility for it, having to be its parent, having to look after it physically, mentally and emotionally—this *thing* that was not of him, not of his desires, and not of anything that he wanted to have happened. It was, he reflected, as though *he* had been raped: that the child growing inside his marriage was not of his doing nor of his volition.

And so he flung himself into his work with ever-increasing vigour. No one from the outside noticed, other than to comment on how much more effective Derek seemed to have become over the past year—much more compassionate, much more caring, much more attentive. No one seemed to notice his gaunt features, the strain on his face, the loss of weight, his jumpy manner, his irritable inability to keep still. Derek noticed though—the pounding heart, the racing pulse, the upset stomach, the loose bowels, the sense of increasing fatigue—but it didn't stop him. On and on he worked, driving himself harder and harder and harder—and it was made worse because he couldn't talk to anyone about it. Anne was mute and ice-like as ever. Certainly, he couldn't talk to Martin... and there was no one else. He couldn't even talk to God. Martin could, not that it seemed to do Martin much good, but it probably helped him more than Derek who didn't even have a God to believe in. In short, Derek bottled up all his emotion and vented his considerable anger on himself. In-turned anger can often cause depression, but not always. In Derek's case it gave him ulcers, restless nights, nightmares, tension headaches, a profound sense of lassitude and a total sense of hopelessness.

And *still* he drove himself on, and on, and on...

*   *   *

As expected, in both Ampthill and Buckingham the yields of wheat were substantially lower than those of the previous year, and the work had been much harder. Neil was satisfied, but not *that* satisfied, and certainly not complacent. Each community had managed to grow about a tenth more grain than it needed—which hadn't been bad guessing on his part. Of course a tenth of the grain had to come from Buckingham to Ampthill in part payment for the food that had been sent in the other direction earlier in the year, but even so it would leave the Buckingham group with enough food for the next twelve months. Nevertheless there were mutterings—many mutterings—and dark surly looks as the grain tithe was prepared for its journey east. 'Why should we have to pay?' was the continual muttered cry, *sotto voce*, of the Buckingham workers. 'We ought just to *share* what we have. Why should *you* take from *us*?'

After a week, Peter finally lost his patience and when one particular group muttered slightly more loudly than the others, he exploded, rounding on them and telling them precisely what he thought of them—ungrateful wretches who'd been all too willing to take up the Ampthill community's offering of grain, expertise and time, yet were not prepared to pay it back when they were able. It wasn't as if the tithe was taking the food they needed—the Buckingham group would have quite enough for the coming year. The Ampthill workers were only taking from the excess, to renew their stocks and pay for their labour, and they were taking back a lot less than they'd given so far.

But still the mutterings continued, and dark-eyed, anxious, haunted men kept meeting and murmuring and looking sideways at the Ampthill workers as the first wagons were loaded.

Eventually they moved out, five cart-loads laden with bags of grain, each wagon pulled by a pair of shire horses under the watchful, and now much more skilled, eyes of Trevor, who if nothing else had taught the rest of them how to use the brakes.

The convoy started out early in the day to transport the first part of the tithe back to Ampthill. By nine o'clock the horses had already plodded the first three miles of the journey. It was hot: the sun was rising ever higher in the sky and the animals were in need of a rest. Ahead of them lay a bend in the road and an avenue of trees which would afford some shelter from the sun.

Trevor turned round and yelled to the others, 'We'll stop in the shade. OK?'

Behind, in line astern the message was passed on from Paul, in the number two wagon, to Peter behind him, to Alan behind him and finally to David who was drawing up the rear. Ahead of him Paul could see Trevor's wagon but he couldn't see Trevor, who was completely hidden from him behind by the towering mass of sacks of wheat but suddenly Trevor's wagon slewed to one side and came to a quick and shuddering halt. Applying the brakes and shouting 'Whoa' to the horses Paul stopped, got down and ran forward to see what had happened. Pulling level with the front of the first wagon, he looked up at Trevor.

'What's the matter?'

Trevor didn't look down at him, but just stared ahead into the middle of the road. Paul followed his line of gaze and there, blocking the road, were four men, dressed in motorcycle leathers, their motorbikes forming a barrier across the roadway.

But what Paul noticed most was that the four of them were carrying shot-guns.

The leader looked familiar. Paul racked his brains trying to remember who he was, wishing he'd a better memory for faces. And then he remembered.

And then he wished he hadn't. Because the man leading the group—a big, burly fat man—was the same man he'd last seen chained to the water pump in the centre of Ampthill, being flogged by Kevin for trying to steal his motorbike...

At times of severe stress, especially when the considerably unexpected happens, the mind often goes off into a sort of dream-like state in which everything is seen to be happening but almost as in a dream—as though everything is unreal; happening, but somehow, not there. De-realisation is the technical term—and it was in a de-realised, dream-like state that Paul found himself obeying the orders of Lew Pritchard and his gang, mesmerised by the sight of four shot-gun barrels all pointing at him, with the sure and certain knowledge that all he had to do was to irritate Lew and he might well pull the trigger. He was that sort of man.

'Down,' said Lew, pointing the gun viciously at Trevor who was too stunned to do anything other than obey. One of Lew's henchmen, Den, advanced along the line of wagons, gesturing roughly to each driver to come down, then gathered them up in a little group that he hustled back to where Lew was standing. The two remaining bikers—Adam and Frankie—practised looking aggressive and waving their shot-guns around while guarding the five Ampthill drivers.

'Going somewhere, were we?' said Lew arrogantly, thrusting the muzzle of his gun at Paul's chin, then jerking it upwards, knocking his head back and cutting his lips in the process. 'Stealing our corn, were you?'

'*Our* corn actually...' began Paul, only to be stopped in mid-sentence by a thump in the stomach from the butt of the shot-gun.

'*Our* corn,' said Lew. 'You're stealing it. Thieves must be punished, mustn't they?' He turned to his henchmen who giggled, as if on cue. 'Is that brat Kevin here?'

'No,' mumbled Paul, still gasping for breath and trying to stem the flow of blood from his face.

'Where is he?'

'How should I know?' said Paul. 'In Ampthill somewhere.'

'Where?' said Lew, putting his face to Paul's and staring him in the eyes.

'I don't know,' said Paul. 'I've nothing to do with him. I can't stand the little so and so.'

Lew—whose IQ was about as low as his size was big—was a bit nonplussed by this. Somehow he'd expected that Kevin would be around somewhere. He gave Paul a further glare, then decided enough was enough and stood up straight again.

'All right, on your way.'

Trevor started to climb up into the wagon.

'Oi you,' said Lew. Trevor stopped as if turned to stone. 'Who said anything about taking the horses with you? Get down.'

Trevor did as he was told, rivulets of sweat pouring off his face and down his huge body.

'All of you, on your way, quick, before I change my mind.'

Meekly Paul obeyed, motioning with his eyes for the others to follow. They walked past the line of bikes with four pairs of eyes and four sets of guns swivelling to follow them.

'Only another twenty-five miles to go,' called Lew after them. 'It's good for you. It'll give you some exercise.' The others sniggered on cue. Lew whistled and five figures emerged from the undergrowth by the side of the road, each jumping up on to a wagon, taking the reins, and swinging the horses round to plod back along the road they'd just come.

The five dispossessed Ampthill dwellers watched silently over their shoulders, still walking so as not to attract Lew's further attention.

'Pity about the horses and wagons,' said Alan under his breath.

'Good job they're *their* horses and wagons,' said David. He was still shaking from the experience. He'd seen too many videos in the past month for his own good, and had been fully expecting a shot-gun blast at close range. After all, that's what happens in all the best violent movies...

But there is a deep inbred resistance to killing other humans, and although Lew and his gang were quite prepared to be violent they weren't prepared to be *that* violent—at least, probably not. Not yet, anyway.

'Good relations between the two communities seem to be on the back burner for a while,' murmured Paul indistinctly from between his now swelling lips. 'What a way to say thank you for saving their lives.'

'Why did you say that?' asked Alan. 'How do you know they're connected with the Buckingham set and not just bandits living off what they can find? That's what they were the last time we saw them.'

'They weren't acting on their own,' said Peter, 'I recognised two of the people with them. They were working on the thresher when I last saw them.'

'What, the ones with the shot-guns?' asked David.

'No, the ones who were hiding in the undergrowth ready to drive the wagons back to Buckingham.'

'Maybe they're in cahoots,' mumbled Alan.

Peter said nothing, thinking. They trudged another half mile down the road in silence, the day getting ever hotter, the perspiration running down their faces and chests.

It still doesn't fit, thought Peter. *It still doesn't fit.*

*   *   *

When none of them had turned up by sunset, as expected, Chris went into a paroxysm of anxiety. They'd known it would be a long and slow journey from Buckingham with the horses and wagons but they should have been home by eight o'clock at the very least. Nine o'clock came and there was no sign of them. By ten the light was fading and in their cottage Chris was getting increasingly worried. By eleven o'clock she was desperate. 'I'm going to look for them,' she announced and went round to ask Anne if she could borrow the Peugeot. She knew the route they would be taking—she'd been down it many times with Paul. Gunning the car off west, she'd travelled for a quarter of an hour, anxiously staring at the road ahead in the beam of the headlights before she spotted them, five exhausted people with blistered feet, hobbling along the road, weary, hungry, thirsty and tired beyond belief. And no wagons. The car screeched to a halt and Chris jumped out.

'What's happened?' she exclaimed and then, seeing Paul's cut and bloodied face, gave out a little cry. 'Oh Paul, what's happened?' The five men collapsed into the car and Peter told the sorry tale of the day's activities as they drove back. They were back in the Market Square by a quarter to twelve with everyone clustering around to hear the news, consternation appearing everywhere when the name of Lew Pritchard was mentioned.

'Council meeting tomorrow,' said Chris brusquely and then turned round to Paul. 'Come on you, let's get you patched up.'

At the cottage Paul collapsed into a chair. 'I feel as if I've just been run over by a steam roller.'

'I don't blame you,' said Chris. 'I'll bring you some water. Oh you poor thing,' she said, dabbing at his face with a cloth. But the injuries were more unpleasant than serious and the cut turned out to be shallow, if bloody.

'You go up to bed,' she said. 'I'll get you some food.' Ten minutes later she came upstairs to find Paul sitting in bed looking a great deal better, if battered, dispirited and exhausted. He wolfed down the supper that she'd prepared together with about two pints of liquid, and then pushed the tray away.

'That's a lot better,' he said.

'You still look a poor thing,' said Chris touching his now subsiding lips. 'Do you want anything else?'

'How about a bit of tender loving care?' said Paul with a grin, pulling her bodily onto the bed beside him and deftly undoing the front of her dress.

'Paul, you're insatiable,' she said.

'I know,' he said, grinning. 'Isn't it nice?'

*   *   *

The council, with the addition of Kevin and Peter, met in emergency session the next day. Most had already heard what had happened but there were a few who hadn't and they greeted the news with a mixture of horror and disbelief—disbelief that the Buckingham residents could have turned against them so quickly, and horror at the thought that Lew Pritchard and his colleagues were on the loose so near to Ampthill.

'But why,' said Mary, 'why should they suddenly turn against us? All we've done is help them. We couldn't have done more—except perhaps not take anything in return, but that wouldn't really be on, would it? Would it?' She looked round expectantly, hoping for some degree of support. Everyone else was too stunned to comment. 'Do *you* think we asked too much?' she asked Chris, who seemed to be the only person paying her any attention.

'It's not as if we were permanently fleecing them,' said Paul, whose lips had recovered somewhat overnight.

'I can't believe it either,' said Susan. 'We do them a good turn—save their lives even—and all they do is turf us out and beat up our representatives the minute we've delivered them their first decent harvest. I mean, it doesn't stand to reason.'

'Well, what are we going to do about it?' asked the Major. 'Send out a raiding party? Take the grain that's ours, do a bit of damage, beat up one or two of them? We can't take this lying down, you know.'

'Hold on a minute,' said Martin, 'just hold on. Going on a revenge attack isn't going to help anybody.'

'We can't be trampled over,' retorted the Major. 'That just isn't on.'

'Maybe,' continued Martin patiently, 'but all you're likely to achieve with a revenge attack is a state of continued aggression and that won't help anyone.'

'So we do nothing, do we?' said the Major, his cheeks going redder. 'We ought to teach the little whippersnappers a lesson.'

'Gunboat diplomacy is all very well,' said Martin, 'provided firstly that you've got a gunboat, and secondly that's it's got something to fire at. Whether we like it or not we have no easy way of inflicting any punishment—even if we think that punishment is the right way to go about it, which I doubt—and in any case we don't know who we punish or how. Short of razing their houses to the ground or burning all their crops—which, bearing in mind what we've just been doing for them, seems a little counter-productive—I can't think of much that we can do.'

'Tie them up and whip them again like Kevin did?' suggested the Major.

'And how do we catch them?' snapped back Paul. 'Do they saunter up, lay down their weapons and allow us to flog them? Go on. Martin's right. Whether we like it or not we can't do anything.'

'And I don't think we *should* do anything,' said Martin.

'You're going back to being a pacifist,' snarled the Major, contempt written all over his face.

'No, I'm not,' said Martin evenly. 'I just have a sneaking suspicion that this is one of those times that we'd be better turning the other cheek. This could easily escalate into a continuing battle in which nobody wins and everybody loses. Let's just draw a line under it, put our losses down to experience and go on from here as though it had never happened—except of course that it'll be a long time before we give them any further aid.'

'And write off half our previous year's crop?' interjected Neil. 'Do you realise what you're saying?'

'How much grain have they got now?' asked Martin.

'What, in bags?' asked Alan.

'No,' said Martin. 'I was meaning in terms of comparison for their needs for the next year.'

'Oh... About ten per cent more than they need for the whole year.
We were actually taking back the difference between what they
needed and what they'd grown.'

'Therefore,' continued Martin, 'we haven't lost half our supplies
of wheat—because we couldn't have retrieved all that amount
immediately. What we've lost is simply their tithe, their ten per
cent. I suppose we could go on a raid and try and get it back by
force, but the difficulties and dangers would be enormous. We certainly couldn't take any more because then they'd be back to square
one and they'd be starving again.

'I agree with you. It's a bitter blow and it's highly unfair on
everybody here who worked so hard in the first year only to see all
the surplus grain wasted in this way, but if circumstances were to be
repeated we'd still have given them the wheat, wouldn't we? We
couldn't have let them starve.'

'We could now,' murmured Paul darkly.

'Martin's right,' said Henry. 'We've only lost the tithe—for this
year at least. It would be nice to have had the tithe for subsequent
years. But we'll survive—though for the life of me I'm still not
clear as to why they've suddenly changed their attitude so much.
Does anyone have any ideas?'

'Peter was saying that the tithe was causing great annoyance,'
said Alan.

'They were all muttering about it while we were doing the
threshing,' said Peter, 'saying it was too much, that they shouldn't
have to pay it back and that we all ought to share. I think we were
just asking for too much, that's all. Maybe if we'd only asked for
five per cent...' His voice tailed off. He shook his head. 'But I don't
know. I can't fathom it out either.'

'Nah,' said Kevin suddenly from the far end of table. 'You've got
it all wrong.' Eleven heads swivelled to look at him. 'You're assuming they're all in it together. They're not.' A muttered ripple of conversation passed round the table.

'Order, everyone,' said Chris. 'Let's hear what Kevin has to say.
Do go on.'

'We've been conned, that's what,' said Kevin.

'We know that,' said the Major huffily.

'Yeah, but you've been conned even more than you think. Who's running the show, who's in charge?' He looked at Alan.

'Well... Lew Pritchard and his friends... I would think.'

'But Dave Wittering's *supposed* to be in charge—the guy in the cottage. Isn't he?'

'I don't follow you,' said Chris.

'Lew Pritchard's in charge of Dave Wittering. Now do you see?'

'Ah.'

'Willingly or unwillingly,' said Paul, his eyes narrowing.

'Waddayermean?'

'Is Dave Wittering going along with Lew Pritchard willingly or unwillingly?'

'He's not Lew's type at all. He won't want to work with someone like Lew Pritchard. No. My guess is that Lew's terrorising Dave Wittering and all the others, just as he was terrorising us.'

Then it all fell into place. It was easy, really—so easy. They all wondered why they hadn't spotted it before. Paul sat back in his chair and uttered a long sigh. 'So *that's* it,' he said.

'What is?' said the Major, who hadn't followed a word.

Paul leaned forward, suddenly eager, quite unlike the reticence he'd been displaying over the past twenty-four hours. He turned to Chris. 'Do you remember the first thing we said when Shaun, Jason and Vince came across that first time? How they all seemed to have a shifty, hunted look about them?'

'That's right,' said Chris.

'It stuck out like a sore thumb at the time, didn't it? It just didn't fit. All these people looking over their shoulder every other second. That's why. They're in fear.'

'How can they be in fear of Pritchard and his mob twenty-five miles away?' said Henry, '...Oh... I see...'

'I'm glad you agree,' said Paul.

'Agree with what?' said the Major, his head moving between Paul and Henry like an umpire at a tennis match..

'They've got hostages,' said Paul. 'That's right, Kevin, isn't it?'

'Course they 'ave,' said Kevin. 'Can I go now? Who's got my six pounds?'

'Sit down, Kevin,' said Chris, looking daggers at him. 'We haven't finished.'

'Will someone explain to me what's going on?' said the Major.

'Hostages, Major,' said Martin. 'Paul and Kevin reckon that Lew and his gang must have some hold over the rest of the people in Buckingham.'

'It stands to reason,' interjected Paul. 'I mean, why else would anybody else stay there? What would *you* do if you were starving and you'd got rid of all the food and livestock in the area around you? Come on, what would you do? You'd move on, wouldn't you? So why didn't *they* move on?'

'Because Lew's got hostages,' said Alan. 'Hang on, that doesn't fit either. Why don't they *all* move on if they're starving?'

'Ah, but they're not *all* starving,' said Paul. 'Do you remember how, although we sent them enough grain, they never really seemed to fatten out?'

'Yes...?' said Alan.

'I'll bet a pound to a penny that Lew and his mob were taking most of it for themselves and that the Buckingham residents were having to exist on the rest. So it wouldn't matter to Lew if everybody around him was starving as long as he had enough to eat, and only when they hadn't got enough to supply him would Lew think of doing anything else.'

'And the first thing he thought of,' interjected Susan, 'was seeing if he could con us for food because he knew we were here and he thought we'd be the easiest touch. Much better than having to up and off and find somewhere else to get food from. Or even grow your own...'

'Well done, everyone,' said Henry, genuinely, without the slightest hint of being patronising. 'I think that's brilliant. Let's see if I can recap.' Chris coughed. She thought it was her job as chairman to recap but Henry seemed to have taken it from her, much as he seemed to take any job from anybody. She coughed again. Henry continued unperturbed. 'Lew Pritchard and his cronies come to

Ampthill in the Christmas of the first year. They try and steal from us.'

'Too right,' said Kevin. 'From *me*, to be precise. Just for the record,' he added, nodding at everyone.

'Lew gets beaten off, courtesy of Kevin's tactics, but not before he realises that we've got a thriving community. After that he goes west, comes across the crowd in Buckingham who aren't thriving, but they don't offer any resistance to him. The original Buckingham group are living off whatever they can find in a parasitic way without giving anything back, basically because they don't know how. Lew and his cronies take over, bully everyone else into submission, probably by taking hostages from their families. As a result everybody in Buckingham has to work for Lew and daren't try to escape because of the hostages.' He looked up. 'Everyone agree so far?'

The nodding heads round the table looked like corks bobbing on waves. 'After a time the food supply starts to diminish, but Lew and his colleagues always get first choice. So while the rest of the Buckingham group starve, Lew and his friends are still living a luxurious enough existence, at least by their own standards, so as not to make moving worthwhile.

'Then the food finally runs out and Lew knows he's got to do something. He's got two options: he could move the whole community off somewhere else—but that's a bit dicey because most of the food in the shops will have gone off, except for the tinned food, and for all he knows, that's already been scavenged by us or other communities nearby. On the other hand he knows that only twenty-five miles away there's a community that's doing quite well. So he sends three emissaries—probably picking the hungriest ones he can find—and tells them that if they breathe a word about him or that he's got members of their families hostage then unpleasant things are likely to happen to those self-same hostages. Similarly, if they don't come back with food, the hostages get it in the neck. And this is why when we looked round Buckingham we saw nothing— because Dave Wittering guided the search party round and conveniently kept us away from places he daren't let us see.

'We send food and aid and knowledge across, which is great.

Now Lew and his cronies have got the food they need—they always take the prime share, you can be sure of that—and gleefully accept the offer of help in teaching their slaves how to farm. After all, this'll keep Lew in clover for years to come.'

'More than that, Henry,' interjected Paul. 'It actually makes the lot of the people in Buckingham worse. They probably didn't want to find food, because that keeps them where they are—and they don't want that. They don't want to continue. They'd like everyone to have to move out because only then will they be able to have a chance of getting the hostages back, which means...

'...that they've got their hostages in a *very* safe place,' interrupted Kevin. 'Of corse they 'ave. What did you expect?'

'So that explains the resentment when we sent the food across,' said Paul. 'It explains why we had that feeling that we were being watched all the time when we went on our trip to Buckingham— because we *were* being watched. And it explains the cow.'

'What cow?' said the Major.

'A cow that shouldn't have been where it was,' said Paul. 'I spotted it on the way to Buckingham and thought that shouldn't be there. If they're all starving, surely they'd have found it by now and eaten it? No. It was one of Lew Pritchard's cows—a bit like one of the deer in the royal forests. "Death to him who shoots a deer"—in the eleventh century I mean. I bet you anything Lew's promised that anyone caught killing or eating one of his cows gets the relevant hostage returned to them, in pieces, the next day.

'I'll tell you something else that bothered me, too—why did Vince and his friends come on bikes the first time? They had enough petrol left. It was all part of the plan to make us feel sorry for them and give them food more readily.'

'We *have* been conned,' said Chris. 'So what difference does this make to our plans?'

'As I said before, it shows that we mustn't retaliate against the Buckingham community as a whole,' said Martin. There was a murmur of assent. 'If they really are in thrall to this gang then what has happened isn't their fault and they mustn't be punished. So what we need to do is check out whether Kevin, Paul and Henry are right—

and I must say I think there's every chance that they are—then see if we can help.'

'Couldn't we go on a raiding party?' asked the Major. 'At least now we know who we're trying to stop.'

'And what happens to the hostages if we do?' asked Martin. 'What if Lew and his gang find out our people are there and capture them? Or if they take it out on the hostages if any one dares to attack? What we need is some intelligence.'

'Are you insinuating that I'm stupid?' retorted the Major, getting very hot under the collar.

'No, no, no, Major, I didn't mean that at all. I said what we need is some intelligence—information gathering.'

'Oh,' said the Major, thinking somehow that he'd rather let himself down, which indeed he had.

'Basically we need to find out whether all this is true. We need to find out if there really are hostages and if so where they are.'

'That's easy,' said Kevin. 'They'll be hidden in that jail thing in the middle of Buckingham.'

'You're right,' said Henry quietly, more to himself than to the assembled company. 'What a clever thing to do.'

'Why's that?' asked Paul.

'As Kevin's just said, it's the obvious place to keep them—nice and secure, built for keeping prisoners in. But the brilliant thing about it is that it's right in the middle. It reminds all the Buckingham residents *where* the hostages are and *why* they're there. Every day of their lives they're faced with the fact that members of their family are being held hostage in their midst. It encourages good behaviour in the subject peoples, does that. It's absolutely brilliant.'

'I can't imagine anything that Lew did being brilliant,' said Paul acidly. 'I don't know about his being as thick as two short planks but I should think between them those four must have the combined IQ of a forest. Lew wouldn't have achieved this brilliant piece of psychological leverage deliberately. He'll have put the hostages in the gaol just because it's a convenient place to put them. He won't have planned it that way.'

'It'll still have the same effect though,' said Henry, 'whether he planned it or not.'

'Can I go now?' asked Kevin, trying to get up.

Chris glared at him again. 'We haven't formalised a plan of action yet.'

'I thought we had,' said Paul, 'or rather, a plan of *in*action.'

'This does rather change things, don't you think?' said Mary. 'But shouldn't we be doing something about the hostages?'

'It's going to be *very* difficult,' said Paul. 'Buckingham's a long way away. If we tried anything, who knows if we'd succeed? We're not violent people. We're not trained in the use of force. We can hardly call in the UN, can we? Don't you think we'd be risking an awful lot if we tried a rescue attempt? What happens if it fails, and then we have Ampthill hostages to contend with as well?'

'We can't just leave the hostages to fester, can we?' asked Mary.

'We'll have to if we can't think of a sensible plan for getting them out,' rejoined Alan. 'There's no point in making matters worse, no point at all.'

'Can I go now?' asked Kevin.

*   *   *

Whatever the situation in Buckingham, by the end of August the harvest in Ampthill was in again and they knew they would eat for another year. At the end of September they had the customary harvest celebrations which Martin led with considerable aplomb. Not that *he* thought he'd led it particularly well, but everybody else did. In fact the strange thing was that whatever might have been happening in Martin's personal life, none of his inner anguish had been reflected in his work or in his professional life—quite the opposite in fact. He was increasingly and widely regarded as able, adept, sympathetic, understanding and a great comfort.

In some ways this had been heightened by the recent events. Unknown to Martin, his admission of failure and his acknowledgement that he had done wrong had worked inside him something that even he was not aware of—a deep awareness of his own foolishness, vulnerability and sheer humanity: so that despite on the surface feeling completely unforgiven, out of favour with God and that everything he touched would turn to dust in front of his eyes, other people found in him a humility that demonstrated quite the reverse. Yet although they tried to explain their appreciation to him, somehow Martin never felt it, nor believed it: he could see a criticism at fifteen miles but wouldn't accept an accolade if it hit him in the face.

And all the while, inside him, was the dreadful, nagging fear, screaming at him—what if the awful secret got out? What would the community say then?

Part III

Part III

- 17-

*W*inter came and with it more work for Derek. By now Anne was in the last stages of her pregnancy and Sarah was running around excitedly, talking about the baby and planning all the things she was going to do with it when it arrived, most of which seemed to involve the baby being born aged three, already capable of walking, singing, understanding and talking. But no matter, thought Anne, if Sarah is happy about it then that's good: she'll learn by experience, and in the nicest way possible.

Anne was due in late November. The date came and went, and nothing happened. Then early in December the first contractions occurred and Derek had to be called back to his own house, as he was visiting a patient at the far end of the community at the time. It was a quick labour—after all, it was Anne's third. The first stage was over in four hours, and soon Anne was starting to push. The delivery was a textbook one. The head crowned, then with the next push, and guided by Derek's gloved hand, came gently out: he felt for the cord round the neck, but it wasn't there. With the next push the shoulders and waist of the baby came out: Derek was able to pull his fingers underneath the baby's armpits and gently lift it out. Then he held it upside down as it screamed blue murder with the shock of the cold air on its skin. A reassuring noise, he thought, distantly, wrapped up in his own thoughts, holding his wife's bastard son upside down by the feet to help him breathe those precious first few breaths, half wishing he could swing him very hard against the nearest wall and bash his brains out there and then, and half thinking how vulnerable, how beautiful, how perfectly formed and how precious this new life was. He tied the cord, cut it and then gave the baby to Anne. Five minutes later, with a little pulling on the cord and a further contraction, the afterbirth came away.

Derek suddenly realised how fast his heart had started to beat and wondered why—until he remembered that this was the point at which Jane had started to bleed, and bleed, and bleed... Thankfully—mercifully—Anne showed no sign of doing the same.

Just to be sure he rubbed her uterus through the abdominal wall to make sure that it went into contraction again; with the contraction a few more drops of blood were expelled: he could feel the womb, tight and firm, low down in the abdomen. Nor did she need stitches, he realised to his relief.

Suddenly he felt how weak his knees were and a wave of exhaustion washed over him, together with a slight sense of exultation as the memories of the only other obstetric delivery he had attended were washed away in the better memories of the recent successful one. It was only then that he realised how anxious he'd been about Anne: how at the back of his mind he'd always feared that, like Jane, she would die in childbirth. It was, he reflected now, a rather illogical fear. After all, mankind had lasted for thousands of years without modern medicine: and women had mostly survived to produce many offspring. It had just been bad luck that for his first delivery he'd encountered an obstetric disaster area: but in times of stress people think emotionally rather than logically, and emotionally he'd been sure that the events of Jane's delivery would be repeated at Anne's. As he had no experience of a successful delivery to fall back on, all he had had was the fear.

Having packed up his equipment, he went downstairs to where an anxious Sarah was waiting, looked after by Susan, their next-door neighbour.

'Well?' asked Susan, looking at him expectantly.

All the eyes in the room focused on Derek and it was only then that the real importance—the real emotional importance—hit him. How not only was he *not* the father, but everybody thought he *was* the father and that from then on he would *have* to be the father of this thing that had come between them.

'It's a... it's a boy,' he stuttered.

'Oh, goody,' said Sarah jumping up and down. 'Can I go and see him?'

'In a minute, Sarah,' said Derek, tiredly. 'Just let Auntie Anne have a few minutes' rest. She'll be very tired, you know. It took a lot of pushing to get the baby out of her tummy.'

'What are you going to call him, Dad?' asked David. He'd come in through the front door a moment earlier carrying yet another rabbit that he'd managed to impale with his crossbow.

'Your mother wants him to be called Julian,' said Derek.

The subtleties of Derek's linguistic niceties were lost on David. He didn't even think to ask, 'But what do *you* want to call him, Dad?' Nor did he notice the convoluted way Derek was referring to his wife, and to David's mother.

'Julian,' said David. 'That's a nice name. Julian Jones. J.J. Hum. Better than Horatio.'

'*Horatio?*'

'That's what I used to call him—before he was born, I mean.'

'Horatio?' said Derek. 'Why Horatio?'

Deadpan, David replied, 'Because we didn't know whether it was going to be a boy or a girl and Horatio of boys to girls is fifty-fifty.'

Derek grinned and tousled David's hair in a friendly gesture.

'Are you pleased it's a boy, Dad?'

'I didn't mind,' said Derek weakly, 'just so long as your mother was all right.' Again the circumlocution. Again David missed it.

'Can we go and see him?'

'Yes, yes,' bounced Sarah, clutching at Derek's leg. 'Let's go and see him. Let's. Please? Can we go now?'

'All right,' said Derek patiently as the two scampered up the stairs. They opened the door, then stopped and turned round. Inside the room, Derek could see Anne with Julian on the breast, tears streaming down her face.

'Why's she crying, Uncle Derek?' asked Sarah.

'She's very tired after the birth,' said Derek gently.

Lies. Little lies. Small things can have great effects, and sins beget more sins.

*   *   *

In the way in which insult is so often added to injury Paul, quite unintentionally, succeeded in jarring Derek's feelings even further the next time they met. For once Derek hadn't been rushing around like a bluebottle in a jam jar. Paul bumped into him in the Market

Square and pumped his hand up and down in an energetic hand-shake. 'Many congratulations, Derek,' he said. 'I tried twice to be first off the mark at repopulating the earth, but you just beat me to it.'

'Oh... yes,' said Derek, with a wan smile which emerged from its receptacle, applied itself to his face, and went back into its receptacle again. 'Thanks.'

'How are you keeping anyway?' continued Paul. 'You look as though you've lost a bit of weight. Baby not keeping you up at night *all* the time I hope?' He didn't wait to hear the reply. 'I must admit I'm a changed person since marrying Chris. She's *so* good, you know. I couldn't have wanted better. She keeps the house spick and span, and always manages to fill it with the things that we need. I don't know how she manages it. Even *I* couldn't manage to make the housekeeping stretch that far. I must admit,' he continued, totally ignoring Derek's vain attempt to get out of the conversation, 'that I've never been particularly house-proud. Chris has made such a difference to me. She keeps on saying that I was too hard before we got married—hard on everybody, I mean. You don't think that, do you Derek? But I do think I've softened.'

Derek smiled weakly again. 'How's Chris doing?'

'Oh fine. Fine. She's coming to see you in another couple of days. Thirty-four-week check-up, I think she said. Anyway, I must go. You must be very proud of young Julian, very proud indeed. See you.'

'See you,' said Derek, wondering what had hit him.

*   *   *

Two hundred yards up the road quite a different conversation was taking place. Susan Rogers was, as usual, wanting more money from her husband, and as usual Alan wasn't having it.

'Why is it,' he moaned, 'that however much I give you, you always want more? You don't seem to be able to make the house-keeping stretch anything like as far as you used to.'

'That's because things are so expensive,' she said. 'I'm not being profligate, really I'm not, but I just can't make ends meet on what you give me. The price of bread has just gone up again, that's about twenty per cent in the last two months. And as for getting coal... that's gone up too. I can't manage, I really can't... and don't look at me like that. It's not my fault.'

'I'm not looking like anything,' said Alan irritably. 'I'll just have to charge more for the leatherwork. I know what you mean about costs though. They seem to be going up all the time.'

*   *   *

Derek scrambled uneasily back to consciousness from an extremely bad dream in which everyone in Ampthill was in a boat which had sunk, and they were now on a very small raft in a very large lake surrounded by choppy seas and high winds. The cries of the drowning were coming at him from all sides and he was trying to save everyone by baling the lake out with a tea cup. When he came fully into consciousness he realised that the cries were not of the drowning but of Julian. Anne was sitting in the corner feeding him and she wasn't having an easy time of it. She'd switched just one small light on to try to keep the room as near in darkness as possible so that Derek could snatch a few precious hours' sleep. One eye open, Derek observed his wife talking gently and softly to Julian, trying to calm him down. It wasn't working. The baby got more and more distressed until with a final cry he vomited the entire contents of the feed halfway across the room. Only then did he seem happy for a moment—but then the hunger got to him again and he started crying for food. Anne picked up a cloth, mopped up what she could of the sick and then put him back on the breast again, anxiously looking down at him and tenderly stroked his forehead.

'There there,' she said, 'hush, little one. Daddy's asleep. You don't want to wake him. Hush.'

Derek winced at the use of the word 'Daddy', and closed his eyes again. The next time he opened them the dawn was just breaking through the window and there was a banging on the door. Leaving Anne and Julian sleeping he staggered downstairs, glancing at the clock in the hall which showed half past six. The banging started again. He pulled the door open.

'Ssh. You'll wake the baby,' he said irritably through bleary eyes to the little lad at his door.

'Me mam says come quick. She's got ever such a pain in her chest.'

'Oh, all right,' said Derek, quickly putting on his clothes and picking up his bag. 'Show me where.'

He didn't get back until mid-morning by which time Anne and the baby were asleep again. She looked worn out, poor thing, he thought, and glanced at the baby in the cot. Julian stirred irritably, let out a small whimper then subsided with a quivering lip. Anne rolled over in bed, briefly opened an eye to check on Julian, and went off to sleep again.

Tiptoeing downstairs again Derek helped himself to a slice of bread and rushed off to his surgery, an hour and a half late.

He returned at four o'clock to find a shattered Anne and a whimpering baby. Only this time the whimpering didn't stop. Anne was tearful, her dark hair lank and stringy, draped across her forehead. She hadn't had time to wash or dress and looked worried to death.

'Everything all right?' said Derek, hoping that the answer would be 'Yes' and that he could actually get a few minutes' peace and quiet, yet knowing it wasn't going to be. Anne turned her eyes away from him.

'What's the matter then?'

'It's Julian... He keeps being sick. I've fed him I don't know how many times, but he won't keep anything down.'

'Any diarrhoea?' said Derek.

'No.'

'Are his nappies wet?'

'No,' she said, 'that's the problem. He's not taking anything in at all. I'm ever so worried,' and she looked up at him from between the rats' tails of hair. Giving off a loud long sigh of exhaustion, Derek went downstairs to get his bag, then went over Julian with a fine tooth comb.

'Fontanelle, OK. So it's not meningitis. Chest clear. Ears normal. Stomach not tender, no masses. No extra bowel sounds. No temperature. *Very* dehydrated. Probably just an infection,' he said, knowing that it wasn't, but it was all he could think of. An infection would almost certainly have given Julian a temperature, and Julian didn't have one. 'I'd just keep trying if I were you. Try feeding him little and often. That sometimes helps.'

He bent over the cot again, then straightened up. 'I've got to go, to see that lady out in Clophill again. You know, the one I was called out to this morning,' and so saying, he grabbed his bag again and headed off downstairs, quietly shutting the front door behind him.

Wearily Anne pulled Julian out of his cot and started trying to feed him again.

*   *   *

'Paul, can I have a word with you?' said Alan, crossing the Market Square to get to him.

'Yes, Alan, what can I do for you?'

'There's something I don't understand and seeing you're the economic brains round here I thought I'd ask you first.'

'Fire away.'

'Have you realised that we've got inflation?'

There was a pause.

'Have we?' said Paul, thinking hard. 'I've been so tied up with the Buckingham problem that I've not really been in touch with the Ampthill community.'

'Susan's just told me that the price of bread has risen by a fifth in the last two months and I know that some of the things I use have gradually increased in price—in fact they've gone up so much that I've had to put up my own prices in order to break even.'

'Really?' said Paul, looking puzzled. 'That shouldn't happen.'

'Well it *is* happening,' said Alan. 'I assure you it is. I know Susan's not the best of people with money but she doesn't lie.'

'That's strange,' said Paul, only half-hearing what Alan was saying. 'I hadn't realised we'd got inflation. Chris doesn't seem to have any problem with the housekeeping. Are you sure it's not because Susan's a bit flighty as far as money's concerned?'

'Well, she is a bit,' said Alan, grimacing. 'A bit of a spendthrift is our Susan, I'm afraid. Always has been. But no, I don't think it's just that.' Just then he spotted Mary coming into the square from the Maulden road. 'Mary, can you give Paul the benefit of your wisdom?' She came across to them. 'Do you think prices seem to be going up?'

'Oh, yes,' she said. 'Up and up and up and up. It's awful. I told you we shouldn't go back to using money. It only brings problems.'

'There you are,' said Alan turning to Paul. 'I told you.'

'How very odd...' said Paul, thinking hard.

'And I've had to put the prices of my eggs up,' said Mary, 'just to match.'

'Classic inflation,' said Alan. 'Prices go up, so you have to put up your own charges to keep up, and then because your charges are up, other people have to put *their* charges up, and round and round it goes.'

'Yes, I know that,' said Paul irritably, giving him the 'you're teaching your grandmother to suck eggs' look. 'That's not the point. The point is, why has it started?'

'Don't ask me,' said Alan. 'Probably someone being greedy somewhere.'

'But *where* did it start?' said Paul.

'What do you mean where did it start?'

'What commodity went up in price first?'

'Search me,' said Alan. He looked at Paul. 'I don't know. It all seemed to happen at the same time really.' Paul suddenly fell very silent, deep in thought. After a moment he surfaced.

'I think I'll have to go away and think about it. It really shouldn't happen you know, not in a simple economy like we've got where you just pay for things as you get them and there's nobody lending money, which always has a distorting effect. It's most odd. It shouldn't happen at all,' and without more ado he bid them a curt good day and wandered off, muttering to himself.

*   *   *

They put Julian to bed at ten o'clock that night, and Derek, desperate to get some sleep—having been woken up throughout the

previous night and then called out early in the morning—tumbled
into bed and was almost immediately asleep.

This time it was a ward—a ward full of crying, vomiting babies.
As fast as he went to one of them, another one would vomit: he'd
settle that one down and a third would start, and as soon as he'd got
that one settled the first one would vomit again, and the noise of
sickness and crying filled the air.

He surfaced from the dream to find Anne sitting in her feeding
chair, next to the small table, with the light shaded so as not to disturb Derek more than she had to. Even at this distance Derek could
see that Anne was quietly and silently sobbing as she looked down
at Julian who'd obviously just been sick again. She reached up her
free hand to brush back the straggly dark hair that had fallen across
her forehead. 'Hush, Julian, hush,' she kept on saying, rocking him
backwards and forwards, two rivulets of tears streaming down her
face.

Julian was crying, but it wasn't the same cry of the night before.
This time it was a fainter cry, a weaker one. Wearily Anne put him
to the breast again, hoping against hope that this time some of the
milk would stay down.

Derek drifted back to sleep again. When he woke a second time
it was four o'clock, but Anne was still in the chair and Julian had
been sick again. This time he was making very little noise, and
Derek was wondering what had woken him when Anne spoke
again. 'Derek, are you awake? I think you ought to look at him
again. He's not at all well.'

Wearily Derek pulled himself into full consciousness and went
to get his bag. Once again he went over Julian from top to toe. No
temperature, chest clear, ears normal, nothing at all wrong with the
abdomen, fontanelle now remarkably sunken, eyes glazed and not
moving. And no diarrhoea. It *couldn't* be an infection—but Julian
was obviously very, very short of fluid. His nappies had been totally
dry for the last twenty-four hours and his skin had acquired that odd
semi-elastic feel where a small mound can be pulled up and does
not immediately stretch back into its original position—in the way
that the icing of a cake can get pulled up, apparently defying

gravity, and sets in that position, corrugated and distorted.

Derek sat back on his haunches, desperation in his voice. 'I don't know what's the matter with him, Anne. I can't find a thing wrong. His tummy's perfectly all right. I've examined him a number of times after he's been sick and each time the abdomen's perfectly normal. I really don't understand it. The only thing I can suggest is that you just keep on trying.' He looked at Anne's white, exhausted face. 'I'm sorry, there's nothing else I can suggest.'

'Perhaps if we tried him on baby milk...?' she said.

'Well you can,' he said, 'but usually breast milk is easier to absorb so I don't think it would help much.'

'I've got a packet downstairs,' said Anne, levering herself up from the chair and giving Julian to Derek for a moment. Derek looked down at the little scrap of flesh, wondering what the illness could possibly be.

She returned in a few moments with a bottle. Julian sucked at it weakly then vomited the whole lot right across the room again.

'What are we going to do, Derek?' asked Anne, panic written all over her face.

'I don't know,' said Derek, 'I just don't know.' By now Julian had fallen asleep again, so Anne put him back in the cot and went back to bed again.

Both mother and baby were still asleep when Derek rose to start the day's work. He'd vaguely been aware that Anne had been up with Julian again at about six o'clock, but as both of them were sleeping he chose not to wake them, tiptoeing out of the room and down the stairs. Perhaps Julian had kept some of the milk down, he thought. At least they were both asleep, and Anne was getting a little bit of rest.

He was away for about six hours. He let himself quietly into the house and went upstairs, trying not to make a noise. He found Anne leaning over the cot, anxiety written all over her face. Julian was lying in the cot staring dully into space and giving off just the occasional whimper. The smell of vomit filled the room. Streaks of it were everywhere—across the carpet, on the bed, up the wall. 'He's going to die, isn't he?' said Anne looking up tearfully at Derek .

'No, of course he's not,' said Derek, panic welling up inside, but trying desperately not to communicate his fear. 'He'll get over it.'

'It's all my fault,' said Anne. 'If I hadn't gone to see Martin that day, then Julian... wouldn't have happened.'

'It doesn't work like that,' said Derek, his lips tightening at the mention of Martin's name. 'You're just thinking emotionally. How Julian occurred has got nothing to do with why he's ill now.'

'It's all my fault,' she said and burst into tears again. 'Oh I wish, I wish, I wish it hadn't happened,' and she bit her lower lip almost until the blood ran.

'Let me have a look at him again,' said Derek. He went over Julian from top to bottom. Absolutely nothing to find, apart from a very dehydrated baby indeed, with a weak, thready pulse. But there was still no temperature, and there was nothing abnormal to find in the abdomen. 'When did you last feed him?'

'About two hours ago.'

'And?'

'And he vomited it all up again.' She pointed at one of the marks on the wall in the far corner.

'I thought you always sat to feed him, on the chair in the middle of the room,' he said.

'I do,' said Anne.

'And the vomit went that far?'

'Yes. All over everywhere.'

Down in the deep recesses of Derek's mind something stirred and then suddenly, as if from nowhere, came the answer. Projectile vomiting. Pyloric stenosis. Commonest in males. He rushed downstairs two at a time, grabbed the textbook of paediatrics and began reading.

'You said you last fed him two hours ago.'

'That's right.'

'Well, feed him now. I want to watch.' Anne put the little infant to her breast again and Julian began weakly sucking. By now Derek had his hands on Julian's abdomen, feeling just underneath the ribs *before* he vomited—as a little knot of muscle formed and grew firmer. Then with a cry Julian was sick. The vomit shot out past

Derek's left ear, narrowly missing the light and underneath his fingers the little ball of muscle started to relax.

'Now we know what it is. It's pyloric stenosis.'

'What's that?'

'It's where the muscle at the exit from the stomach gets too strong, and won't relax to allow the stomach contents out into the intestines. So the only way for the stomach to get rid of its contents is to throw them back the way they they came. Projectile vomiting. It's typical.'

'Can we do anything?' said Anne.

'That's the problem,' said Derek, looking worried. 'Normally you need an operation.' Anne went wide-eyed. 'It's a simple one,' said Derek. 'All you need to do is cut into the thick band of muscle so that it can't squeeze as hard. So the outlet from the stomach can open instead of being forced shut.'

'Can you do it?' she asked.

'You don't always need to do an operation,' said Derek looking at the textbook again. 'Sometime it will go away with time.'

'But we haven't *got* time,' said Anne, still wide-eyed. 'I mean, look at him.' Julian had gone back into the whimpering half-world of not being quite awake and not being quite asleep. He opened his mouth as if to give off a cry, then seemed to think better of it and closed it again. Probably it was too much effort.

'Derek, he's going to *die* if you don't do something.'

'I know that,' said Derek angrily—but it was fear, not anger that motivated his irritation. 'There are some medicines we can try. I'll go and get them.' He shot downstairs, leaving the front door open behind him and dashed to the chemist's in the Market Square.

At least he's showing concern about Julian, thought Anne. It's the first time he's shown any emotion towards him at all. She looked at the little scrap of human being in the corner of the cot, then picked him up and cradled him in her arms.

'Don't die, my sweetie,' she said. 'Don't die,' and started gently stroking his forehead again.

Derek was back in five minutes.

'I've found some,' he said triumphantly. 'It's an old use for it, apparently the newer textbooks don't recommend it at all, but it's all we've got... The idea is it paralyses the stomach muscles so they can't contract quite as quickly. Let's put a couple of drops in his mouth and then you can try to feed him again in a few minutes.'

'All right,' said Anne weakly. 'Let's hope it works.'

To their profound delight it did and the next feed went down and stayed down. So did most of the one after that—and Julian began to look at least a little less like the survivor of some famine-ridden country in East Africa.

- 18 -

*T*wo days later Alan called a meeting with as many of the council as he could find. In the absence of Chris—whom Derek had told to rest as her blood pressure had started to go up—Henry decided to take the chair, much to the annoyance of the Major.

'Paul, you called this meeting, didn't you?' he began.

'Actually, *I* did,' said Alan. 'I went to Paul first and he didn't know what was going on so I thought we'd better tell everybody. There's some odd things happening. We've got inflation.'

'I told you having money wouldn't work,' said Mary. 'It's quite simple. People are just being greedy, putting up their prices too high.'

'I don't think it's as simple as that,' said Martin. 'Everybody I've talked to says they've put their own prices up because they can't afford to pay for the things other people are selling, not the other way round. I don't know of anybody who's been making a killing.'

They argued the pros and cons for some time. And all the time Paul was silent in the background, thinking, apparently not contributing to the debate at all, just listening, calculating, working it all out. Finally Henry cottoned on to the fact that Paul hadn't said anything, and turned to him.

'What do you think about it, Paul?'

Paul paused, looked down at the table for a moment, then looked up. 'I think we've got a thief,' he said.

'I beg your pardon?'

'We've got a thief.'

'Why on earth do you think that? We've got inflation, not missing money.'

'Our money was stable to start off with, wasn't it? How long did we have it before everything started to go wrong? Six, eight months?'

Henry nodded. 'That's about right.'

'And then suddenly we've got inflation. Well, we've got to have a thief. Somebody else has access to extra money which they're using; now there's more money chasing the same number of goods, so prices are bound to rise.'

'But, Paul, theft isn't the reason for inflation,' said Alan in his usual blunt way. 'We had inflation in the past before the plague and no one said anyone was stealing anything.'

'It was more complicated then,' said Paul, 'and we experienced inflation for other reasons. Look—we use money to buy things. If we have too much money, and too few goods, then the price of those goods will go up; because with more money around somebody will always be prepared to pay more to get what they want. Then once the price has gone up, other people will have to try to raise their prices to follow suit, as otherwise they won't be able to buy those ordinary things they need just to stay alive. In the past inflation started because we had too much money in the system, either because governments printed too many bank notes, or else because banks lent too much.'

'I don't follow that,' said Mary. 'What's it got to do with the banks?'

'When banks loaned money too readily it was as if they themselves had printed a few more bank notes. They'd increased the amount that the people could spend: so again there was too much money chasing too few goods.'

'But we don't have any banks now,' said Mary, 'or hadn't you noticed?'

'That's just the point,' said Paul. 'That's why I know we've got a thief. We should have a static amount of money. But the amount of money in the system has increased, and its value has declined. There's only one way that can happen. Somebody's found a cache of money and has introduced it into the system.'

'But that's wrong, surely. That can't be the case.'

'No,' said Paul, 'I'm sure you'll find that's the answer.' And then suddenly he went very, very quiet, almost as though he'd said something extremely wrong, slanderous, blasphemous even.

He had. He knew he had, and now he knew exactly who the thief was.

* * *

The medicine worked for the next forty-eight hours and Julian began to pick up. But the next night Derek awoke to find the same events happening again, with a distraught Anne trying to console Julian who'd gone back to pumping up ever-increasing volumes of milk all over the wallpaper. They increased the dose to its maximum, but it wasn't working. The medicine was still in date—having learnt his lesson over Alison's insulin, that was the first thing that Derek checked.

During the first forty-eight hours of remission Julian had put a little bit of weight back on, and had actually had one wet nappy, but soon the old routine started up again, and within twelve hours it was obvious that they were fighting a losing battle for the child's life.

By ten o'clock that morning, in desperation, with a great deal of difficulty Derek tried to put a drip up and was at least managing to give Julian some saline that he had found in the health centre, but that would never feed him. It would only stave off the inevitable.

By noon Julian had rallied slightly, but then started to go downhill again, getting weaker and weaker until the exhausted and frightened Anne could stand it no more.

'Derek, I want you to do something for me,' she said. 'Just this once, and I promise I'll never ask you again.'

'What is it?' said Derek.

'I want you to tell Martin.' Derek opened his mouth in protest. 'I know,' she said quickly, before he could say anything. 'I know. I promise I won't ask you ever again. But I want you to tell Martin. He is Julian's real father, after all, and I think he ought to know. I think he's a right to know.'

Derek gave his wife a long hard stare, then sullenly and slowly descended the stairs and walked slowly through the Market Square, past his once beloved Dynevor House and up to the hated Old Rectory. Martin answered the door quickly and his face fell when he saw Derek.

'Anne's sent me to tell you,' began Derek, and a cold clammy hand grabbed at Martin's heart. He knew what was coming without being told and all he could think of was the story of David and Bathsheba... *And the child died.* He knew it was his fault. He shouldn't have done it and this was God wreaking vengeance on him. 'She wants you to come,' said Derek. 'She asked me to fetch you.'

'Oh... er... yes,' said Martin. 'Of course. Does she want me to baptise him then? Is he that ill?'

'I don't know what she wants,' said Derek curtly. 'Bring your things anyway,' and then turning on his heels strode off back down the drive. Martin collected his equipment for the baptism, and hurried down the drive after the departing figure of Derek. When he got to Lime View Derek had got there before him. Timidly Martin knocked on the open door, and when no one answered, cautiously pushed it open. There was no one there. He decided to go upstairs, came through the doorway into the main bedroom and for the first time saw his son—*his son*—cradled in the arms of Anne. Anne didn't even look up at him.

'Anne, I'm so sorry...' he began, and then stopped as Julian briefly looked up at him and closed his eyes in distress. 'Oh, the poor little thing,' said Martin totally unaware that by now he'd got tears streaming down his face. 'Oh you poor little thing.' He knelt down by Anne's side, the better to be near Julian and touched him—*his son*—gently on the forehead and on the arm that didn't have the drip in. Turning his head to the side he looked at Anne. 'What do you want me to do?'

Anne slowly shook her head from side to side, staring wordlessly at Julian. Martin looked up at Derek.

'What's going to happen?'

'He's going to die. There's nothing more we can do.' Martin felt all the muscles in his head and neck tighten; his tension headache worsened until it was pounding away in his ears.

'Are you sure?' he said, trying to control his panic. 'I mean you've got a drip...'

'That won't last for ever...'

Martin turned to Anne again. 'What do you want me to do? Baptise him, anoint him, pray for him?'

'Pray for him?' said Derek in disgust. 'Who says anyone will listen to you?' Martin hung his head in shame, and the words kept going through his mind again and again and again... '*And the child died*'.

'I'll do all three,' said Martin. 'If only for Anne's sake.' He got out a bowl of water and dipped his finger in it. 'What do you want him called?'

'Julian,' said Anne.

'Anything else?' asked Martin, swivelling his head between her and Derek.

'Just Julian.' With his finger Martin drew a cross in water on the child's forehead.

'Julian, I baptise thee in the name of the Father, and of the Son, and of the Holy Ghost. Amen. God the Father, God the Son, God the Holy Ghost, bless, preserve, and keep you, this day and for evermore. Amen.'

He withdrew his hand.

'Thank you,' mouthed Anne, though no noise came out.

'You can go now,' said Derek. Anne fixed Derek with a hostile glare.

'Derek's right,' said Martin. 'I ought to go, Anne. I'll pray for Julian. I'll pray for you all.'

'Thanks a million,' said Derek acidly. Julian stirred, opened his mouth to cry but no sound came out either. Martin packed up his things and went back to the Old Rectory, his mind in a turmoil. All he could think of was the turbulent memory ricocheting round his head—'*And the child died.*'

Reaching his room—the room where it had all started, where Julian had begun—he flung himself down at the side of the bed and, like King David before him, began to plead with God for his child's life, for a miracle, for *anything*. But the great King David had pleaded for his child's life, and the child had still died. So why should he, Martin, think that God would deal any differently with him?

It was dark when he finished. He hadn't noticed the sun going down, nor the shadows lengthening over the grass, nor the cold still air of the late afternoon as the frost descended. For hour upon hour Martin remained there, apologising to God for what he'd done, pleading for God to take control of the situation, desperate for God to hear him. He didn't stop to eat or drink—he didn't want to do either. All he could think of was...'*And the child died.*'

'No,' he kept on pleading, 'please no. Please in your mercy and grace forgive, in your love heal Julian. Please Lord, I am so sorry. I wish it had never happened, but I can't undo that now and it isn't Julian's fault. I'll do anything, *anything* you want me to, if only you will heal the child.

'...*And the child died*...' For hour after hour he knelt there, praying, pleading.

Then suddenly, around midnight, he knew he'd said enough, and prayed enough, and that there was no more to do. Exhausted he got off his knees and rolled forward into bed, collapsing exhausted on to the pillow, and within minutes was asleep from sheer fatigue. Perhaps Julian was already dead. Maybe that's why he felt he no longer had to pray. It was over. The whole awful thing was over.

*   *   *

But Julian didn't quite die that night. Somehow he held on with that ferocious tenacity that threatened young animals sometimes exhibit, though by the morning his pulse was feeble, his eyes permanently closed and his heart only just beating. Derek and Anne remained sitting by the cot, waiting for the inevitable to happen.

Dawn broke; the sky lightened, and the sun rose. The room became lighter, to reveal Julian lying motionless, with Derek and Anne sitting on each side, staring dully at him, willing him to live, but knowing that he wasn't going to make it.

Anne, too, had prayed that night—not in the well-formed way of Martin, but silently, in half-sentences, half-formed phrases, single words, like 'Please help... I'm sorry... Look after... Please... Jesus... Julian... Dear Lord...,' nothing that was remotely coherent or intelligible as far as anyone human would have been concerned. She just stayed there, watching, her lips silently moving from time to time.

And still Julian held on. Outside they could hear the noises of the Ampthill residents as they started to go about their daily business, in the far-off, unreal world outside their window.

Then from far in the distance out to the east came an unaccustomed sound, the rumble of heavy goods vehicles as a small convoy of three heavy vehicles slowly drew near and climbed past their house, crashing their gears to begin the descent into the Market Square. The front lorry had what appeared to be a snowplough on the front, and bringing up the rear was a caravan.

- *19* -

Without a word Derek leapt up, stormed down the stairs at least four at a time, and ran down the street after the lorries, yelling and waving his arms like a madman, begging them to stop, and not accelerate out of the other side of the Market Square. With a squeal of brakes the first lorry ground to a halt and out stepped the thin, aloof figure of Nicholas.

'Hello, doctor,' he said, to the flying figure of Derek coming nearer. 'Where's the fire?' and then the look on his face changed as he saw Derek's face. 'What's the matter?'

'What are you doing here?' said Derek, gasping for breath.

'I just thought I'd come. I don't know why really. I haven't been past here for ages. I thought I'd look you up.'

By now Derek had nearly got his breath back. 'My son,' gasped Derek, oblivious to the inaccurate use of the personal pronoun, 'my son... back in the house there... Oh, we're in a different one. No time to tell you... Six weeks old... Pyloric stenosis... But you may be too late,' and grabbing Nicholas by the sleeve almost pulled him off his feet in his haste to get him up to Lime View.

When they got upstairs Nicholas looked at the inert tiny body in front of him, and at the tube coming out of Julian's left arm.

'How long's this been in?'

'Twenty-four hours.'

'You've not done one of these before, have you?'

'You've guessed.'

'That's why Julian's not getting better.'

'Why?' said Derek.

'The drip's tissued. You haven't set it up correctly. There's supposed to be a drip chamber so that you can see that fluid is going out on a regular basis. 'Look here...'

He pointed to where the needle was in the flesh. There was a bulging area around it where the needle was stuck in Julian's arm. 'The needle's come out of the vein. Some of the fluid has gone into the tissues around, but then it can't get anywhere so it's stopped. The whole drip's blocked. Julian isn't getting any fluid at all. And you see that chamber there?' He pointed to a bit of the tube that had a bulbous part to it, in which was a white plastic float. 'That's supposed to be half air, half water so you can see the drips coming down from the plastic bag and measure how fast or slowly the drip's running.'

'Oh,' said Derek, '*that's* what it's for. I thought you had to get all the air out of the system before you set up a drip—in case you got air into the veins.'

'Yes, but you won't get any air into the veins if you set a drip up correctly. Watch.' He disconnected the drip from the plastic bag of fluid that was hanging off the back of a chair, let some of the fluid run out of the chamber containing the white ball until it was half full of air, then reconnected it to the bag of saline. Then taking a thin hollow needle with what looked like two green wings at the back, he inserted the needle in, of all places, a vein on Julian's scalp, waited till the blood oozed up the tiny tube behind the needle, and connected it to the main drip. Using some clear tape, he stuck down the wings of the needle, fastening them against Julian's head so that the needle was fixed firmly in place. Finally he used a tiny rotating wheel on the drip that ran up and down a piece of plastic which looked like one-half of a clothes peg to regulate the flow, and Derek and Anne watched as the fluid ran drip, drip, drip into the chamber with the ball in and then into the tube that was inserted into Julian's scalp vein.

'There you are,' said Nicholas. 'That should sort him out.'

'Is that all?' said Derek.

'Yes,' said Nicholas. 'We just rehydrate him,'

'Pardon?' said Anne

'Put back the fluid, and when he's a bit more chirpy we'll do the operation.'

'Operation?' said Anne, suspiciously.

'Ramstedt's operation. There's a muscle at the end of the stomach that's contracting too violently, and we have to cut into it to weaken it, so that it will let go enough to let the stomach's contents go into the rest of the gut. It's very easy. It'll only take a few minutes.'

'And it's that simple?' asked Anne, not quite believing what she was hearing.

'There shouldn't be any trouble,' said Nicholas. 'We'll pump enough fluid into little Julian until his biochemistry comes back to normal, and then when he's good and ready we'll put him to sleep and do the operation. Maybe about twelve hours. All right by you?'

'Yes,' nodded Derek, weakly.

*   *   *

'How *could* you, Chris?' asked Paul. She was ashen-faced, staring stonily at the empty fireplace.

'I don't know, now. It seemed a good idea at the time. But how did you know it was me?'

'It had to be either you or somebody who was forging your signature.'

'But how did you find out?'

'We've got inflation, or hadn't you noticed? There's only one way you can get inflation in a simple economy like ours—that's if somebody's found another stash of money and is using it, diluting the value of the rest of the money. We hadn't officially increased the money supply, because we were still using the same amount that we started with. So someone somewhere had got access to extra money which they'd started using. But to make that money useful in our system we first had to have your signature on it, didn't we? To prove it was "Ampthill" money.'

Chris nodded weakly.

'So I knew that someone somewhere had found a stash of money and had been putting your name on it, then using it as though they'd earned it. Either someone *else* found some money, and forged your signature, or else *you* found some more money, and signed it yourself. I looked at hundreds of bank notes—and they all looked like your signature to me, all done with the same type of pen.'

She nodded again, blankly.

'Where did you find it?'

'In Woburn, when I was looking for a wedding dress. I went upstairs in one of the old houses. To this day I don't know why I peered under the bed. I think I must have dropped something and stooped to pick it up... and there it was—in boxes.'

'How much?'

'About a thousand pounds in all.'

Paul let out a long whistle.

'No wonder we've got inflation. We've only got a total of six thousand pounds swilling round the whole system anyway. You've diluted it by nearly twenty per cent. That fits. And then you took it home and signed it so that you could pass it off as our money.'

She nodded silently again.

'*Why*, Chris?'

'It... it seemed a good idea at the time,' she said. 'I didn't realise I was doing anything wrong. I didn't realise I'd give everybody a quick dose of inflation. I didn't, honestly. You're the one who knows things like that. Not me.'

'Oh, Chris, love,' said Paul. 'What shall we do?'

Chris pulled herself together. 'Well, *you're* not going to tell anyone, are you?'

Paul looked away, torn between his responsibility to Ampthill, of which he'd effectively become honorary treasurer, and to his beloved wife.

'*You're* not going to tell anyone, Paul, are you?' said Chris firmly, looking him in the eye.

He opened his mouth and shut it again like a fish.

'No Paul, you are *not* going to tell anyone, because *I'm* going to tell them what I've done.'

'No, Chris,' Paul said in a panic. Visions of what the council had done to him when *he'd* been caught out suddenly flitted in front of his mind. He'd been strapped to the town pump and lashed. *But Chris was pregnant.* They couldn't... They wouldn't... Oh, no. Not to Chris.

He stared up at her. 'You can't. You mustn't.'

'I'm going to. I'm going to tell Henry.' And pulling on her jumper over her growing bump she waddled off determinedly in the direction of Dynevor House, shivering against the unexpected cold.

*   *   *

As Nicholas had planned, they performed the operation late that evening, inside the mobile theatre in one of the HGV vehicles in Nicholas's entourage. Derek couldn't believe the speed of it all. One minute Julian was being anaesthetised, the next minute he was asleep, and Nicholas was probing away with instruments inside a small hole that he'd made in Julian's upper abdomen. Within seconds, Nicholas pulled up a loop of shiny white thickened tissue, which he held between finger and thumb.

'There you are, Derek,' he said, 'there's the problem.'

To Derek one bit of bowel looked like any other and it was only with great difficulty that he made out the extra large bulge at the point where the stomach narrowed down into the duodenum. Deftly

Nicholas picked up a scalpel and cut lengthways along the tube at that point. The muscle beneath bulged out. With a pair of forceps, he split the muscle fibres apart until Derek could see a shining membrane glistening at the bottom of the split. 'See that? That's the internal lining of the pylorus—the exit from the stomach.'

Picking up a swab Nicholas dabbed the blood away from the area, and closed the bleeding points with a cautery. Then just as quickly and deftly he replaced the now weakened pyloric sphincter back in its original place, and before Derek could blink, was sewing up the layers of the abdomen one by one as he retraced his steps, coming out towards the skin. He closed off the skin with two tiny sutures then placed a dressing over the top. 'There you are,' he said, 'one son, back in one piece. Or at least, he will be in a very short time.'

'Now,' he said, pulling off his gloves, 'I think you owe me a drink.'

- 20 -

*L*ittle Julian had a peaceful, if not entirely pain-free night. As soon as Anne started feeding him again it was obvious that things had got back to normal. Gone was the projectile vomiting, the look of distress on the face and the hunger pains that followed. Early the next morning Nicholas was able to take the drip down, and Derek noted with satisfaction that Julian had taken in enough fluid to be able to produce wet nappies again. For the first time Anne looked as though she'd had a decent night's sleep; Derek looked considerably relieved, though still his usual gaunt, anxious self.

Nicholas pronounced himself well-satisfied with the way his patient had performed, and, standing up after bending over the cot, stretched—for he was a big man—then turned round to Derek.

'Well, doctor,' he said. 'As I was going to say yesterday morning before I was rudely attacked by this strange man flying down the hill after me, have you any other cases you'd like me to see?'

Derek thought for a moment. 'Yes,' he said. 'I've got someone that I don't understand at all. Let's go back to the surgery and I'll tell you about her.'

They left Anne and the baby there, basking in the freshness of the morning sun. As they walked back to the surgery Derek told Nicholas the long, involved, and to him quite harrowing story of Mrs MacKenzie.

'Makes you angry, does she?' said Nicholas staring at Derek over the top of the half-moon glasses which he'd taken to wearing.

'Well, now I come to think of it, yes she does. Why do you say that?'

'Just a hunch. Let's have a look at her notes.'

Derek led Nicholas into the surgery and presented him with Mrs Mackenzie's notes, by now a full two inches thick. No wonder— Derek had seen her about twice a week for the past year. Although he'd got absolutely nowhere, each time he'd assiduously examined her, recorded his observations, and tried to prescribe for her. It made for a lot of paperwork.

'I haven't a clue what's wrong with her,' he said finally. 'I've tried absolutely everything, and all she seems to do is get worse.'

'Oh *I* know what's wrong with her,' said Nicholas, 'or, at least, I'm pretty sure I do.'

'Really?' said Derek suddenly alert. 'What is it?'

'Let's just wait until I've examined her, shall we?' said Nicholas patiently. 'Can you get her here?'

'With pleasure,' said Derek. 'She's probably due in the surgery any minute if you must know. She usually turns up about this time.'

As luck would have it, she didn't, so Derek had to spend an annoying twenty minutes trying to find out where she'd got to. She was in her house, baking. When Mrs MacKenzie learned that there was a real doctor in the town her joy knew no bounds. Immediately she took off her apron and bustled down to the surgery in a most self-important way, which irritated Derek even further.

'Good afternoon Mrs... er... MacKenzie,' said Nicholas, putting on his best consultant manner and looking over the half-moon spectacles again. 'I gather you've been seeing my colleague quite a lot recently.'

'Oh yes, doctor,' she said, 'but I'm afraid I'm no better. We've tried everything. No, now you mention it I do think I might be just a little better on the last prescription he gave me. That was quite good. Or was it the one before that? Of course it was nothing like as good as that medicine they gave me when I was up in Scotland two years ago, but Derek can't work out what it was, so unfortunately we can't use it.'

Inwardly, Derek fumed. Nicholas went through all the routine questions and then asked Mrs MacKenzie to get up on the couch to be examined. He looked at her abdomen very carefully, then turned her on her side and performed a detailed rectal examination, followed by a procedure in which he pushed a long thin metal tube up her back passage.

'This is a sigmoidoscope,' he said gaily, producing a long wand about eighteen inches long and an inch wide. 'Don't worry, it looks more fearsome than it actually is. I'll just insert it in the back passage... like so... and you'll feel a funny sensation as though you want to go to the toilet because I'm gently puffing up the inside of your gut with some air, so that I can see inside a little better.' Gently he introduced the sigmoidoscope up to its hilt. Mrs MacKenzie opened her mouth slightly as if to protest. The instrument looked so long that Derek could have sworn that when she opened her mouth it was to let the sigmoidoscope out at the other end, but then he could have been mistaken. Finally Nicholas withdrew it.

'Do dress up, Mrs MacKenzie,' Nicholas purred, and suddenly looked very serious.

'What is it, doctor?' said Mrs MacKenzie suddenly startled. 'I haven't got anything serious, have I?'

Nicholas paused. 'That depends on what you mean by serious,' he said.

Alarmed Mrs MacKenzie sat down with a bump. 'I've not got...' and her hand flew to her mouth '... the big C, have I? Oh no, tell me it's not that...'

'No, it's not that, Mrs MacKenzie.'

'Well, what is it then? Has Derek missed something? Oh, I'll never forgive you if you have, Derek. All these times I've been to see you and you've missed something. Well, that's just too bad, it is. Really it is.'

'No, Mrs Mackenzie,' said Nicholas, 'and you can stop having a go at Derek, too. Let me tell you. There is nothing wrong with your abdomen and nothing wrong with your gut. It's all in your mind.'

'*I am not imagining things*,' said Mrs MacKenzie indignantly. 'Oh, the very idea. How *dare* you say things like that?'

'Do hear me out, Mrs MacKenzie,' said Nicholas, lacerating her with a stare. 'Listen to me, and listen to me carefully. There is nothing physically wrong with your stomach at all, and you do feel pain—real pain: but it's not coming from your stomach, it's generated by your mind, and the real reason why you are experiencing pain is because of anxieties that you've had for a very long time. Derek's told me all about you, so I know your past quite well. Do you know how some stressed people get ulcers?'

'Yes,' she said cautiously.

'Those are people who've put all their anxieties into their stomach—and then they don't feel so anxious because much of their anxiety has gone from their mind and has been "put" into their stomach.

'Some people get chest pain because they're anxious. They put all their anxieties into their heart, and because they have real pain to worry about, it stops them worrying about their anxieties. And I'm *sure*,' and he emphasised the last word, 'that this is what is happening to you. I've talked with Derek, who incidentally has done an excellent job over the past year. He hasn't missed anything *physical* in your abdomen. But what I'm going to ask him to do is to talk with you about the things that have made you anxious and angry in the past, because I'm sure we'll find that events in the past are, even today, still returning to haunt you.'

The relief at not having cancer was evident on Mrs MacKenzie's face.

But Nicholas still looked very concerned. 'You asked me right at the beginning "Is it serious?" Yes, it is serious because unless you acknowledge and deal with the causes of stress within your life, then you will *never* get better, because they will continue to cause your stomach pain. And if you try and imagine that your stomach is the real cause of your pain then you'll never find the answer.'

For once Mrs MacKenzie was struck dumb.

'Oh help,' said the gerbil in her subconscious.

'*Oh help*,' said the lion in her subconscious. 'I've been sussed.'

'*Gotcha*,' said the lion in Nicholas's subconscious.

*   *   *

'But how did you *know*?' asked Derek as the retreating rear of Mrs MacKenzie waddled out of the door in her characteristic fashion and she retreated up the hill, muttering under her breath.

'Twenty-five more years' experience than you've got, Derek my lad. She's a hysteric.'

'I thought hysterics ran around in a frenzy.'

'So do most people, but most people are wrong. Hysterics make *other people* run around in a frenzy. They love tying them up in knots. She had you tied up good and proper, didn't she? Whatever you suggested she found a way to evade it.'

Derek nodded ruefully.

'And you found yourself getting angry with her, didn't you?'

'Yes, but that wasn't because I couldn't cure her.'

'Oh no,' said Nicholas. 'It wasn't that at all. You aren't angry with her because you can't cure her. You're angry with her because *she makes you angry*, because that's how she works. Her game is to try to make you impotent, and she succeeded very well. It wasn't the fact that you didn't try or couldn't help her that made you angry. You didn't get angry about Susan when she had her gallstones, did you? Or when Mrs Summerfield died of cancer?'

'No,' said Derek slowly, 'should I?'

'Not at all—that's the point. Even though you couldn't make Susan better it didn't make you angry, it just made you frustrated. But Mrs MacKenzie *did* make you angry, and it wasn't because you couldn't make her better, it was because of the way that she would slip out of your grasp every time you tried to help her, and the selfishness with which she did it, too. I bet if you go into her history you'll find some very interesting things about her early life—perhaps the way she played her mother off against her father or the other way round. She's just learned to behave like that, that's all—to deal with her problems by denying them, confusing others and making them go round in circles. It's not your fault Derek—you just got in the way.'

'So what do I have to do now?' asked Derek.

'I don't know,' said Nicholas thoughtfully. 'Hysterics are very difficult people to deal with. I know full well what she'll be doing now. She'll be going to her next-door neighbour and complaining about that awful surgeon who thinks that she's a mental case and look at her of course she's not mental she's got this real pain in her stomach... all in one breath, of course. And *of course* she's got a real pain in her stomach—but it doesn't come from there, it comes from her head: but she won't be able to appreciate that. So you've got somebody here who's a chronic case, who's never going to get better. It's almost a bigger problem than if she did have "the big C" that she dreads so much. I don't think you've got a chance with her. She needs skilled psychotherapy, from someone who won't be manipulated by her, because they understand the game she's playing, and the way she's playing it. We're neither of us skilled in that area, are we? So I think—I'm afraid—that for the moment Mrs MacKenzie is effectively incurable. Still, at least you know enough not to be frightened by her in the future, because she was always working on your fear that you couldn't control the situation.'

'But how did you *know*?' said Derek.

'It's the anger,' replied Nicholas. 'Hysterics nearly always make their carers angry.'

Derek sighed.

'Now, have you got any other patients for me?'

Derek thought for a moment. 'No,' he said slowly. 'I don't think so. I think everything else is under control.'

'Are you sure?'

'Yes. I think so. Why?'

'I think you've missed someone.'

Derek thought again.

'No, I don't think so.'

'I'm *sure* you've missed someone.'

'Who?' asked Derek, wondering how he could possibly know.

'You,' said Nicholas.

'Me?'

'Yes, you. You look like death warmed up. You've lost at least
two stone since I last saw you. You've a complexion that looks as
though it's inhabited a mummy's tomb for a couple of thousand
years, and only just been let out. Tell me about it.'

No, thought Derek, I can't. I'm sworn to secrecy. And suddenly
he realised he wasn't sworn to secrecy because he could tell his own
doctor, and Nicholas was his own doctor.

And so he poured out the whole sorry story. Of the stresses and
strains of trying to be a doctor with inadequate teaching and inadequate supervision. Of how at first it was a privilege, then electrify-
ing fun, then frightening, and finally draining beyond belief. Of
Martin and Anne and Julian. Of how, as a reaction, he'd thrown
himself into his job, and worked himself into the ground. Of how
Anne had sworn both Martin and him to professional silence, so
they weren't allowed to tell anyone else what had happened, and so
he couldn't off-load to anybody. All this he related over the space of
half an hour, with Nicholas gently coaxing him into letting go of the
ghosts and ogres that had haunted him for so long.

A trouble shared is a trouble halved, and just through the telling
and in the off-loading Derek was able to see that some of the problems that he'd previously regarded as immense were not as large as
he had imagined them to be. He shed a tear or two that day, especially when relating how Anne, the love of his life, had in a moment
of madness gone off with, of all people, her vicar, and how in that
one small event she had managed to kill off the marriage as though
she had nailed a stake through its heart. The 'something' that had
been between them had gone, evaporated into thin air like the early
morning dew. And now he was left with another man's baby to look
after and no one to be able to talk to about it.

Nicholas listened patiently and then gently but systematically started asking him questions about his physical health. Did he smoke? No. Were his waterworks OK? Yes. What about his bowels? Any recent change? Yes, there'd been a little bit of discomfort and some diarrhoea, but that was obviously the anxiety. No, he didn't get too many headaches—just occasional ones when he got stressed.

'OK Derek,' he said, 'up on the couch.'

'You what?'

'You heard. Up on the couch.'

'Why?'

'Because I want to examine you, that's why.'

Derek shrugged. 'If you say so.'

'I do say so.' Nicholas went over Derek with a fine tooth comb and Derek found how odd it was to be examined medically when now he knew what the examiner was looking for: how when Nicholas placed the bowl of the stethoscope against the left-hand side of the breast-bone he was listening to the mitral area of the heart and now, at the front of the chest telling him to breathe in and then breathe out and hold it, he was listening to the aortic valve. It was just as he, Derek, had done, so many times in the past, but it was so strange to be on the receiving end. Nicholas asked Derek to lie down again for the abdominal examination. 'Any pains,' he asked, 'when I do this?' His fingers moved relentlessly and remorselessly around the abdomen, kneading, probing, pressing.

'Just a little there,' said Derek as Nicholas's hand passed over the middle of his abdomen, deep on the left. Nicholas stared over his half-moon glasses again.

'Over on your side.'

'What, why?'

'Sigmoidoscopy time.'

'Why?' Suddenly there was terror in Derek's voice. 'Why? What's going on? What's happened?'

'Calm yourself, Derek,' said Nicholas. 'Let's just find out what there is, shall we?' Deftly he inserted a clean sigmoidoscope, and puffed up the little balloon at the eyepiece end. Derek thought that his gut was just about to burst, or alternatively that if he opened his mouth too wide the sigmoidoscope would come out and then he'd have something to bite on to ease the discomfort.

'Yes... Aha... Yes... Good... Right,' said Nicholas withdrawing the instrument for the last time.

'How're we doing?' said Derek, sitting up. 'Is everything all right?'

He then looked at Nicholas's face. For once Nicholas had let the mask of bonhomie slip, for a second, but it was enough for Derek. His heart began to race, and his mouth had suddenly gone very dry.

'What do you think's the matter with you, Derek?'

'Well, I *thought* that it was all anxiety and stress,' Derek gulped, trying hard not to look an anxious coward, too.

'You're undoubtedly right. Some of it is... but you've also got a cancer sitting there in your colon, and that's the real reason why you look so ghastly. You might lose weight if you were just anxious, but you wouldn't go anaemic and you wouldn't have that horrible pasty look. I knew you'd got something as soon as I clapped eyes on you.'

'Cancer?' mumbled Derek indistinctly. 'Are you sure?'

'As sure as I can be without taking samples and sending them to a lab, and I can't do that.'

'But I'm only forty-six.'

'I'm afraid that doesn't stop you having cancer, my friend.' He put his hand on Derek's forearm. 'But the good news...'

'Yes.'

'... is that I think that I can get it out. I *think*. I don't know. It looks as though we might just have got it in time and as you know cancer of the colon is actually quite easy to treat, and has a high cure rate. *Cure*. Got it?'

'Why's that?'

'Because there are fewer ways for the cancerous cells to spread in the gut. You know your anatomy, don't you? Of course you do. The gut is a long thin tube inside the abdomen, rather like a snake inside a balloon, tethered at each end. All the gut hangs off the back of the abdominal wall at the bottom of a thin curtain of tissue called the mesentery. When we were at medical school we were always told the gut was like a pipe that was passing along the bottom of a curtain. The pipe is the gut, the curtain is the mesentery. This means that if you get a cancer in the gut, the only easy way it can spread is up the mesentery. It doesn't jump across to the abdominal wall all that often. So with a bit of luck, if we find a cancer early enough and chop it out with wide enough margins and cut back the segment of curtaining—the mesentery—on which it hangs, you may get rid of the whole thing. It's actually quite hopeful, if you must know. If you're going to have cancer, have it there.'

'Can you do the operation?'

'Of course.'

'Have you got enough anaesthetic?'

'Yes,' said Nicholas unequivocally. 'I've been very careful only to use it on the people who really *have* to have a general anaesthetic. You couldn't do an operation like this under a local anaesthetic or without any anaesthetic at all.'

'I'd rather not have cancer at all,' murmured Derek, suddenly feeling extremely tired. Then a thought struck him. 'Hang on, what's going to happen while I'm ill? Who's going to look after everybody here?'

'Aha,' said Nicholas, pushing the glasses back firmly back on to the bridge of his nose. '*Quis custodiet ipsis custodes*, eh?'

'What do you mean?'

'It's Latin. Or to put it in its modern context, "Who cares for the carers?" Well, I can tell you who will look after your patients—I will.'

'You?'

'Why not? I am a doctor after all.' A little twinkle came into Nicholas's eye.

'No, I didn't mean it like that,' said Derek, suddenly embarrassed. 'I mean, you like to move around.'

'There's no reason why I have to, is there? I can stop here for a bit, take up a house if there's one spare or else live in the caravan for a bit—for maybe six or eight weeks while you're getting better. It'll be good for both of us—you'll get a rest, I'll see some different cases and maybe I'll sort out one or two of the things that you've been a bit puzzled about.'

'Well,' said Derek, 'that would be nice.'

'Of course, there is the question of payment.'

Oh no, thought Derek, not again, and visions of overpriced surgeons, manic vicars with shot-guns at the ready and tankers full of petrol all flashed through his mind in one swift instant.

'I don't mean for the operation itself. I wouldn't charge you for that.'

'That's kind,' said Derek.

'One has a duty to treat one's professional colleagues for free.'

'Really?' said Derek. 'I didn't know that. But anyway I'm not a proper doctor.'

'I think you're quite good enough to be one,' said Nicholas. 'I'm most impressed, and I'm quite happy to extend the normal professional courtesies to you.'

Derek suddenly felt a mixture of exaltation, elation, deliverance and fear at the same time. It was so good to be able to unload his problems and off-load his cases onto someone who could handle the debris. He felt better already.

'The remuneration I'm talking about is what the community will need to pay me while you're unwell. Locum fees, if you like.'

'I'll go and see Chris about that, shall I?' said Derek, suddenly becoming rather numb with the shock of it all. He paused. 'Are you *sure*?'

'Sure of what?'

'That it's cancer.'

'Of course I'm sure,' said Nicholas. 'There's no real chance that it's anything else.'

'Oh God,' said Derek suddenly, though he didn't believe in Him. His life seemed suddenly to be at a dead stop. He'd lost half his family, his wife, and now his health.

'And when you get better,' Nicholas said, looking at him again over the half-moon glasses with his penetrating stare, 'you will not, repeat *not*, wear yourself out as you've been doing. Do you understand? It's not professional and it's certainly not good for you. If you'd looked after yourself better you might have spotted what was happening a bit earlier, don't you think?'

Derek nodded dumbly. How could he have been so stupid as to miss it? The diarrhoea, the cramps, the loss of weight?

'Right,' said Nicholas. 'You gather yourself together and I'll go and tell Anne.'

Derek made as if to protest. Nicholas held up his hand. 'No, Derek, we'll do it my way. I'm in charge here now.'

*   *   *

Nicholas did tell Anne—very effectively, very enthusiastically and very comfortingly. He made it sound as though getting over cancer was the easiest thing in the world and that it was just a matter of a few weeks before Derek was up, about and running around as normal. Once the shock had worn off Anne felt very positive about the situation.

Nicholas negotiated, apparently successfully, with Chris over a suitable fee for his locum arrangements, so the next day a starved and prepped Derek lay drowsily awaiting the anaesthetic which as usual was administered by one of Nicholas's drivers. Nicholas got the tumour out, reconnected the gut and closed Derek up.

It took six weeks for Derek to recover, during which he felt as weak as a kitten. This was partially due to the operation, but more to the sudden cessation of stress and activity which as so often happens, leads to a reactive depression and exhaustion, once the adrenaline of activity has gone away. Derek was surprised at how smoothly it had gone, but found it quite unnerving being on the receiving end of medicine, knowing rather more about it than the average layman. It's a frightening experience for a doctor to be faced with his own serious illness, because there are no holds barred and no way of glossing over the potential problems; no chance of talking of 'a little bit of thickening here' or 'a few nodes there' when what those phrases so often mean is 'secondaries have occurred—the cancer has spread'. For Derek there was no hiding place. He knew the odds, the warning signs and what could go wrong. He knew the percentage chances (which were in his favour) but he had the awful job of learning to live with this uncertainty at a far more intimate level than most lay people ever have to experience.

But he got stronger, and as the days grew longer, the air grew
warmer and Julian grew bigger, Derek quietly started to recover.

*   *   *

Shortly after Derek's operation Chris went into labour and fourteen hours later was delivered of a healthy, robust girl weighing in
at eight pounds eight ounces. Paul just looked at her, and looked,
and looked.

'Emma,' he said to Nicholas, choking back his tears. 'She'll be
called Emma. That's what we agreed.' He turned to Chris. 'That's
what you wanted, wasn't it?'

Too exhausted to say anything, Chris just nodded, amazed by
Paul's soft centre that had suddenly appeared.

It was only afterwards, outside the bedroom, that Paul confided
to Nicholas his fears that what had happened to Jane would also
happen to Chris, for he was *terrified* of losing her. It took him days
to calm down: even he hadn't realised how concerned he'd been,
underneath it all.

*   *   *

While Derek was out of commission after his operation,
Nicholas acted as his locum, though he had an easy time of it and
never seemed to have to work anything like as hard as Derek. In part
this was because, like all doctors, Derek had developed a personal
following of those who valued him for himself as much as for his
medical ability, and who found consolation and comfort in his bedside manner. Nicholas, although much more highly qualified,
hadn't built up this rapport and so people were more reticent in
coming to see him. But in addition Nicholas, being the better doctor, technically speaking, was able to make diagnoses much more
quickly, and with a greater degree of certainty, and had an extra
quality of pharmaceutical and therapeutic expertise, so cases under
his care took less time to sort out.

Strangely, to the patients, this often seemed as though Nicholas
was being abrupt with them—Derek would have spent half an hour
sorting them out whereas Nicholas dismissed them in three minutes

flat! So in some quarters Nicholas—although a 'proper' doctor—wasn't held in as high standing as Derek, who wasn't.

Nicholas, of course, got wind of this, but wasn't in the least worried, because he'd been used to it. It had always been a source of cynical amusement to him that doctors had been held in the highest regard in the Victorian and Edwardian eras, at a time when in truth they could often do little for their patients; and yet in more modern times, when they had much more effective drugs and vastly more complex surgical techniques available to them, the medical profession was criticised much more frequently.

Although Derek's convalescence had been physically trouble-free, emotionally it had been anything but. Lying there after the operation, sedated by some of the last vials of morphine, he started thinking about what life was going to be like for the citizens of Ampthill in the future, when the morphine finally ran out; what life would have been like in the present had not Nicholas turned up at the right time; and what life definitely had been like in the distant past when surgical expertise, anaesthesia, and painkillers were simply not available because they hadn't yet been invented or discovered. The implications simply appalled him.

Before the plague Derek had thought of the world as being rather an enjoyable place, often very beautiful, but really quite placid and in some cases almost Elysian. A week after the plague struck he'd realised that this placid Nature had to be *fought* with to yield up enough food to eat; and he was gradually realising, through the initial selfishness of Nicholas—before they had become friends, that is—and later on through the cruel way of life of Lew Pritchard and his gang, that the world was full of evil selfish people. In many ways Derek was just making a secular reassessment of the same discoveries that Martin had already made concerning his theological reassessment of the nature of man.

But for once Derek had gone one further than Martin, philosophically speaking. Because he had experienced at first hand the discomfort and pain of being seriously ill and of the operations necessary to get him better, he realised perhaps earlier than Martin what a dreadful world it is, full of illness, pain, suffering, remorse, double-dealing, deceit, dishonesty, deception, pain, lies, anguish and death.

Martin, doubtless, would have said that as well as man being fallen, the whole of the universe was fallen and that included nature: that the face of God had been turned away from the world—hence death, decay and destruction, the great white shark, TB, Legionnaires' disease and malaria. Derek, being Derek, and without any such religious faith, could only look at the world and despair in a particularly complete way. Martin at least had a hope of an after-life that would be better—perfect, even—where God would return to the world in a permanent and intimate way, to create a new heaven and a new earth where pain and suffering would be unknown, where the lion really would lie down with the lamb, where beloved daughters no longer died of diabetes nor friends in childbirth: and there were no such things as children conceived out of wedlock.

But Derek didn't have Martin's faith: so he shuddered and turned his face to the wall again, counting the spots on the wallpaper and the days before he could get back into action again—activities designed to smother the exhaustion and the sadness that now threatened to overwhelm him.

*   *   *

Martin was settling neatly into a dual-function role. On the one hand there was the obvious and increasing demand for his pastoral care and spiritual advice. The episode with Anne notwithstanding, his pastoral and spiritual gifts were consistently valued throughout the community and even those who didn't agree with his religious viewpoint all said that he was a courteous, kind and effective counsellor, an excellent listener, and a source of sound and mature advice.

But this wasn't the only string to his bow, for, like Trevor, Martin also seemed to have a way with animals. His first job in the community, right at the beginning, had been to milk the cows and look after them, and in the same way that Derek had changed occupations successfully, so Martin found an alternative occupation dealing with farm animals. He had that indefinable knack of being relaxed in their presence. They too sensed his calm, confident approach and in turn responded to him. He didn't acquire any formal training—unlike Derek, Martin didn't start reading any of the farming or veterinary medicine text books—but even so he just seemed to have a way with all animals, whether it be training young puppies, encouraging sheep who'd just given birth to suckle their lambs, or catching and controlling rogue cows—and on one occasion a rogue bull—that had managed to break out of their field and go on the rampage.

It was natural therefore that Martin was among the first to be involved with the breaking in of the new foals that were gradually arriving. When Neil and Paul had first begun to plan for the future they had recognised that the role of the internal combustion engine was strictly limited and that the community should look elsewhere for its transport. Horses were the obvious choice. There had been a number of stud farms in the area before the plague, and many mares were already in foal. As soon as they had found some shire horses, they too were encouraged to breed.

Martin had never ridden a horse before, never mind having the job of breaking one in, but he'd seen it done on the television, so he had a rough idea of what was required. First he got to know the horse, offering it titbits of food—sugar lumps of course were a thing of the past. Then, when the horse was comfortable in his presence, he would slip a simple halter over its neck and allow it to canter around freely. The next job was to add a long leash so that the horse had to walk round in a circle. Then Martin would back him— putting a rug over his back and lying across it.

Next he would put a saddle on the horse so that the horse could get used to it over a few days. Finally—and this was the difficult bit—Martin then had to try to get into the saddle for a few moments for the horse to feel comfortable with him there, and then he would get off again.

After this the next procedure was to get the horse to walk forwards with the rider in the saddle and a second person holding the long leash so that the horse gently walked round in a circle. Gradually the animal would become accustomed to the process, accepting bridal, bit, harness and saddle without demur. With a willing horse the whole process was supposed to take as little as two to three weeks, but with a determined, high-spirited or unwilling horse it could take considerably longer.

The first horse he trained was a beautiful chestnut. Judging by the number of teeth, he'd only just been born when the plague struck. Not knowing whether he'd been called anything else before the plague, they named him Seamus. He was a haughty, sprightly but nevertheless very gentle beast, who had, quite obviously, never been broken in.

All went well at first. After several days of coaxing Seamus Martin managed to slip the first-stage halter on him. Seamus tolerated it well, and within a few days was walking round in a circle at a command. The next day Martin backed him, and it was only a few more days before he strapped on the saddle, which Seamus accepted with good grace, walking round happily and obediently.

The day after that was the big event. Martin and Trevor put the full harness and saddle on Seamus, let him out into the middle of the field and, with Trevor holding Seamus' head, Martin gingerly lifted his leg over into the saddle and sat down.

Martin had never flown in his life before—certainly not without an aeroplane—nor had ever he been an acrobat. Approximately two seconds later neither of these statements was true any longer. He didn't know quite how he got there, but he landed on his buttocks in front of Seamus' head, having executed a complete somersault in the process. Seamus had bucked him with incredible ferocity and speed.

Shaken, Martin got up gingerly, went across to Seamus, who was by now pulling at the traces and whinnying, bringing up his head and staring, with the whites of his eyes showing—as horses always do when they're afraid of something near and are trying to bring the feared object into focus in the only part of their eye that can see close objects, the part that normally looks down at the grass.

It took Martin five minutes to calm Seamus down, after which, bravely, he tried again.

This time he lasted a lot longer—a hundred per cent longer, to be precise. It was about four seconds before he came off, this time sideways, landing heavily on his right arm. He got up, brushed the mud off as best he could and went to comfort Seamus again.

Five minutes later he tried again.

There seemed to be a geometrical progression in the amount of time Martin stayed in the saddle. This time it was nearer ten seconds before Seamus threw him, the time after that about half a minute, and the one after that, two minutes. But eventually Martin did it, sitting nervously on top of Seamus waiting for the reaction.

As if sitting in the saddle wasn't enough, getting Seamus to walk with Martin held aloft was an even bigger problem. For the first two days Seamus refused to budge at all, resisting all entreaties, prods in the belly from Martin's heels, tugs from Trevor on the halter or sheer bribery in the shape of titbits of food held two feet from his nose. Then, when Martin was beginning to doubt if he'd ever manage to break Seamus in, without warning, and to Martin's complete surprise, Seamus responded meekly and without any fuss at all, walking round in a circle three or four times.

Martin leaned forward in the saddle. 'Good boy, Seamus,' he whispered in his ear. Seamus responded by bucking violently, throwing Martin off head over heels again.

But it was the last time that Seamus responded that way, and from then on he really was broken in. High-spirited, yes: powerful, yes. But finally Seamus proved to be obedient, responsive and reliable. By the end of the three weeks Martin would have trusted Seamus with anyone.

From then on Seamus and Martin became like inseparable friends. To Martin it felt as though Seamus seemed to respect him as his rightful master and genuinely seemed to enjoy riding out with him, much more than anyone else. In turn—and on a very fast learning curve—Martin soon became a proficient horseman, his knack of communicating with animals once again displayed, which, though he never intended it to, earned him nothing but further admiration from the rest of the community in whose eyes his standing increased daily.

It was a good job they didn't know about Anne.

*   *   *

In the first week of May Nicholas had pronounced himself satisfied with Derek's recovery, and Derek had decided that he was ready to take the reins again, so without much ado, and with profuse thanks on the part of Chris, and especially Derek, Nicholas gathered up his things, got into the lorry with the operating theatre inside and trundled off noisily in search of further patients.

Meanwhile Derek returned to work, tired and weak but determined to get back into harness. His enforced rest had done him good—in one sense—and bad in another. The good was because at last he'd been forced to stop and give himself the physical and mental rest that he so desperately needed. The bad was that he was put into greater contact with the very reasons why he had driven himself onward in the first place: his wife, and Julian. Half of Derek was glad of the period of rest, the other half couldn't wait to get away from Lime View and back into the community again.

Within days of returning to work, Derek was up to his old tricks again, fully immersed in his practice, finding more and yet more work to do. It wasn't that he'd forgotten Nicholas' advice to take it easy, to be balanced and professional about things, and to look after himself—he remembered Nicholas' words all too well. The trouble was that he just couldn't bring himself to carry them out. There was always something he could be doing, always another useful activity into which he could throw himself, another set of health checks to carry out, another elderly person to visit... He knew he was doing it again, but he couldn't stop himself: it was just too painful being at home with Anne... and Julian. He could hardly bring himself to mention the child's name. In fact he could hardly bear to be with Anne, so great was his sense of loss: Anne, the woman he'd loved all his life—the *only* woman he'd loved, the one he'd always desired above all others, and who had repaid his fidelity with... with Julian. If work was murder, it was even worse being at home, so near to the woman he loved, and yet so far away, with a constant reminder in the squalling little infant of the chasm that had come within his marriage.

Derek's patients, of course, loved him for his extra attention: they had even more of him all to themselves, for even longer. Daily his stature grew within the community—especially by comparison with that off-hand shirker Nicholas who was soon perceived to have every single one of the vices of the medical profession, whilst Derek possessed every one of the virtues.

The real casualties, of course, were the onlookers—David in particular, and Sarah. Anne was a casualty, too. She knew she'd done wrong, but somehow couldn't bridge the gap between them: sheer embarrassment at what she had done somehow prevented her from saying effectively those two words that mean so much—'I'm sorry'. Instead she retreated into her shell and created a hard-glazed exterior around herself, trying with all her might to cocoon her emotions away, emotions that were threatening to break her in pieces just as much as the sadness and anger within Derek were threatening to break him in pieces, too.

Throughout the summer Derek toiled away, devoting himself to his patients. Having recently read a book about how the doctor himself is part of the medicine, Derek concluded that even though he had fewer drugs available to cure patients, the doctor's presence itself was a mightily powerful drug, and he resolved to use it as much as possible: in fact, he'd soon convinced himself that this was the only way for him to go, now that so few medicines were left. All he had was himself—and the more he could give of himself to others, the more quickly would they recover. And so Derek gradually became like the doctors of old—with little in their bags that actually worked, but with a powerful presence that made the patient feel good just because they'd walked in through the door.

It was a pity that Derek hadn't read another, more bitter, modern medical aphorism: 'Divorce at forty, coronary at forty-eight.' At the rate he was going, he'd got just two years left.

*   *   *

It was June when it happened—flaming June, the month of strawberries, heat, long summer evenings and the slow gentle ripening of the corn under the heat haze. At the insistence of the council,

Susan, Alan and Anne had between them set up a school to teach the
children some of the lessons they needed. It was quite a different
school from those in the past: out went the Latin and geography
lessons; in came farming and survival programmes. Gone were the
days of absconding, truancy and why-bother-with-learning-what's-
the-point, to be replaced by a sense of urgency—that old crafts and
skills shouldn't die out.

And, as in the past, that sense of urgency conveyed itself to
the children. In the nineteenth century, when many villagers still
couldn't read or write, to be able to go to school was considered a
privilege not to be turned down. Many an illiterate worker would
scold his child for not being attentive to the important matters of
reading and writing, when these might later make a difference
between a job that fed you and one that didn't. In the latter half of
the twentieth century, when schooling was taken for granted (or, in
some quarters, preferably avoided altogether) there was no such
urgency. Why should one bother? ran the argument—we'll eat anyway. What's the point?

With the advent of the plague all this changed. There was a sudden desperation to get information and expertise: part of this came
from the adult population who were all too aware of the knife-edge
on which the community rested; and part came from the children
themselves who could see with their own eyes the difficulties of living, and who knew only too well that if they didn't work, if they
couldn't contribute, if they didn't learn the skills, then it was they
who would go home hungry, cold, or ill-dressed: there was no fall-
back. So the children went out with their parents to help tend the
crops, mend the equipment, cook, sew, build and clean: it was 'all
hands to the plough'—the community couldn't afford to have
mouths that had unproductive bodies attached. And (Derek's learning of medicine notwithstanding) it was quickly realised that skills
were difficult to learn from books, and that the wisdom and experiences of a lifetime's work with cattle, wood or metal was better
passed on from person to person—and that if these skills weren't
passed on soon they would die out with their original owners, never
to be replaced. There was no longer a safety net for this, either.

With the urgency for acquiring knowledge, the needs for schooling changed: although it was fun to learn disciplines that were of theoretical importance—such as foreign languages, particle physics, and the geography of distant lands—these were luxuries, to be indulged on special occasions. The practicalities of botany, horticulture, and engineering were of vastly greater relevance.

Paradoxically, as schooling became less learned and more like an apprenticeship, the more the pupils enjoyed it, because they could see its immediate relevance. One day they would be taught about working with metal: the next they would find themselves helping to mend some item of agricultural equipment, and would return to the classroom full of questions that were born of experience and genuine difficulty. Gone were the theoretical questions: 'A factory producing polyester fibres has a ten per cent rise in costs...' and in came the practical ones—how much grain would be needed to sow that polygonal field? How much load would a beam take? How does an engine work, and—more to the point—what do we do when it doesn't? Even the more theoretical problems could be seen to have relevance for the near future—how could engines be converted to use rapeseed oil, and how many acres would we need to grow each year to sustain the vehicles?

It was from this hands-on, practical approach that David, many months earlier, had had the idea for the crossbow, which he had made from the wishbones of an old car.

Susan and Alan—as always at daggers drawn—produced a surprisingly well-rounded course. As an ex-science teacher, Alan naturally took the lead in engineering, with some practical chemistry, physics and maths thrown in. Susan took the more 'arts' subjects, with great emphasis on cooking and the creation and adaptation of garments: she also filled in on the one area of science where Alan was weak—botany and horticulture. Anne, as an ex-junior school teacher, naturally gravitated towards the little ones, such few as there were, giving them an enjoyable entry into basic numeracy and literacy.

It was while Susan was teaching the older children about potatoes (nutritional value, growth, pests and storage) that it happened.

David was at that moment slicing up a potato, and putting an 'eye' under their one and only microscope to observe the growth point when he snagged his long baggy-sleeved top on the back of an adjacent chair, pulling the sleeve up. Hurriedly he pulled the sleeve back down again, but not before Susan saw the two large, purplish bruises on his upper arm.

'Where did you get those, David,' she asked, suddenly alert.

David mumbled something and looked sheepish.

'What did you say?'

He mumbled the same syllables again, pulling his sleeve further down.

'I can't hear you. Speak clearly. Where did you get those?'

'It doesn't matter. It's not important.' David moved to look down the microscope but Susan put her hand over the eyepiece.

'I want an answer, please. Where did you get them from?'

'I fell over,' came the sullen reply. He looked up at her, and then away again, giving as good an impression of a guilty lie as any Susan had ever seen in her considerable previous experience of teaching in a deprived neighbourhood.

'I don't believe you.'

'Don't then. Does it matter, anyway?' He looked away again. 'I want to use the microscope, please.'

'Come with me, David.' She led him into an empty room, then pulled up his other sleeve. There were bruises on that, too. 'Pull your trousers down.'

'No!'

'Oh don't be silly, I only want to see your legs. You've got underpants on, haven't you? Now do it.'

Sullenly he obeyed. His legs were a mass of bruises and welts, some new, some old.

'And you fell down?' The disbelief showed in the voice. David looked away, then down at the floor.

'Something like that, yes.'

'All right, you can go back to the class.'

Pulling up his trousers, David almost ran to the door.

*   *   *

'Alan,' said the voice across the empty fireplace.

Alan lowered his book and looked at Susan with a questioning frown, wondering what he'd done wrong now.

'I think I've got a problem with David...'

'Fire away.'

'He's got bruises and welts all over his arms and legs. It looks as though someone's been beating him.'

Alan closed the book and put it carefully on the table beside him, then gave Susan his full attention. He paused. 'Did he say who...?'

'No. Sullen as ever. Said it was a fall. It wasn't. Anyone could see he was lying.'

'So...?'

'So he's been beaten, you ignoramus.'

'By whom?'

'Derek.'

'*He said that*?'

'Not in so many words. But who else is there? Anne couldn't— she's far too small. David towers over her now. No, it's got to be Derek.' The amateur psychiatrist in Susan had the bit between her teeth now. 'Come on—who else is there?'

'*Derek*? I don't believe it. You're crackers.'

'*I AM NOT!*'

'All right, all right... calm down.... I agree with you, there isn't likely to be anyone else, but... I can't believe it's Derek... he dotes on the lad, especially after Alison's death. No, it *can't* be Derek— he's just too fond of him. And he's too gentle a character to beat up his son.'

'Rubbish. You never can tell by appearances. Didn't you learn anything from teacher training? "Abuse can happen in any family, rich or poor, professional or manual. Even in the church." It's got to be Derek. Who else is there?' She leaned forward, the logic pouring out, now unstoppable. 'Look, he's under stress, isn't he—a job he can only just do...'

'I never said that...'

'I know you didn't, he did. A job he can only just do, one that loses him sleep and has him out at all hours... You know. You've seen him. He never stops, does he? *And* they've just had a new addition to the family... disturbed nights, upset balance of power within the family: wife not paying as much attention to him because of the new baby....

'I must admit they don't seem to be talking to each other as much as they did in the past...'

'See?... I told you so. It's Derek. It's got to be.'

There was silence as the awful prospect unfolded itself before Alan's eyes. *How do we deal with this*? he thought to himself. We can't exactly go up to Derek and say 'Hi, Derek old fellow, been beating your son recently, then...?'

'Well, what are you going to do?'

'Why me?'

'You ought to be the one to tackle this.'

'But I'm not even sure...'

'Oh, don't be so wet. Who else is there?'

'I don't believe it was Derek,' replied Alan, sounding unconvincing in his denial.

'Oh come off it,' said Susan scornfully. 'Well, if *you're* not man enough to do anything about it, then *I* will,' and she flung down the book she'd been holding and stormed out of the room.

Alan watched her ample, retreating figure and shook his head. At the door she turned. 'Are you coming with me or aren't you?'

Out of duty, he came.

*   *   *

They went next door, firstly to speak to Anne. She was in the middle of making cheese, the curds hanging in tight white muslin balls suspended from a string which traversed the width of the coolest room in the house, the almost-underground store-room opposite the kitchen. Even in the summer it was cool, though the bees buzzed outside the window, inspecting the flowers in the beds above them. Instinctively Alan put out his hand, palm up, to feel the cheese, firm in the cloth. Just in time Anne slapped his hand away.

'*Don't!*' she said brusquely. 'You'll ruin it. Don't you know any-thing? You mustn't squeeze it. If you want to find out whether the fluid's all drained off you must touch it gently, with the back of your hand. Like this.'

As she leaned forward to demonstrate, Julian, whom she was holding in her left arm, stirred and began to moan. Anne looked down and made soft soothing noises to him. Julian stirred again and fell asleep on her shoulder. Gently she extricated him and laid him in the pram at the back of the room.

'Now, what can I do for you?'

*   *   *

Anne didn't believe them. Alan knew she wouldn't, though the manner of her disbelief didn't seem quite right. There was a certain edginess, an off-hand, matter-of-fact denial on behalf of Derek that didn't seem to fit with the caring, loving couple Alan remembered from their first encounters. She denied that Derek—or herself, for that matter—had any knowledge of the situation, or indeed anything to do with it, but her voice was flat, uninterested. Too calm, thought Susan. She knows something. She's not letting on.

'Can we see Derek? Is he in?'

'No,' came back the flat reply. 'He's never in. He's gone off to see someone—in Maulden, I think he said.' The irritation showed in her voice at last. Anne wiped her hands on a cloth, then pushed the pram out of the room into the hall. 'I can't help you beyond that. You'll just have to wait until he returns. If you want to, that is.'

*   *   *

Derek didn't know what hit him that evening. It was long after dark when he got back, hoping that the rest of the house would be asleep, and finding to his annoyance that although Alan and Susan had gone back home to bed an hour or more earlier, Anne was wait-ing for him with a face like thunder.

The denials came in thick and fast, and the more Derek denied anything, the more Anne was sure he'd done it. He was stressed; he was tired; and, yes, they'd had a few of the usual teenage troubles

with David, which Derek had said he'd sort out—but not like that,
Anne said, not like that. And the more he protested, the more she
disbelieved him.

The next morning Alan and Susan came round, early, just to
make sure they caught Derek before he started work. They nearly
didn't make it: Derek had spent a sleepless night, tossing and turning, and had decided shortly after first light that he might as well get
up and get about the day's activities: he could travel to his most out-
lying patient and get to her by six o'clock, when he knew she'd be
up—the day started early for everyone now.

Alan and Susan got there first, doorstepping Derek just as he was
about to leave. The guilty party leaving early to evade the questions? thought Susan, giving her husband a knowing look.

From Derek's point of view the nightmare of the previous
evening was just about to start up again. The more he denied any
involvement the more they disbelieved him, and the more they disbelieved him the more they asked questions. After a time even
Derek began to doubt if he believed his own story, which he still
stuck to, nevertheless. By that time Alan and Susan were beginning
to wonder if they could handle it on their own, or if they'd have to
bring in other members of the council—Martin, perhaps—because
Derek was proving a difficult nut to crack.

It was a good job they didn't tell Derek of their intentions,
because he would probably have finally lost his temper with them
and become violent, and then his goose would have been well and
truly cooked. Although he kept his anger buttoned down it was a
near thing: the effrontery of it all! He became more and more
enraged with the accusations. Susan had learned the trick of dropping her voice in order to make it more insistent, but Derek hadn't
learned that and raised his, so that while his accusers' voices got
softer, his got louder, making his guilt seem the more obvious.

Eventually he lost his temper, demonstrating to all and sundry
that here was a man out of control.

'Why don't you ask David?' he thundered, finally. 'Go on, ask
him. You obviously don't believe a word I'm saying. Ask him.'

Alan and Susan looked at Anne, who shrugged. At that moment

Julian began to wake up in his bedroom upstairs and cry for food. Anne rose to go to him. At the door she turned. 'I'll get David. Stay here.'

Two minutes later a tousled and sleepy David stumbled into the living room.

'About these bruises...' began Susan, calmly, with all the cold efficiency of the SS or the Gestapo.

'Oh, not again....' breathed David, embarrassed, looking from one to the other of them. Finally his gaze rested on the nearly-apoplectic Derek. His mouth dropped and his head swivelled back to Susan, then back to his father again. 'You don't think... Dad?...' He gave off a long sigh and sat down with a bump on the sofa, blinked, thought for a moment and then began to speak again. 'Oh, I suppose I'd better tell you...'

'Tell us what, David?' asked Anne, suddenly, with a quick and dagger-like glance at Susan.

'I got them picking strawberries...'

'*David!*' Anne interjected crossly. 'That's ridiculous. Stop wasting our time with this nonsense.'

'I did, Mum, honest.... With Kevin. Only they were the Major's strawberries, and he saw us. The first time...'

'You mean you've stolen the Major's strawberries more than once...'

David looked sheepishly at the floor.

'The first time he spotted us we managed to get away, but I fell getting over the wall at the back of Avenue House, where he grows them... which is why I got the bruises.' He pointed to the older bruises, now yellow-green and fading.

'We went back four days later. That time he caught us. He'd rigged up some form of a man trap and the first thing we knew about it was that a net dropped on top of us as we went up the path in the woods leading to the strawberry field.

'Then the Major came up and started hitting us with his belt... We couldn't get out of the net... or at least, not at first, but then Kevin got out and started threatening the Major while I cut myself free. And then we both ran away...'

It was Alan and Susan's turn to look sheepish, while Anne continued to wear her uninterested look.

It was Alan who broke the silence, clearing his throat in an embarrassed fashion. 'I... er... I'm sorry Derek. We did have to ask, you know.' He turned to David. 'And if you'd told us earlier what had happened to you, then none of this would have been necessary.'

'You never asked me,' came back the surly reply. He was beginning to sound just like Kevin, thought Derek, annoyed.

'Perhaps we should go and interview the Major?' suggested Susan.

'Don't you think you've done enough damage for today?' retorted Derek, suddenly very angry indeed. 'How do you think he feels, spending ages tending his strawberries only to find that two people think they can help themselves?'

'Well, he could have told you about it, got you to do something.'

'Like give David a good hiding, you mean? Then you *would* have had something to complain about. Now, if you don't mind, I've got work to do.'

Susan was silent. Alan beckoned to his wife to leave. Outside the door she turned on him. 'Why did you let it get that far?' she hissed. 'You didn't think he'd done it, did you? Then why didn't you stop me?'

Alan just shut his eyes and said nothing. Derek would understand, he thought... he hoped... Derek would know that it hadn't come from him.

Inside the room the silence lasted a little longer, broken only by tiny sucking noises from Julian as Anne put him to her breast. Finally Derek looked up at David and shook his head. 'You don't learn, do you? Not only do you go scrumping, you get caught *twice*... You deserve everything you got from the Major.' He shook his head in disbelief, then picked up his bag and without a word walked out of the house and off on his rounds.

It was going to take a long time before the dust settled on *that* interlude, thought Alan, as he watched Derek's retreating back going over the brow of the hill towards the surgery. And all over a few bruises.

How suspicions can be aroused over the smallest of things! Little things are sometimes significant—and sometimes not. Derek, tight-mouthed, trudged towards the surgery, slowly shaking his head in disbelief and anger. Yes, he was under stress, he knew that—though no one other than Martin and Anne knew why, or to what degree. Yet the only response of those who'd suspected he might be under more stress than he could bear had been to increase his stress, not lessen it. If Alan and Susan had suspected that Derek was suffi-ciently out of control as to batter his own son, then they'd had a curious way of dealing with the situation: neither Susan nor Alan had once thought to ask Derek if there was anything either of them could do to help *him*.

*   *   *

In fact Susan and Alan's visit *had* had a beneficial effect, though they could never have known it at the time, and certainly not in a way they could have suspected. Although David was bemused and not a little embarrassed by the episode, and Derek was enraged and further stressed by it, its effect on Anne was to bring her up with a shock, opening her eyes to the damage that was happening to her family as a knock-on effect of her affair with Martin. Just as Alan and Susan had misread Derek's stresses, so everyone—Martin included—had misunderstood Anne's response to the events of that fateful winter night the year before.

For the truth was that Anne wasn't angry with Derek, or Julian; she wasn't angry with David or Sarah; and most specifically—and surprisingly—she wasn't angry with Martin: she was mainly angry with *herself*—with a bitter hatred so comprehensive that it spilled out into almost everything she did, touched or thought. At least Martin had explored his reactions to the affair and had hought through them to some extent: but Anne couldn't get even this far. Her burning self-disgust was so immense, so vicious, so potentially destructive that it had to be contained, suppressed, chained down into her subconscious, because there was no knowing how she would respond if once it welled up into her conscious—suicide, possibly. She hadn't forgotten the affair of course—she couldn't possibly repress those memories: but the self-hatred afterwards—that she could repress, and did, denying to herself that it existed. It was too dangerous to do otherwise. Wisely, her subconscious buried it for her, camouflaging it, for the most part holding it down when it threatened to surface in its self-destructive hostility. The only thing her subconscious couldn't disguise was that there was *something there*—a great, big, black something whose existence couldn't be denied, even if its true identity could be concealed. And that great black something was creating psychological shock waves of enormous height which reverberated round her brain, producing in her a tide of anger and aggression that was matched only by her conscious inability to connect it with its true source.

The intensity of that anger and aggression was overwhelming, uncontainable. It had to come out somewhere—and so it did, spilling out onto whoever got in the way, whoever irritated her: the children, Derek, Martin—anyone and everything.

But even that wasn't the end of it. At a conscious level she'd been taught (inappropriately) that a Christian was never supposed to show anger, so even this expression of her overflow of emotion was denied her.

And the only way she could cope with *that* was to bottle up *all* her emotions: so she became an icicle—tart, unemotive, dismissive, uninvolved. It wasn't that she didn't want to be involved—oh, how she longed to be back in her husband's arms again, and once again have Martin for the good (if fallible) friend that she knew he was! But her self-loathing stopped her, and so she stayed an icicle, hurting others, but hurting herself more.

Surprisingly, the one person she wasn't angry with was Martin. Oh yes, he shouldn't have gone as far as he did. *But she should have stopped him*, because at the time she was the stronger of the two. She had the support of her partner: Martin was lonely, and didn't have such support. It was her fault, hers more than Martin's, she reasoned: and so her current rejection of Martin was only cutting off her nose to spite her face. Deep down she was desperately fond of him (in a non-sexual way) and hated herself all the more for having led him—the innocent—into their physical affair.

It would have been better—*far* better—if she had had someone on whom to unload all this detritus, someone to whom she could confess, who could bind up the emotional wounds, lance the emotional boils and let the black pus out: someone who could tell her that there are occasions when it's right as a Christian to be angry—to be angry with sin, to be angry with those who deliberately cause harm to others, but that righteous anger should never turn to rage, should never become vindictive—rage against others, or self-destructive—rage against oneself. But in the absence of a priest, other than Martin, there was no one she could turn to—and she certainly couldn't turn to him!

A psychiatrist or counsellor could have helped her approach the blackness of her self-loathing: not that a psychiatrist could provide forgiveness, but at least he could help her understand the true nature of the dark and loathsome self-hatred currently embedded in her subconscious, and could 'go with her to look at it', without risking her committing suicide first because the stress of seeing it for what it was might be too great. Once she had dared approach her self-hatred, she would then know what it really was, and where it came from, and why her response to it had had such an effect on the rest of her emotions.

But she had no counsellor, no psychiatrist, and no priest—and as long as she was unable to confront her self-hatred she couldn't begin to do anything about it.

She'd already prayed for forgiveness: and in truth, what Anne had left wasn't true guilt, but guilt *feelings*—quite a different matter. Like Martin, Anne had to learn to forgive herself. Inside her she *longed* to let go: more than anything else she wanted to be back in her husband's arms, as his lover and his lifelong friend—but the enormity of her self-hatred meant that somehow she could never bring herself to do it, feeling that, purely to punish herself for her failings, she should at all times deny herself the love that undoubtedly she wanted and needed.

And so the great, unstated, nightmarish, black entity in her subconscious overrode any attempt to give herself any respite, for whatever reason, in the realm of her family life, and her family and her friends became victims of it in the process.

So Anne became the icicle—on the surface, at least: the warmth inside was perpetually smothered by an internal winter whose coldness and fury reached Siberian proportions. It wasn't that she didn't love—it was that something inside her prevented her from expressing her feelings, a barrier that was as final, as unyielding, as impersonal and as implacable as the Cold-War Berlin Wall.

*   *   *

It has been a fair summer. The weather hasn't been too bad: early on it was wet, but from June onwards it's been sunny and dry and although the hay was late coming in, the wheat was on time.

As Neil told us, the ground has taken time to recover from its previous dependence on fertilisers and weedkillers. The crop last year was down, as predicted—but not as badly as the worst Neil had suggested. I suspect he was overstating his case just to make us all sit up and take notice! Or maybe it's his natural farmer's pessimism coming out. This year the yields have been marginally better, so presumably the land is starting to return to its natural fertility. The measures we've taken to limit the spread of crop diseases have been remarkably successful—always rotating the crops and letting the hedgerows grow. But it's still strange to see fields of vegetables laid out in small strips rather than in whole fields—it's the only way we can get to weed them without treading down the ground too much.

Over the summer Peter, Alan, Trevor and Mary took two of the narrow-boats down the Grand Union Canal into London to see if they could obtain more supplies, especially candles, condoms, soap, matches, light bulbs and detergents, none of which we can make— or else, not in sufficient quantities. Isn't it surprising what we've run short of! Before the plague if I'd been asked what we'd run out of first, I'd never have said any of these!... On second thoughts, perhaps I'd have mentioned matches. They also picked up as wide a variety of CDs and videos as they could sensibly find—instructional ones as well as entertainment—together with some special business computer programs, and CD-ROMs as well, for all the information they contain.

Peter said that London looked much the same—after all, what could have changed it?—though the shops were now much dustier and dirtier, and weeds were growing all over the streets. Imagine it!—weeds on Oxford Street!

We've had to stop the school over the summer, so that everyone could help with the harvest, children included. As usual, it's been a busy time...

Susan paused, thinking, and a little trickle of sweat rolled down the side of her face. In Bedfordshire, August could be a very hot month indeed! She had the windows open, but the stink of the horse manure on the unswept streets made the place smell like a farmyard.

We haven't had any further problems with the Buckingham crowd. They haven't dared come here for many months now. We're all upset about their hostages, but no one has any decent plans for their rescue. We may just have to let them get on with it, awful though that sounds...

She couldn't bear it any longer: she'd just *have* to shut the window and brave the heat and humidity inside the house.

*   *   *

As the summer went on, and the nights drew in again to yet another winter, Martin was feeling wretched. For him the Old Rectory was no longer a place for welcoming silence and solitary contemplation but a prison, a place of isolation, in solitary *confinement*. He missed the contacts with Derek: he'd always enjoyed Derek's company, and in times past had enjoyed many a long philosophical chat with him deep into the night. He also missed Anne dreadfully—not for any sexual reason, but, quite simply, because he enjoyed her presence and her company, her companionship, her understanding and the sharing of their common interests. Had it not been for his one physical dalliance with her he would have been quite content to know her as a close friend, without in any way feeling that he was trespassing on her and Derek's marriage. He missed the rapport with Anne; without her, life had an emptiness that nothing seemed to fill. He missed her touch as well—again, not in a sexual way but for the friendly, comforting person-to-person 'I care' manner in which she would occasionally put her hand on his arm or shoulder. We English are so bad at touching, he said to himself, and yet it means so much. Why can't we be more like the continentals or the South Americans, and be more tactile people? And involuntarily his mind went off to pictures he'd seen of baby elephants and their mothers, where the trunks of the mothers were always around the baby, touching, guiding, saying 'I'm here, I'm here' and he longed—how he *longed*—for a more physical communication between himself and the outside world. It was one thing for people to say 'thank you' to him—which they did very frequently and quite genuinely, often after he'd been his usual wise and helpful self. He just wished one or two of them would do as Anne had so often done and put a hand on his arm when saying it.

And they did, quite genuinely, mean 'Well done'. In the eyes of the community Martin was the one to whom everyone went when they had a knotty problem and needed wise and sensible counsel, and Martin would always rise to the occasion like a swan—gliding apparently effortlessly across the surface of the river: but no one could see the legs paddling furiously underneath.

Martin himself felt anything but wise, anything but helpful, purely a sham. Daily he waited for the hammer-blow, when the secret got out, when the community knew at long last that their minister was nothing but a hypocrite, a fraud, not worthy of the name of Christian, not worthy of anything.

For once it hadn't been helped by the music. Among the trophies from London, Alan had brought him a CD of Mendelssohn's *Elijah*, a work he knew about, but for some reason had never actually heard. One evening he put it on and was instantly enthralled, enraptured and terrified—enthralled by the music, the vividness of its portrayal of events in the life of the prophet, but appalled by the opening and its implications.

Without any introduction or overture, the oratorio plunges

straight in with the words of Elijah. 'As God the Lord of Israel liveth, before whom I stand, there shall be neither dew nor rain...' Over the next two weeks the music and the words haunted Martin— the grandeur, the vast historical stage on which it was enacted, the power of God that was portrayed and the awfulness, the *awfulness*, of those first few words.

'*Before whom I stand*...' For Elijah it had been a privilege to stand in the presence of God. For Martin it was nothing less than torture, as though all the spotlights in the world had focused on him and he was there in front of God, hanging his head in shame.

'*Before whom I stand*...' It dogged him day and night, running through his mind, shouting at him, screaming at him. Surely it wouldn't be long now before somehow the cat was let out of the bag and people found out just what he'd done and how awful he had been, when, like David and Bathsheba, his affair was made public—to his own vilification and, what was much worse, by implication, the vilification of God. He could just hear the whispers—*what can God be like if this is how his servants behave*? He couldn't think of anything else that could more effectively undermine the work he was trying to do in the community.

And his agony was made the more intense because he had to face it alone. There was no one he could tell. He had no counsellor at all. He could, he supposed, talk to Derek—but under the circumstances that seemed less than helpful. And he hadn't got Anne to share it with because Anne, the icicle, would no longer speak to him, look at him, go up to the Old Rectory to meet him or have any communication or contact with him at all—and he missed her. He missed her wise counsel over his own needs, her emotional warmth that could have said to him, 'Don't you think you're taking this the wrong way? Can't you let go of the past?' And he missed her charm, her warmth, her kindness, her sensitivity: and the more he missed her the more lonely he became, the more isolated, and the more morose.

The more she stayed away, the more lonely he got, and the more lonely he got the more morose he became, and it didn't occur to him—not even once—that possibly his spiritual life was tied to his emotional state of mind more than ever he might have suspected. Had he had a wife, or at the very least a close confidant, who could have supported him and given him emotional stability, he might perhaps have realised that there were alternative approaches to his problem.

But he had no one—and so he had to go the long way round. If only he could have seen the answers... All the clues were there, all the instructions, all the information he needed but he just couldn't fit it together.

He'd got to the stage where he couldn't pray about it, could hardly read his Bible, could seldom do anything on his own with any confidence: in company, with other people he was his usual wise self, and the others (just to add insult to injury) kept on saying he was *wonderful*. Little did they know, he thought to himself bitterly: but doubtless they would soon find out.

- 21 -

*I*t was October when the inevitable happened. Jason Harbury, Shaun McCluskey and Vince Andrews suddenly turned up in the Market Square demanding to see the leader of the council. Jason in particular seemed to have lost his hunted look as the three of them came confidently—arrogantly, even—to see Henry, who in the June elections had formally taken over leadership of the council from Chris, much to the Major's disgust.

They were shown into the hall at Dynevor House.

'Good day, gentlemen,' boomed Henry confidently. 'Come into the library, will you.'

Jason and Vince walked across the hall, looking in that same arrogant fashion at the beautiful decor and the elegance of the rooms. 'Sit yourselves down,' said Henry. 'Now, what can I do for you?'

'We need more flour,' began Shaun.

'Do you now?' said Henry, staring at him. 'So why are you asking me?'

'Because you're in charge here,' said Vince.

'I seem to remember the last time we sent you food, you repaid us by stealing the wheat that was being paid us for our earlier help.'

Vince looked down at his feet. 'We didn't have a choice about that.' The other two looked at him angrily, as though he were letting the side down.

'No, we need more,' said Jason. 'What you left us with wasn't enough. That's why we took the rest back. The way we see it, you were stealing it from us.'

Henry gave him a hard stare. 'Do you know,' he said affably, 'I don't believe a word of it.'

'It's true,' blustered Shaun. 'We don't have enough grain. Our last harvest wasn't good enough.'

'If that's the case then your stocks have run out remarkably quickly,' replied Henry. 'We left you with quite enough for the numbers you told us were living at Buckingham. You should have enough for another six months, even if this year's harvest wasn't good. So we won't want to give you any more—quite apart from the fact that you stole what was due to us anyway. We're not going to be interested. I'm surprised you bothered to come. You'll just have to go and tell your friends in Buckingham that they'll have to make do with what they've got. You were stupid enough to kick us out— so we won't be involving ourselves with you any further, as obviously you don't want us to interfere. Now if you'd like to go, the door's over there. I've got things to do.'

Vince started to get up but Jason and Shaun stayed where they were, staring at Vince, trying to force him not to break ranks.

'It's not quite as easy as that,' said Shaun.

'Oh?' said Henry. 'You do surprise me.'

'We're not here to *ask* you for corn, we're here to *demand* it.'

'Really?' said Henry sarcastically. 'And what, may I ask, entitles *you* to demand anything from *us*? We've bent over backwards to help you, and all you've done is kick us in the teeth—quite literally, if I might remind you.'

Vince looked down at his feet again.

'You have quite enough to eat,' said Shaun, 'and we don't. It's only fair that you share what you have with us. And we're here to tell you that if you don't give us more then we'll come and take it.'

Henry remained silent, staring at Shaun poker-faced, leaving Shaun with not the slightest doubt that Henry didn't believe a word of it, wasn't going to be conned, blackmailed or threatened by anything and that Shaun was on a totally losing wicket as far as any negotiations of this nature were concerned.

Eventually Henry spoke. 'I gather that's your final offer.'

'Yes.'

'I shall of course take it to the council, but I can tell you now what their response is going to be and I suggest that the three of you get on your bikes and disappear off west as fast as your little legs will carry you, because otherwise you may find that one or two people in the town, on hearing of your presence here, might see things just a little differently and beat your brains in. Now, get out.'

The three looked at each other. They hadn't expected this. The conversation was definitely not going the way they had planned.

'And that's your final word?' said Shaun, despairingly.

'Yes. Now get out—unless you want us to keep you here as hostages like your people are being held hostage.'

The three of them jerked—convulsed, rather—as one person.

'How... how... how did you know?' said Vince eventually in quite a different tone of voice. Henry raised one eyebrow quizzically and waited for a few seconds. Vince swallowed hard and tried again. 'How did you know they'd got hostages?'

Henry ignored the question, his face totally expressionless.

'How many are there?'

'How many what?'

'Hostages.'

'One from each family... at least. Mainly women and children.'

'Where are they?'

'We don't know.'

'Oh come on, you can do better than that,' snapped Henry. Vince looked up at him, almost recoiling with the force of his words, throwing up his arms in reflex to protect his head. There was no more pathetic demonstration of their fear and vulnerability.

'I don't know,' he repeated. 'None of us knows. If we knew we could do something about it. Perhaps.'

'Well, you'd better tell me what you *do* know,' said Henry, a little more gently. 'You can sit down—I'm not going to hit you.'

'Sorry,' said Vince. 'Habit.'

'Tell me,' said Henry. 'And tell me *all* about it this time. Nothing missed out please. Not like last time.' He gazed slowly at each of them in turn, outstaring them until each averted his eyes and looked down at the floor.

'We're sorry about that,' mumbled Shaun. He cleared his throat and looked up at Henry. 'Honestly. We're sorry. We had to do what we were told otherwise they...'

'So I gathered.'

'We were fine until Christmas that first year... well, sort of. We'd all survived the plague in one way or another and we'd all clustered together in Buckingham. But we didn't have anybody to show us how to farm so we just lived off what food there was and killed what animals we could find. We thought that maybe when the food ran out we'd just move somewhere else—maybe west, towards the Cotswolds. And then just after Christmas four people turned up on motorbikes...'

'Lew Pritchard and his cronies,' interjected Henry.

'Yes—how did you know?'

'We'd tangled with them before.'

'Oh... well, they came along in early January. The first thing they did was round up about thirty of the women and children. Made no bones about it. Said that if we didn't work for them and give them food then they'd take it out on the hostages.'

'And did they?' said Henry. Vince shuddered.

'When they threaten to send you the finger of one of your children, baked in a pie, you soon learn to do what they say.' He shuddered again.

'As vicious as that?' Henry leaned forward, appalled.

'There was no one to stop them...' Vince's voice trailed away.

'Go on.'

'That's about it, really. Lew and his friends commandeered whatever food we had, so even if we starved they had plenty.'

'And of course,' continued Henry 'you all knew that if you didn't give Lew any food there wouldn't be any for the hostages.'

'That's right,' said Shaun.

'So while you all starved, Lew and his friends got fat and kept control, because you knew that if you didn't keep giving them the food they demanded then your relatives would die of starvation; and you couldn't move out because that would mean leaving the hostages... Didn't anyone try to rescue them?'

'You can't do much when the other side have shot-guns.'

'Couldn't you get shot-guns yourselves?'

'And how do you get hostages out safely without risking their lives? We're not the SAS you know. None of us has any experience of using guns. Nobody's been in the army... I mean, for goodness sake, we're just ordinary people. We wouldn't know how to go about a military exercise like that.'

'So where do they keep the hostages?' asked Henry returning to his original theme.

'At first they were in the gaol—you must have seen it, the town gaol, in the middle of the square.'

'The obvious place to put them.'

'Well, it was at first,' said Shaun, 'but it's not as secure as you might think—not now it's been turned into a museum.'

'It looks strong enough from the outside.'

'It is and it isn't,' said Vince. 'The original walls are very thick—solid stone—but one side has been turned into a shop. There's a way straight through into the exercise yard and from there into the cell area. The cells don't have locks with keys, only bolts worked from the outside, so it's easy to get in and open up the cells. We managed to get half the hostages away one night before Lew woke up and found out what was happening. The next day I got one of my wife's fingers delivered to me in a package. It still had the wedding ring on...' He shuddered again, pain written across his young face. 'They took the hostages back again. We think they keep them in one of the houses on the far side of the river, but we're not sure which because they seem to move them around from time to time. Whenever someone finds out which house they're in they always move them a few days later. They won't let us go anywhere near the area—except for the monthly visits. They let us meet our relatives for a short time...'

'...just to remind you how vulnerable they are, and how much they'll suffer if you don't do what you're told...'

'Precisely.'

'How many are there in the gang?'

'Four.'

'And how many of your people have gone over to their side?'

'What do you mean?'

'How many of your people are in their pay so that you can't trust them?'

'None of them,' said Jason. 'No one wants Lew and his lot around. But nobody can do anything because we've all got relatives among the hostages. Any sign of trouble and...'

'Right,' said Henry, standing up. 'You've told me all I need to know.'

'So what are you going to do about the corn?' asked Vince, anxiously thinking of his son's fingers.

'Look, I can't do anything myself,' said Henry. 'I've got to ask the council. They won't be able to meet for twenty-four hours and we'll give you an answer after that. You just have to go back and tell Lew and his colleagues that we'll think about it.'

'They'll come and take it by force if you don't give it them,' said Shaun.

'That's what they told you to tell us, isn't it?'

'Yes.'

'Well, now you've told me; and we'll think about it; and we'll give you our official reply...'—mentally he ticked off the days—'...let's say in four days' time, just to be on the safe side.'

'Aren't you going to help us?' asked Vince.

'How can I?' said Henry shrugging. 'You lot are miles away, and as you said we're not exactly the SAS. Mind you, I wouldn't tell Lew that you've said any of this. He might not take it too kindly.'

Vince winced.

'Just tell him that you've delivered the message, that I can't possibly make any decision without the council, and he'll just have to wait for another four days. Now, you'd better be on your way.' He ushered—almost shoved—them down the steps outside the house and shut the door behind them. He paused for a second, his hand on the inside latch and then let out a sigh. 'Clever Kevin,' he said. 'Clever little jumped up so-and-so. I must go and talk with him.'

*   *   *

At the rate that the council were using him for advice, Kevin reckoned he'd be a millionaire by Christmas. They had, of course, needed to meet again, and everyone—quite genuinely—was full of congratulations for him over the way he'd assessed the situation and predicted what was likely to have happened over in Buckingham.

The council now had to decide what to do about it. Henry reported the happenings of the previous day, then opened the debate up to everyone.

For once it was Martin who started the ball rolling. 'It seems to me that we have a simple choice: to accede to their demands—in which case we'll be under their thumb for the rest of our lives—or to fight back.'

Mary stared at him in dismay. 'You're not actually advocating violence, are you?' she said bitterly. 'I thought you were a pacifist.'

'I'm not advocating anything at the moment,' replied Martin. 'I'm just exploring the options. If we give in now and give them what they want, they'll just come back for more in three months' time... and three months after that, and three months after that. They'll want more, and more, and more. And perhaps for good measure they'll come across and take a few of our people hostage as well, just to make sure that we keep on behaving, too. Or, on the other hand, if we say we won't play their game, either they'll take it out on their own hostages, or else they come here with guns and take what they want.'

It is amazing how a succinct assessment of a situation cuts through unnecessary discussion. Martin had encapsulated the problem in about the fewest words possible and had left nothing further to be said.

'I'm still surprised you're advocating violence,' repeated Mary.

'I'm not,' said Martin. 'I just said we had a choice, that's all. It's a pretty unpleasant one, I grant you, but it's still a choice. We can knuckle under or we can fight. There are no other alternatives.

'That's one issue. The second is, that I think we have a duty to try to get the hostages out. We can't leave them to rot, can we?'

'I thought we'd said that was impossible, the last time we talked about it,' interjected Henry.

'No, Henry: with respect, at that time we didn't know for certain what was going on. Kevin had made some assumptions which seemed plausible, but it's only now that they've been proved right.'

'But everything else that we said is still true, isn't it?' retorted Henry. 'We don't have any military training: we haven't got any experience in this sort of thing. You need well-trained people to get hostages out safely, especially where the other side have guns.'

'Don't *we* have guns?' asked the Major.

'Actually,' said Martin, 'no. I'm sorry to have to tell you this but we used the last of the shot-gun cartridges yesterday.'

'Can't we find some more?'

'We've already searched for more cartridges over quite a wide area. We use them a lot you know—for shooting rabbits and pigeons and keeping vermin away from the crops—and I'm not sure how long it will take us to find some more supplies. Anyway, could anybody here really point a shot-gun at a fellow human being and pull the trigger? All right, so it happens in films, but when it came to the crunch would any of us really do it?'

There was an embarrassed silence as each of them acknowledged to him- or herself that they would find it very difficult. Only the Major had had any experience of shooting at other people, but as he was seventy, with permanently shaking hands as a result of the gradual onset of Parkinson's disease, no one in their right mind was going to entrust the Major with a shot-gun, especially if there was a need for accurate shooting to hit the gaoler rather than the hostage.

'What about the crossbows?' said Kevin.

'What crossbows?' asked Susan.

'The ones me, Trevor and David made. They're dead accurate and lethal with it.'

'Um,' said Paul, sucking on his pencil. 'Now there's a thought.'

'So what are we going to do?' asked Henry.

'We're going to get the hostages out,' said Martin. 'Eventually.'

'Are you sure?'

'We haven't got a choice, have we? We can't sit by and let them suffer.'

'Even if it means hurting or killing Lew Pritchard and his cronies?'

'Let's hope it doesn't come to that, Henry. Let's see if we can find a way of getting them out without fuss and with the minimum of violence. But what we can't do is let them stay where they are.'

Again, a silence.

'Are we all agreed?' said Henry. 'Any objectors?'

Mary raised her hand.

'Is there anything else that you'd rather we did?' asked Henry, gently.

'Not that I can think of,' she began, 'but I don't like the use of violence.'

'If you haven't got any alternative ideas, then do you have any option? That is, other than to give in now and recognise that the hostages will stay where they are for the rest of their lives.'

Faced with the bare logic of it all, Mary gave in. 'I feel I'm being a traitor to myself,' she said.

'You don't need to,' said Alan, kindly. 'We do appreciate your sensitivity on this Mary, but there's likely to be more suffering if we do nothing.' Mary was tight-lipped, white, lost for words, her hands clenched in her lap. She hated herself for agreeing with him, but really she couldn't think of anything else to do.

'We need a war council,' said Paul. 'Who's got experience of this sort of thing?'

Only the Major put up his hand, shakily.

'Well,' said Paul, 'can I suggest the Major, Kevin, Henry, Peter and myself? And we'll call in anybody else as needed.' He held up his hand and ticked the people off on his fingers one by one. 'The Major—because he's had experience of military matters, even if physically he can't take part; Kevin—because he's a good tactician; Henry—because he's a good leader; Peter—because of his police experience: me—to help plan it.

'Before we do anything more we need intelligence. We need to know where those hostages are. We need to know whether the three emissaries that Henry saw yesterday were telling the truth, and that everybody except the bikers is ultimately going to be on our side...'

'Can I interrupt?' said Henry. 'I deliberately didn't tell them about what we might do, or even that we might even be thinking about supporting them. In fact I gave them the impression that we were going to do nothing.'

'That wasn't very kind,' said Susan.

'Oh, I think it was,' said Henry. 'The last thing we want is for any whisper of our interest or involvement to get back to Lew's gang. We don't want to alarm them or warn them. We want to lull them into a sense of false security. If they think we're not going to be interested in their problems, then so much the better. They can spend their time instead worrying about whether we'll deliver enough food to them to satisfy their needs.'

'Quite right,' said Paul. 'We also need to buy time, so I suggest that we tell them we agree to give them some more food, but that it'll be a one-off contribution to help them until they get their harvest in.'

'Do you think that'll stop them?' asked Susan.

'No,' said Paul, 'but it'll put them off for a bit and give us a bit of time. The last thing we want is them breathing down out necks.'

It was only after the council meeting had ended that Chris realised that Derek hadn't said anything: he didn't look as though he had the energy. He was beginning to look gaunt again and was little more than a shadow of his former self. As usual he'd been overworking but that didn't really account for his waxen complexion. But Chris had other things on her mind, didn't remark on it, and instead hurried off to talk to Martin.

*   *   *

The war council met for the first time that evening. Chief among
the problems was the distance from Ampthill to Buckingham, the
lack of knowledge of the local situation, the lack of information
about the hostages and where they were being kept, and a complete
and total absence of ammunition. Other than that, things were fine.

Paul's first action was to co-opt Derek onto the war council. He
should have had him on from the start he reflected: was he losing
his touch since Emma's birth, he wondered? He valued Derek's
advice, and besides, he had a couple of specific questions to put to
him, chief among which was the psychology of how to deal with
hostage takers.

*   *   *

Three days later Vince returned—with a wagon, which was duly
loaded up as requested, not with grain, but with flour. After all, as
Lew had said to his cronies, why ask for wheat when we could save
ourselves trouble and let them do the grinding for us as well?

The wagon was piled high, and Vince was sent on his way a sor-
rowful man—because he'd hoped that the Ampthill community
wouldn't supply the flour, and then the Boss would have to decide
whether to risk attacking Ampthill or not: at the very least he hoped
that it would bring matters to a head, and then his wife and child
could be released. Somehow he couldn't see Lew taking on the
whole of Ampthill and winning, but then the four of them had taken
on the whole of the Buckingham group and weren't exactly losing
at the present... So he was downhearted that no resistance was being
offered, other than a grumbling acrimony of the type that Peter had
experienced when collecting together the tithes that a year earlier
should have gone from Buckingham to Ampthill.

Those who were loading the wagon were in fact playing a role.
They'd been let into the secret of what was going to happen ultimately but only in as much detail as they needed to know; they'd
been told to make a good job of looking sullen and angry so Vince
would be taken in and would report back appropriately. 'After all,'

Kevin had said during their briefing, 'we don't know whose side Vince, Jason and Shaun are on. For all we know they're in with Lew, but making out that they're poor downtrodden citizens.'

Vince had also come with a message—that in a month he'd be back wanting the same again. He also demanded petrol, diesel, horses and a tractor. Sullenly Paul agreed to look into it. Then he made secret plans.

*   *   *

Meanwhile the concerts continued. The social life of the community had been greatly enhanced by Anne's efforts in setting up regular concerts and artistic events of one sort or another, and she saw no reason to stop now—indeed, there was every reason to continue: if Derek could throw himself into the life of the community, expending on it all the mental and emotional energy that otherwise he would have put into his marriage, then so could she. Rapidly she became the life and soul of the artistic community, sublimating her energies into the concerts and presentations. Sometimes these were musical, sometimes literary: and there were not a few budding artists who enjoyed having exhibitions of their work from time to time.

It was generally agreed that the community had been greatly enriched by these events. It was all very well living to work to get food in order to eat: but there was a dimension of man beyond this that was not satisfied by mere physical things, or by food, a dimension that longed for conversations about Meaning and Truth and Existence. And art was a royal road into this dimension.

The community was about to embark on their most ambitious project to date, a rendition—for good or ill—of Gilbert and Sullivan's comic operetta *The Mikado*. Because they hadn't got enough instrumentalists to form a useful orchestra Martin was to be the accompanist, on the piano. Anne had been persuaded to join in herself, rather against her will, and had been cast as Pish-Tush: but even so, would only look at Martin when he was giving them musical directions, and otherwise would make a point of staring in any other direction but his. Henry, who had a fine bass voice, seemed

the obvious contender for the role of the Mikado himself, whilst
the diminutive, shy Peter excelled himself as the tremulous Ko-Ko.
Derek—pale, thin and exhausted—would like to have been involved but couldn't stand the thought of acting in the same production as Anne, and in any case couldn't guarantee that he wouldn't
be called away on the night.

The plum role of Poo-Bah went to the lean and angular Alan who
had to be padded out very considerably for the part. Some observed
dryly that it might have been better to cast his wife, as she already
had the appropriate build... but not, unfortunately, the baritone
voice.

The casting was done in October, once the last of the summer
work in the fields was over, and soon rehearsals started in earnest.
Anne threw herself into learning the role, and found a marked sense
of relief in being able at last to find a genuine reason not to be at
home.

*   *   *

At the same time as Anne was starting to rehearse her first song,
Derek was alone in Lime View: as usual when Anne was out Susan
was baby-sitting Julian next door, in case Derek too was called out.
Exhausted, Derek had struggled upstairs to his bedroom. He looked
at himself, yellow-tinged, in the mirror and then lay down on the
bed, gently but desperately feeling the upper right side of his
abdomen. And he could feel it—just underneath the line of the right
lower ribs where there should have been nothing, there was a
craggy rocky mass, like a cliff edge made of hard granite. Sweating
with both the effort and the fear he sat upright, struggling to focus
his mind and make himself think. Surely Nicholas wouldn't have
told him a lie deliberately? Maybe he wasn't such a good surgeon
after all and hadn't spotted the secondaries? No, thought Derek, that
wasn't true either. He'd seen far too much of Nicholas to believe
that he was anything less than a supremely competent surgeon. No,
the secondaries had grown since Nicholas had done the last operation, which meant either that they were in a very significant place,
blocking the exit of bile from the liver which would account for the

jaundice, or else—and he swallowed hard—they were growing very quickly indeed. He thought yet again—no, it couldn't be a tiny cancer blocking the bile duct. That might cause the jaundice but it wouldn't cause the massively enlarged liver that he knew he had now.

So it was secondaries—and pretty swiftly growing ones too. His mouth now dry, hands shaking, Derek approached the mirror again, pulled down his lower right eyelid and for the fourth time that day stared at the beginnings of the sickly yellowing of the whites of his eyes. It had only been—what, nine months?—since Nicholas had operated on him and in that time the secondaries had spread to engorge the whole of his liver. If it were that fast then how much longer had he got? He tried to swallow again but now his mouth was so dry he couldn't even do that. The trembling in his knees increased to such a point that he just had to collapse into the chair by the fireplace and in the silence of the evening, surrounded by the blackness of the night outside, with no one in the house to comfort him, he began to shake uncontrollably.

- 22 -

*T*he midweek Bible study group continued to meet despite the continuing absence of Anne, who was sorely missed not just by Martin but by the others in the group. They all enjoyed her vivacity and enthusiasm and Martin missed—oh, how he missed—her sensitivity. When they came to study Elijah he *longed* to put on the CD of the Mendelssohn oratorio, which so wonderfully portrayed what had happened during Elijah's life—but the music would have been lost on the Major or the Higginbottoms. If only Anne had been there, to listen, to understand, to share...

Once Martin had got over the utter calamity of the first few words—'As God the Lord of Israel liveth, *before whom I stand...*'— the next part of the oratorio always had him entranced, with its

blow-by-blow account of the battle between Elijah and the prophets
of Baal—how there was a contest on Mount Carmel between the
two groups: each set up an altar, prepared an offering and then
invoked their god to prove he was there by bringing down fire from
heaven to burn up the offering. The music wonderfully conveyed
the increasing pandemonium as the prophets of Baal danced around
the altar, whipping themselves into a frenzy, calling with increasing
desperation upon their god who couldn't see, couldn't hear, and definitely didn't answer.

And then, by contrast, Elijah prays to God in measured, almost
quiet tones, not commanding, nor invoking him like a magic spell,
but simply and quietly *asking* for a miracle—and God responds,
and sends down fire to burn up Elijah's sacrifice. Exit prophets of
Baal, stage left.

Martin got to know and love the piece so much that when he
came to read the biblical account out loud he couldn't do it without
hearing the music at the same time in the back of his mind, and feeling its emotion; and each time he slowly but surely recognised the
fact that when the prophets talked *to* God and *of* God they were
quiet, not noisy, peaceful, not agitated; and when the prophets asked
the people to turn from their sins and back to God again, they knew
God didn't want vast sacrifices or abject prostration, but a simple
apology, and a turning away from what was wrong to what was
good.

The study group had come to the time immediately after the
episode on Mount Carmel. 'I know this,' said the Major happily,
glad for once to find something familiar.

'Would you tell us what happened?' asked Martin. The Major
obliged, relating how, in an episode of exhaustion and depression
after the stress of the contest with the prophets of Baal, Elijah had
suddenly begun to feel afraid that God was no longer able to protect
him from the evil King Ahab and his queen, Jezebel, and had run
away in a panic. Silly man, thought Martin, wondering how it was
that a devoted prophet could see his prayers answered, fire come
down miraculously from heaven, and immediately afterwards still
feel that God somehow couldn't protect him.

Then he thought again, a little more charitably, remembering
how after a huge mental effort anyone can feel exhausted, drained,
and not a little depressed. It had happened at college when he and
his friends were doing their finals: they'd been promising themselves all sorts of enjoyable activities as soon as the exams were
over but the let-down afterwards was so great that none of them did
anything much. Elijah was only being human, after all, thought
Martin.

And then he noticed what happened next, hearing it with ears
that seemed to perceive it for the first time, so great an impact did
it make on him. Frightened, exhausted, fearful and not a little dis-
obedient, Elijah had run away to a cave on Mount Horeb: even so,
God said he would reveal himself to him. So Elijah stood at the
mouth of the cave, with his eyes covered because God was too awesome to look at.

The Major's voice continued, hesitantly. 'First God sent a
mighty wind that shattered the rocks; but God wasn't in the wind.

'Then there was an earthquake—but God wasn't in the earthquake.

'Then there was a fire—but God wasn't in the fire.

'And after the fire, came a still, small voice, which said, "Elijah?
What are you doing here?" '

It was the stillness and the smallness that made the impact on
Martin. Dimly in the back of his mind he could hear the Major and
the Higginbottoms chatting away happily, with the Higginbottoms
filling in the background, helping him to see the episode in context.

But Martin wasn't aware of what they were saying, for his mind
had gone back to that day, that dreadful day, in the vicarage when
the plague had erupted on London and what seemed like the whole
world had passed by him, dying in the process. Once again Martin
lived out the awfulness and dreadfulness of the situation, and the
sadness and the desolation that he felt, sure that God couldn't be
there if things like this were allowed to happen.

'...and God wasn't in the fire....'

He paused for a moment to take it all in. So the sadness, the
destruction, the plague, the killing off of civilisation—that hadn't

been God's doing, hadn't been what God wanted! But, *after* the fire... Martin grinned inwardly to himself, chuckled almost, remembering the number of times when things had just gently and quietly fallen into place, not with a proverbial sound of trumpets but just with a satisfying tiny 'click'. And just as Elijah had emerged from his cave to be told—very gently—that, actually, he was in the wrong place altogether, but never mind, God could cope with that, so Martin felt that he, too, was now being told something, something very quiet. That he too was in the wrong place.

Well, of course he was in the wrong place, he thought to himself, thinking of Anne and of Julian. Totally in the wrong place. And suddenly the guilt and anguish flooded over him again like a wind, shrieking at him that he had no right to call himself a minister of the Gospel, no right to be involved in the church, no right to be a leader in the community. He felt himself going redder and redder and hoped that the other three people in the room hadn't noticed.

After they'd finished and gone home Martin went to bed, too. For hours he lay, tossing and turning, staring at the ceiling, while what seemed like all the demons in hell flooded past in his mind.

*   *   *

That night, two hundred yards away, another person was lying awake unable to sleep and every few minutes his hand would reach out to feel something underneath the ribs on the right-hand side of the upper abdomen—the craggy hard line of a diseased and distended liver. He too stared up at the ceiling and wondered about the future, a future that now he knew would be measured only in days—not even in weeks, and certainly not in years.

*   *   *

'The first thing we need is information,' said the Major to the others in the war council. 'We can't even *begin* to work out how to deal with the hostages until we know where they are.'

'I'd thought of that,' said Paul.

'We'll have to mount a reconnaissance,' said Henry grandly, knowing that he wouldn't be the one going on it.

'What we need,' said the Major, 'is a quick in and out—get the information and scarper as fast as we can before anybody knows that we're there.'

'But we won't be able to drive into the centre of Buckingham and have a look round. It would be—how can one say—a little obvious?' replied Alan.

'Yes,' said Henry, 'but there's no reason why we shouldn't drive to about four miles from the centre and then walk in quietly, at night. No one will be expecting us.'

'I don't know about that,' said Kevin.

'Do you really think that they'll have guards out?' retorted Henry. 'There are only four of them: they've got to sleep some time *and* they've got to guard the hostages. The only way they could mount guards is if the guards were the actual Buckingham residents themselves, and they're not exactly going to be too eager to report intruders, are they?'

'Well, we hope not,' said Paul, 'but Kevin has got a point. If *your* wife were being held hostage, wouldn't you co-operate?'

'Why don't you take the Porsche?' said Alan. 'It's very fast, and even if they've got a car or two that we haven't heard about, you could use its speed to get away from them if you needed to.'

There was a slightly awkward pause while Paul considered it.

'No,' he said finally. 'I don't think that'll work.'

'Why not?' said the Major. 'I think it's a very good idea.'

'I... er... I haven't got it any longer,' said Paul. There was a brief, embarrassed silence.

'Oh,' said the Major. 'Oh yes. I'm sorry...' They were all thinking of Chris and her fine for her misbehaviour. And then something very strange happened, something that nobody would have predicted.

'Why don't I go?' said Kevin. 'On my motorbike. It's just as fast as the Porsche and it's easier to hide—under a hedge or somefink. It's not red, it's black, so it'll be harder to spot. Why don't I go there at night, hide the bike and myself, make sure I'm not discovered and then go spying the next night?'

Paul was amazed. It was, to his knowledge, the first time that

Kevin had volunteered for anything. 'Are you sure?' he said, looking at him. 'It'll be risky. What if you're found, or captured, or taken hostage?'

Kevin shrugged. 'What, me? Nah, I'm too clever for that. They won't catch me.'

Paul gave him a hard stare, then realised he was looking a gift horse in the mouth and gratefully and graciously accepted Kevin's offer.

*　　　　*　　　　*

By now it was obvious to everyone that Derek was very ill. Martin knew that he would have to go and see him sooner or later, if only to ease his own conscience. He couldn't let Derek die without saying to him what had been on his mind for so long.

It took him some time to summon up the courage, but after nerving himself for the fray he walked up Woburn Street and knocked on the door of Lime View. Anne greeted him, tight-lipped, refusing to look him in the eye.

'I've come... to visit...' Martin said hesitantly. 'Do you think he'll see me?'

'I'll ask.' She went upstairs and came down again a few moments later. 'He says yes. Don't be long, he's very weak.'

Martin climbed the stairs. Derek was in the tiny room at the top which looked out onto the back garden and over the plum and apple trees, whose leaves were starting to drop. It wasn't the Derek that Martin had remembered. Skeletal in appearance, he looked as though he'd lost at least four or five stone. The jaundice was increasing every day, and what should have been the whites of his eyes were now a sickly dark yellow. Martin stood for a moment at the foot of the bed, wanting to know how to begin, ashamed for himself, saddened, but appalled by what had happened to his former friend.

'How are you, Martin?' croaked the voice from the far end of the bed.

'Not so bad, thank you. How are you?'

Derek made a gesture of despair.

'Derek,' began Martin, hesitantly, 'I just wanted to say something. Please hear me out: don't send me away. I just want to tell you how bitterly sorry I am for what I did to your marriage. I've always been fond of Anne but never in the way you imagine. I don't want to make any excuses for myself, but things somehow got out of hand when I was very low. There was no plan to deceive you. I just wish to God that Anne had never come up to the Old Rectory that evening. I'm sorry for the rift that it's made between the two of us, and I'm even more sorry for the rift that it's made between you and Anne. I've killed your marriage and I'm not at all sure that in driving you to work yourself so hard, and not recognise until too late that you'd got cancer... I'm not at all sure that I haven't killed you as well...'

'Martin...' the voice croaked from the end of the bed. 'Sit down. You didn't need to say all that. I know you too well. I know you mean it. I forgave you long ago, you know.' Martin's eyes widened. 'Oh yes, I had. It's just that you never came near me after that. I suspect *you* haven't learned how to forgive *yourself*.'

Derek paused, fighting for energy. 'And you haven't killed me because even if I'd spotted was going on I'd still have had to wait for Nicholas to come back, so it wouldn't have been operated on any earlier.'

Derek lifted his arm slightly. 'Hold my hand, Martin.' Tentatively Martin put out his hand. Derek's grip was surprisingly strong. 'I mean it, Martin,' he said. 'I forgave you in my own mind long ago. I won't even mind if you marry Anne after I'm...'

'*Derek!* I've told you there's nothing between us. We've hardly seen each other since. But thank you for being so kind and forgiving. It's more than I could have expected... more than I ever deserve. You're right—I haven't learned to forgive myself. But then I did an appalling thing.'

'It helps to talk about it,' said Derek.

'I know,' said Martin, 'but I hadn't got anyone to talk to.'

'No... Anne was insistent, wasn't she? Keeping the secret to myself nearly destroyed me...'

Martin looked down, shame-faced.

'... but then Nicholas came and I thought—well at least I can talk to him. He'll keep it in confidence. He's my doctor. I can tell him. So I did.'

'Did it help?'

'Enormously. I only wish you'd been able to find someone to confide in, too. Maybe it would have lifted your burden as well.'

'That's kind of you.'

'Anyway,' continued Derek, 'enough said about that. Let's forget it. What's past is past. We mustn't let it come between us in the last few days that are left to me.'

Totally wrong-footed by the complete turnaround of events, Martin was lost for words. He'd gone over and over the conversation in his mind trying to work how best to say the things to Derek, always working on the premise that Derek hated, despised and loathed him, and would preferably have nothing to do with him. Everything Martin had planned had hinged upon that idea. He found it so difficult to comprehend that Derek was actually forgiving him, and was friends with him once more. The enormity of it all, the goodness of it all, the kindness of it all overwhelmed him and made him feel, if anything, even worse than he had before. It was wonderful to know that he and Derek were friends again—that was unchallengeable. But the manner in which Derek had re-established their friendship made Martin shame-faced with embarrassment and guilt, yet amazed at the consideration that Derek was showing for him.

Too overwhelmed to speak he got up, went across to the window and stood for a moment looking at the apple tree in the garden. There was something else he wanted to say, something so deep, so important, so loving: something that Derek needed to hear desperately, yet something that was going to be one of the most difficult things for Martin to say in his whole life.

For Martin had come with two messages. He'd expected to be ignored, vilified, despised and hated but even so he had determined to deliver the second message because he cared for Derek so much. And the fact that Derek had forgiven him had temporarily taken the wind out of his sails, and wrong-footed him completely.

What he wanted more than anything else was to tell Derek about Jesus, knowing that this was possibly the last chance he would ever have of hearing the Christian gospel. Yet he knew that Derek had always professed agnosticism or atheism, was unlikely to be interested, and while always courteous in the face of Martin's beliefs, had always gently but firmly and politely rejected them.

What Martin *wanted* to say was, on the face of it, easy. He wanted to tell Derek that when God first created the world He had made it perfect, but that man had wrecked it by choosing to go his own way: and that by that sin had come death, disaster, destruction and, ultimately, the cancer that was eating Derek alive. And yet that same spurned God hadn't deserted the human race, but had taken the only course available to rectify the situation: He had sent his Son, to live as a man among us, ultimately to die on a cross as a sacrifice to pay the penalty for what we'd done. Then simply by asking that God forgive our sins in the name of his Son we could be forgiven for all that we'd done that was wrong, be at peace with God and that after death we would go back to him and live with him for ever.

That was what Martin wanted to say. That was the theory. What actually came out was completely different. Martin wasn't a natural evangelist—he was good with people, an excellent listener, kind, courteous, sympathetic and wise. But he wasn't an evangelist. Somehow he never managed to make evangelistic conversation sound anything other than stilted and awkward, and this conversation was going to be more stilted and awkward than most, bearing in mind his own behaviour in the not-too-distant past.

'Derek,' he began uncertainly. 'I'm sure you know you're going to die...' Derek held up his hand in a gesture of weariness and resignation.

'You're going to try and evangelise me, Martin, aren't you?'

'I'd like to.'

'Save yourself the bother. I made up my mind long ago and I'm not changing it now. Tell me, did you come here just to evangelise me? Was it me you were interested in, or was it your conscience that was pricking you?'

Martin went red. His conscience was pricking him like mad—how could he possibly evangelise Derek when he'd shown by example what an unchristian life he, a professed Christian—a professional Christian even—could lead?

'I came because I cared for you, Derek,' Martin replied. 'I cared enough and I still care enough to want to face you, to talk to you, to tell you about the things I believe in because I think they're important and I came out of consideration and care and love for you. And it was very difficult coming, I can tell you, because to be honest I didn't think that you'd want to let me in the room and I could quite understand why.'

Derek's hand flopped down on the bed. 'I'll believe you, Martin,' he said. 'Thousands wouldn't...' And then he looked up at him and grinned. 'No, that's unkind. I really do believe you. Thank you for wanting to try anyway. I do accept that, honestly I do, and I'm grateful to you for having the guts to come...' The rattle in his throat got louder and he coughed. 'And I'll hear you out, Martin, if only for your sake—so that you know that you've said all that you want to. I know it means a lot to you.'

Martin tried to tell him what he wanted to say, but it all went wrong. He told him about Jesus, he told him that even at this late stage Derek could still make his peace with God, but that after he died it would be too late, that judgement and hell awaited those who had not chosen for God, and that eternal peace and life awaited those who asked God for forgiveness. But somehow Martin's words didn't carry their normal conviction—it wasn't that he didn't believe in what he was saying, just that he didn't put it across very well, somehow. But at the very least, he said it sincerely, and Derek knew it.

When Martin had finished, Derek held his hand for a moment.

'Thank you for telling me that, Martin. I'm afraid it doesn't make any difference. I still don't feel any different. I still don't believe in anything. I'm sorry for you that I can't see it your way, but there it is. But thank you for trying. I appreciate your concern, and your care, and your love.'

All Martin experienced was a ghastly sinking feeling inside his chest. He was sorry, above all, for Derek. Martin truly believed what he'd said about heaven and about hell, and found it difficult to contemplate how this good, kind, loving man whom he, Martin, had so grievously wronged, could be so gracious as to forgive him completely and yet was going to end up as a non-believer, as an enemy of God with all that implied. The knowledge that he, Martin, might have contributed to that by his own actions, by his own demonstrations of how appallingly badly it is possible for a Christian to behave—that knowledge nearly drove him frantic. Looking down at his dear friend who had meant so much to him, the man who had helped him so much when he had been deep in the depths of depression, drinking himself senseless, Martin could only feel a great sense of lostness, of sadness watching this good, kind man disintegrate slowly in front of him at such a dreadfully early age.

Derek sensed something of what was going through his mind. 'Cheer up, Martin,' he croaked. 'It's my decision and I'm standing by it. I made it long ago and nothing I've seen since has made me want to change my mind. You've done your bit. Thank you. Thank you for being so kind and thoughtful to come round and see me. I'm very grateful,' and he grasped Martin's hand again, firmly. Then, suddenly, his grip lost its strength and his hand dropped to the bed. 'I think I need to rest now. Thank you for coming. Goodbye, old friend.'

'Goodbye, Derek,' Martin's lips said, but no sound came out. Quietly he walked out of the room and shut the door gently behind him, blinking away the tears. Anne was at the bottom of the stairs. He tried to smile at her but she looked away.

'Goodbye, Anne.'

'Goodbye, Martin.'

*   *   *

The end came two days later. Derek had had a restless night but eventually drifted off to sleep as dawn broke. Anne, who'd never known quite how to face him since the adultery, had looked after him impeccably but in a curiously impersonal way, almost as though she was going through the motions of caring without

actually doing it. Towards midmorning Derek's breathing became
noisier and harsh. Gradually he slipped from sleep into a coma,
from which he was unrousable. Throughout the morning Anne sat
patiently by the bed, looking at him. David had come in earlier but
had found it difficult to stay and had rushed out again in distress a
few minutes later, unable to cope—not that there was much that he
could do. His father was no longer able to respond to him, and
would never be able to respond to him again.

Gradually Derek's pulse became weaker and his breathing more
irregular. At about half past eleven his breathing stopped, then after
a few more moments started again, then stopped again. Anne felt
the pulse at the wrist. It was there for a moment and then it was
gone, and Derek's sightless eyes stared unseeing at the ceiling from
his jaundiced and skeletal face.

In that moment all the agonies and guilt of the past year and a
half burst on Anne. She grabbed hold of Derek, buried her face in
the pillow beside him and cried and cried, crying for the man that
she'd married, the father of their two children, the one whom she'd
ultimately betrayed, the one to whom she'd owed so much and
finally given back so little. She cried for him, for David and for herself. And in a distant, numb sort of way she too felt just like Martin
—that Derek would have to go on from there to face an awesome
God on an awful Judgement Day and the knowledge that she might
have had something to do with what would then happen to him
made her feel as wretched as it is ever possible for a wife to feel.

With the tears came anger—anger at Martin for what he'd done,
anger that he should have known better, should have behaved in a
more disciplined manner, that as a minister of the gospel he should
have been better equipped to deal with his own passions, been in
control, able to resist temptation; anger that as a Christian he had
betrayed her and him and God and Derek all in one fell swoop,
anger at herself for letting herself be deceived; anger at God for letting her family become the disaster area it now was with her daughter and her husband both dead, far, far too early. For a quarter of an
hour she sobbed her eyes out, her tears soaking the pillow next to
the jaundiced head of her dead husband.

Derek couldn't hear her now, couldn't respond to her, couldn't love her, as he'd always done even though it had been difficult when first she'd told him of the pregnancy. Even so, Derek had never actually stopped loving her, though under the circumstances it had been difficult for him to express it, and the love and the care and the consideration that he had shown and the lust and the uncare and the inconsideration that she and Martin had demonstrated seemed all the more shocking by comparison.

She was left with a single question on her lips: 'Why should it happen to Derek—good, kind, considerate, unselfish Derek—and not to Martin? How would God look at Derek on Judgement Day? Good, kind, considerate, loving, forgiving Derek? Why should Martin gain entrance to heaven when Derek didn't?' All these and a thousand other related questions rushed round in her head, tumbling over and over until she stopped crying and withdrew into herself, numb, becoming almost mute with sorrow and grief and guilt and anguish and anger and rage.

*   *   *

Martin had, of course, to conduct the funeral and everybody, but *everybody*, in the town attended to pay their last respects and tell Anne what a wonderful person Derek had been, how kind and considerate, and—though they knew he wasn't a proper doctor—how wonderful he'd been when he treated them. To Anne it made little difference. Her eyes didn't see any of it. Her ears heard nothing. She stared ahead, numb, shocked, almost senseless throughout the whole service, anxiety, guilt and fury almost overwhelming her.

Martin felt much the same, only probably even more guilty, though he kept his emotions well under control, appearing on the surface to be appropriately calm and sad. It was, quite simply, the worst funeral he had ever attended. It is bad enough for an atheist to attend the funeral of a friend, feeling certain that the friend has gone into oblivion never to exist again; but for a Christian to be present at the funeral of an avowed non-believer is even worse, because there is the fear that not only has that person gone from this world but that they will then have to face another world which is distinctly less pleasant. The funeral of an atheist attended by a believing Christian is one of the most pitiable, sad and exhausting experiences that can ever be imagined on this earth. The knowledge that a friend has gone to eternal damnation, and the feeling that surely that there must have been *something* that could have been done to help change his or her mind, is a very heavy burden.

All through the service the thought hammered at Martin's brain. The service began, of course, with the words that are meant to be so comforting, but which under the present circumstances had turned into a curse.

' "I am the resurrection and the life, saith the Lord: he that believeth in me, though he were dead, yet shall he live: and whosoever liveth and believeth in me shall never die," ' intoned Martin, leading the coffin, with the sickening knowledge of the unspoken implication that he that doesn't believe in Jesus shall *not* have eternal life. All the comforting words of the funeral service about faith, hope and a lasting resurrection to a better existence, all were as barbs in Martin's brain, with the knowledge that, had he done differently, had he behaved more wisely, things now might be very, very different, that perhaps instead of mourning a lost soul, he might be exulting at another of God's children entering heaven.

Like Anne, Martin's mind soon became numb and he could think about it all no more. He just went through the service automatically. If anybody thought he was affected by the service they would think it very natural. He and Derek had been very close at the beginning and everybody would understand that Martin would be greatly upset by the loss of a friend, so there was no need for him to fear that anyone would think differently of him if he faltered during the service. But he didn't. He simply conducted the service by rote. Afterwards he didn't remember the interment, or the final words said over the coffin as it was lowered into the ground. Nor could Anne, staring straight ahead and avoiding looking at Martin. She couldn't think of anything at all.

- 23 -

*T*hey came the next night, two black-clad figures furtively moving down Woburn Street in the dark. The one who'd had the field glasses knew the layout of the town intimately. There was just the faint sound of smashing glass as they let themselves into a house. The first thing the occupants knew about it was when they awoke to torches being shone in their eyes and shot-guns pushed, none too gently, against their necks.

'Where is he?' hissed the one with the field glasses. Alan tried to struggle and got the stock of a gun in his solar plexus for his pains. Susan's eyes widened and she tried to scream but the hand over her mouth was too tight. She indicated with her eyes to the next bedroom.

The two ran across the landing, grabbed the sleeping Darren and, still pointing the shot-gun menacingly at his parents, bundled him down the stairs, handcuffed him to one of the bikes they'd pushed along the road with them and then just as swiftly swung into the saddle.

The roar of the high-powered engines split the silence of the night. Lights came on in the houses and cottages down Woburn Street as the two bikes shot off into the night, back to Buckingham.

*   *   *

Next day Paul had to deal with a distraught Susan and Alan, whose misfortune was made worse because even at this most difficult of crises, they still couldn't agree, and the simmering rift between them was, if anything, worsened. Sometimes a crisis shakes the protagonists up and makes them realise that there are more serious issues at stake than petty bickering: but at other times a real problem blows apart what remnants of a relationship remain. The current crisis was threatening to do just that.

'But can't you *do* something?' said a tearful Susan to Paul. 'I mean, can't you chase them and get him back *now*? *Do* something, today, before it's too late, before anything happens to him.'

Paul shook his head.

'I don't believe this,' said Susan. 'You're supposed to be in charge of our war council and you're doing nothing.'

Alan tried to intervene. 'It's better to do the right thing slowly than the wrong thing quickly,' he offered.

'Oh shut up. What do you know about it?' She almost spat the words out. 'If you were anything like a man you'd go after him yourself.'

'That wouldn't get us anywhere,' replied Alan, forcing himself to remain calm under extreme provocation. 'It would be likely to end up in a bigger mess, and then there'd be two of us to rescue, not one. There's no point in my getting blown to bits, or captured.'

'That's it, isn't it? That's the bottom line. You're only concerned about whether *you* get hurt, not about Darren. Paul, *you* tell him. Tell him to get off his silly backside and do something instead of fiddling around with radio sets all day long.'

'It's very important,' said Alan, 'the weather.'

'Blow that,' she said. 'What's more important to you, the weather or your son?'

After another five minutes of this, Paul gingerly tried to put an oar in. 'I don't want to appear to take sides, Susan,' he began gently, 'but Alan's right. There isn't any point in making the situation worse. We've got to think carefully. Besides, they'll be expecting us to mount some form of rescue and they'll be waiting for us.'

'I knew you'd take his side,' said Susan. 'You men are all the same. I'll obviously have to do something myself.' She got up and was about to storm out of the door when Paul jumped up from his seat and physically blocked her way.

'Do you want to see Darren back?' he said, giving her his most lethal stare. She buckled.

'Well, yes, of course I do... What a stupid question.'

'If you want to see him alive again,' said Paul, slowly, and in measured tones, 'can I suggest that you don't do *anything* without first consulting the war council and getting our permission.'

'I don't need your permission to do anything,' she snapped back.

'If you want to make things a great deal worse, put Darren's life at risk and maybe the lives of the people who are going to rescue him, then just continue as you are, Susan. You do want to see Darren again, do you?'

'I told you, of course I do.'

'Then don't *dare*, don't even *think* about trying to rescue him yourself. All you'll do is put the plans we've already made at risk. Do you understand? *Do you understand*?'

Finally it got through to her. She subsided, irritably. 'If you say so Paul, if you say so.'

'I do say so, Susan,' he said. 'I do say so.'

'All right, if you insist. Can I go now? Is that all right, *sir*?' and with a snort she brushed past him and out into the street.

Paul turned to Alan. 'Make sure she doesn't do anything, won't you?'

'How?' said Alan, spreading his hands expressively. 'The best way to make her go on a rescue mission would be for me to suggest that she *doesn't* do it.'

'All right,' said Paul, a resigned look on his face, 'just let me know if you think she's planning to go off on her own on some form of rescue attempt. She won't get anywhere, and all she'll do is jeopardise the plans we've already made.'

'I promise I'll tell you if I find out,' said Alan, 'but I can't guarantee that she'll tell me.'

'Well, let us know if she seems to be getting things together for a journey. OK?'

'OK.' He paused. 'Do you really think we'll get Darren back?'

'I think so but it's going to take quite a time.'

'How long?'

'Four, five...'

'Days?'

'Months, Alan, months. We're in for a long haul here. We've got to make sure we get it right first time. We'll only get one decent bite at the cherry. We need to lull them into a false sense of security, and then we'll strike. Just don't push it, that's all. We'll go when we're ready, and not before.'

The prospect of so long a wait appalled Alan.

'*Months*?' he echoed. 'Months. Why can't we do it in ten days?'

'We don't have the information. We've got to know exactly where we're going before we do anything. Information, Alan: we need information. We can't act without it.'

*   *   *

Far from speeding up the process of rescuing the hostages the capture of Darren had expanded the time-scale considerably. There was no point in even thinking about a reconnaissance for another five or six weeks. For a start, the bandits would undoubtedly be on their guard, and probably jumpy and trigger-happy to boot. In addition, if they'd got any sense—which Paul wasn't quite sure was true—they'd be moving the hostages around quite frequently, just in case they were being watched.

The war council was in total unanimity about the time-scale. Surprisingly, Paul found that he was depending more and more on the Major for tactical advice. Whereas Kevin was the strategist—the one who seemed to be able to read the minds of the bandits—the Major was the tactician, the one who could very ably plan a campaign once he knew what the objectives were. While he was never the sort of material to make a brigadier or a field marshal he was, nevertheless, extremely competent in the lower levels of management of battle tactics and Paul came increasingly to respect his opinion and trust his judgement. Crusty, hide-bound and antiquated though the Major was in many ways, in the area for which he had been trained he was an extremely able performer.

From then on the Major went up several points in Paul's estimation.

*   *   *

The immediate need was to get information. As previously planned, Kevin would take the Harley-Davidson on a circuitous route, aiming to come into Buckingham, not by the direct road between Ampthill and Buckingham, but on the road from the northeast. He would leave the bike about three miles from the town centre, then lie low for twenty-four hours to make sure that he'd not been discovered. The next night he would get into the city centre, hide somewhere appropriate, observe during the day, then in the early hours of the next morning return to the bike and come back home.

That at least was the plan. Everybody knew that it was fraught with danger: if spotted, Kevin would instantly be recognised as a stranger—and if he were spotted by the wrong people the bandits would soon know that they were being spied on and take instant evasive measures, thus rendering instantly obsolete all the information gained by Kevin's reconnaissance.

And if Kevin were recognised, stopped and captured... Just as Paul had discovered how the Major was a great deal more resourceful than he had previously imagined, so he discovered that Kevin was considerably braver than he had previously believed. It had been Kevin, of course, who had whipped Lew Pritchard for daring to steal his Harley-Davidson, and Paul had no doubt that if the tables were turned, Lew would do the same and much, *much* worse to Kevin. In that instant his respect for the twenty-year-old rose significantly, too.

So now they had the plan, but the timing was the most important thing. In the meantime, all they could do was wait and try to behave as normally as possible. Perhaps, in turn, the bandits were watching them, as they had done in the past, and it was important that they got no inkling of any special preparations, so life just had to go on as usual.

- 24 -

*W*inter has come early this year—or maybe it's because we've lost Derek that we all feel so cold. It's been a miserable few months. And no one's doing anything about Darren, least of all Alan. He says he's concerned, but why doesn't he do anything towards rescuing him? What a wimp.

Nicholas has come back again. Somehow he found out about Derek, and was here within a couple of weeks. The good news is he's decided to stay permanently, so we've still got medical help. The bad news is that no one likes him—at least, not by comparison with Derek. He's so quick—no time for anyone. He doesn't visit like Derek used to. In fact, he hardly seems to do anything: although he's now permanently based here, he takes patients over a much bigger area and often travels to Harpenden, and the other communities to consult. How he can do this when Derek found it so hard to look after just the inhabitants of our community, I don't know. I'm sure Nicholas is short-changing us on the amount of time he spends on each case.

At least he's here and he's a doctor, so we're safe again for a time. Until he decides to go, that is. I'm sure he has no great interest in the community—apart from financial, that is. He's also told us that he's now run out of anaesthetic completely. What will we do if someone needs another operation?

And what are we going to do about Darren?

Susan put down her pen again and stared out into the blackness of the night.

$$*\qquad\qquad*\qquad\qquad*$$

In his new abode in Dunstable Street Nicholas settled down comfortably to read in front of a roaring fire, a glass of wine at his elbow and chestnuts roasting on the hearth.

$$*\qquad\qquad*\qquad\qquad*$$

Perhaps it was the maturing of the years; or maybe it was his marriage to Chris, or else the birth of Emma, but for whatever reason Paul seemed to be moving into a more tranquil phase of his life. The waspish display of his aggressive humour seemed to be less frequent, his self-centred arrogance (which had always been a defence against his own insecurities) was less often displayed, and he seemed to have mellowed with the years. It didn't make him a less calculating planner, however, because he still possessed the aggressive, ascerbic, incisive analytical mind that he'd always had, but he seemed more relaxed somehow, less of a go-getter. He even seemed to have time to talk with Martin, whom in the past he'd passed off as a useless appendage on society, both in his professional status and as an individual.

Paul's pride in his new offspring was evident, and he was often to be seen towards the end of the day taking Emma out in a pram or pushchair, and showing her the sights and sounds of the countryside. By chance Martin met him one day, standing with Emma at a five-barred gate at the end of Woburn Road, pointing at the cows on the other side of the fence and making mooing noises. Somehow baby-talk and Paul didn't seem to fit together too well, though Paul seemed quite unconcerned about it. Martin grinned inwardly to himself as he strode past, observing Paul's face as he realised he was being watched and suddenly changed his voice from baby-talk to normal English-speak.

'Good evening, Martin.'

'Hello, Paul.'

Martin crouched down to speak to Emma. He had learned long ago that to a child a bow is a threatening gesture, and that an adult who bends down to talk looks most aggressive, but that squatting down by the child is much less alarming. 'Hello, Emma,' said Martin, letting Emma grab the index finger of his left hand which she jerked up and down with her whole arm. 'Are you looking at the cows?'

Emma, who was only seven or eight months old at this stage, had no idea what 'cows' meant, never mind the other interesting noises of 'are', 'at', 'looking' etc. Nor had the full philosophical implication of the word 'you' even begun to impinge upon her brain. Nevertheless, she looked at Martin and went 'goo', chuckled, and bounced both her hands up and down in delight, kicking out her legs at the same time and managing to hit herself on the forehead with Martin's hand. The bottom lip curled.

'Oh dear, Emma,' said Paul, bending down to pick her up and cradle her in his arms. 'Now don't cry. Uncle Martin's a friend.'

'*Uncle*?' thought Martin to himself. 'I am on the up and up.'

Over in the mid-distance a black and white cow mooed and lumbered over to have a closer look at them. Emma's attention diverted itself neatly from the knock on her forehead to this great lumbering monster coming nearer and nearer.

'You look very happy,' said Martin amiably to Paul.

'I am,' Paul replied, picking up a piece of grass and chewing it absent-mindedly. 'I think family life changes us, don't you?' He'd intended it as a friendly statement of fact, but Martin felt the daggers go in yet again. For a moment his mouth tightened, thinking that Paul was winding him up again.

Paul suddenly realised that perhaps he'd not quite said the right thing, bearing in mind that Martin had presumably never experienced human closeness of the sort that he, Chris and Emma were now enjoying, and hastily added, 'I'm sure you've noticed that in other people.'

'Oh yes,' said Martin, relaxing, realising that the barbs for once had not been intentional, only to be replaced a few moments later by the worry that maybe they were intentional, that perhaps Paul knew but wasn't letting on that he knew, or at least not letting on very obviously. Desperately Martin tried to push the thoughts down, out of the way.

The sun was beginning to set, its orange rays shining through the black branches of the wood to their right. 'It's a funny thing,' Paul continued, quite oblivious to the sudden surge in Martin's adrenaline level that he'd inadvertently caused, 'I used to think I was happy before, with all the money and the flat, and Jane, and the job, and the Porsche. I wasn't, you know.'

'Really?' said Martin, his pulse rate just starting to settle.

'No,' said Paul taking the end of the piece of grass out of his mouth and spitting a broken-off bit of it into the hedge. 'No, I used to think that was the height of enjoyment but it's strange—I'm much happier now, and yet I've not got half the things I used to have.'

Martin suddenly realised he'd not seen the Porsche around for some time. He started to say something, then checked himself.

'Mind you,' continued Paul. 'It can't last for ever, can it?'

'There's no reason why the community here shouldn't go on for a long time.'

'I didn't mean that. It's a funny thing but with the onset of a new life—' he nodded towards Emma, who by now was reaching out her hand to the oncoming cow that was lumbering up, steam pouring from its nostrils, 'one does tend to be a bit more aware of one's own mortality—the next generation following on, and everything.'

'I suppose that's true,' said Martin, still looking at the sunset. 'That's where, I suppose, people like me come in. You know,' he said smiling, looking at Paul sideways, 'useless people like me, and useless professions like the priesthood.'

'Yes,' said Paul with a grin. 'I've never really had much time for the church.'

'But you've never believed in God, have you? So you wouldn't.'

'That's true.'

And then Paul asked the question which, afterwards, he didn't know why he'd asked. A silly, stupid question to which he didn't even want to know the answer. But the question came out anyway. 'Why *did* you become a priest then?'

As soon as he'd asked it, Paul realised that he didn't want to know the answer, and braced himself for the evangelistic spiel that he was sure was about to come. Martin looked at him again, then leaned on the gate and stared at the sunset. He sniffed.

'Do you want the honest answer?'

'I suppose so.'

'Then I don't think I can give it to you. I went into the ministry for all the wrong reasons. It seemed a good idea at the time. I suppose I thought I could change the world, do good, help people... I don't know. I certainly didn't go in for any cogent reason that I can think of now. I just sort of fell into it.'

'No great lights in the sky, apparitions, voices in the ears, blinding conversion experiences, miracles, raising of the dead, gathering up of enough money to save the clock tower...?'

Martin turned to Paul and grinned. 'You do have a way with words Paul, you know... No, nothing like that. I learned afterwards though.'

'When—afterwards?'

'After the plague. I'd trundled on, not being a very good priest, not being particularly effective. Then when the plague came I had to rethink everything.'

'Such as how your nice, caring, loving God could ever allow a plague like that.'

'Something on those lines, yes.'

'Which is precisely why I have no time for the church,' replied Paul.

'Yes,' said Martin looking at the sunset again. By now the cow had reached the gate and was looking at Emma curiously in the way that only cows can.

'I'm not sure that I understand it any better now,' said Martin finally. 'I had a great catharsis at the time the plague came and it knocked me sideways for a bit and, like you, I got to the point of thinking that God wasn't there. But then I realised that I hadn't learned my lessons properly and I certainly didn't understand human nature properly. And once I'd realised that man is capable of very great evil and at heart is selfish then a lot of things fell neatly into place.'

'I'd heard,' said Paul. 'Derek told me.'

'Well, there you have it,' said Martin, embarrassed, and started to move away. Paul remained curiously transfixed and suddenly, underneath all those psychological sweatshirts that he'd been wearing for so long, the inner Paul came to the fore, the one that was insecure, the one that need reassurance and meaning, the one that needed loving, the one that needed to feel loved.

'You still haven't told me why you believe what you believe.'

'Haven't I?' The cow breathed again, great clouds of hot damp air coalescing around her. Then with a 'thrump' she slowly turned away, settled down on the ground and began amiably to chew the cud. And so with Paul staring at the sunset, and Emma staring at the cow, Martin told Paul quite simply how man had gone against God, had chosen to go his own selfish way and had estranged himself from God in the process: and how God—who really *was* a God of love whatever natural disasters might occur—elected to send Jesus on a rescue mission. He told him how sin put a barrier between man and God, how wrongdoing had to be paid for in the final analysis by the death penalty, and how God sent his Son to tell us about God and to pay that price on mankind's behalf by being crucified.

Paul drank it all in—but only up to a point. He agreed whole-heartedly with Martin about the selfishness of the individual. He knew all too well how self-centred he'd been in the past and had had many a twinge of guilt about the vengefully dismissive way in which so often he'd treated others. And it was a nice story about God sending his Son to tell us what God really was like, and to die and rise again to prove that he was who he said he was. But, try as Martin might, he could not get Paul to understand the point of the crucifixion. Martin went through all the analogies he could think of. He told him about the tabernacle in the wilderness and how the priests couldn't approach God without first having sacrificed an animal; how the High Priest wasn't allowed to go into the presence of God unless he could first pour the blood of the sacrificed animal out over the place where the stone tablets with the Ten Commandments lay. Martin even tried the old and often-used analogy about the magistrate who sentences the convicted man to pay a huge fine but, because the prisoner is genuinely sorry for what he's done and asks for forgiveness and mercy, the magistrate pulls his wallet out and pays the fine himself, acting as judge, jury and prisoner at one and the same time.

Martin tried everything and still Paul couldn't see it. He could understand how a loving God might send his Son to show us that we ought to love each other, even to the point of death, but he couldn't understand further than that.

They stayed, silent, for a few more moments, watching the sun cast its last rays over the frost of the field in front of them. Finally Paul turned to Martin. 'Well, thank you for explaining that: I can't say I agree with you, but at least I know a little bit more about why you think the way you do.'

The cow snorted and Emma jiggled up and down in his arms. Paul sensed a hot wetness towards Emma's rear end. 'I think we ought to be going, Martin,' he said with a grin. 'A change of nappy may be indicated.' Putting Emma back in the pushchair they walked slowly back to Paul's thatched cottage in Woburn Street. As they came to the gate Chris bustled out of the house.

'Where *have* you been?' she said . 'I was beginning to get quite worried.'

'I've just been chatting with Martin,' said Paul. 'Emma's wet. I'll go and change her.'

'Oh, thanks, that'll be a help.' She gave him a quick kiss as he passed her on the path.

'Hello, Martin, how are you? I haven't seen much of you lately.'

'Not so bad, Chris and you?' She looked a bit downcast. 'The fine still hurting?'

Her face reddened. 'I'm sorry,' said Martin. 'I didn't mean to hurt you or remind you. I was only trying to be helpful.'

She put her hand on his arm. Bliss, he thought, somebody's touched me.

'I know you didn't mean to hurt—it was very kind of you to ask, and I'm very grateful. We're managing. It was a bit difficult at first.'

'Paul had to sell his Porsche to pay your fine, then?'

'Oh no. Didn't you know? Paul gave it...' She suddenly realised what she was saying and put her hand to her mouth.

'Go on,' said Martin gently.

'I'm not supposed to tell anyone... Well, I'd *like* to,' she said defiantly. 'If nothing else for Paul's sake...'

'Don't tell me if you don't want to.'

'No, I do want to... He gave it to Nicholas. You know when Nicholas came—when Derek was ill.'

'I though Nicholas did the operation on Derek for free.'

'He did. But he needed paying for the locum work. Paul paid Nicholas to do Derek's locum work... with the Porsche.'

'He did *what*?' said Martin. 'I thought the community had paid.'

'We couldn't afford it,' said Chris. 'Paul volunteered.'

'*He gave him his Porsche*?'

'That's right.' Martin opened his mouth to say something but nothing came out. He knew just how much *PIG 1* had meant to Paul.

'I never realised...' he said finally.

'That's why I wanted others to know, but I suppose I shouldn't really. Just keep it between us, would you?'

Martin walked slowly back into town, totally gobsmacked by the news. Somehow he couldn't imagine the Major, a committed churchgoer, ever giving up so much in such a dedicated way. And here was Paul, an avowed atheist, no connections with the church, who had given up the most precious personal object in his life, simply to help Derek. Why was it that Christians could so often be out-shone over things like this? Surely being near to the things of God should make people even more generous, and yet it didn't always seem to. Shaking his head in amazement Martin walked slowly back to the Old Rectory, musing on the possibility that greater love hath no man than that he lay down his Porsche for a friend.

- 25 -

Martin was beginning to despair of his ability to convince anybody of the validity of the Christian faith. He was all right in the company of the Major, or Edna and Fred Higginbottom, or in happier times Anne, but somehow he never seemed to be able to pass on his beliefs in the way that others could. In truth he was actually somewhat embarrassed about his conversation with Paul and rather hoped that he wouldn't bump into him for a bit. As it happened he didn't, but in any case Paul was far too busy plotting war games with Kevin, Henry and the Major to be bothered with the niceties of philosophical belief for the moment.

Then at two o'clock on an ice-cold February night, when no one was looking, Kevin quietly slipped away into the darkness, having first hidden his motorbike by the Westminster pond. Dressed entirely in his black leathers and black helmet, he was almost invisible as he padded quietly up the Woburn Road, retrieved his bike and, out of earshot of the town, roared off into the night. Only Paul knew he'd gone. They weren't taking any chances that a passing remark by one of the Ampthill community could by any possible means get to the ears of the bandits: there was of course the additional possibility that the bandits might strike again to take a further hostage, and neither of them wanted any such hostage to know what was being planned.

*   *   *

Meanwhile *The Mikado* was reaching the last stages of rehearsal. It was due to be put on for three nights at the beginning of March and rehearsals were going well, though Martin and Anne were still not looking at each other. Susan was still scolding Alan for the amount of time he spent on the production instead of working to get more money, and there were the usual actors' tiffs, production problems and technical nightmares to deal with, but all in all, as productions go, it was proceeding well.

The first night came and went; tolerably successfully, everyone thought.

The next night Chris, Paul and Mary came. Susan had been prevailed upon to baby-sit Emma, and Chris and Paul were really looking forward to a good night's entertainment.

The council had specifically been approached for permission to use the lights on the stage at Parkside Hall: all the other lights in the town had to be turned off while the production was on but everyone had jovially agreed to this. Neil, who had suddenly found his artistic metier as a producer, had capitalised on the fact that the rest of the town was in Stygian darkness and had deliberately kept the house lights as low as he could while Martin played the overture. The house lights dimmed to blackness. Silently the curtain opened—and then Neil, who was also doubling as lighting engineer, flicked the switch to open up every light that he'd got at his command. Suddenly the stage was awash with light, kilowatts of it, pouring in from all directions, giving the impression of brilliant daylight in Japan. The effect on the audience was stunning, almost as though the sun had suddenly come out from behind clouds after a gap of twenty years, and each night there was an audible gasp from the audience at the blaze of light on stage, and the panache with which it had been displayed. It was by far the brightest light at night that anyone had seen for more than two years—dazzling, almost as dazzling as the brilliance of a single bulb had been a few months before to a group of people whose previous brightest light at night had been individual candles.

From then on the production never faltered—Neil had them on the edge of their seats from the word go. Perhaps it was the light that did it, but the quality of music and the standard of the singing and acting meant that the audience really enjoyed themselves, losing themselves totally in the production itself, absorbed by the strange tale of the village of Titipu. There was Henry dressed as the Mikado, a bloodthirsty ruler at the best of times who seemed to enjoy nothing better than a quick execution before supper, Alan as the grotesquely vain Pooh-Bah padded out for the occasion, and Ko-Ko, the timorous Lord High Executioner.

As Gilbert's witty—if totally unbelievable—tale unfolded the audience laughed in all the right places, tapped their feet to all the right tunes and, like audiences for the past century or more, enjoyed the patter songs most of all. On swept Peter, looking suspiciously like something cloned from a willow pattern plate, to sing about how he'd

'...got a little list
Of society offenders who might well be underground
And who never would be missed—
They never would be missed.'

And as he rattled off the list of all those whom W. S. Gilbert would have liked dealt with, unknown to each other, Paul and Mary made their own lists. Definitely Lew Pritchard was on it, as were all the other members of his gang. Paul's list included Kevin—sometimes—though ruefully he was beginning to understand that there was more to Kevin than met the eye. In fairness Paul did wonder how he was getting on, and fervently hoped he would return safely.

Mary's list was much longer, much more varied and in many ways much more interesting. Right at the top—far out in front of anyone else among people she would like 'underground, and not

missed'— was Paul. Oh, how she would *love* to pay him back for
the emotional anguish and turmoil he had caused her. And then both
Paul and Mary spent the next few minutes feeling guilty about the
people they'd put on their list, recognising that there were good
points about them all and perhaps thinking that they were wrong to
be so cutting and damning about other human beings.

And then came the exchange on stage which was to change Paul
forever. The Mikado, like any visiting dignitary, expected to be
pampered a little: and for the Mikado, 'pampering' meant cutting
somebody's head off. Unfortunately Ko-Ko, the frightened and
insignificant Lord High Executioner, and the pompous Poo-Bah—
Lord High Everything Else—had a problem: they hadn't executed
anybody in weeks. Nor did there seem to be any criminal conveniently available for the purpose. The penalties for disobeying the
Mikado were dire: Poo-Bah was anxious to lose none of his status
(to say nothing of the top twelve inches of his anatomy) and he and
Ko-Ko spent some time discussing the problem. How were they
going to find a victim to satisfy their great and terrifying ruler, the
Mikado?

'I'm afraid that, unless you can obtain a substitute...,' said Anne
as Pish-Tush, moving downstage.

'A substitute?' said Ko-Ko, turning to the officious and self-
important Pooh-Bah (the Lord High Everything Else). 'Oh, certainly—nothing easier. Pooh-Bah, I appoint you Lord High Substitute.'
The audience laughed, as if on cue.

Lord High Substitute!

Paul felt as though there'd been an explosion inside his head: it
seemed as if the operetta in front of him was taking place in just a
tiny part of his mind as the rest of him contemplated the awesome-
ness of the whole puzzle, now that the final piece had dropped into
place with what seemed like an almost audible clang.

Lord High Substitute.

Suddenly, unbidden, Paul was transported in his mind's eye, not
to Japan, but to Jerusalem: everything that Martin had told him
about the crucifixion fell into place and at last Paul understood how
Jesus, the Son of God, had come earth to be Lord High Substitute

and to die on his—Paul's—behalf. The enormity of it—the sheer
enormity of it—took his breath away.

Lord High Substitute.

Then came the challenge. He had a choice to make.

Paul didn't take much notice of the rest of the concert. He said
the right things to the right people, nodded and smiled at Chris at
the right moments, bought drinks in the interval and carried out all
the small talk that goes on these occasions without once engaging
his conscious mind. All he could think of was the magnitude of the
decision that had opened up before him—and it was his to make,
one way or the other.

They went back into the hall for the second act. In the distance
he could vaguely see Martin playing for all his worth, totally
unaware of what he'd started those several weeks earlier, just like
the concert before their first harvest where he'd played the
Rachmaninov Prelude and had had the audience in tears, without
understanding what he'd done on that occasion either.

And suddenly it was over. The audience cheered and clapped.
The actors and singers took their bow: Martin and Neil were invited
on stage to take their share of the applause and Paul could see
Martin, moving bashfully to the middle of the stage and hating
every minute of it.

Then the curtains closed for the last time, the house lights came
on dimly and everyone went out, babbling excitedly about the blaze
of light that had bathed the make-believe town of Titipu. All, that
was, except Paul.

'You're very distant tonight,' said Chris, holding his hand as they
walked back to the thatched cottage.

'Am I?' said Paul, his mind on other things. 'I'm sorry. I was just
thinking.' He left the conversation unfinished as they walked the
short distance home. Chris put her arm round his waist.

'How about an early night tonight?' she said with a sort of gleam
in her eye that made it quite clear that an early night and an early
sleep were not necessarily one and the same thing.

'What did you say?' said Paul detaching himself from his own
inner thoughts.

'You heard,' she said with a wink.

'No,' he said. 'No. I want to go out. I want to think.'

'Oh, very well,' she said, suddenly becoming cold at the rebuff, 'if you must. I'll see you later then, shall I?'

'Yes,' said Paul absent-mindedly. Chris was going to give a vehement retort but something about Paul's manner stopped her and instead they parted at the gate of the cottage, Chris having first given him a peck on the cheek.

'Don't be too late, will you?'

'No, I won't,' he said, again absent-mindedly. Chris watched his retreating back as he walked slowly up Woburn Street towards the Market Square.

'Paul Greatorex,' she murmured to herself, 'when I think I know you, I don't know you. Ah well, I wouldn't have it any differently,' and went into the cottage to relieve Susan of the job of baby-sitting.

Like so many before him, Paul knew what he should do; he knew why he should do it; and he knew that it was his choice, and his choice alone. No one was forcing him, but he was being asked, nevertheless. Which way would he choose? The enormity of the decision lay in front of him. He knew all too well what the options entailed—being in charge of his life or being accountable to God. Again, like many before him, Paul didn't feel pleased, happy or contented at the prospect—he felt *angry*, angry at being challenged, angry at the upheaval it might cause him, angry for having his current happy and relatively easy lifestyle disturbed.

Along Woburn Street he walked, over the crest past the Queen's Head, and down towards the Market Square, oblivious to everything happening around him. Straight as an arrow he headed for the White Hart, all the time feeling the rage rise and rise inside, until he was immensely, intensely, furiously angry—angry at the choice he was being offered, angry at the responsibility he faced, angry even at being asked. With a face like thunder, he entered the White Hart and for the first time in his life proceeded to get energetically and systematically blind drunk.

*   *   *

Kevin got back from Buckingham that night, at four o'clock in the morning, cold, half-starved and more tired than he'd ever remembered being in his life. Cursing himself for not looking after his house more effectively he surveyed the unmade rubble of his bed, but collapsed into it anyway, still in his cycle leathers, and fell asleep for twelve hours.

When he awoke it was nearly dark again. He managed to get some food together, splashed cold water on his face and then went out in search of Paul. A cross-looking Chris answered the door. Evidently Paul had returned at two o'clock that morning and was currently suffering from the biggest hangover he'd ever had in his life. It hadn't extinguished his rage though: he wasn't cross with Chris and he was his usual loving self with Emma, but internally his anger blazed like a fire that was totally out of control.

Nor was he angry with Kevin. In fact he was utterly charming with Kevin. 'Good to see you,' he said. 'I'm glad you got back safely. Chris, can we rustle Kevin up some food?'

'Sure,' said Chris, giving Paul a covert hard stare. Kevin noticed the look and wondered what had been going on in his absence. Kevin was going to say that he'd just eaten, but not being one to turn down the offer of free food—and hot food at that—he nodded his head enthusiastically.

'Are you *sure* we haven't got any coffee left?' asked Paul pointedly, holding his head. 'Not anywhere?' Chris shook her head, her lips pursed.

'You'll just have to suffer,' she murmured *sotto voce*.

'Right,' said Paul sitting down opposite Kevin, who by now had a plate of freshly baked bread and butter and a steaming mug of soup in front of him. 'So what did you find out?'

*　　　　　*　　　　　*

When Kevin and Paul had finished, Kevin thanked Chris for the food and then walked the few yards up Woburn Street to Susan and Alan's house to tell them that he'd seen Darren, if only from a distance, and that he was all right.

'When did you see him?' said Alan.

'*How* did you see him?' demanded Susan.

As Paul had suggested, Kevin kept the details to himself. 'He's orl right. Really 'e is,' he said, sniffing loudly.

'Poor Kevin,' said Susan. 'You must be starving after all that reconnoitring. Do sit down. Do you want something to eat?'

Gosh, thought Kevin to himself, three meals inside one and a half hours. Can't be bad.

Over food he told Susan and Alan everything he could about Darren, carefully leaving out the details of exactly where he was being kept, and embroidering other details enough to make them feel comfortable. Darren had been gone five months and by now Alan and Susan were delighted to hear any news whatever, however scrappy or incomplete, of their eighteen-year-old son.

It was completely dark when Kevin left Susan and Alan's house to walk back to his own place. Walking up Woburn Street he found himself behind the unmistakable figure of Paul. Kevin called out to him but Paul seemed oblivious to the sights and sounds around him as for the second time in twenty-four hours he headed for the White Hart.

Paul got drunk again that night; and the night after; and the night after that. Chris, who at first had been angry, and had then tried to laugh the matter off by suggesting that Gilbert and Sullivan wasn't as bad as all *that*, had started to become extremely worried, and had sought guidance from Martin. Normally she'd have gone to Derek first, but that wasn't possible any more...

Chris told Martin all she knew, which wasn't much: just that they'd been having a great night out, and suddenly Paul had gone all indrawn and morose. Martin couldn't help—not surprisingly, under the circumstances, because he didn't have the vaguest idea of what was happening to Paul.

'Has he ever done anything like this before?' he asked.

'No, not as far as I can recall,' said Chris, 'though of course I've only known him for the past three and a half years. There was the problem with the heroin, which you know about, but that seemed to be over. I know he's inclined to put the knife in on other people from time to time but he's been quietly growing out of that ever since we got married—and especially since Emma was born: but I don't recall him ever going off the deep end like this before.'

'Maybe he's having a midlife crisis,' said Martin, half-jokingly. To Chris it was anything but a joke. She was hurt by Martin's off-hand attitude but more than that she was concerned for what might have happened to Paul or what might be happening to him.

'At thirty?' she said angrily. 'Come off it, Martin.'

'Actually I mean it,' said Martin. 'Being a family man, having a child for the first time, does make you look differently at the world.'

'How would you know?' snorted Chris. Martin winced inwardly at the thought of Julian, then brightened up a little. At least Chris didn't know. She'd just told him that.

'Friends of mine,' he mumbled. 'I recall a lot of them saying how differently they looked at life once they'd had their first child.' He leaned forward and put his hand gently on Chris's arm. 'Don't worry Chris, I'm sure it'll pass. Maybe it's the problem with Darren that's getting to him. It's an awful responsibility for him, you know.'

'But what do I do?' said Chris.

'Just love him,' said Martin. 'Just be there for him. You do love him, don't you?'

'Oh yes,' said Chris, shaking her head sadly. 'That's what makes it so painful.'

'I know it sounds as if I'm spouting platitudes,' said Martin, 'but, you know, I think that'll help him more than anything else. If he knows that he can come back to you, if he knows that you're there, secure, that you won't stop loving him just because he's going through a difficult patch, then it may give him the confidence to get through whatever it is that he's facing at the moment.

He paused. 'Maybe it *is* Darren,' he said. 'Maybe he just can't cope with the pressure any longer.'

*   *   *

That evening Paul headed for the White Hart yet again, and yet again, as before, angrily and systematically got himself blind drunk. His next-door neighbour, Trevor, and another friend dragged him home at two in the morning, legless and vomiting. Chris had waited up for his arrival and gently and tenderly put him to bed. By now some of the alcohol had worn off and Paul was in the morose phase, the self-abasing, self-deprecating, apologetic phase of drunkenness.

'What's the matter?' Chris said to him.

'Nothing... I am sorry Chris, really I am... I am... Oh, please help me, Chris. I do love you... I am sorry... I don't mean to hurt you...'

Chris held both his hands tightly.

'*Please* tell me what's the matter.'

Paul turned his head away from her as she got into bed beside him. For once Chris was lost for words, then, ignoring the stink of alcohol on his breath and his mild but ineffectual protestations at the intrusion upon his life, gently but firmly she did the only other thing that she could think of to convince Paul that he was loved and that she loved him more than anything else in the world—she held him, clutched him, cuddled him, caressed him. Sometimes she had to hold him as one would a child having a tantrum, to stop the arms and the legs hitting or kicking in anger: sometimes she had to touch him to make him open up instead of withdrawing his arms and legs into a foetal position, but gradually her physical caresses, her concern, and her love for him broke through and at long last he responded to her intimacies, changed by her constant loving attention from the hurt, withdrawn, frightened creature that he had become. It took her a long time, a time during which she was constantly caressing him, touching him, giving herself to him, telling him by deeds not words that he really was loved—and that he was worthy of her love, too, whatever had happened, whatever his problems were.

Gradually the intimacies progressed until at last Paul wanted Chris as well. It wasn't the most elegant love-making Paul had ever taken part in. For a start the alcohol had given him the colloquially named brewer's droop, which didn't help at all—but that just made Chris more determined than ever to make sure that they'd finish what she'd started.

They lay there for nearly two hours, touching and being touched, loving and being loved. Afterwards when it was all over Paul looked

straight into her eyes, mouthed the one word 'Thank you' and
promptly burst into tears.

With the exception of that celebrated concert the day before the
first harvest, Chris had never seen Paul shed even the beginnings of
a tear, but now he lay in bed against her, tears pouring down his
cheeks, heaving great convulsive sobs. Chris simply held him
against her as tightly as she could. It lasted twenty minutes, after
which the sobs became less frequent and less deep, and eventually
Paul drifted off to sleep. By now Chris was physically exhausted but
alert, her mind in a whirl. She lay back on the pillow, staring at the
ceiling, wishing that sleep would come and finding that it wouldn't.
Every few minutes she would turn her head to look at the drunken,
smelly body lying beside her and more than once she turned over to
touch him on the arm or the shoulder or the trunk knowing that even
though the conscious part of him couldn't feel her, maybe subcon-
sciously he could sense her presence and could be more secure and
more supported by it.

'Oh Paul,' she said, more than once looking at the snoring head
three inches away from her nose, 'what *is* the matter with you?'

- 26 -

*T*he war council met the next day, both to debrief Kevin and to
consider the options available to them. It turned out that Kevin's trip
had been remarkably successful. As far as he was aware he'd gone
completely undetected, and the information he'd acquired was first-
rate.

The first night he'd travelled to within three miles of Buckingham, hidden his bike carefully and had found somewhere safe to
stay, where he could observe what was going on during the day but
where he himself wouldn't be spotted.

He'd chosen the most obvious, and yet the most unobvious place
in which to secrete himself—in the gaol, right in the centre of the

town! He knew already that the cells had no keys and that in the old days prisoners were locked in simply by an outside catch on each cell door. Vince had already told them that the hostages had at first been kept in the gaol, but following a rescue attempt in which they had simply been let out of their cells by a brave intruder, the bikers had realised how insecure the place was and had moved elsewhere. Kevin had guessed—rightly—that no one would be using the gaol for anything else, so in the dead of night he made his way there.

He found it to be a big, castellated building with thick stone walls and an outside door that would keep a marauding army out for a considerable time. However, a chain is as strong as its weakest link, and just as householders fortify their front doors with ironwork that wouldn't look amiss in the Tower of London yet leave the back door guarded by a tiny three-tumbler lock, the gaol was equally vulnerable: at some time before the plague a tourist office had been created, let into the east wall, with a front door to the street and a back door opening into the gaol's exercise yard. In turn this led to the corridor containing the cells.

Getting inside the gaol was a doddle. The front door of the tourist office wasn't even locked, and the back door was shut and locked—but from inside the office! All Kevin had to do was unlock it with the key provided and go through. Cautiously he walked into the small exercise yard in the centre of the gaol, looking up at the sky which showed as a slightly lighter patch against the high-walled blackness of the gaol building surrounding him. Looking and listening intently, he crossed the courtyard and tried the door leading to the main corridor. It wasn't even shut properly.

Silently he padded inside, finding himself in a high-ceilinged corridor, with an internal gallery above him reached by stone steps on his left. On the right was a row of four gloomy cells which backed onto the exercise yard: above him, off the gallery, was a second row of four cells. Silently Kevin climbed the stone steps, went to the far end of the gallery, and let himself into the end cell, having first made sure that the outside catch couldn't slip down inadvertently. Then he settled down to sleep.

He woke late, as little light came into the cell from the small window overlooking the exercise yard. Cautiously, he let himself out onto the gallery again, glad to find that the cell door still opened! After that, from time to time he risked going out of the cell, down through the exercise yard and into the tourist office, from which he could furtively observe the comings and goings within the town.

The tourist office was useful. Not only had it been his means of entry into the gaol, but it contained a good number of maps of the town. He collected a few for use later in planning: one he kept as his own personal copy, which he marked up as he discovered various prime locations.

His big stroke of luck came that afternoon. Hidden behind the wall at the front of the shop, he managed to overhear some of the conversations of the residents as they passed in front of him in the street. The front of the tourist office seemed to be a natural place for the people to stop and talk, and Kevin picked up a number of clues in the process. He also saw some of the bikers, grandly and arrogantly zooming around the town on their machines, grinning as they aimed their bikes at groups of the residents who had to run to get out of the way. They reminded him of the SS guards he'd seen in war films of the concentration camps.

Kevin waited until long after night fell, then, dressed in his black biking gear, skulked off under the cover of the shadows to reconnoitre more widely, returning before dawn to his hiding place.

For two nights Kevin stayed in the gaol watching, and waiting. Then on the third night he slipped out of his cell for the last time to investigate the western end of the town which seemed to be the direction from which the bikers came and went.

It was then that he had his second big stroke of luck, for he stumbled almost immediately on the place where they were keeping the hostages. They were simply using a house, but a well-selected one for all that, situated near the river in an estate of houses of similar design. It was a three-storey affair with patio doors at the back and ample space upstairs to keep the hostages, whom Kevin could see from time to time, walking round inside. The four bikers were using the house next door as their base, with one biker—with shot-gun—

on duty at the front of the hostages' house at all times. Kevin wondered why the hostages couldn't escape until he realised how effectively they were locked in: the glass in patio doors may be transparent, but it will resist a sledgehammer, and window locks can be used to keep the occupants *in* as much as intruders *out*. In addition, because it was a three-storey house it would be a very dangerous task indeed to escape from one of the uppermost windows, even if it could be opened or broken: the drop to the ground would probably kill or disable anyone attempting to get out that way. And the siting of the house was such as to give the guard a clear view of all approaches, and adequate warning of any attack.

Yes, the house had been very well chosen indeed.

Having achieved all he set out to do, Kevin had made his getaway, slipping back to his bike just as secretively as he had arrived. It was undisturbed. At four-thirty in the morning he started it up and roared off into the night. If any of the Buckingham residents heard him they would have assumed it was one of the bikers and left it at that, asking no questions. (It didn't do to ask too many questions in Buckingham.)

When Kevin finished his story, Paul—who had been listening attentively, despite the blinding headache from yet another hangover—leaned back in his chair, thinking hard and sucking the end of a pencil. He opened his mouth to speak but the Major beat him to it.

'I have to say,' he said a little gruffly, searching carefully for the right words, 'that was as good a piece of reconnaissance as any I've ever seen in my professional career. Well done lad, well done.'

Kevin sniffed. He was going down with the beginnings of a cold, courtesy of the three bitter nights he had spent out in Buckingham. 'Does that mean I get my money now?' he said, wiping his nose on the back of his hand. 'It was freezing in that there gaol.'

Paul glared at him, but not quite so acidly as usual. He was developing a sneaking respect for Kevin, who always seemed somehow to come up with the goods. He leant forward again to study the map Kevin had carefully prepared. It was all creased and rumpled, a function of being kept for a considerable time in the back pocket of Kevin's jeans. Then he puzzled over the hand-drawn map of the estate where the hostages were kept, brow furrowed, headache banging away inside his skull.

'Where did you say the dairy was?'

What on earth has a dairy got to do with it? thought Kevin, but pointed at the map anyway.

'There,' he said truculently, looking puzzled.

Paul sucked on his pencil again. 'Right,' he said at last, 'here's my plan.'

*   *   *

Two hours later they'd finished. Then they disbanded, each to go his own way—Kevin to spend his new-found riches, and Paul to the White Hart again. With every step from the meeting he seemed to get angrier and more morose, with a tightness about his mouth that no one had seen before. No one knew, no one suspected what was going on in his mind: and had they known, they wouldn't have believed it anyway. All he could think of—when he wasn't concentrating on rescuing the hostages—was The Mikado and the Lord High Substitute. It dominated his thinking, looming over him like a cliff that was about to topple over and crush him.

If he hadn't got drunk he would probably gone back to using cocaine or morphine; but he was wiser now, and wasn't going down that road again. Or he could have got into a fight—which was, after all, what he was just preparing to do, but in an institutionalised way, in Buckingham—so at least that could let out some of the aggression within him.

With each step on the road his anger rose and rose until, as he walked through the front entrance of the White Hart he could cheerfully have picked up one of the bottles on the counter and flung it against the display of bottles behind the bar for sheer, unrestrained, tormented rage.

*   *   *

They brought him back at two o'clock again, legless; and again Chris was there to meet him, kindly and lovingly. This time he was so far gone that nothing would have roused him, so she put him to bed, cradled him in her arms and went to sleep herself. At least if he woke up during the night he would know that she was there, and that she cared.

The next evening was much the same except, surprisingly, he came back at ten-thirty; he didn't smell quite so much of drink and the eyes weren't so haunted and the mouth not quite so tight and set as before. This time he went straight to bed without a word, without even saying good night to her, and went to sleep, deliberately isolated and deliberately alone.

- 27 -

*M*artin was sitting in his study preparing the Passion Sunday service and, as usual, feeling totally guilty about the whole thing, when Paul knocked on the door. It was a surprise to see him there: the Old Rectory was out of everybody's way, which was why Martin had picked it in the first place. People didn't drop in while passing—they had to make a deliberate point of coming to see him.

Martin opened the door wide, wondering what it was about.

'You win,' said Paul, standing on the step.

'I what?' said Martin.

'You win.'

'I... er... don't... follow you. Come in anyway.' Martin closed the door behind them.

'As I said, you win.'

'Win *what*, Paul?'

'About Christianity. I've come to enrol. What do I do?'

Martin swallowed, thinking how totally unworthy he was to lead *anyone* to Jesus.

'You really mean it?'

'I don't say things like this for nothing, you know. Of course I mean it.'

'What brought this on?'

Paul told him—of the results of the chance conversation with him; and Emma, and the cow and the gate; of *The Mikado*, and how Ko-Ko's fateful words 'Lord High Substitute' had suddenly made him realise how it all fitted together; of how he'd spent the next ten days fighting furiously against it, and after a long and protracted struggle had finally chosen to give in and accept what at heart he now knew to be both inevitable and right.

'Do I have to be inducted into the church or something?' asked Paul. 'Or baptised? No. I've been baptised, haven't I? I was baptised as a child. Not that I remember. Does it mean anything? I mean, what do I do?'

'Do you want to follow Jesus, and live as his friend?' asked Martin.

'I should have thought that was obvious.'

'Are you sorry for the things you've done that God wouldn't want you to do?'

'Of course.'

'Would you like to start a new life with Jesus in charge?'

'Yes. How do I begin?'

'Just pray. Tell him that you're sorry for what you've done, that you acknowledge that he's Lord, and that from now on he'll be your master and you will do—try to do—what he wants.'

Paul stayed looking at Martin, attentive, waiting for the next instruction.

Nothing happened.

'*Is that all*?'

'Yes,' said Martin. 'And from that moment on you'll know that everything in your past has been forgiven, that you're starting a new life with Jesus in charge, and that you'll have a new future for which he's got a purpose.'

'I don't have to give away everything I own, wear sackcloth and ashes, or keep holy vigils at dead of night?'

For a minute Martin wondered whether Paul was winding him up, then decided that he wasn't and that Paul was both perfectly genuine and very confused about certain aspects of Christianity.

'It's much simpler than you're making out. Why don't we pray about it together?' he asked.

And so they did. Martin, still feeling guilty about his own past actions, yet at the same time amazed and privileged to be finding himself in this position, prayed with Paul, leading him to acknowledge that God was his Lord and Master, and also his friend, and to ask for forgiveness in the name of Jesus, that same Jesus who had come to die on the cross as Paul's personal Lord High Substitute. They only prayed for a short time—a couple of minutes or so—then Paul sat back, opened his eyes and smiled at Martin, a mixture of relief, peace and happiness. It was, thought Martin, the nicest smile he'd ever seen on Paul's face. Which was a pity, because about three seconds later it was wiped off almost completely.

'You realise of course what one of my first activities as a new member of the church?'

'No?'

'I'm probably going to have to go out and kill someone.'

Martin looked puzzled.

'The hostages... remember?'

Martin's face registered it all and for a moment was lost for words.

'Oh...' They never said anything about *this* at theological college! He struggled for the right thing to say, jaw working, but no sound coming out, like a badly dubbed film. 'Not the easiest thing for a new convert to do, I suspect,' Martin sighed eventually. 'Life isn't the pretty, easy thing it's made out to be in the films, is it? Not even Christian life.'

*   *   *

Paul told Chris what had happened, of course, and embraced her and hugged her and thanked her for being so loving and understanding while he'd been so repulsive over the past ten days. She was just glad to have him back, buried her head on his chest and hugged him tightly and he hugged her. Finally he extricated himself. 'I must get on, Chris,' he said. 'We've got a lot to plan.'

'When's D-Day?' she said.

'Five days, we think. There's lots to do before then. I'd better be going.' He walked up the path to the gate. She waited at the door, paused, then ran after him.

'Paul...' He turned round, one hand on the gate. She ran up to him, squeezed his other hand warmly, looked him in the eyes and then gave him a quick kiss. 'I'm so glad... Glad that you're happy.'

*   *   *

That week the Wednesday evening meeting had an additional member. As Paul entered the room he was warmly welcomed by the Higginbottoms. The Major was a little more reticent—after all, he couldn't get out of his head the idea that Paul was little more than a jumped-up yuppie, though he was gradually mellowing about it— no mean feat for a man in his seventies. On the other hand the Major did have a certain fixity about the way he looked at life, and in his eyes Paul had always been tainted after the episode with the pethi- dine. So the Major welcomed Paul politely, if a little guardedly, and they sat down to discuss the evening's topic.

As it happened that week they were finishing off a three-week study of Gideon, in the book of Judges: Martin didn't see any rea- son why they should change the format or content of the midweek group just because Paul had joined it, so rather than being sent down the usual road for a new convert of reading the Gospels, the Acts and then the Epistles before turning to the Old Testament, Paul found himself flung in at the deep end.

Paul found the meeting interesting—different, maybe, but quite fascinating. He enjoyed studying about Gideon too, and Gideon's faith in God; but as he walked slowly back down Holly Walk to his house he deliberately went on his own, contemplating deeply.

That evening Paul stayed up late, reading and rereading the story of Gideon, and thinking very hard indeed.

*   *   *

Palm Sunday approached and Martin, his mind on other mat- ters, for once failed to do much preparation for the service. It was, after all, a fairly standard service, one which came round with unfailing regularity! As a result, he got quite a shock.

The day was a typical late March day, bright but with a thin wind—the sort of day that promises much to come in spring and summer, but doesn't quite deliver it yet. There was a slightly bigger congregation than usual for the morning service and, as usual on Palm Sunday, Martin prepared to read the account of the entry of Jesus into Jerusalem, at the beginning of the last week of his earthly life.

Ever since the deepening of his personal faith which had occurred some two and a half years earlier, Martin had been delighted to find nuggets of information stored within the Bible in places that he'd never believed they could be. Like a yoke, which actually makes a burden lighter, not heavier. There were many references—often agricultural—to practices, events and ideas that previously had passed right over Martin's head, ideas which in an industrial world had seemed to have no importance, relevance or meaning. But now that they were living a more hand-to-mouth agrarian existence, many of these pictures came alive in front of him with a vividness all of their own.

Martin, however, was not in the mood for reading anything. Weighed down by his worries, constantly anxious that people would discover his awful secret, constantly insecure and almost frightened by his own shadow, he was having a very bad week of it, and this particular Sunday was even worse, the more so because the high days and holidays of the church merely served to emphasise how low he felt, how little he felt he belonged, and how much he felt he had no right to be doing what he was doing or even wear the vestments of his office.

As usual, in the middle of the service he began to read the gospel account of the triumphant entry of Jesus into Jerusalem, and how he had sent his disciples on ahead to find the donkey which had never been ridden before, on which he was to ride into Jerusalem.

It was as if the floor suddenly opened up in front of him. He suddenly felt a sort of dream-like quality coming over him—derealisation—and suddenly understood the implication of what was being said. In the distance he could hear his own voice continuing to read the gospel story, but all he could see in front of him was Seamus the horse and how it had taken him many, many painful hours to break him in with all the accoutrements of the riding school equipment: Seamus, like all animals to begin with, had not wanted to be ridden and it had taken a long time to get his confidence—to say nothing of a considerable number of painful meetings between rider and earth in the process. And yet here was Jesus, calmly riding on a donkey which had never been ridden before, and on which the only preparation was a cloth spread over its back! *How did he do it?* thought Martin. How *did* he do it? It just wasn't possible—normally that was.

In the distance he heard himself finish the rest of the gospel reading, and after a time lost the sense of derealisation. But he didn't lose his sense of wonderment, of another priceless nugget that had been lying there for centuries, waiting to be rediscovered.

*   *   *

The rescue attempt was planned for just after the time of the full moon: they needed some light, but not too much. Broad daylight was out of the question—and the pitch blackness of a moonless night was just as bad.

Peter had begun to assemble a list of somewhat obscure items from various parts of the town, including the police station. He didn't find what he wanted, so with a certain amount of trepidation decided to look for the remainder of the items in the police station at Kempston, risking the possibility that the plague was still active in the dead bodies that were still lying around. He stayed in voluntary isolation for the next three days, just in case, but thankfully remained well.

Then they packed, ready to set off for Buckingham. They were to take a long, circuitous route, finally coming in from the west, not the east, just in case their arrival was monitored.

When they were ready to go, the Peugeot was piled high with equipment, food and sleeping bags, with a long folding ladder on the roof-rack. Finally Paul went to consult Neil about the weather forecast.

And then they unpacked again. It was clear from the weather satellite that a string of fronts was coming in from the Atlantic and that clear skies and bright moonlight were certainly not going to be much in evidence over the next week.

Paul went off to Susan to make his apologies. They weren't going to get Darren back for at least another month—if, that was, they could get him back at all. By now it was April, and although the nights might be brighter, they were also shorter, which didn't give as much time for activity. Nevertheless the days were warmer, too, a distinct advantage when preparing to camp out without being able to light a fire or prepare hot food. Susan was understandably upset at the delay, but had by now become so numb and despondent about ever seeing Darren again—and as usual, blaming it all on Alan's lack of virility in not going off in the first instance to retrieve their son—that she barely commented.

She would just have to wait. There was nothing else to do.

- 28 -

*T*hey slipped out of the town in the middle of the night in the Peugeot, five of them in all. Paul was driving, with Peter in the front passenger seat. Kevin, David and Alan were squashed together in the back, with the equipment piled round their legs, on the roof, and in the rear end of the estate.

By then it was late May. The weather satellite had showed a minimum of cloud over the Atlantic, so at long last the rescue mission was on. Anne had been reluctant to let David come, but Paul had been very persuasive. After all, David and Darren had been very close—if nothing else they were next-door neighbours—and David wanted to do anything in his power to help free Darren.

So David went, and Anne watched him go with a mixture of pride and sheer terror. She'd already lost two of her family—was David going to be the third? Time after time she wondered whether or not she'd done the right thing in allowing him to go. But Paul had insisted that David had a talent which they needed, which was unmatched by anyone else in the community, and that they really couldn't do without him.

So Anne said goodbye, hoping and praying that she'd see him again, and wondering how on earth the five of them could rescue the hostages when they all knew the bandits had both guns and ammunition. The Ampthill residents might have guns but for them ammunition was a thing of the past.

They were all quiet in the car as they travelled on the long arc leading to Buckingham, each thinking his own thoughts.

During the preparations for the raid Peter had noticed a change in Paul, though he couldn't put his finger on quite what it was. Paul hadn't said anything to the others about his conversion, largely because he was still working through the experience and sorting out his life in a new and different direction, but the changes in him had already become obvious to others, even if they weren't always obvious to Paul himself. Like a seed that grows and bursts out from the confines of its original shell, so Paul's personality flowered, breaking out from under the confines of the mental sweatshirts that he'd been carrying around with him for so long, sweatshirts that had been confining his spirit and constricting his growth as effectively as if they had been a strait-jacket. Gone now was the inner gnawing uncertainty. Gone was the sense of not being loved, gone was the sense of insecurity, the need to prove himself. Gone was the dislike of himself that constantly had driven him on to prove himself better than other people, usually by humiliating them. Instead came a flowering of the intellect and abilities that Paul had, but a flowering that was humble, that didn't draw attention to itself. From now on Paul could have designed the best five-year plan for Ampthill, known that it was the best ever, but not bothered that it was he who had designed it.

It wasn't a big change, merely a subtle shift of emphasis—but the effect was like being on another planet. Suddenly, instead of the need to prove himself to all and sundry, Paul could get on with doing the things he was good at without worrying about what others thought, which made him even more centred and even more certain—not in a big-headed way but in a more confident way. Yet although he was undoubtedly an even bigger and more effective personality he was also more gracious and kindly—there was more largesse about him, more diffidence, and certainly more humility.

It was noticeable to the others more than it was noticeable to Paul. All that Paul knew was that instead of feeling fear he now felt a great calm. Previously he'd carried his psychological sweatshirt messages in layers. The first had said, 'Gee I'm great, I'm a wow in society.' The next layer down had said, 'Actually I'm not, everybody points at me, laughs at me and doesn't really like me.' The third sweatshirt had read, 'But I don't care.' The fourth layer had said, 'Yes I do, deeply.' The fifth quite simply had said, '. . . . . the lot of them,' but the next, the deepest, the one closest to Paul's personality, the one which was the thing that was nearest to his heart, had said, 'I'm so frail, so vulnerable that I'll do anything—*anything*—to avoid revealing the depths of my frailty.' This, the last message, had been so frightening and so deep that his conscious mind had never really known of its existence except in odd terrifying moments of anxiety and fear, and it was this message that had at long last disappeared, to be replaced, quite simply, by a message that read 'I *am* me, I *am* frail, not what I would like to be, often a failure, often unkind, but I am loved by Jesus for myself, warts and all, and therefore I am afraid of nothing.' And because this sweatshirt—this, the deepest message, the closest to Paul's heart and personality was now a positive, not a negative message, it didn't need to be wrapped up in other more superficial layers each protecting the next layer down, like codicils to a legal document, or subjunctive clauses in a simple sentence. Because at heart the deepest sweatshirt message had changed for the better, the others—the constricting strait-jacket sweatshirts—were no longer needed and were in the process either of being discarded, or else were burst asunder by the expanding personality welling up from within, blossoming out into the beautiful creature it was always designed and intended to be.

* * *

On that first night they crept in from the west, cautiously, quietly, with the lights on the Peugeot switched off, navigating solely by moonlight. It wasn't difficult. The moon was just past the full and once their eyes had become accustomed to the night they could see almost as well as if it had been daylight, except in black and white: colour vision in the eye only works in bright light. On through the night they rumbled quietly, unobtrusively, sweeping south and west, taking a huge detour in order to come in from exactly the wrong direction and retain the element of surprise. The roads, being country ones, were mostly clear, though there were some awkward moments with the odd knot of silent sepulchral cars, motionless, standing stark in the moonlight like metal tombstones—which in many cases was exactly what they were.

As they approached Buckingham the town seemed quiet, with no lights anywhere. They stopped shortly before they came to the town itself, found a convenient patch of woodland and drove the Peugeot in among the trees. At least it wouldn't be obvious there, unless someone were to stumble upon it directly. Then, taking their equipment, quietly and carefully they walked the remaining four miles into the centre of the town, moving noiselessly, in single file and without lights, guided by the dimming rays of the now-setting moon.

After a time Kevin motioned them to stop and beckoned to gather round. 'We're getting very near,' he whispered. 'The road to the hostages' house is on the left, round the next bend.'

'Why don't you and Peter go ahead and just check out that everything's all right?' whispered Paul. 'We'll wait here for you.'

Kevin and Peter disappeared off into the darkness—for by now the moon was low in the west behind them and the moon shadows were lengthening, obscuring much of the ground. Five minutes later they were back, two dark shapes detaching themselves from the blackness of the shadows.

Kevin waved the wrecking bar in triumph. 'We're in,' he said.

'That quick?' asked Paul.

'Yep,' said Kevin, pleased with himself.

'That's good. Well done. Let's get a move on before it gets light.'

Further down the road, Kevin again motioned them to stop. They were about to pass the opening to the estate, ahead, on their left.

'We're in full view of the hostage house when we cross the next road,' he whispered.

'Where's the house we're going to stay in?' asked Paul.

'Over there,' Kevin whispered. 'There's a back garden wiv a high fence round, so no one can see in.'

'You go first,' whispered Paul.

'OK.'

The estate was built in an elongated rectangle, with a central open area. The entrance to the rectangle was by the short road they were just about to cross, which widened and split as it entered the rectangle at one of its ends. Dimly at the other end they could see the house where Kevin had last observed the hostages.

It was quiet and unlit. Paul had a twinge of panic. Suppose the hostages weren't there? What if they'd been moved since Kevin was last here? He forced himself not to think those thoughts. You're crossing bridges before you even know there's a stream there, he thought to himself. Suddenly Kevin was gone, scurrying at a crouch across the road, conscious that for a brief moment he was in full view of anyone looking out of the hostages' house. The house he was aiming for was at the near end of the oblong, on the short side of the rectangle, directly opposite, but some way from, the hostage house. Warily, out of the corner of his eye Paul could see the back garden gate open briefly and then close behind the crouching figure.

Peter was next with Alan, at either end of the collapsible ladder. Before they left the shelter of the shadows to venture across the road they'd spent a few minutes glancing anxiously at the moon. There wasn't much cloud about, but for a few moments a wisp of it obscured the moon more than usual, and taking advantage of the dimmer light, Peter and Alan carefully crossed the road, desperately hoping that the ladder wouldn't make any form of metallic noise or bang against anything.

Then it was David's turn.

'You go next,' whispered Paul in his ear. 'Take care.' David started to cross the road, tripped, stumbled and fell flat on his face, inadvertently giving off an 'Ooooof' as his chest hit the ground. The noise seemed to echo round the empty estate. For a moment Paul's heart stood still. Any minute now, he thought, there would be lights, shouts, people giving the alarm. Winded, David lay prone on the ground, not daring to move, glancing anxiously up the road and into the square. There was no movement from within the hostage house. After what to Paul seemed like an eternity, David decided that he really hadn't been seen, struggled to his feet and limped across the road, through the back gate and into the garden.

For a full fifteen minutes Paul remained on the far side of the road before he dared try to cross it himself, thinking that if anyone had been awakened by the noise and chose to look out, that perhaps after this length of time they might decide that there really was nothing wrong, and go back to sleep again. Again choosing a moment when a stray wisp of cloud partly covered the moon, carefully and noiselessly he padded across the road, thankfully opened the back gate and let himself into the sheltered and secluded garden. The back door of the house lay open in front of him. He went inside, closing it quietly behind him, and jumped as a hand touched his shoulder. He whirled round.

'Where on earth did you get to?' asked Peter.

'Don't do that,' whispered Paul, clutching at his chest. It was all right. His heart was still going. Very quickly.

'Sorry. I wanted to make sure you didn't use a torch on the stairs. The landing has a window which looks directly out down the square.'

'No, I wasn't going to do that,' said Paul, letting go of the torch that he just happened to be feeling in his pocket. 'Is the house clear?'

'Yes, we checked.'

'Good. Where are we staying?'

'Top floor.'

There were three flights of stairs. When Paul finally got to the top he found Kevin, David and Alan already laying out their equipment in the room facing away from the square. Gratefully he put his rucksack down and stood up straight, stretching.

'First things first,' said Peter, grabbing the wrecking bar off Kevin. 'I'll go and do the floorboards.'

'No,' hissed back Paul urgently. 'Leave it. Do it during the daytime. Nobody notices noise during the day. At night it's a dead giveaway. Anyway we've made enough noise for tonight already,' he said, glaring at David who was glad that in the gloom no one could see that he'd gone pink.

'Sorry about that. I think I must have caught my foot on a manhole cover or something.'

'Never mind,' said Paul. 'I don't think anyone spotted us. Let's go and have a look, sh..'l we?'

'What, outside?' asked Alan.

'No,' whispered Paul, 'in the front room.' The five of them trooped out of the back room and carefully opened the door into the front bedroom. The window of the room looked out along the length of the estate to the hostage house at the far end.

The hostages' house was exactly similar to the one they had just entered. The building itself consisted of two semi-detached houses—tall ones, three storeys high, with a pair of double garages side by side in the middle at the front and a porch on the outermost side of each.

'The hostages are in the left-hand house,' whispered Kevin. 'At least, they were when I was last here.'

'That was a long time ago,' said Paul. 'They might have been moved since then. Have you seen any sign of movement?'

'Not yet,' said Peter. 'Alan was looking while we were waiting for you to get across the road.'

'We wouldn't really expect any movement at this hour,' said Alan. 'All sensible mortals are in bed asleep.' He yawned.

'Good idea,' said Paul. 'Alan—you, David and Peter get some sleep. I'll take the first watch.'

'Don't I sleep?' said Kevin.

'No, I need you for a bit,' said Paul. 'I want you to tell me where everything is. Have you got the field glasses?'

'Right here,' said Peter handing them to him. 'As I said, we couldn't see any sign of activity.'

'You three go and kip down,' repeated Paul in a whisper.

When the others had left the room he turned to Kevin. 'Is this the best place to observe from? What about downstairs?'

'The window sill's higher here,' said Kevin. 'Less chance we'll be spotted.'

Careful not to go too near the window in case he could be seen, Paul found that if he stood on the bed he could get a good view whilst being right at the back of the room and in the least visible position.

'OK,' said Kevin. 'They're all in that end house, on the left—or they were last time I came.'

'Got it...' said Paul, surveying it carefully, minutely with his glasses, letting them travel slowly from the ground floor up to the roof. The houses were made of brick, with imitation slate roofs in a simple inverted V-shape front to back.

'They've got a guard-room at the front—one of the bandits always sleeps there. I've never seen any of the hostages come out, but there's always a guard just inside the door.'

'Where are the hostages then?'

'Upstairs. First and second floors.'

'Maybe they've barricaded the stairs,' said Paul, thinking out loud, 'or cut them down. That would do just as well, wouldn't it? Where do the rest of the bandits stay?'

'The house next door.'

'What do you mean—the right-hand of the pair at the end—the semi-detached house attached to the hostage house?'

'Nah,' said Kevin. '*Next door*. Next building. Next house. In the corner on the right.'

'Got it,' said Paul again surveying it minutely. It was exactly the same design. His eyes travelled slowly up to the roof. Ground floor—garage and front door; second floor—two large windows; third floor—two much smaller windows.

Suddenly outside the window a sparrow started twittering, sounding so loud that it made the two of them jump. Kevin looked at the sky which was lightening almost imperceptibly. 'Dawn's coming.' After a moment the sparrow was joined by another, and another: then other birds joined in until the noise reached a crescendo—the dawn chorus, nature's alarm clock.

The two stayed there, yawning, for the next hour, waiting for any sign of life.

'Are you sure this is the right place?' said Paul putting his glasses down for the umpteenth time.

'Of course I'm sure,' said Kevin. 'Whaddya you take me for?'

'No, I didn't mean it like that,' said Paul.

'Well, it sounded like it.'

'It wasn't... I just meant... Are you sure we've got the right estate? Houses can look very similar, you know, especially in the middle of the night.'

'Course I'm sure,' whispered back Kevin, crossly. 'I was here long enough, wasn't I?'

'Yes, all right, I'm sorry.'

They surveyed the house again. 'Maybe they've moved on,' said Paul. 'No, hold on... No, you're right. There they are. Look.' He pushed the glasses at Kevin who put them to his eyes and saw movement at the first floor window of the hostage house. Someone was standing behind the glass, stretching and yawning.

'Darren,' said Kevin, handing Paul the glasses.

'Are you sure?' said Paul. Kevin looked at him.

'Why is it that whenever I do something, you say, "Are you sure"? *Yes I am.*'

Paul almost didn't hear him as he was concentrating too hard.

'You're right, it *is* Darren.'

'I told you I was right,' mumbled Kevin. Paul put down the glasses.

'I'm sorry Kevin, I really didn't mean to criticise you. I really didn't mean that I thought you'd got it wrong. What I actually meant was, have they moved on since last you saw them?'

'Ah well, that's all right then,' said Kevin, sniffing. 'If that's what you really meant,' he added, in a tone which implied that that was probably *not* what Paul had meant.

But Paul had his glasses to his eyes again. 'And here comes the guard...' In the sunlight which was now pouring into that end of the

square, Paul could see one of the bikers, Adam, come out of the corner house, go across in front of the pair of double garages and knock
on the front door of the hostage house, on the left. He waited, then
knocked again. The door opened and the tousled, unkempt and
totally unmistakable figure of Lew materialised in the doorway. The
two conversed. Paul stared down the binoculars, desperately trying
to make out whether there was any urgency about the conversation,
any indication that their presence might be suspected. Adam
seemed agitated and kept pointing at the first-floor window above
him. Paul's heart sank. They're on to us, he thought. They know
we're here, they know we're coming. We've lost our element of surprise.

The discussion continued. Then Lew walked to the bottom of the
short drive, turned round to face the hostage house and through the
glasses Paul could clearly see him indicating to Darren to get away
from the window. Reluctantly Darren obeyed. The animated—and
to Paul, quite silent—conversation between Lew and Adam continued, with the body language clearly indicating that Lew was telling
Adam off for not impressing on the hostages who was boss.
Eventually Adam replaced Lew as guard, leaving Lew to wander
across to the bandits' house, presumably to have some breakfast.

'OK Kevin,' said Paul, putting down the glasses, 'you've done a
great job...'

'That's what I told you,' said Kevin, sniffing.

'No, I mean it... Anyway, time for you to get some sleep now. I'll
take the first watch.'

'Suits me,' said Kevin, shambling into the back bedroom, opening up his rucksack and eating a couple of biscuits before getting
into his sleeping bag.

Paul stayed in the back of the front room, observing for hour
upon hour, watching how the bandits worked, seeing them as they
came and went: noting the hour when they brought food into the
hostages, who were obviously locked in at all times. Yes—unbreak-
able patio doors and window locks can make a very effective prison,
he thought to himself. And doubtless the bandit on duty downstairs
has some form of weaponry with him at all times.

At about eleven o'clock Adam was replaced by Frankie, who seemed much the weakest personality of the four of them: straight afterwards Lew, Adam and Den got on their bikes and, carrying their shot-guns, roared up the road towards Paul. For about the fifteenth time that day Paul's heart skipped a beat, and he was halfway off the bed and into the other room to warn the others that an attack was coming when he realised that the sound of the bikes was fading in the distance as they roared off towards the centre of the town.

He looked at his watch. It was time to wake one of the others. He went into the back room and gently he shook Peter, who took some time coming to. He'd been dreaming of his wife and children again, as he had every night since they'd died in the plague, and his face fell visibly when he realised that he was back in the land of... well, the living, but not necessarily the ones he wanted to be living. Paul knew how much Peter had missed his family and had mourned for them, and suddenly felt humbled by the degree to which Peter obviously cared for and loved the family that was no longer able to love him back.

'Time to do the floorboards. Warn the others, would you?'

Quickly Peter woke the rest of the sleeping group. 'Floorboard time,' he said to each of them. Sleepily they raised themselves into consciousness and then one by one went to the various windows in the top of the house to keep watch. Meanwhile Peter and Paul pulled back the carpet to uncover the rectangles of pressed board that formed the floor. Using the wrecking bar, they levered up a board. The nails shrieked as they were prized out of their places in the supporting joists. Paul stiffened, listening. The watchers at the windows anxiously surveyed the square outside and the main road behind, but there was no one there. No one moved, no one raised the alarm. Gently letting out his breath—as if the process of simply breathing might draw attention to their presence—Paul tried again. There was a further prolonged squeak, and then the board was free at one end. Holding the flashlight Peter anxiously scanned the joists underneath. He looked up. 'Front to back, as we thought.'

'Are you sure?' said Paul, ducking his hand under the board for confirmation. 'OK, let's put it back.' They levered the board more or less back into position, pressed it down with their heels, then put the carpet back over the top. 'Anyone hear us?' he hissed.

'Well, we heard you,' said Alan, 'and probably the whole of Buckingham if the truth were known—at least that's what it sounded like.'

'No,' said Paul irritated, for by now he was getting extremely tired. 'You know what I mean.'

'Yes, I know what you mean,' said Alan wearily. 'No, not a dickie bird.'

'Right,' said Paul, 'I'm shattered. Time for some kip.'

*   *   *

It grew hot in the house that day as the five of them rested, watched and waited. While Paul slept, Alan and Peter took careful note of all the activities that went on in both the hostages' house and the house that the bandits were using as their own residence. Once or twice a couple of people—presumably Buckingham residents though none of them recognised who they might be—tried to get into the square to attract the attention of the hostages but were quickly shooed away by whichever bandit was on duty. Presumably, thought Alan sadly, they were relatives of the hostages hoping to get a glimpse of them, to wave, to pass on a greeting, or just to be near each other.

It was a hot May day. They couldn't open the windows, of course, as it would have been an instant give-away that there was someone in the house so they had to sit and swelter, all the time watching through the sunglasses and waiting.

At eight o'clock they woke Paul with the news that nothing much had happened since he'd gone to sleep. The hostages had been brought some food at about seven o'clock, and the guard had been changed twice more, but that was all.

It had begun to get cool again with that same odd weather so common in May, hot days and cold nights, made especially cold because the sky was cloudless and the heat of the earth was radiating back off into space. For the next hour they went over their plans, yet again rehearsing the roles each of them had to take and the jobs each had to do. In the distance the sun was setting, throwing the hostage house into silhouette and temporarily blinding them as they looked almost straight into its rays.

And then it was night. For half an hour candles showed in the bandits' house and also in the hall of the hostages' house, where presumably the current guard was sitting: the hostages didn't seem to be allowed any light at all. Presumably they weren't worth wasting candles on, thought Peter bitterly, wondering what it must be like inside the building after so many weeks and months.

Before the plague everyone had lived according to the clock and with the benefits of electric light had been enabled to stay up long after sunset, often going to bed well past midnight. Since the plague, and in the absence of electricity—especially in Buckingham—the hours of rising and going to bed had changed to be more in tune with the daily rhythm of natural light and darkness. In summer, sunset was the time to go to bed. There were no lights on in the town after half past ten, and by eleven Paul judged that they could get started. 'You're sure about the dairy?' he whispered yet again to Kevin.

'Of course I'm sure,' said Kevin scornfully. 'Why do you keep asking?'

'I just want to check things, that's all. I told you, it's nothing personal.'

'Nah,' said Kevin. 'I believe you. Farsands wouldn't.'

'OK, Alan,' said Paul, looking at his watch. 'Time you were off. Let's synchronise our watches, shall we?'

Quietly Alan gathered up his equipment, padded softly downstairs, cautiously checked from the doorway to see that no one was watching, and then let himself out of the back door. Checking much more carefully as he inched open the back gate, he looked up and down the street then padded off silently in the direction of the town centre. It was much darker than the night before—for a start, the moon always rises fifty minutes later than the time of moon-rise on the previous day, and in addition was by now well past the full, so that the amount of light it gave off was much less.

The minutes ticked by at a snail's pace. If Paul looked at his watch once he looked at it thirty times during the next forty-five minutes, amazed that three-quarters of an hour could ever pass so slowly. Kevin kept on the lookout, his eyes glued on the hostage house.

Paul was in the process of checking his watch yet again when there was a hiss from Kevin. Then Paul saw it too—a brief flash of light from a torch coming from the top of a short rise behind the hostage house.

'He's there.'

'OK everyone. Alan's in position. Let's go.'

They gathered up all their equipment, bulky though it was and cautiously and carefully went downstairs, letting themselves out this time not by the back, but by the front door, fanning out into the shadows until they had taken up their positions halfway along the square.

All except Paul. Paul had a job to do. Taking the top off a small tin from his rucksack, he went into the front lounge, and emptied its contents liberally over the furnishings and the sofa. When he'd finished the whole place reeked of petrol. Opening the windows for good measure he went outside and checked his watch. A minute to go. He could hear the beat of his heart pounding loudly in his ears—so much so that he began to think it would be audible to others in the square. While he waited, he used the remaining forty-five seconds to collect his thoughts and—a novel event for him—to offer a brief prayer for the success of their mission and that it would achieve its object with a minimum of violence. He remembered what Sir Jacob Astley, a commander in the English Civil War, had prayed before the Battle of Edgehill: 'O Lord! thou knowest how busy I must be this day: if I forget thee, do not thou forget me', and mouthed it silently. It would have to do.

The second hand crawled up towards twelve on the dial. Using one of their last matches, Paul lit a piece of rag, tossed it through the open window and dropped to the ground. It was a good job he did so, as by then much of the petrol had vaporised. It didn't catch fire as much as explode with a satisfying whoomph and a shower of glass from one of the windows just above his head. Within seconds the front room was an inferno. Those who have never seen a house fire usually imagine it must start quite slowly, gathering momentum. It doesn't. It starts very quickly indeed—especially when helped by petrol—and simply gets faster from there on.

In seconds the whole of the front room was blazing fiercely, flames licking out of the window. A spiral of smoke drifted upwards from the doomed house. Paul crawled along in front of the open window and then ran as fast as he could round the border of the square in order to avoid being silhouetted against the flames. In front of him the hostage house was garishly illuminated in the yellow light and he could see faces of the hostages pressed against the windows in the upstairs rooms as they climbed across to see what had happened. Good, thought Paul. Any moment now...

The four were ranged across the square about half way along, lying flat on the ground. There was still no response from the downstairs guard who was probably still asleep so, feeling around, Paul picked up a handful of gravel and flung it as hard as he could at the downstairs windows. His aim was good and the gravel landed with a satisfying rat-tat-tat against the glass of the door and the hall.

And then it happened. The door opened and a sleepy, tousled and much bemused Adam poked his head out, gun in hand, looking anxiously at the fire that had appeared as if by magic in the square immediately opposite him. Rubbing his eyes to get rid of the sleep he stared around uncomprehendingly.

'Now,' hissed Paul and at the same instant four powerful battery spotlights—courtesy of the police stores at Kempston—were switched on, picking out Adam as he stood helplessly in front of the door. In the dark each of the four assailants rolled over quickly until he came to the next lamp that he had placed a few minutes earlier on the ground, switched it on, rolled over again and switched on yet another set of lamps.

It all happened too quickly for poor Adam. Three minutes earlier he'd been asleep in his bed in a quiet house dreaming of Harley-Davidsons, then suddenly the house opposite had exploded in flame and now there were twelve flashlights pointing at him.

The bullhorn in Peter's hand crackled into life as he pressed the 'speak' key. Old habits die hard. He nearly started off by saying, 'This is the police,' but checked himself at the last minute. 'Drop your gun,' he said imperiously. 'You are surrounded. We won't harm you but you are heavily outnumbered. Step forward and drop your gun.'

Curt and imperious. Police-speak. Commands, not requests. Police-speak doesn't sound good on television programmes, thought Paul, thinking back to the awkward way in which the police often came across in interviews, but it worked brilliantly in situations like this.

Still half asleep, Adam jerked as if stung, but the gun stayed in his hand.

'Put down the gun,' said Peter's curt, clipped voice through the megaphone. Adam's jaw dropped. He wasn't a brave person—in fact like most bullies he was a very weak person indeed—and when faced with what appeared to be odds of at least twelve to one, (never mind however many were standing behind the men with the lights) he knew when to give up. He dropped the gun.

As he did so he became aware of a peculiar noise from behind him—a sound as if of an avalanche. But his attention was swiftly brought back to the front of the house.

'Now step forward,' hammered the voice out of the darkness. 'Put your hands in the air. You are in no danger as long as you do what we say.'

Adam obeyed.

'Lie down.'

Paul raced forward with one of the plastic handcuffs that Peter had given him, quickly pinned Adam's hands together behind his back, then with a loop of wire, tied his feet together and pulled his heels towards his hands so that he was trussed up, totally unable to move.

Dimly Paul could hear shouting from the bandits' house and was aware of Peter speaking again through the megaphone, but the sound he was really listening for was coming from behind the hostages' house. At least, he *thought* he could hear it. He wasn't sure because without warning there was a bang from behind him as a shot-gun went off from the direction of the bandits' house, and a peculiar whizzing noise filled the air, as though he'd just been buzzed by a small, silent aircraft.

*   *   *

When Alan left the security of their temporary accommodation at eleven o'clock he had padded off, burdened with the aluminium ladder which had been carefully bound with cloth to stop it squeaking. Glad of the darkness he walked quickly along the streets, meeting no one and being challenged by no one, until he came to the dairy. There were a number of battery-powered milk floats inside the main shed, already loaded up for the morning's delivery the day the plague struck—before the owners, the drivers and everyone else had run for their lives.

He got into the driving seat of the front float, and taking out his torch quickly scanned the controls. They were simple enough. He put it into gear and pressed the accelerator pedal, but the cart just gave out a curious whimper, moved about a foot, and then shuddered to a halt. He went on to the second, which didn't even move at all. With a sinking heart Alan began to wonder whether he'd have to put the reserve plan into action—a plan that was much riskier, because it would be much noisier. He got into the third vehicle and, wonder of wonders, it whirred into life with that peculiar electrical noise that only milk floats make, a sound that is so completely associated with four-thirty in the morning, the noise of muffled feet along paths and the quiet clink of bottles on the doorstep.

The float was empty of crates, which saved him at least one job. Loading the ladder onto the back of the van and tying it down with rope he'd brought especially for the purpose, Alan got back into the driving seat and, without any lights on, drove the van quietly and carefully out of the yard and off down the road towards the hostage house, stopping after a quarter of a mile at an old building site where he loaded the van up with bricks, beams of wood and anything heavy he could lay his hands on. Then he set off again.

Almost noiselessly the milk float chugged along the road,

making its quiet whine, but without the clinking sound of bottles. Alan went slowly, avoiding all bumps and potholes in order to minimise any extra noise. He didn't go to the front of the house but instead took a back path which led to a small knoll above, behind and to one side of the house. In the pale moonlight he could see between the van and the house a short sweep of grass, then a low fence of thin wood. Noiselessly the float climbed the knoll and Alan turned it round to point directly at the house. Quietly he got out, taking the ladders, stepped over the fence and placed them on the ground well to the right.

He was early. Looking at his watch, he waited for a further five minutes until it was quarter to midnight, then lifting his torch twice and shielding it from the view of the hostage house looming large on his left, he winked it briefly in the direction of the house where they'd been staying, at the other end of the close.

As soon as he'd switched off the torch he looked round cautiously in case anyone had seen him or come to investigate. At first there was no sound, but then there was a sudden rustle in the hedgerow behind him and a snuffling noise. Alan whirled round, only to come face to face with a startled hedgehog which sniffed, and then wandered off with a curious panting, rustling noise, looking for snails and grubs. His heart beating wildly, Alan got back into the cab.

Suddenly he saw the mushroom of fire erupting from the downstairs window of the house they'd been living in, illuminating the close in its garish light. Still he waited. Nothing happened in the hostages' house. Then he saw the spotlights snap on, and heard Peter's voice, crisp and precise, coming through the bullhorn.

It was time for action. He waited thirty seconds, then started up the milk float. Getting it up to maximum speed, Alan charged down the knoll. The fence splintered, offering no resistance whatsoever to the combined weight of the milk float and its heavy load. Even in the short distance from the knoll to the house it had got up to quite a tidy velocity. Hoping desperately that by now all the hostages were awake and had been attracted to the front of the house by the fire and the noise—and hoping particularly that Darren was still a very light sleeper—Alan aimed the milk float for the back end of the side wall of the house and wedged the accelerator with a brick.

The float charged down the lawn towards the house and at the last minute Alan flung himself free, rolling into a ball to get out of the way as fast as possible. Still making its curious whining noise the float bounced over the flower beds and ploughed into the side wall of the house with a satisfying crump.

Brickwork looks strong, and *is* strong—very—so long as it's in a state of compression. Bricks can safely be used one on top of the other to build structures that are hundreds of feet high, but the minute brick or stonework is pulled—put into tension—it becomes very weak indeed. An earthquake knocks buildings over by putting them into tension—by vibrating them up and down, the mortar drops off the bricks and suddenly a wall that is solid becomes anything but.

Exactly the same happens when a wall is pushed hard by a heavy object. The pressure stretches the wall, and because masonry is very weak when stretched it starts to give way very quickly. The more the wall is buckled the more it fails.

As if in slow motion Alan watched it all happen. The milk float hit the side wall of the house at about twenty miles per hour—not a high speed, but enough, bearing in mind the momentum of its load. The side wall buckled, then caved in as the float buried itself in the back kitchen. For a moment Alan thought nothing was going to happen, and then gravity did the rest. With a dull roar the side wall of the house collapsed, both the outer brick wall and the inner block walls, as if they had been peeled off. It had happened almost noiselessly—at least, compared to the row that was going on at the front of the house. With a bit of luck, thought Alan, none of the bandits would realise what had happened.

He noted thankfully that the house had been built in exactly the same way as the house they had briefly occupied. The beams *did* run from front to back. His nightmare had been that he would take out the wrong wall, the one supporting all the first- and second-floor joists, and that the whole of the side of the house plus its occupants would cave in, throwing the hostages out on to the ground from some three floors up. But they had guessed correctly. Above him Alan could see the first and second floors still securely supported, the joists travelling across his field of vision from front to back of the house.

Inside the house the hostages didn't know which way to turn. At first they'd been attracted—as Paul had intended—towards the front of the house by the sight of the house in flames at the far end of the square, and by the commotion in the square beneath them. Then suddenly moonlight and fresh air had rushed in as without any warning the whole of the side wall of the bedrooms behind them had fallen away. Thankfully the hostages stayed where they were, petrified, unable to move, taken aback by this strange set of occurrences.

All the hostages were on the upper two floors. As Paul had surmised, Lew and his gang had cut away the lowest part of the stairs, marooning the hostages upstairs. The only method of communication had been a rope on a pulley to bring up food and water. Anyone who'd attempted to climb down had been severely beaten for his pains: they couldn't have got out anyway because all the ground floor doors and windows were locked, bolted and barred.

This method of keeping the hostages secure benefited the rescue operation: if the hostages couldn't get down, then by the same token the bandits couldn't get up. So there was time for them to effect an orderly escape, even for those on the top floor—before anyone was likely to be able to get up to the first-floor level and do anything about it.

Picking himself off the ground amid the clouds of dust emanating from the collapsed piles of brickwork, Alan ran across to where he had placed the ladder, hoisted it into the air and extended it. Securing the bottom of the ladder firmly, Alan placed the top against the first-floor floor-boarding, then, switching on his torch, ran up the ladder and waved the torch around in front of him. There was an instant clamour of voices but Alan motioned them to be silent.

'Quiet,' he said. 'With a bit of luck the guards still don't know what's happened. Quickly, all of you, down the ladder, and when you get to the bottom, get away. Go and hide. Just don't stop, don't hang around once you're out.'

He rushed up the stairs between the first and second floors, taking them two at a time, both to repeat his message and to make sure that everybody was awake.

It was only then that he finally took in the sight that was in front of him.

It was like Belsen. He'd expected to see healthy people waiting to get out but instead he saw thin emaciated wretches almost too weak to move. There were a few babies, some toddlers and the occasional older child staring at him dully, pleased that he'd come, but almost too tired even to get down a ladder to safety.

Alan couldn't afford to be polite—there was no time. Goading them, helping them, pulling them, pushing them, he guided them down the stairs to the first-floor level, then helped them down the ladder into the garden beneath and watched as they slowly dragged themselves up the knoll behind and off into the night.

Except for one. One of the hostages lay on the top floor on a bed in filthy conditions. Thin, emaciated, skeletal, she looked about fifty-five, except that she was twenty-two. Two of the fingers on her left hand were missing, and the hand itself was gangrenous and putrid. 'Come on,' said Alan, pulling at her other hand. 'Hurry up, you'll be late,' but she was cold, and very, very stiff...

He jumped as a hand descended on his shoulder.

'Hi Dad,' said Darren. 'I knew you'd come eventually.' Alan whirled round and played the flashlight on his son's face. The two briefly looked at each other and smiled and then hugged each other. Darren, who hadn't been held hostage as long as the others, hadn't got their skeletal look, but he was obviously weak and didn't look at all well.

'That's Sophie,' he said by way of explanation. 'She's only just died. Two days ago. She's Vince's wife. Remember?'

'No time to remember,' said Alan. 'Tell me later. Let's get you out first. Anyone else left up here?'

'Yes,' said Darren and from a cot in a corner he picked up a small bundle, a three-year-old with fair hair, thin legs and an emaciated face, and very, very deeply asleep. 'This is Tom,' he said by way of explanation. 'Sophie's son. I've been looking after him.'

'Here, let me have him,' said Alan.

'No, Dad, I can cope.'

'Are you sure? Are you strong enough?'

'Dad, I'm all right. *I'm* looking after Tom at the moment.'

They were the last three to go down the ladder—Darren, carrying Tom, followed by Alan. They were half-way down when the first shot rang out, the noise echoing off the faces of the buildings in the square.

- 29 -

*S*atisfied, Lew ducked his head back in behind the safety of the doorway. He'd never fired a shot-gun before—except as an act of bravado, and then it was up into the air—but to his delight one of the lights had disintegrated as the hail of shot poured into it. Hopefully, thought Lew as he quickly reloaded, that will have taken out one or two of the attackers holding the lights as well.

'I wouldn't do that again if I were you,' roared Peter's metallic voice down the bullhorn. 'You haven't hit anyone. Can I suggest that before you think about firing again you take a look at this?'

On cue, David, who had all this time been lying still, pinned to the floor, took aim with the crossbow and fired. There was a twang and with a peculiar whizzing noise the quarrel sped away to embed itself in the lintel over the front door, eighteen inches from Lew's head. The bullhorn crackled into life again but from a different position. Peter had rolled ten yards to his left, both to have a better view round the corner of the garage, and to give the impression, as did the lights, that there were a large number of people attacking the bandits.

'That's just for starters,' said Peter amiably, his voice roaring off into the night with the hard metallic edge and the occasional

whistle that bullhorns give off. Lew, who'd put his head round the
corner to try to work out what was going on, drew it back as if it
were spring-loaded. Almost immediately another quarrel—from
Kevin's crossbow this time—thudded into the woodwork above his
head, sticking in at almost 90° to the first.

'You will notice,' continued the bullhorn, 'that those two shots
came from completely opposite directions. You are surrounded.
Throw down your weapons and come out with your hands up.'

By now all the lights had now swung to illuminate the doorway
of the bandits' house. Inside the house Den, in a panic, was trying
to get out of the back door but Alan, realising what might happen,
had gone round and had put his torch on the hedge at the back of
the house, pointing towards the doorway. Anxiously Den withdrew
back into the house and went out of the front door again to where
Lew was standing, occasionally risking a glance round the edge of
the front of the garage.

'They're round the back as well,' Den whispered urgently to
Lew. 'We're surrounded. I'm going to surrender.'

'No, you're not,' hissed Lew. 'They can't hurt us. They can't
even shoot straight. Look, I've already taken out one of them at
least.'

'The trouble with a crossbow,' continued the bullhorn, inexorably, 'is that it makes no sound when it's fired and there's no
flash, so you don't know where it's being fired from. You can't work
out where are our marksmen are, can you?' Peter's voice developed
a harder edge to it. 'Now come on out, Lew. Put your guns down
and come on out with your hands in the air.'

'I don't believe you,' shouted Lew back. 'I don't believe you've
got marksmen. We've got guns. What good are bows and arrows
against that?'

'Where shall we put the next one?' roared the horn. 'I know. You
see the quarrel that's sticking out of the door-post just above your
head? Two inches to the left of that.'

Thanks, thought David looking down the sights. Of the two of
them—Kevin and David—David was much the better marksman,
renowned for being able to pick off a rabbit at two hundred yards.

But to hit a rabbit at two hundred yards, when it doesn't matter too much if you miss, is one thing; to put a second quarrel two inches from the first one, when your heart is beating and your hands are shaking, is another matter altogether. But the challenge had been laid down, and David was not one not to ignore a challenge. Lining up carefully along the telescopic sight he'd built on his apparatus— which seemed all the deadlier for being home-made—cautiously he squeezed the trigger. The same whizzing noise swept through the air as the quarrel embedded itself deeply in the woodwork, two inches to the left of the first quarrel.

Hidden behind the return wall of the garage and squeezing himself into whatever protective space he could, Lew swivelled his head round to see where the quarrel had struck. He gulped.

'I've had enough,' shouted Den behind him. 'I'm coming out,' and to Lew's fury, he rushed out into the open. As he advanced beyond the end of the garage four lamps swivelled to pick him out, an almost unnecessary action, because the light from the burning house—which was now fully alight on all of its three floors—was quite enough to show him up in its garish yellow light.

'Put your hands up and lie down,' came Peter's clipped tones from yet another position. Crouching, Paul ran across to Den and trussed him up as he had trussed Adam three minutes earlier, though by now it seemed half a lifetime away.

Frankie was the next to give in. There was nothing that the fuming Lew could do as the scared face of Frankie ran past him.

Three down and one to go.

'Come on out, Lew.'

'All right, I'll come,' shouted a voice. 'Don't shoot,' and round the corner of the garage came the bulky, burly figure of Lew, still clutching his shot-gun.

'Stop, where you are.'

But Lew didn't stop.

'Stop where you are or we fire.'

Still Lew didn't stop. Kevin fired at him—but missed, the quarrel whizzing past the back of Lew's head—and Lew was still coming.

It was in that instant that David realised for the first time that life and videos are not the same thing. In the videos the heroes would have shot—probably from the hip—the man who was threatening them and what's more, would have shot him without compunction, and without a second's thought.

Only it doesn't work like that in real life. David had his sight fixed on Lew's head—on Lew's left eye, to be precise. He wanted to pull the trigger. He knew he'd been asked to pull the trigger but there was something inside him that prevented him, that told him not to do it, that refused to pass the message on down the nerves to his finger. It was always all very well David locking on to a rabbit and pulling the trigger, but doing it to a man was very, very different. When it came to it, David found he couldn't bring himself to kill.

On the far side of the square, and furious with himself for missing at such a crucial moment, Kevin reloaded—but it takes time to pull back the string on a crossbow, fit the quarrel, bring the stock back up to the shoulder, then take aim and by the time he was ready Lew was another ten yards nearer.

'Stay where you are,' bellowed the voice from the bullhorn. Suddenly Lew pulled the shot-gun up to firing position and let fly again in the direction of the only thing he could be certain of. He couldn't see the two archers—he didn't know how many there were, for that matter. Not all the lights moved, so he couldn't be quite sure who was behind them or not, but he knew for certain that there was someone behind the bullhorn, someone goading him, someone annoying him, someone telling him to do things that he didn't want to do, and so in blind fury and anger and panic and guilt, with the knowledge that his whole world was crumbling round his ears, and with the last action of a despairing man Lew let fly in the direction of the bullhorn.

That second shot was what did it for David. It's one thing to kill a man in cold blood. It's quite a different matter when your own life and that of your friends is at stake. But still he couldn't pull the trigger when the cross wires were over Lew's head. Almost instinctively he dropped his aim a few inches down and a foot and a half in front. With a twang the quarrel sped away, transfixing Lew's right arm, and pinning it to the stock of the shot-gun. At the same time Kevin let fly from the opposite direction, hitting Lew squarely in the side of the left thigh, the quarrel embedding itself completely in Lew's fat and oversized leg. With a howl Lew collapsed, writhing, on the ground, his hand convulsively pulling again on the trigger, but by then the gun was pointing uselessly skywards and the shot roared off in the general direction of the moon. Simultaneously Kevin and Paul leapt on Lew, pinning his arms and binding his feet as Lew screamed out in agony. Injured he might have been, but he was still strong enough to thrash around. Paul called out to Peter to come and help them but eventually he and Kevin managed to tie the writhing figure up on their own.

'Thanks for your help, Peter,' called out Paul tartly—and then wished he hadn't, for out of the blackness a shaking David appeared, aware not just of what he'd done to another fellow human being, but also knowing that an instant before, Peter had taken the full force of the last but one shot on his head and face, and had died instantly, his head pulped by the blast, spraying David with his blood in the process. For a minute Paul thought that David had been hit, and that this was why he was staggering, but he soon realised that David was safe—in body, at least.

'*If only I'd fired earlier,*' David kept on saying, anguish written all over his face. 'If only I'd hit him before he fired at Peter. I could have. I had him in my sights...' and he sat down on the low wall at the front of one of the houses and began to shake uncontrollably.

- *30* -

*I*t was a slow and miserable homecoming. The raiding party's relief at releasing the hostages—and especially the knowledge that Darren was safe—was tainted with their almost unbelievable grief at the death of Peter, and the knowledge that Sophie, Vince's wife, was dead also.

The noise of the battle woke many of the Buckingham residents, who converged on the site in droves once word got out that the hostages had been released. Though Vince was overjoyed to see Tom back again, his grief on hearing of his young wife's death was pitiful to see. Paul was left empty, knowing that had they made the attempt a month earlier, as planned, Sophie would still be alive. Correction, he thought to himself—only if we'd been successful. There would have been cloud and we might not have been able to see what we were doing, so we might not have been successful and there could have been a higher death toll. And then he kept thinking of whether he could have planned it any differently.

They bundled the three fit bandits into the gaol in the centre of Buckingham knowing that no one, but no one, was going to help them escape. Vince put himself in charge of the party that was guarding them: nothing would induce him to let anybody else take control or responsibility for them. They were his prisoners and he was going to make sure they stayed where they'd been put.

At first light they moved Peter's body onto a plank which they carried into the centre of the town, laying it in the exercise yard in the centre of the gaol. It seemed as good a place as any, and anyway they had no easy way of transporting it back home.

Lew was a different matter. Initially they put him in the gaol, still stuck fast to the butt of his gun with the quarrel that had gone straight through his upper arm. Removing the quarrel proved surprisingly easy. At first they'd tried to pull it out the way it had come but it was deeply and solidly embedded in the butt of the gun, so after a moment's thought Paul simply pulled the quarrel through completely, in the direction in which it had been going. Lew howled a bit, but it actually came out more easily than Paul had imagined. There wasn't as much bleeding as he expected and it was quickly staunched with a pad.

The other quarrel wasn't so easy. It had embedded itself completely in Lew's massive thigh, having glanced off the bone in the process: had it not hit the bone it would probably have passed through his thigh and out the other side, such was the force that their home-made crossbows generated. 'I think this is one for Nicholas,' said Paul after a few more moments looking at it.

But there was no way that they could transport Lew safely in the Peugeot without risking further violence, so they left him in the gaol, promising Vince that they would return as soon as possible both to pick up both Peter's body and to take the four bandits away.

Then there was nothing left to do. They collected the Peugeot from its hiding-place and a grateful band of residents and hostages gathered round to see the raiding force off, patting them on the back, cheering and shedding not a few tears, knowing what had been done, what had been risked and what had been sacrificed. To the waves and thanks of the Buckingham residents, Paul slowly and tiredly slipped the car into gear and started off east, for Ampthill.

The journey was a silent one, each of them alone with his thoughts. Alan was overjoyed to have his son back safe and well, if a little thin, but appalled at the price that had been paid to get him back alive. David was sitting in the back of the car, teeth chattering, almost in a panic, blaming himself for not having fired earlier—because if he had fired as instructed Lew would be dead and Peter alive. And Paul, tight-lipped, was thinking for the hundredth time that morning whether if he had planned it differently they would still be talking with Peter now.

At eleven-thirty they reached the outskirts of Ampthill and two minutes later were in the Market Square pulling up in a cloud of dust. News of their arrival seemed to have travelled with the speed of light for suddenly everyone seemed to be in the Market Square, congratulating them, asking how it went, delighted, overjoyed, overwhelmed to see them back. Susan collapsed into the arms of Darren in tears, having half given up hope that she would ever see him again. She wasn't particularly pleased to see Alan back but, she supposed, if he'd rescued Darren then he still had his uses.

And then they found out about Peter. The whole Square fell silent as if a huge and heavy hand had descended upon it and Susan, discourteously, wished under her breath that Alan had been taken and Peter spared.

At first, Anne had thought that David had been injured, because he was still covered in blood and shaking violently. It can't happen to me again, she thought: not again. Not to another member of my family—and she almost fainted on finding out that David wasn't hurt.

Then she too heard about Peter. Of anyone, Anne had been the nearest to Peter—not that anyone could really get near to him because he'd always been too dazed and too demoralised by the loss of his young wife and family really to enjoy living from then on. She simply let out a very deep, long sigh, looked down at the ground, looked up and said, 'Well, he's with his family now. He never really wanted to live after they'd gone, you know.'

Then Kevin spoke up. 'He saved our lives.'

Paul's, Alan's and David's head all swivelled to look at Kevin in incredulity.

'What do you mean?'

'He saved our lives, didn't he? He kept talking down that bull-horn. He was the only thing they could aim at. They didn't know where the rest of us were. He almost committed suicide.'

Thinking back, once again Paul realised just how accurate Kevin had been. Unlike Police Officers in a siege, Peter had kept talking, going on and on, and had effectively drawn the fire of Lew and his cronies, sacrificing himself so that the rest of the little band would be safe.

His quiet unassuming bravery was simply astounding. No one had really given much thought to Peter in the past: a solitary, lonely figure, he had made few demands on anyone, and all had known that in truth he was sobbing his heart out over the death of his family. In some ways he'd had, not a death wish, but a wish not to live any more—not an active wish to die, as much as a passive wish not to live, an attitude that didn't make him uncaring about his own life in a negative sense, but one which meant that he knew he could best use it by expending it for the sake of others.

David, though proud of his role, was still upset at the nearness of death, and of his involvement with Lew's injury and the possible prevention of Peter's death. Anne led him away shaking to get some food, a debriefing of the emotions, and a lot of sleep. Alan sauntered away quietly on his own—probably to talk to no one but Schrödinger—and Paul fell into Chris's arms. She'd not said anything to anyone but she'd known what the plans were and it had terrified the life out of her. On paper at least it should have been Paul who was most at risk, because it was Paul who was going to have the job—without any training—of immobilising each biker as he surrendered.

Which left Kevin. One might have thought that the death of a policeman or, at best, a former policeman, might have given an ex-East End lout like Kevin some simple satisfaction. After all he had frequently, in the past, been caught shouting abuse at the police, taunting them and writing 'Death to Pigs' on any available wall.

Which didn't explain anything, because slowly and deliberately Kevin walked out of the Market Square on his own in a cold fury, back to his house, seething at the death of Peter. Perhaps it was the common kinship, the common bond of having originally been fighters on opposite sides that made Peter's death so important to Kevin. Or maybe it was just that he liked Peter with his common-sense and down-to-earth approach; or maybe that, unlike some of the police he'd remembered from his past, Peter seemed to have a depth of sensitivity and an awareness of other people's needs that struck a strange chord in Kevin.

Or perhaps it was the basic gut common-sense that both of them possessed, in different ways and in different areas and expressed in a different manner, but Kevin suddenly felt as if he had lost a brother and all he wanted was vengeance and retribution.

- 31 -

*T*here had, of course, to be a trial. After all, it was, inconceivable that having killed Peter and Sophie, Lew and his friends should simply be set free to roam, possibly to do the same thing again, either to the same people at Buckingham, or else to some other unsuspecting group. Besides, if there were no trial and no punishment, Paul was quite sure that Vince would take matters into his own hands and probably somewhat unpleasantly.

But there was the more immediate problem of Peter. After due thought, Paul decided that they would simply *have* to use yet more of their dwindling stocks of diesel on a lorry trip to Buckingham, mainly to bring back Peter's body, but also to transport the four bandits, chained in the back. Any other method was fraught with danger. There was no way that the burly Lew could successfully be restrained in a car. Even with his hands manacled behind his back he could create mayhem. Then again, it would mean one trip per prisoner—not a good use of resources.

After a moment's pause, Alan volunteered to drive the lorry to collect Peter. Martin went with him in order to conduct the burial service for Sophie. He was beginning to get quite despondent at the number of funerals he'd had to take. In fact, they were fewer in number than in the days before the plague, but because each one at Ampthill was personally known to him, and because, through Vince's account, he felt that he had known Sophie so well, it seemed each time that he was losing a personal friend. Burials seemed somehow more tragic now that each person was known to everyone within the community.

The burial was a desperately sad affair. Weary and disillusioned, Vince, delighted to be reunited with Tom whom he hadn't seen for more than nine months, but aghast at the loss of his lovely wife, stood mute at the end of the grave, holding his son in his arms. Revenge in the making, thought Martin, looking at him and rather glad for the four bikers that they were about to be transferred from Vince's guardianship across to theirs, at Ampthill.

What Martin hadn't been prepared for was the way in which Alan—the only one of the rescuers present—was fêted. As one of the party that had successfully stormed the hostages' house in the face of live guns he was lauded beyond belief, being treated with a combination of reverence, gratefulness, exuberance and awe. As soon as the crowd realised who he was and what part he'd had to play, they were swarming round the lorry like bees round a honey pot. No sooner had his feet touched the ground than they left it again—to be hoisted high onto the shoulders of those townspeople who'd had relatives who were hostages. *Nothing* was too much for them to do for him. He only had to ask politely and quietly for something for five people to rush off and bring it to him. He asked briefly for a glass of water—and within minutes, ten bottles of home-made wine were pressed into his hands. He wanted to see what was left of the hostage's house after the battle—twenty people volunteered to accompany him down there: he asked for a quick bite to eat after their journey and found himself festooned with food of all types, pressed on him by people who looked as though they could do with the food themselves, but would still rather that he ate than they did. For a man who for so long had been deprived of love at home, this sudden level of quite genuine affection and attention proved almost overwhelming, especially as in his own eyes he'd done very little. He'd just rammed a vehicle into the back of a house, put up a ladder and guided people down it. No one had even thought of shooting at him. But they were *so* grateful and Alan, in turn, was grateful back: glad for the affection and attention, but gladder still that the hostages were out—or nearly all of them.

After Sophie's burial, the Buckingham men had reverently placed Peter's body in a makeshift coffin in the back of the lorry, then none too gently frog-marched Adam, Frankie and Den onto the back of the lorry as well, manacling them to the platform, far enough apart so they couldn't touch one another.

Lew still had the quarrel stuck firmly in his left thigh, where it was starting to fester. He had to be carried—all eighteen stone of him—from the gaol to the lorry, where he was laid down next to Peter's coffin, then manacled hand and foot to the lorry floor, like the others.

Alan started up the lorry for the journey back. Out of respect for Peter the crowd in the Square fell silent, and Alan drove the lorry slowly through a gap that opened up in the crowd, with people who waved and smiled at him but who, eerily, did it in total silence, their smiles a glassy mixture of gratitude and sadness, mingled with hatred for the four convicts in the back who had done so much to harm, disturb and defile their lives.

As with the journey home on the previous day, it was completed in almost total silence. Alan had by now gone into the exhaustion phase that is so common after frenzied activity. It reminded Martin of the discussions in the midweek study group about Elijah after his triumph against the prophets of Baal: how after an enterprise that has taken much emotional effort, even if successful, it is common to find that an element of depression sets in temporarily. Halfway back, it was obvious from Alan's driving that he wasn't really concentrating at all. At one place he nearly put the lorry off the road.

Martin turned to him. 'Alan, you look awfully tired. Won't you let me drive?' Gratefully, and sensibly, Alan decided that enough was enough and swapped places. As it happened Martin had never driven the lorry, and knew it was going to be unfamiliar, while Alan had driven it a lot—which was why, naturally, he had taken the driving seat. But it was all just too much for Alan, and a novice driver who was alert was a great deal safer than a good driver who was mentally so exhausted that he could hardly see the road ahead. Gratefully Alan ceded the driving seat to Martin, and spent the rest of the journey home staring blankly out of the passenger window thinking of what was in the back, and of what had happened over the past few days—like the others, going over it again and again, hoping and wishing that somehow it could be re-enacted, that different decisions could be taken, that different events could have happened.

They arrived back in Ampthill in the late afternoon, with the tank showing less than empty and Martin wondering if they weren't running on thin air after all. Stopping at the police station in Woburn Street they untied the four bandits and manhandled them one at a time into cells. Then they went on to St Andrew's where Peter's coffin would lie in state overnight.

Anne was one of those who saw them arrive: quickly she plaited a wreath of wild flowers and placed it on the coffin as it lay in the nave.

There would be yet another burial tomorrow.

*   *   *

And the day after there would be yet another trial. One that, surprisingly, no one was looking forward to—least of all the four bikers. But the council were not particularly enamoured of the problems the trial presented them with; nor, as it happened, did anyone envy them their position.

Except Kevin. Tight-lipped, but with angry eyes that flared whenever anyone spoke to him, he wanted blood and vengeance. Or, perhaps that ought to be rephrased—because Kevin didn't want revenge as much as justice, and in his eyes justice for Peter meant retribution for the bikers.

Just before the council were due to meet to decide how to handle the matter, Kevin banged on Chris's door.

'I wanna do the prosecution,' he said peremptorily. 'Yer know, Perry Mason in reverse.'

'Er... Come in, Kevin,' said Chris, playing for time, and somewhat taken aback by the brusque nature of his request.

'I wanna do the prosecution,' he repeated defiantly, the eyes flashing again under his lean and slightly gaunt features.

'I don't see why not,' floated Paul's voice from the other room where he was busy changing Emma's nappy. He wandered in with Emma cradled in his arms. 'After all, someone's got to do it, and we might as well pick somebody who believes in what he's saying.'

'Whadda yer mean? You mean yer don't believe that they ought to be punished?' said Kevin looking up at Paul.

'No. I didn't say that,' said Paul. 'Perhaps what I should have said was, "You more than anyone else want them punished." '

'Oh,' said Kevin. 'Yer.'

'Do you think anybody will object?' asked Chris.

'I don't see how they can,' said Paul. 'There's nothing wrong with having prosecuting council believing thoroughly and utterly in the accused person's guilt, is there? It seems to me the problem's going to be who's going to defend them. Who's going to believe in them? Who's going to speak up for them? If you want to have a fair trial you've got to make sure that your best lawyer is acting for the defence, not the prosecution.'

'You mean you don't think I'm any good?' retorted Kevin.

'No,' said Paul as patiently as he could. 'No, I didn't mean that.'

'Yes, you did. You just said it.'

'No, Kevin, what I *meant* was...'

'I wish yer'd say what yer mean the first time instead of having to explain it twice, especially when it changes what yer said in the first place.'

Paul sat down beside Kevin. 'Look,' he said, staring him straight in the face in a not unkindly way. 'It's good that you want to act as prosecution. You believe passionately in what you're going to do and say. Fine. I'm glad you're doing it, but if we're going to be fair we've got to have somebody who can talk for them as well. We don't want to feel afterwards that they've been punished unfairly or unjustly sentenced. In this case the prosecution's got the easy job. It's virtually cut and dried, which is why that I said that you need your best lawyer for the defence.'

'There you go again,' said Kevin, 'telling me I'm no good.'

'You haven't exactly taken a degree in law, have you?' retorted Paul. 'Or a course in debating...?' And then he stopped, because in his mind's eye there suddenly flashed a vivid picture of his own trial. He wasn't a lawyer either, and although he'd taken part in many a debate when at school and at university, Kevin had somehow managed to run rings round him at the trial itself. He subsided. 'I'm sorry, Kevin,' he said, 'yes, you're right. You *are* good at putting your point of view across. Yes. I apologise.'

Kevin sniffed. 'Orl right then.'

Paul looked down and then looked up at Kevin again. 'Kevin... I think I may have treated you... a bit unfairly in the past.'

Kevin sniffed again.

'And I just wanted to say... I'm sorry. I've misjudged you. I thought the worst of you rather than the best and I've judged you on your background rather than what and who you are and I apologise. Will you forgive me?'

Kevin looked at him in an odd sort of way, sniffed again and then stood up and walked to the window, hands in his pockets. He turned round. 'S'pose so,' he said flatly.

'I mean it,' said Paul, holding out his hand. 'Shake on it.'

'Yer, if you want,' sniffed Kevin again. 'Do I get to do the prosecution then?'

'Yes, if you want.'

'I do want. I've just said so, haven't I?'

'He was agreeing with you, Kevin,' said Chris amiably. 'It's just a manner of speaking.'

'Oh... right,' said Kevin, still not quite believing what had happened during the last three minutes.

'Who would you pick to defend them?' asked Paul of Kevin.

'Me?' He sniffed again. 'You, of course. You're the brightest of the lot of them... After me of course.'

Paul shot him a sideways glance, not quite sure if he was being serious or not. He opened his mouth to say something.

'Of course, that's just my manner of speaking,' said Kevin with a gleam in his eye. 'Like you did before.'

Chris giggled. And then Paul giggled. And then Kevin giggled. And all three of them spent the next thirty seconds howling with laughter, tears running down their faces while Emma looked on uncomprehending and chuckled along with them.

*   *   *

But Paul didn't act as defence counsel. Whilst agreeing with Kevin's premise that mentally speaking Paul was the ablest of them all, the council reckoned that as he'd master-minded the plan to get the hostages out it really rather precluded him from taking on the role of counsel for the defence. Eventually it fell to Henry to do the job. Although he'd been on the war council, he'd not had any personal contact with the bikers, so he wasn't biased in that sense: he had an able brain, and the right sort of background and attributes to take on such a difficult role, and his wisdom and maturity from long years of negotiation in various parts of his life had made him adept at explaining, reaching compromises and putting the best point of view on a particular situation.

He went down to the cells at the police station to see the bikers and to try to get a bit of background information. The treated him in a surly, defiant manner but Henry—amiable and convivial as ever—somehow managed to get them to talk. The most truculent of the bikers, surprisingly, was not Lew, who was too ill to be his usual obstructive arrogant self, but Adam, who was a mixture of fear, anger and terror. He was certain that they wouldn't get a fair trial and felt that whatever happened they'd all be butchered afterwards.

At this Henry put down his sheaf of notes and his pen and looked Adam squarely in the eye. 'Believe you me,' he said, 'if the council says you can go free—which I have to say is a bit dubious—then you'll go free. And if they say they just want to kick you out of the area, then they'll kick you out of the area. They'll take you to the far corner of Buckinghamshire and leave you there and you'd be able to make your own way in the world afterwards. *If* that's what the council says.'

Adam's eyes spoke volumes. Maybe that was what would happen if the council said they were to be outlawed, but he very much doubted if that would be the decision. Inwardly, Henry recognised as much but chose to say nothing. After all, he was there, not to do what he wanted, but to act as their mouthpiece. Whether he believed in them or not, it was still his job to make sure that he presented their case as well as he possibly could. It wouldn't be just to do anything less.

And so the trial started. The four bikers arrived at the court house manacled, and were promptly chained to their seats. Lew had to be carried in, and remained unwell throughout the proceedings, as Nicholas was away in Harpenden and unavailable to treat him.

Kevin, flushed with his new-found role—for the time being—of leading the aspirations of every single member of the community, and the Buckingham community to boot, stood up and presented his case. There wasn't much that needed to be presented. It was, to quote a pun, dead simple. Lew had fired at Peter, killing him. The bikers had all connived to take the hostages prisoner and keep them under appalling conditions, ill-fed and ill-housed. They'd cut off two of Sophie's fingers at different times in order to force her husband and the rest of the Buckingham residents to obey them, and Sophie had died after the second assault as a result of the ensuing infection. Two murders and a lot of hostage taking. That was enough for Kevin. He didn't really need to call witnesses, but he did, and rightly the court insisted that he did, for form's sake. The witnesses all agreed that Lew had been the ringleader, that the three others were to some extent under his spell and his guidance, but that at all times any one of them could have opened the door and let the hostages go free.

Then it was Henry's turn, the man with—as far as he was concerned—the worst job in the world on that particular day. He didn't really want to represent the bikers because he believed in their guilt no less than did Kevin. But in the interests of fairness and justice they had to have a mouthpiece, and Henry was it. He did the best he could under difficult circumstances. He pointed out that Lew had fired twice that night, on neither occasion knowing what he was firing at, so he couldn't be said deliberately to have set out to kill Peter. Nor had they deliberately set out to kill any of the hostages. It had happened as a by-product of the hostage taking, not as intent to murder. Then he told the court how much the other three feared Lew, and were under his spell. How the three of them had had deprived backgrounds with lack of discipline in the home, absent or non-existent fathers, poverty, poor schooling, no chance in life. Every social stone that could be upturned, Henry turned.

Inwardly Paul had a sneaking admiration for the job that Henry was doing. He knew he didn't believe a word of what he was saying, yet there he was, putting the case for the bikers as forcefully as if they had each been pure as the driven snow. If there was a heartstring to be tugged, Henry tugged at it. If there was an opportunity to be taken Henry took it. His delineation of the miserable lives of the four miserable people in the dock was masterly to the point where Paul actually began to feel sorry for them.

Henry sat down.

Kevin stood up. 'Rot,' he said. 'Pure rot.' He rounded on Henry. ' "Poor deprived childhood"; "absent fathers"; "illegitimate"; ah, my 'art bleeds. Henry, you could have been describing me. So why am I here and they're in the dock then... Eh? "They didn't know what they were doing..." Eh? I suppose if you take hostages and don't feed them then they're not supposed to die. You make me sick. All this waffle about "they didn't know what they were doing" and "it's their background, you know".' He said it in a sneering, baby-ish voice. 'All I'd say is—*of course they knew what they were doing*. They just thought they could get away with it, that's all. And never mind their background or 'ow they grew up. What they did was wrong, and they knew it. They could choose, and they did, and they chose what they wanted to do. That's right, innit?' He glared at the four defendants in turn.

And then an idea came to him—an idea that he'd heard someone else say... Peter! That was who. About lawyers who tried to split the law down into small pieces and change it by redefining everything. He paused, desperately racking his brains to remember what Peter had said, and how he'd put it. There was a little shuffle in the court as Kevin appeared momentarily to be lost for words. And then it came and he knew what he was going to say and he knew why. 'Do you remember what Peter said—about his own trial, before the plague? How the lawyers tried to say things were different to what they really were? He said, it's like a dive. Where are the swimmer's feet when he dives? Are they on the diving board? Nah, because that's before he's dived. Are they off the board? Nah, because that's after he's dived. *So when does he dive then?*'

He paused for effect and looked round the court. 'It's all right yer saying it's their background or they didn't know what they were doing. Yer all looking at it too closely. Yer've got to stand back, haven't you? Did they know what they were doing? Yer, corse they did. Did they know it was wrong? Corse they did. Did they know it might end up with someone dying? Well, if they didn't they should 'ave. Did Lew mean to kill Peter? If he didn't really want to hurt anyone he should 'ave fired up in the air. Stand back. Look at it all. They're guilty as hell.'

Kevin sat down to a roar of applause. As defence counsel, Henry rose to do what he could before the final decision was made, but there wasn't much point and he knew it.

And then the council retired to consider its verdict... and the sentence.

*   *   *

'So are they guilty?' said Chris to the rest of the council members—minus Henry, of course—stuffed in the tiny back room of the courthouse. 'There are three counts: taking hostages. Do we agree they're guilty?' Everyone nodded. 'The murder of Peter?' Again everyone nodded. 'The murder of Sophie?' Everyone nodded.

Except Mary. She cleared her throat. 'Are you sure that was murder? Not manslaughter?'

'Oh, come on Mary,' said Susan acidly. 'They didn't exactly contribute to her health and happiness, did they?'

'Aren't you supposed to *intend* to kill somebody for a true verdict of murder?' Mary continued.

'I think that's right,' said Martin furrowing his brow. '*Mens rea*, or something like that. You've got to have the intent to kill, or at the very least to inflict serious injury. So maybe they didn't intend to kill her at all...

'We don't have to accept the legal definitions that people used in the past,' said Chris, 'or do we? Perhaps we ought to remember what Peter used to say. Are they guilty? Does it feel like they've done a crime or not? Remember what Kevin said about the dive. Like analysing a dive bit by bit, slice by slice, you can probably do a salami technique on it and prove that there wasn't an obvious point at which a murder took place, but when you stand back it's pretty clear, isn't it? There was a crime, and it killed Sophie.'

It was obvious, really, when put like that. 'Do you still say "not guilty", Mary?'

Mary thought about it. 'No,' she said. 'You're right, Chris. When you stand back there *was* a crime, and a very big one too. We ought not to let little legal definitions or niceties get in the way. Guilty.'

Chris took a deep breath. 'All right, everyone. That's two counts of murder and one count of taking hostages. Obviously Lew's the only one who's guilty of the murder of Peter, but who's guilty of the murder of Sophie. Lew? All of them?'

'They're all in it together,' said the Major. 'As Kevin said—' he almost coughed over the name, '—stand back and look at the whole picture. It was a crime. They all knew what was going on. Any one of them could have prevented it. Therefore each one of them is guilty of it.'

'And the punishment?' said Chris to no one in particular. A ripple of unease spread throughout the room. Had they *really* got the right to do what they were contemplating?

'Let's do what Peter said,' said Paul. 'What punishment fits these particular crimes. Flogging? Fining?' There was a shaking of heads. 'Imprisoning them? Are we really being fair to Sophie and Peter if we merely deprive these four of their freedom for a bit?'

There was a sort of shuffling, a nodding of heads and a shaking of heads all at the same time. 'Stand back' they could hear Peter saying. 'Stand back and look at the whole thing.' No, imprisonment wasn't enough.

Paul didn't want to say it. He really didn't want to say it. 'Do we hang them then?'

'Yes,' growled the Major.

'Yes,' said Alan.

'Yes,' said Susan, agreeing with her husband for only the second time that year. Chris looked around the table at the two remaining people.

'Martin?'

He took a deep breath, but said nothing.

'Mary?'

'I don't think we hang them,' she said. 'How *can* we hang them? What right have we got to take somebody else's life? No, I say we lock them up for a long time.'

Paul suddenly looked up straight at Mary.

'Would you have hanged Hitler?'

'Oh yes,' she said. 'I mean... six million Jews, to say nothing of the Russians and the Poles and the Americans and the English and the French...'

'Would you have executed him if he'd only killed three million Jews?

'Of course,' she snapped back.

'A hundred thousand? Twenty? Five? Two? One? So someone who kills a lot of people is more guilty and deserves to die more than someone who only kills one person? I'd have thought a mass murderer was more in need of psychiatric care than someone who does a single evil act, wouldn't you?'

'But who are we to judge someone else?' said Mary.

'They've already judged Sophie and Peter and deprived them of their lives for no good reason,' said Paul, levelly. 'If we don't execute them we say to everybody else that their lives are of less value than those who did the killing in the first place. And how many more do they have to kill before you think that we ought to execute them? Isn't one dead person enough? If we *don't* hang them what will it tell other people about how we value Sophie's and Peter's lives? And what people can get away with, if only they push hard enough?'

'But what if we hang innocent people?' said Mary.

'There's someone who's been dealt with unfairly in every single crime,' said Alan. 'The victim. Don't forget that.'

Mary bit her lip. Her choices were narrowing very quickly. 'Oh, very well,' she said. 'I don't say it willingly.'

'I don't think any of us are doing this willingly,' said Martin. 'It gives me no pleasure. I just think we've got to act responsibly, that's all, and we don't act responsibly if we let people get away—quite literally—with murder.'

'Do I take that as a "yes" for hanging?' said Chris.

'Unfortunately, I think that's the only option.'

'Well, I agree with all of you,' said Chris. 'When? Tomorrow? *And who's going to do it?*'

*   *   *

The sentence had been as the four bikers had expected. Belligerently they talked about civilisation and mercy but knew it was futile. Martin too was thinking about civilisation and mercy and decided that to show mercy inappropriately was a very uncivilised act indeed. There had been no sense of apology from any of Lew's crowd, no sense of regret—other than of being caught; no sense of guilt at having done wrong; no sense of remorse, only anger at the position they found themselves in and a tendency to blame every one else but themselves for what was, quite clearly, their own decision, their own fault, and their own guilt.

Martin, in his function as priest, tried to visit them in the cells , but they didn't want to see him. Next morning the four prisoners were escorted to the centre of Ampthill Park by Trevor who—in respect for Peter, of whom he had been rather fond—had volunteered to act as executioner, thus ending another awkward problem.

Judicial hanging is quite different from lynch-mob hanging. In judicial hanging the noose is put, reversed, round the neck of the condemned man. When the trap-door is loosed the convict falls six feet, whereupon the rope tightens, snapping the head back, breaking and dislocating his cervical spine, killing him instantly. That the convict is left to hang for a further hour is merely to satisfy judicial niceties.

Without the necessary apparatus of a scaffold and a trap-door, judicial hanging was out of the question, and the lynch-mob technique of a rope over the branch of a tree would have to suffice. It was the same method as was used in the old days, when felons were turned off a ladder and allowed to suffocate as their own weight pulled the noose tight. It took longer to die that way, which was why friends and relatives of the condemned man or woman would often pull on their legs to hasten the onset of death.

There was quite a crowd for the hanging. Martin began to think that maybe this was rather more barbaric than he had anticipated. It couldn't exactly be done privately, but reverting to public executions was a little bit medieval he thought—until he realised that before the plague everyone had done the same sort of thing when they ogled at video pictures of car crashes, or buildings collapsing or people being shot by a firing squad. If you see it on film then it's still a public act.

Martin walked with the convicts to Ampthill Park in the forlorn hope that perhaps one of them might want or need his presence. By now the doubts had begun to re-emerge and he remembered that although it said in the Ten Commandments 'Thou shalt do no murder' (which, he acknowledged, didn't preclude judicial executions or acts of war), a few lines further down was the statement 'Thou shalt not commit adultery,' and he wondered for a fleeting moment why it was that he wasn't being hanged as well. Maybe he deserved it—after all the Old Testament punishment for adultery was stoning to death, a procedure still carried out just prior to the plague in many a Muslim country and all for good Old Testament reasons.

It was all over very quickly. Trevor lined the bikers up on a variety of stepladders and other supports, their arms and legs bound together, a noose round the neck of each, strung out along the same bough of a large oak. In the distance Martin could see Vince, who had come to watch, together with Tom. Quite deliberately he kept Tom's face pointing in the other direction, hugging him tightly. Vince hadn't come for vengeance, but to see justice done, to see those who had murdered his lovely wife and Tom's devoted mother die for their crime. Then justice would be done and some degree of civilisation would return to his shattered life.

As a last despairing act Martin said the Lord's Prayer, and then one by one Kevin pushed the bikers off the ladders, leaving them to jerk and convulse until unconsciousness supervened and death followed close behind.

From a little distance Vince watched until the last movements had ceased. Then he pulled Tom from off his shoulder, looked him in the eye and said quietly, 'It doesn't bring her back, Tom, but I feel her life's more valued now.' Then wordlessly, he led him away, pointing out to him the beauties of the wood and the birds and the trees and the flowers.

*   *   *

Between them Trevor and Martin buried the bikers that night in an unmarked grave on the north side of the church, the place traditionally reserved for such matters. There seemed little point in conducting a formal service—after all no one would be coming. Nevertheless Martin fulfilled his priestly duty according to the Rites and Ordinances of the church and read the burial service over them. Then wearily he helped Trevor push the soil back into the grave on top of the bodies.

- 32 -

*T*he nagging sense of doubt, insecurity and guilt continued in Martin unabated. Every time he passed the church and looked at the freshly dug mound of earth by the north wall his doubts increased. The bandits had murdered two people. He'd murdered a marriage. Was there much difference? Wasn't he just as guilty as they? It was with a heavy heart that he went back to his house to lead the mid-week meeting yet again. He was late—he'd been called to attend one of his parishioners who was ill out in Clophill, and by the time he had ridden back to the Old Rectory and put Seamus back in his stall he found that the others were already there, talking away at nineteen to the dozen.

'Jolly good idea of yours for flushing out the bandits,' said the Major to Paul. 'Using spotlights to surprise them and give them the impression that there were many more of you. I'm very impressed.'

'Yes, it *was* a good idea,' said Fred Higginbottom.

'It's not original, you know,' said Paul with a twinkle in his eye.

'Really?' said the Major. 'Where did you get it from?'

'You should know,' said Paul.

'Me. Why?'

'You read the story.'

'What story?'

'Gideon. We studied it a few months ago, remember? He defeated the Midianites using a small group of men, each carrying a light hidden inside a jar. They crept up to the Midianites' camp at night, then smashed their jars so the lights suddenly shone out. The defending army thought they were surrounded by a much larger force, panicked and started fighting among themselves. That's where I got it from, if you must know.'

'Well I never,' said Edna Higginbottom. 'That *is* good, Fred, isn't it? I say.' And she chuckled to herself.

'What are we studying tonight, Vicar?' said Paul mischievously, as Martin sat down. He might have lost his cutting nature but he'd certainly lost none of his humour. Martin flushed slightly, wishing to goodness that he could just go away and hide—anywhere, so long as it was far away.

'I thought we'd start looking in the New Testament,' he said. 'Especially for you, Paul, it would be good to study something about the life of Jesus.'

'Fine by me,' said Paul. 'Incidentally, why's he called the son of David?'

'Because he was,' said Edna Higginbottom, 'or strictly speaking, descended from David.'

'That's right,' said Martin. 'Look at the beginning of Matthew and Luke's Gospels. You know the Jews and their love of family ties. The first thing Matthew does is is tell us where Jesus comes from.' He opened his Bible. 'Here it is, right at the beginning. "Abraham was the father of Isaac, Isaac of Jacob... and so on and so on... and Jesse was the father of King David." Now this is the important bit. This is where King David comes in. "David was the father of Solomon (his mother had been the wife of Uriah)..." '

Martin suddenly stopped, swallowed hard, and couldn't believe his eyes. *The wife of Uriah was Bathsheba*! There it was in front of him, in black and white, in the Bible, almost hidden, because who reads genealogies in detail? He'd always jumped across that bit whenever he'd read the beginning of Matthew.

Martin became aware that three pairs of eyes were looking at him. 'Er... sorry,' he said, trying to gather himself together and finding a great knot welling up in his throat ' "...David was the father of Solomon (his mother had been the wife of Uriah), Solomon of Rehoboam..." and so on, "... Jacob of Joseph, the husband of Mary, who gave birth to Jesus called Messiah." '

Martin didn't know what to say. *So Jesus was descended through Bathsheba*! And although his birth had been foretold long before King David had even been a twinkle in his father Jesse's eye, his lineage had been known—through Bathsheba, the adulterous woman for whom King David committed murder. Never in a million years would Martin have thought that could happen. Surely the Son of God would be descended from the virtuous line where there

was purity, and not from a union that had been illicit from the beginning—begun with adultery, sealed with a murder? And yet Jesus
was descended from the very line that had been started as a result
of that illicit relationship and that illegal act. Martin swallowed
again.

'I thought Jesus was born from a virgin?' said Paul. 'So why the
fuss about who the father was?'

Yes, yes that must be it, thought Martin. Of course, Matthew
traces the lineage of Joseph and clearly says that Joseph wasn't the
father of Jesus but just the husband of Mary who was the mother of
Jesus. Yes, yes that was it. That must be the spiritual linkage of
David to Jesus. Of course *that* could go through Bathsheba and
Solomon. No problem. And virtue triumphs.

'There's another genealogy in Luke, which is different,' prattled
on Edna happily, hands across her ample lap. 'Scholars think that
the Matthew genealogy is of Joseph whereas Luke—being a doctor
you know—is more concerned with the lineage of Mary, though the
Bible doesn't say this specifically because in the style of the time,
as a woman, her name's missed out and in any case both genealogies are abbreviated...'

Yes, yes that was it! Frantically Martin found the relevant passage in Luke which, just to be awkward, was the opposite way
round. Matthew had given the father first and the sons second. Luke
did it the other way round.

'Hang on a minute,' said Paul. 'This just seems to be Jesus'
genealogy through Joseph again, but different "the son, so it was
thought, of Joseph, the son of Heli..." '

'As Edna said,' interjected Fred, 'that's the way it was done in
those days. Just as a woman in England a hundred years ago would
change her surname to her husband's on marriage, so names in old
genealogies can be difficult to interpret for similar reasons. Instead
of reading "son of", try substituting "of the family of" and you'll get
the idea. So Jesus was of the family of Joseph, whose *wife* was of
the family of Heli; Heli came from the family of Matthat... and so
on. That's what the Jewish genealogists always told me it meant,
anyway.'

Yes, yes, thought Martin, anxious to get away from the technicalities, and reading out loud as the list of Mary's ancestors went back in time, ' "*...son of Menna, son of Mattatha, son of Nathan, son of David.*" ' Nathan, one of David's many sons. Yes, that was right, the maternal line was descended through Nathan. But which of David's many wives was his mother? Martin got up to consult a concordance. 'Nathan... Nathan the prophet... Nathan the son of David. Here we are.' And his voice faltered. *Son of Bathsheba.* Whether he traced the lineage of Jesus back through Joseph's side or Mary's side the answer was still the same. The Son of the Most High God had come from the line created as a result of King David marrying Bathsheba and *that* had come as a result of... In other words, nothing was fixed, nothing was final and nothing was *ever* beyond forgiveness. All that was needed was the sorrow and the contrition that King David had shown when he realised the enormity of what he'd done.

David and Bathsheba! The words had been running round his brain ever since that fateful night so many months ago, shouting at him, screaming at him, telling him that the wages of sin was death, rule off, end of discussion. And the lineage he'd just read showed twice over that it wasn't the whole answer, that he need no longer be obsessional over what he was or what he'd done, and that each day he could start afresh.

The rest of the evening passed in a blur in front of his eyes. His mind couldn't concentrate on anything other than the enormity of what he'd just discovered. Automatically, reflexly, he finished the Bible study, teaching Paul in particular about the origins and person of Jesus, but all the time in the back of his mind a still small voice was murmuring away, telling him that always there was hope and that there was no corner so tight that hopelessness inevitably followed. When he thought of the waste of the past eighteen months, though, he shuddered. All that time spent worrying inappropriately!

*   *   *

The meeting ended early, which was fortunate, because there was something Martin needed to do, had wanted to do ever since

Derek's death so many months ago, but the time hadn't been right nor the occasion appropriate. He didn't expect that anything positive would come out of it, but nevertheless he felt that he ought to go and do it, just the same. He had to go and talk to the icicle Anne.

There was no time like the present. It was only half past nine— time to walk down to Lime View and back again with his deed done, difficult though it was likely to be.

He trudged down Holly Walk, steeling himself for the occasion, hoping that it wouldn't go too badly. Anne had very pointedly avoided him for the past nine months since Derek's death, but he had to say something, and it needed to be said, and anyway, he wanted to say it.

Summoning up his courage he tapped the knocker.

'Oh hello,' said Anne in a dull sort of voice. 'It's you.'

'Can I come in?' said Martin hesitantly. 'To talk?'

'I suppose so.'

'Privately?'

'If you want.' She showed him a chair. 'Sit down.'

'Thanks.' He looked down, clasped his hands together until they were white at the knuckles and then looked up, determined.

'Anne, you know how sorry I am about Derek's death. I feel so awful about what I did to drive a wedge between the two of you. You were two of my dearest friends before and I feel so... *responsible*. I just want to apologise again. It was a total betrayal of the trust you had in me, and I let you down. There hasn't been a day since when I haven't thought about what happened and regretted it bitterly. It destroyed your marriage and it undermined our friendship, and I've hated myself for doing both of those things.'

She looked at him coolly, wordlessly.

'Er...' he faltered, lost for what to say next. 'How's Julian?'

'Fine.'

Martin swallowed but the words wouldn't come.

'Why are you here, Martin?'

'Anne... will you marry me?'

The saga will continue...